NO WAY BACK

ALSO BY MICHAEL CROW

Red Rain

The Bite

NO WAY BACK

a novel

MICHAEL CROW

HarperCollins*Publishers*

This is a work of fiction. The characters, incidents, and dialogue are products of the author's imagination and are not to be construed as real. Any resemblance to actual persons, living or dead, is entirely coincidental.

HarperCollins books may be purchased for educational, business, or sales promotional use. For information, please write: Special Markets Department, HarperCollins Publishers, 10 East 53rd Street, New York, NY 10022.

FIRST EDITION

Designed by Christine Weathersbee

Printed on acid-free paper

Library of Congress Cataloging-in-Publication Data
Crow, Michael.
No way back : a novel / Michael Crow.—1st ed.
p. cm.
ISBN 0-06-072583-4 (alk. paper)
1. Illegal arms transfers—Fiction. 2. Undercover operations—Fiction. 3. Bodyguards—Fiction. 4. Korea—Fiction. I. Title.
PS3563.O7714N6 2005 2004061581
813'.54—dc22

05 06 07 08 09 ❖/RRD 10 9 8 7 6 5 4 3 2 1

For C.R.M., who wasn't always just an attorney.

Some people still turn pale when they hear his name.

Special thanks to Marjorie Braman
for helping me stay on target.

NO WAY BACK

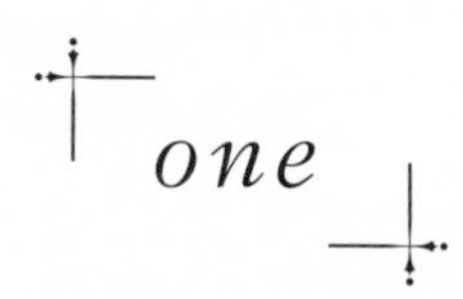

one

"THAT MISTAH KIM, HE'S A TIGER, I SHIT YOU NOT," SAYS THE FAT Buddha, smile wider than it needs to be, his eyes glittery obsidian slits. We're slouched in supple Italian leather chairs, face-to-face across a hand-oiled maple burl table. This Buddha, a serious heavy, knows very well his dark gaze unnerves most people, but he is not trying for that effect now with me. He's loose, he's relaxed, beer in hand, being about as sociable as he's able. He answers to Sonny. At least with those few he permits to reach a certain level of familiarity.

"I believe it, Sonny," I say.

"Good. So, you know that old Chinese proverb thing, the one talks about riding the tiger?" Sonny (official name Park Sung-hi) asks.

"More or less, yeah." Now I'm about to receive some scuffed plastic pearl of oriental wisdom. And I have to be polite about it. Though even a genuine one—if any exist, and I've heard enough to deeply doubt that—wouldn't engage my interest at the moment. It's deep night, we've been cruising seven miles above the Pacific for too many hours, there's an aggressive headache deployed in the back of my neck and moving up fast. The others on board have long since drifted into sleep, lulled by boredom and the steady dull hum of the plane's engines. But Sonny, on maybe his sixth bottle of Red Rock, apparently believes I'm in need of education.

"Everybody understand," he says, "you got to be some kinda goddamn fool, you jump on tiger's back. Everybody know this very, very well. Never mind. Lotta people, they trying it anyway. Total craziness, eh?"

"Absolutely," I say. "Completely."

"Not Sonny. No way. Never. Me, I'm completely happy as tiger's assistant only." He's shucked his suitcoat, but not the custom shoulder rig carrying twin mini-Uzis—very old tech but absolutely reliable, absolutely devastating at close quarters. "You happy, Mistah Prentice?"

"Couldn't be more," I say. Prentice, Terence, is the name on the Canadian passport bearing my photo, the one I'm carrying in my breast pocket. Sonny knows it isn't genuine, knows the name's a ghost name. He may or may not be aware of other passports in other names, other nationalities. They're secured behind the lining of my attaché.

"That's fine. That's very good, Mistah Prentice. Damn straight. Mistah Kim, he love happy assistants. Makes him feel good. Makes him feel happy." The Buddha smile widens fractionally, broad cheeks narrowing those hard black slits from which Sonny looks out at the world.

"Does it? I've been wondering a little sometimes," I say, hoping my tone suggests this information is enlightening, a revelation of something I never saw or sensed during these weeks in the almost constant company of Sonny, and sufficient face time with Kim himself.

"For sure, for sure. So you knowing it's smart to help him stay that way, you bet."

Sonny drains his Red Rock. I watch him put the bottle on the table, shift his shoulder rig slightly so he can sink deeper into the cradling down cushions of his chair.

This Buddha's conscious I'm ex-military as positively as I am he served in the Republic of Korea Army. He understands I wouldn't be here if I didn't have the same skill set he acquired. Since we're both post-Vietnam generation, his experience had to be black ops. Scary midnight strikes through the DMZ. Nasty actions nobody admits happened afterward. Slitting throats, trading fire up in the evil hermit state of the DPRK. Democratic People's Republic of Korea, likely the world's final Stalinist theme park.

He knows I've played the same hard game, anywhere from the Mog, rocking skinnies in the Casbah, to Bosnia to Taliban-stan or Mindanao. Almost any point on the compass, in fact, since my primary employer has global interests beyond comprehension.

And we did have to give each other a short, sharp demonstration (body count: five) quite recently, though it wasn't our choice, we didn't feel like talking much at the time, and haven't said a word about it since.

But just because certain things are never said does not mean they aren't heard, loud and clear. Too loud for me, in my current condition. I only want to shut it all down, go deep into the pain that's wracking my head, kill it, and sleep.

That smile. "You and me, we stay happy, we get along fine," he says.

Oh, outstanding, Sonny. Until I look the wrong way or say the wrong thing out where we're headed, and you feel it's your duty to cap me to keep your Mistah Kim bright and content. But right now my Buddha pal lets himself settle even deeper into his chair, sighs once or twice. As the Master said, in serenity lies virtue. He's asleep in less than a minute.

* * *

I am lacking in virtue, apparently. Sleep eludes me, even after I dominate the throb in my temples, even though I'm so tired my eyes are scratchy. I have the most unsettling sensation of being a stranger inside my own head, seeing and feeling extraordinary things that are happening to someone I do not know. Or I'm watching a movie starring an actor who looks remarkably like Luther Ewing, from the very last row in an utterly deserted mall cineplex with a very small screen.

There are a few facts I've grasped. Mister Kim, he *is* some kind of business tiger. That's why I'm armed and airborne in his corporate jet. Not a Gulfstream, or any other normal private plane. His very own 747, like none other flying. Kim bought it from some failing airline, maybe Swissair or Pan Am, and had it transformed into something that resembles a yacht custom-fitted for a man whose name repeatedly appears on the *Forbes* annual billionaire list. What had been the first-class section and the hump above it are Kim's private lounge and bedroom. I haven't been in there, but it's no challenge to extrapolate what it must be like from the main compartment, where Sonny's low snoring is beginning to sound like the first warning growls of some jungle beast.

Pure luxe in every detail. If the sycamore-and-brushed-steel sideboards, the maple burl tables, the twelve matching Saporiti chairs weren't discreetly bolted to some light, synthetic, but completely convincing imitation of sixteenth-century marble flooring—which, in turn, is a display for antique Tabriz and Isfahan carpets—you'd be certain you were in the VIP lounge of a five-star European hotel. The bulkheads, front and rear, are paneled in pale sycamore. The paintings hanging there—contemporary work by artists I can't identify—are almost certainly museum-grade.

Aft of the lounge there's a galley that looks like a kitchen straight out of *Architectural Digest*. And beyond that, at least a half-dozen private cabins, each with a bed and full amenities.

A slim Japanese girl, with a face that would be exquisitely beautiful if it weren't lifeless as a porcelain doll's, materializes at my side. In a whisper that sounds like a love song she asks if I require anything. I don't. She bows, makes Sonny's beer bottle disappear, and fades back to the galley, the rustle of her kimono scarcely audible. She leaves only the faint scent of some flower I can't name.

The scale of this wealth is much too great for me to absorb. Kim is some big tiger. Beyond imagination, even though I've been briefed by my employer. I've also been educated and made over so I'll pass as a tiger's assistant, had a smooth and stylish veneer laid over this ex–Special Forces slob with offensive habits. I applied myself to the process. Most any observer, checking out my clothes and manners and demeanor, would take me for an experienced member of a major corporate entourage. That is what Kim demands of his assistants. Most especially those like Sonny and me, whose job descriptions have nothing at all to do with business.

Security cannot look like security. That is Kim's nonnegotiable requirement. He's a tiger, after all. It is a matter of face for him. But I wonder if he knows he may presently be taken for the ride of his life on the back of a much larger, meaner, tiger.

And suddenly I'm hearing approximate lyrics from one antique Talking Heads song looping over and over—something about how you may say to yourself: This is not my beautiful house, this is not my beautiful wife, this is not my large autombile. And you may ask yourself: How did I get to this place? . . .

It's not a question, really. I can call up every encounter, every move in the four-month trip that put me here. I can hear Westley, pitch perfect, stating the contract. Feel how his eyes, more than his words, seal the deal. Remember every detail of the prep that follows. It's all hi-rez in my memory bank. No confusion, nothing vague or shadowy about any of it.

Except why I did it.

I'd done it before. I'd sworn never again, after the first time. I'd even refused a second offer a few years back. But my past somehow keeps bleeding into my present.

When this first started happening, I believed I'd figured all the whys and wherefores, most ricky-tick. Simple cause and effect, I'd concluded: a lifetime of training, informal and formal, followed by some fairly ferocious real-world action, and what was basically only downloaded software mutates to something permanently embedded in your frontal lobes, something that ignores or overrides conscious commands when it wants to. Add a head wound, the plate in my skull, the meds I'll have to drop four times a day every day for the rest of my life—unless I dig unpredictable, sudden seizures that put me thrashing wildly on the floor, eyes rolled back and foam bubbling from my mouth.

No wonder there's some leakage.

So. You're leaking? Pressure bandage works, usually. Everybody knows this very, very well, as Sonny would say. But my friend Annie, who's a psychologist as well as the woman who knows me better than any other, started wondering out loud after she saw one or two of those bandages get so saturated I had to toss them and slap on new ones. She says I'm going to hemorrhage one day. Past and present, all one deep-red arterial surge flooding my brain, leaving me unable to distinguish between what I've done and what I'm doing, what was then and what's now, who I was and who I am.

"Don't go. Please don't go. You need some serious intervention. You need it this minute, Luther. Or the real you may not make it back," Annie'd said to me just before I left. I didn't listen. Maybe I should have.

Too late. Change the bandage again. Press hard. Stop the time leak, for the duration of this job anyway. But first just let it bleed a while. I can do that. I can rewalk my own twisted trail, find the the sense of it.

two

GO LOUD.

It's high summer. There's scarcely time for Agent Francesca Russo to've settled into her grave before she comes around to haunt and harrow me.

Not as a soul-shadowing spectre with a lovely, unmarked face above a gaping hole where the tender skin of her throat should have been. Not as stop-action eyelid replays of her own attack dogs ripping that throat out and leaving her corpse twitching in the dust. Not as nightmares of blurred, bloody fury that yank me awake, sweating with fear and the horror.

I'm immune to—or numbed beyond feeling—that sort of torment.

No, she does it with bureaucracy. From the cold, cold ground she gets payback, using the system she'd been trying her best to subvert in life, relying on rules she'd casually broken or ignored. And I can almost hear her familiar "Luther! You punk!" followed by clear, untroubled laughter.

She's handed me over to Internal Affairs, or IA.

"You're surprised or something?" my partner, Ice Box, says one morning in our usual place of business—the narc squad room at Baltimore County Police Department headquarters in Towson, where for the last four or five years I've been punching the clock before going out undercover, hunting dopers and dealers. It's maybe a week after Internal Affairs started squeezing me—including, besides intense chats, close examinations of my spending patterns, my bank account, and all my financial records.

"Like, this is some mystical event?" IB goes on. "The finger of God pointing down from a dark cloud, big deep voice booming, 'Luther did it, Luther fucked up again!' Major phenomenon like that?"

He shakes his head. "Man, you begged for it. Did I or did I not advise you to walk away from Russo? Didn't I say be patient, let her own people get wise to her?"

"Yeah, I heard something along those lines."

"Didn't register, though. Oh no, it did not. Luther Ewing never listens to advice. He never needs to, he's so totally smart."

"Thanks for the encouragement, IB," I say. Not fifty feet away, the IA dick is locked in an office with my boss, Captain Dugal, deciding my future. "Appreciate your support."

"Least I can do, considering all the wonderful law-enforcement adventures I'd have missed without you. Like getting shot at by Russian smack dealers and redneck meth merchants, other thrilling stuff.

"And don't worry, bro," he says. "I'll be there for you too while the IA rips off all your fingernails one by one with needle-nose pliers. Or whatever really awful, painful punishment they're planning."

Neither of us wants to mention that the punishment might very well be job chop: instant dismissal from the department.

Nobody's blaming me for Francesca's death. The Maryland state troopers did the usual crime-scene routine, asked me the questions, cop to cop, over crullers and coffee, and finished their investigation rapidly. Russo's employer, the Drug Enforcement Administration, efficiently moved to conclude its own subtler but deeper probe. Deeply ironic, I figure, since it was me who turned those Doberman–pit bull crosses she'd bred and trained herself on her and her best hit man. Which, at a particular and highly lethal moment down on her Eastern Shore farm, was a desperate maneuver to keep myself alive.

But the troopers and the DEA agree: the hitter wasn't Francesca's employee, only a mean ex-con drug dealer who, feeling heat from Russo and me, moved first and fast. Came to the farm to kill us. Got her, but got dead in the process.

And that should have been that—except Francesca, ruthlessly clever, left behind a few notes and one goddamned tape I never knew she'd made. Which the DEA reviewed, adroitly edited, and thoughtfully passed on to the IA chief of my own employer, the Baltimore County Police. The IA dick was delighted, since he'd considered me borderline at best almost since I made my first drug bust.

Nobody—not our IA, certainly not the DEA—wants truth here: that agent Francesca Russo was mad, bad, and as bent as they come. That she was well on her wicked way to creating and ruling a crystal meth empire. At least ten executions behind her, probably more on the agenda, since major drug trafficking isn't a forgiving sort of trade.

The DEA, for all I know, may've already had some suspicions about her when she was killed. But they're revealing nothing. They never will. Fed Rule Number One: do not permit anything—anything—to tarnish your agency's image, no matter how massive the lies that must be told, how broad the deceit that must be sustained. So the DEA very publically lets it be known that Francesca was a stand-up, dedicated drug agent who died tragically in the line of duty.

The local cop who was there and survived? No hard proof he's dirty, but fuck him anyway.

So it's been one grilling after another, getting tighter and meaner with each interrogation. Must be pure sadistic pleasure for the IA dick, because I admit from the first moment that, yes, I did take some crystal meth from the BCPD evidence locker without authorization and plant it in Russo's Corvette. Seems clear enough to me, though, that I had excellent reasons to bend the rules a little. There was some urgency involved. The IA dick doesn't quite see that. His conception of rules is that they're brittle as glass, no pliability at all. He buys the DEA hint of impure motive because it suits his ends.

I'm confined to desk duty until the inquisitors hand down a verdict, which is why I'm sitting around wasting IB's time instead of out chasing drug dealers. Not cool. Not cool at all, the way this Russo matter worked out.

Like so many other things in my very uneven life. "Might as well have 'Born to Lose' tattooed on my forehead, right, IB?" I say.

"Somebody already did that in invisible ink or something before your mother took you home from the hospital. You got a very special talent for attracting troubles. Troubles love you, man. Any bored trubs just hanging out with nothing to do, they say, 'Hey, there's always Luther. Let's go see him. Luther digs us.' "

"Probably genetic," I say.

"I don't care what it is, long as it's not contagious. I wake up with a pain in my gut every morning already, just from knowing I'm going to be spending most of my working hours next to you. It's high-risk even being in your general vicinity, mostly."

"Worst case, you'll never be in my vicinity again once IA's done with me."

"Aw, man, don't go there." IB suddenly looks forlorn, regretful.

"I mean I'll probably be back in uniform, instead of undercover with you," I say, for his sake. Knowing I'll do the job chop myself before I'll accept that. "Down in the cage on graveyard shift, booking recovered stolen property. High-end mountain bikes, DVD players, super laptops, all that good loot."

"Yeah, it'd have to be that," he says, brightening back up. "They definitely ain't going to let you anywhere near evidence. Especially seized-drug-type evidence."

Just then Dugal's office door opens, the IA dick and his two senior acolytes exit. So stiff with rectitude their knees don't bend when they walk. All three wear identical dark gray suits and white button-down shirts (the acolytes do risk differently striped ties, though), and their usual ecclesiastical faces. But the IA head doesn't look as righteously satisfied as I imagined he might. I'm expecting at least a sneer of muted jubilation from him. He doesn't even glance my way.

I don't want to read too much into impressions like that, though.

"Feels like lunchtime, IB," I say. "I'm booking."

"Right, man. Best to leave a decent interval for Dugal's blood pressure to drop forty or fifty points, so his brain's not swelling so much against his skull. Vanish for a while."

The sun's blazing, it's humid as the Panamanian jungle where I trained back in my army special-ops days, but the sprinklers are whirling on the County Courthouse's green manicured lawns, creating split-second rainbows, once each revolution. My shirt's sticking to my skin by the time I make the hundred meters or so over to Flannery's, a pub I favor because almost no other cops ever go there. The blast of super-cooled air that hits me as I walk inside tightens the muscles in the back of my neck. A headache's likely to follow, but I figure that's a reasonable price of admission. I take a seat at the end of the bar, well away from anyone else.

"Hey, Luther, what's going down?" Frank the bartender says when he wanders over.

"Steak sandwich, bloody. If that retarded quadriplegic you got in the kitchen can manage it. And two Cokes. Cans, not from the taps. If you can manage that."

"Hoo-ah," Frank says softly, holding my eyes a little longer than usual. Former Marine lifer, like my father. He's never said how or why he came here. Probably just wise enough to know anything's better than joining the creaky legion of Corps retirees bunched on the drinking side of cheap bars in cheap towns around Camp Lejeune, boring themselves and each other with bitter bullshit about how exciting life used to be, before that thirty-year clock stopped. "HOO-ah."

"One of those days, Frank. Sorry."

"Sorry-ass excuse. So instead of letting that steak even touch the grill, how about I have the quad give it to you raw?"

"I'm good with that."

"He'll be pleased. Hates that grill, since he has to flip everything with his teeth." Frank goes off laughing. He reaches into a cooler, slides two cans of chilled Coke down the bar. Little bit after that, he puts a thick white plate before me. The steak's perfect, charred outside and nicely red and juicy in. "Chow down, hog," he says.

I do. For two or three savory bites. But then I can't help it, I start thinking options, outcomes. No matter how I try to twist and turn and rearrange them, they still form up as poor to truly shitty. My lunch starts heading in that direction, too. It was a certifiably insane move, trying to burn Russo the way I did. I knew it, did it anyway, so what's that make me? Now I'm facing double trouble. No matter what the IA rules, I know I'm going to be on the DEA's radar for the rest of my life. No way to get under it, no way to slip off their screen. Goddamn Francesca. I never wanted her in my life, never wanted her working my case, and I absolutely never wanted her dead. Just wanted her gone. Away from me. Someplace far away.

But not the place she wound up.

I'd had enough of putting people there, well before she came along.

It seems like I spent most of my adult life doing it, first as a special-ops soldier and then as a narc. No regrets and no guilt. At least none my conscious mind will admit to, since most of the fucks deserved it and I was only doing my job. I'd got trained for it and I'd got paid for it. A profession, and me an enthusiastic practitioner. But sooner or later—unless you're a homicidal psycho, a personal possibilty that haunts me worse than Russo or anyone ever will—you hit the wall. You do not want to do that kind of work anymore. You begin to feel you cannot.

You tell yourself to get out, get into something fresh, clean. Wipe the past.

Easy to say. Much harder to do. All sorts of complications, some real-world, some purely mental. Memory's a major player. Memory has its ways of evading all orders. Soon I'm spiraling deep into dark regions I'd really rather not revisit. Soon I'm so far away on that joyless tour I'm oblivious to my surroundings. For God knows how long I'm not even aware someone's slipped onto the stool right next to mine. Some instinct finally clicks, much later than it should have. Bad lapse. A quick peripheral check then: just another suit on that stool. Okay, I decide. Ignorable. Flannery's is always full of suits—lawyers and civil servants from the courthouse. They never bother anyone, they're too concentrated on selling whatever they've got to whoever they're lunching with.

So I fall right back in. My spiral tightens. I'm no longer eating that sandwich, just staring at it. But seeing something else entirely. Scenes appear, play out, others start. With no regard for the real chronology in which I lived them.

Then the suit speaks.

"Word is you may have some time on your hands. We have an opening that should match your skill set. Discuss?"

A flat, perfectly anonymous voice. The forgettable voice of a man with a forgettable face, the kind who moves through the world leaving little or no impression on anyone. But I snap to full alert, tensed about as tight as I get.

Anonymous. Forgettable. Yeah. Except I'd heard those exact words, in that exact voice, seven or eight years ago. I was underemployed at the time, restless, edgy, unhappy. He seemed to know that when he approached me. Just like he seems to know something now even I'm not sure of yet.

I had discussed, then. Not very much, either. Just enough. I had accepted the offer: independent contractor for a heavy outfit with major international interests.

And then I'd done a year in the worst place on earth.

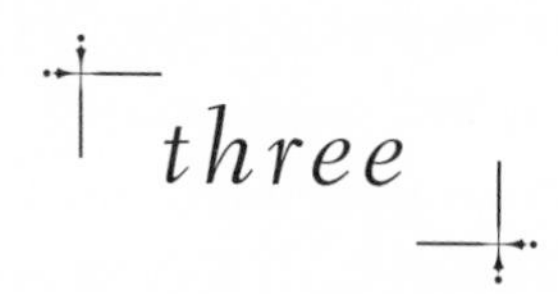

three

FLICK FROM THREE-ROUND BURST TO FULL AUTO. GO LOUDER.

"Suspended. Six months." Captain Dugal's tapping his pen faster and faster against a white legal pad. No beat at all, just tap, tap, tap. It's his version of a facial tic. He won't meet my eyes, though we're face-to-face across his conference-room table. "Without"—taptaptaptaptap—"without pay."

I don't say a thing. I focus on the second hand sweeping around my wristwatch, around and around. Dugal's pen is denting paper faster after one minute thirty. After three, he can't stand it anymore. He looks up from the perfectly blank page, glances at me.

"It was the absolute best I could get for you, Luther. IA pushed very, very hard for dismissal. Morgan even mentioned criminal charges."

Morgan's the IA head. Total failure as a street detective, one of the poorest felony-conviction records ever. I know because I had a savvy friend hack into his file on the BCPD computer net. Five years ago, when he hit fifty, the chief nudged him onto the sidelines, promoting him to captain in charge of Internal Affairs.

I look steadily at Dugal. Now he looks back.

"I went to the mat for you, Luther. Even though this act of yours put me in a very tenuous place. It cast a shadow on my leadership of Narcotics and Vice, threatened to discredit my command and control of those units. You understand this?"

No reply from me.

"I'll assume your silence means yes," Dugal says, leaning slightly forward. "Just so you know, I took the risk of going upstairs on this. To the top. To the chief."

I nod. He's expecting gratitude. He isn't getting it. The pen starts again. Taptaptaptaptap.

"Are you thinking of appealing this, Ewing?" he asks sharply, temper rising now. "We all know the union will back an appeal. They don't care about waving our dirty laundry around in public. Are you going to make that happen, Ewing?"

"What for?" I say. "I could use a nice long break. And it'd only cause you trouble with the chief."

Dugal drops his pen. Surprise, and an odd mix of great relief and extreme discomfort flicker across his face. He wouldn't give a good goddamn what he did or who he screwed if he were ever in my position, so long as he managed to save his own ass. But he's self-aware enough to know it. So it's hard for him to deal with people who don't share that trait, or the obsessive ambition he's had on open display ever since I first met him.

"Goddammit, Luther! None of this had to happen," he says. "Why in the world didn't you come to me with your suspicions about that DEA agent?"

He knows exactly why: he wouldn't have believed a word, or lifted a finger if he had. And he's ranting because some small part of him he usually suppresses is feeling shame. I let him rant, let my mind drift back an hour or so, to the lunch I never finshed. As soon as the suit, name of Mister Westley, said, "Discuss?" I took a ten from my wallet, placed it on the bar, and walked away without looking at him. Nothing to look at, really. "The Man Who Isn't There." That's what we used to call Westley, those of us who discussed and accepted.

We were wrong. He's always there. He must have the instincts of a vulture. He circles, circles, circles. Always looking, always cautious, wary. Then suddenly he's on the ground beside you, and if you're not careful, he'll eat you for lunch.

It's a talent, a natural gift, I suppose. Or the Company wouldn't still have him out there after all these years. He must meet or exceed whatever quota he's given for recruiting contractors: wet-work specialists, covert-action types mainly. People who never have any true contract. If they get killed, get blown, fall into unfriendly hands, the CIA never heard of them. No connection, no relation. And no interest at all in their fates.

They did take care of me after I got shot in Sarajevo, but only because it was less risky to get me out than to leave me where my identity and employer might come to light. So what could Westley want with me now? It'd been years since I did a job for him, and working the suburban narc beat hadn't exactly kept me in special-ops shape. My mind is weighing every possibility it can come up with when Dugal breaks the process.

"What in the hell is the matter with you, Ewing!" he snaps. "Has anything I've said registered with you? You are an outstanding detective who has just been suspended without pay for a serious breach of department rules, and you are simply sitting there like a lobotomized moron. Can you explain this? Am I losing it, or have you lost it, Ewing?"

"Ah, I'm just tired and dazed," I say. "This whole ordeal has been draining, sir."

Dugal unwraps a little. "Yes, yes it has. Not only for you, to some degree, at least. But going forward, let's keep in mind that it could have been worse, much worse. You'll report back in six months—same rank, same duties. All clear?"

"Clear."

Dugal rises, reaches across the table to shake my hand. "Go on home now, Luther. Come in tomorrow, clear out your effects, turn in your badge. I will personally hold on to that, and I look forward to personally handing it back when you return. Good luck."

I take a deep breath of chill, machine-generated air that's been cycling through the plane since we left San Francisco. Not bad recall for a guy as disassociated as Annie's labeled me, I reckon. I down the dregs of my Red Rock, put the bottle on the table. I know if I slip off to sleep now, the delicate Japanese girl who appears and disappears like a fairy will tidy up without disturbing me, though the scent she leaves in her wake may enter my dreams. An hour or two or three ago we touched down in Anchorage, topped up the fuel tanks. Odd. Commercials mostly make nonstop runs from San Francisco to Seoul. Kim must be a nervous flyer, some kink about his air yacht running out of gas over the vast, cold North Pacific.

Kim stayed in his private quarters during the stop. Sonny insisted I go with him to the tacky old passenger terminal, have a look and a laugh at the enormous Kodiak bear that lives there in a glass case. It was a laugh; judging by the mangy fur and the clownish posture, whoever did this monster was having a really bad taxidermy day. It was a laugh, too, when Sonny revealed his secret vice, cleaning out the place's entire stock of Snickers bars.

"You never saw that, Mistah Prentice, okay?" Sonny said as we headed back across the tarmac to the plane, bulging shopping bag in each hand and grinning big. Koreans have two smiles, one genuine and one that's a sign of deepest embarrassment. This Buddha was definitely wearing the second.

The 747's cabin lights are as low as they go. I look out the nearest oval window. The moon's off to the southeast, brilliant though it's only a sickle. We're cutting an arc over the globe from Alaska toward the big, bustling Korean port city of Busan. I'm on an arc with an end point unknown. Because I discussed.

Westley's timing was perfect. He just waited.

Waited past the little going-away party my friend Annie—Detective Lieutenant Annie Mason, head of the Sex Crimes Unit—throws at her house down on Federal Hill in the city. It starts cheerful enough, under the circumstances, rapidly turns loud and boisterous as beer and whiskey consumption increases exponentially, like an old-fashioned Irish wake. It's a good crew, every one of them too cool to even allude to the fact that my suspension's a rank deal, or rant about IA being some kind of asshole conservancy set up and financed by misguided do-gooders totally deluded into believing assholes may be an endangered species.

I can't get drunk—more than one beer or one glass of wine on top of my medication, my brain turns into a kind of toxic and potentially lethal tapioca. But I can flow along with those who do, even when Radik, head of Homocide, falls into some slobbery gratitude about a little help I gave him on some killings related to the Russo case, then staggers into incredibly fluent (for a man who can no longer focus his eyes) descriptions of outstanding crime scenes. He even gets through the classic urban-legend one: teenaged crackhead puts her two-month-old son into the microwave and nukes the kid because he won't stop crying. Nobody's too upset when Radik falls asleep on a sofa.

I get the married men like Ice Box, who's got a terrific wife and adorable twin girls at home, in a state of wistful envy, and the young single guys drooling when I describe how I'll be spending the next six months, though Annie and the other women don't display the same appreciation for most of the details. I say I'm going to do something I haven't done since I was a kid just about to ship out with my Special Forces team: take a long road trip. Leave town in my Audi TT, drive all the way down through Mexico to Merida, then still farther south along the Yucatán coast to Belize, stopping at every likely-looking beach, bay, and *laguna,* snorkling and working on my tan. And in the nights—ah, you can't believe how hot the pretty little señoritas are down there. If you're over thirty and haven't kept yourself aerobically fit as a twenty-one-year-old, you'll be dead of cardiac arrest before morning, they're that wild. I oblige demands to elaborate, and pretty soon I'm half-believing my own bullshit.

Only two people see right through the act, sense the dread of empty time that's hollowing me out already. One's Dog, a rock-hard, super-chilled black city narc. Who took a bullet in the face when we were working on the takedown of a smack gang that left him in a wheelchair for a year, and still on crutches now. As the party's ebbing, I sit on the arm of the chair where he's been parked for most it. I want to tell him how I'm really feeling. But the man already knows.

"You one jive nigger, Luther," he growls. Dog has a master's in criminology, he's more articulate than I'll ever be, but after fifteen years on the streets popping gangbangers, it's hard for him to shed his camouflage. "You be believin' your shit, I let you push mine, faggot."

"Kiss my ass, shorty. Your butt ain't that cute since you been sittin' on it so long."

Dog smiles. "So you know I been there, man. Wake up every morning, nothin' but a blank facing you. Dead hours. Lots of 'em. Damned soon, you be goin' to bed every night hopin' you won't wake up."

"Guess there ain't no stallin', man."

"Maintain. You hearing me, Luther? You just gotta maintain. Do your time, like in the joint. Nigger like me can do it, you a bigger pussy than I ever thought, you got any problems at all maintainin'. Know what I'm saying?"

I feel ashamed when we punch fists.

Feel the same a little later, Annie and me alone in the kitchen, her eyes probing mine. It's all there, clear in her gaze: I'm weak and whipped, loaded with self-pity. And for what? Because I'll be missing the action, the big rush of busts and raids? She sees. She's that good. She works hard at being my friend, does an amazingly graceful job of deflecting my deep romantic interest in her, which she can't or won't return. But I'm losing her respect on this one.

The very last thing in the world I want to happen. I say some things to Annie I hope will stop that. I go home half-believing myself, but less sure Annie believes a word.

No sign of Westley, no word from him since that day at Flannery's. He gives me nearly a week after the party to bounce off the walls of my suburban condo, nearly a week of thinking today will be the morning I throw my duffel into the TT and drive. But never doing it, just sinking deeper into intertia. Nearly a week to reach some volatile combination of frustration, boredom, ennui, and restless, unfocused anger. Then one afternoon he's waiting for me in a government-issue Ford some shade of dark when I leave the condo to go to the nearest mall, objective being to restock my freezer with meals I can microwave and rent a bunch of videos. Leans over when he spots me, opens the passenger door, says, "Let's go for a drive."

It's certifiable. It violates every instinct, and all resolve to maintain, as Dog advised, but I get in. He drives. The opening he's got sounds too easy: no sniping in a war zone, no covert terminations, no wet work at all. Not even clandestine. Just openly shepherding a valuable package around some sensitive parts of North

Asia for a little while. I've never been a baby-sitter before. He knows that.

"Why me?" I ask. "You gotta have guys who specialize in that line."

"None available that I trust. You may have noticed on CNN that we're fairly busy these days, fairly stretched. Afghanistan, up in Kurdish Iraq, even Baghdad. And numerous other places CNN doesn't know about," he says in that flat, lifeless voice. If a polygraph expert asked him if he was Napoleon—or Angelina Jolie, for that matter—he'd answer yes and the polygraph would read he was telling the truth.

"None of our old Asia hands will do; they might be recognized. I need a fresh face, one that comes with your combat and escape-and-evade skills. Someone with no known connection to us, someone who's been out of the game long enough to go unnoticed. There are some few around who fit within those parameters, but none I feel certain won't simply empty all their magazines and make a huge mess if any little thing goes wrong. Not that I'm expecting an incident. I'm expecting smooth and seamless. No jolts. A casual stroll in and out again. But I like to allow for contingencies."

"You forget—I *am* the kind who likes emptying magazines."

"You were once, yes. You were younger, you'd fallen into bad company. But I think that would be your last resort in a situation now. I think you'd choose a quieter exit, in a situation."

"And exactly what sort of situation are you not expecting? What sort of situation that I'll think, instead of shoot, my way out of?"

"The simplest sort. Someone might try—it's highly unlikely, but fools abound—somebody might try a snatch. There will be people with you to deal with any fools. Competent people. If they go to work, all you'd have to do is disappear. With the package."

"This package? Place, time, possible threats?"

"No details until we've come to terms. Then you'll be fully prepped," Westley says.

We discuss. We discuss.

Nothing's any clearer, any more specific a half hour later when Westley drops me back at my place. Except that I've accepted his offer. I spend a long night considering this decision. It's humbling, humiliating. Every reason I come up with seems, under close examination, as stupid and immature as all the bad choices I've made since the first and worst, during Desert Storm. I even seriously entertain the notion that this will be my very last action, and then I'll walk away from it all, including being a cop. But walk to where? What skills do I have? Could I make a living selling cars, or real estate? Could I find contentment—or even resigned acceptance—in any sort of quietly normal existence? I'm starting to feel hopelessly trapped when I hit the one answer that may be true. Then it turns intolerable. I am simply scared shitless that I'm facing six empty months, six months that might well be a preview of what I've got to look forward to for the rest of my life, if I quit the game.

Next day I call a few people, make a quick good-bye. Longer one with Annie, at her house that evening.

"You're really heading where you claim you are, Luther?" she says, giving me the grin she must have a patent on, because I've never seen one on any other woman that made me want her so much. "Swear you're not going off elsewhere, into something truly stupid?"

"Absolutely. All I want is some peace and quiet. Maybe I'll have some fun. If I can get past missing you."

She laughs. "You're so full of it sometimes."

"Am I?"

"Yeah. We've been seeing each other every day for years and it never got in the way of all the fun you managed with a half-dozen pretty young things, most of whose names I can't remember."

"Substitutes, Annie."

"I think maybe you've convinced yourself at some level you want something you wouldn't really like that much if you got it. Self-delusion, Luther. We're good as we are."

"You go right on thinking I'm deluded, if you like. Just let me go on being sure I'm not."

"Haven't I always done that? Or, more accurately, haven't I always failed in my efforts to disabuse you of your whacked notions?" Annie laughs. "But we'll keep dealing with that when you get back. Right now, I just want some more reassurance that you really are just going beach-bumming and will be back."

"No problem. Hey, I won't even be carrying. Don't want to wind up in some south-of-the-border jail I won't be able to bribe my way out of, on a stupid weapons charge."

"Go carefully." Annie kisses me on both cheeks. "You'll have your cell?"

"Won't work in the Yucatán. I'll be calling you, though."

The grin vanishes. Her eyes narrow.

"You're lying, Luther." She stares at me for a long minute, then says, "If I thought there was even a slight hope it'd make a difference, I'd ask you not to go."

When I'm out on the porch, she searches my eyes for a moment, then turns and quietly closes her door.

I don't sleep that night. Next morning I drive the TT to an address in Washington. I go in, disappear into another world. One of Westley's young men goes out, takes my car, and makes it vanish, too.

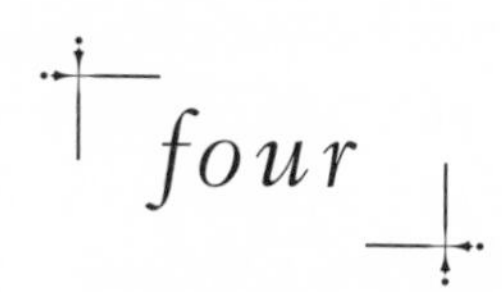

four

WESTLEY AND HIS SPOOK HOUSE. FOUR STORIES, DARK STONE, absolutely identical to every other house lining the block just off Dupont Circle, like a platoon of Marines in dress-blue parade formation. Even has six buzzers beside the front door, names and apartment numbers beside each, since all the other rowhouses have long ago been chopped into apartments, home to young GS mid-grades, lobbyists, Hill assistants, law-firm associates doing their years-long boot camp of eighty-hour weeks, dreaming of making partner. Clever touch, the buzzers. They'll account for all the people coming and going.

I've just put my duffel down on the foyer floor when Westley appears. First thing he says is "Lose the hair." I haven't cut it in maybe two years, it's well past my shoulders. He scans my baggy cargoes, the long-sleeve waffle knit with a Billabong T worn over it. Second thing he says isn't to me. "Get him some decent clothes, too," he tells a young woman I haven't even noticed, who's leaning against a sideboard on the other end of the foyer. Third's a question: "Your Russian up to speed?" When I admit it's rusty as hell, he says he'll have a tutor from Langley come over to work me out for a couple of hours every afternoon. Then he goes back into the room from which he emerged.

"Well? You ready?" the girl asks me, smiling. She's about my height, slim, with a clean-featured face, straight dark brows above amber eyes, but hair a golden brown. Like toast. Very tidy, at ease in her standard-issue officewear.

"What? I don't quite fit in, fashion-wise?"

"Something like that," she says. "You look like every other plainclothes drug cop I've ever seen. Never seen one on this block, though. You guys get your clothes from some specialized catalog or something?"

"Oh yeah. It's called Narcstyle, very limited mailing list. Cool street looks, plus professional discounts and stuff."

"Thought so. My name's Allison, by the way, and I'll be your style guide and personal buyer today."

"Cool, Allison. I'm really ready for a total makeover. Been feeling so five-minutes-ago lately."

Her laugh is perfectly natural. The Company teaches them things like that. No detail too small. "You must have been a star in acting class at the Farm, Allison," I say.

She doesn't even blink. "So let's do it, Luther," she says, swinging open the front door and leading me down the steps and a few houses east, where she keys a British green Mini-Cooper with a white top, the vehicle that's elbowing the Volkswagen Bug as car of choice for her demographic cohort. The engine has an appealing alto hum as she pulls out, shifts into second, swings surely onto the Circle and off three-quarters of the way around.

So Westley's given her my real name. Means Allison here's a senior and trusted member of his team, despite her youth. Probably also means she's a field agent, her name isn't Allison, and she's got the full set of spook skills. So I'm watching her, not where we're going, and she catches it.

"Do you always think so loudly? Or are you feeling we've only just met and there's an instant chemistry so you don't need to be quiet? Maybe even wondering how much time I'll be spending at the house while you're there?" She tosses me a quick smile, then refocuses on threading through the traffic web. "The answer is we'll be together a lot. It's not a crowded house. But you have a lot of work to do. A killer workload. Let's do hair first."

Fucking Westley. I'd love to get a look at the psych profile he has on me. I just know I'm going to be doing most of my prep work with a bunch of Allisons.

She finds a parking spot only a Mini could squeeze into. We walk half a block to Wisconsin Avenue. I haven't spent much time in D.C., but I know we're in Georgetown. She leads me into a hair place called Cutz. Allison tells the cutter what to do. "Short, but not too. A little tousled, sort of a Brad Pitt thing. But brushable down to corporate?"

"No problem," says the girl with the scissors, fingering my ponytail. I feel kind of like a show dog about to be groomed for exhibition. "Great hair. Thick. Good body. The split ends'll all wind up on the floor. A no-gel cut, though, right?"

"Exactly," Allison says.

I'm looking in the mirror, seeing a familiar face, the one I've lived behind all my life. "You're, like, really unusual, man," says the cutter, who has a black Maori tattoo on her neck, an opal stud in one nostril, and two blood-red streaks in her blond hair. "Cool bones."

"I'm Patagonian," I say. I hear Allison stifle a chuckle when the cutter says, "Wow! Never seen one of those before. Where is Patagonia? South Seas, like Tahiti or something?"

"About as south as it gets," I say. Why should I tell her I'm what came out of a union between an Afro-American Marine and a Viet girl with a touch of French blood? I don't look much like either my father or my mother, anyway. My skin's light copper, I've got a large Gallic-type nose, and my hair is as straight as if it's been ironed. High, sharp cheekbones, moderately full lips. My eyes have a slight Asian cant, but they're gray-green, not black. When I was in Special Forces, the grunts called me their Comanche; what would they know about Native Americans? So I went with that, passed myself off as a full-blood. They dug it.

"Do all Patagonians look like you?" the cutter asks between snips. "I mean, the cool bones and great skin and eyes and all?"

"Oh yeah," I say. "I'm average, totally."

Half an hour later we walk out, Allison saying, "Great look. Suits you, Luther, though no Brad Pitt. He's about your age now, imagine that. God, the crush I had on him when I was in high school and *Legends of the Fall* came out. He was so beautiful."

I'm thinking I look a lot more like a not-so-young assistant to a Democratic House member from Massachusetts than any actor this kid had the adolescent hots for. But not real uncomfortable about it.

Can't say the same about the suits. We drive a long way out Wisconsin to a very upscale mall in a very upscale, very close-in Montgomery County suburb. Saks Fifth Avenue has a branch there, and Allison takes me to the aspiring-to-be-CEO menswear section so directly I'm thinking she must shop here a couple times a month. I stand there like a tailor's dummy while she and the salesman pull half a dozen Oxxfords or Hickey-Freemans or whatever youngish executives in conservative corporations wear off the racks. The salesman only slips the jackets on me. They all seem a size too large. She settles on four: deepest navy, two grays so charcoal they're almost black, one dark blue with the faintest pinstripe. "Oh, never mind that. We have a little man who does it just right," Allison tells the salesman when he wants to call out the tailor for alterations. "Just put them in garment bags, please."

Then it's shirts: a dozen white oxford button-downs; ties: three muted paisleys, three rep striped regimentals, all silk; socks: a dozen black merino over-the-calves; shoes: one pair of wing tips, one pair of cap-toes, one pair of dress loafers, all black and all Church's.

It's a one-stop for everything else: the store's Polo boutique. That's where I finally say "You've got to be kidding," and Allison says, "Negative. You know what it's about." A pair of khakis, a pair of jeans, a couple of polos, two cashmere V-necks. "Boxers or jockeys?" is the only question Allison asks, and scoops up a dozen when I answer jockeys. She carries a couple of the shopping bags but I'm listing under my load when we leave the store. It takes maybe ten minutes to find a way to stow everything in the Mini's tiny trunk and rear seat area.

"Hey, that was fun, wasn't it? Come on, admit it, Luther," she says brightly as we're cruising back to the spook house.

"Terrific. Loved every minute." I'm bored, tired, already fed up.

"You were billed as a professional. Misinformation, or are you just really, really rusty? Too much time on the shelf?" Her voice isn't bright now. I know she's going to report every detail of our little expedition to Westley, with a concentration on my behavior and attitude. And Westley, this early, could easily cancel my contract without the mess of canceling my ticket, too. It's all role-play, and time for me to switch mine if I want to stay on this job.

"Hey, Allison, you might want to consider lightening up. I'm just giving you a little of what you expected. Small-time narc, not too clever, attitude problem, way below Agency officer standard. Only asset he's got is close-combat skills. And why the hell do we have to use low-life contractors like this Luther guy, anyway? That's what you've been thinking. Correct me if I'm wrong."

She glances at me once, then once again. "Everything's a test."

"I know. They really drum that one into you at the Farm. Takes years to get over it."

She keeps her focus on the traffic ahead, but I see a hint of a smile playing about her mouth.

Then I know this: Allison's going to be my main handler during mission prep.

Could be worse.

My room's on the third floor of the spook house. It's nice enough: comfortable double bed, easy chair, a desk with a neat NEC laptop, and a full bathroom with tub, shower, hotel towels. Someone's unpacked my duffel, hung up my clothes in the armoire, placed my weapons—still in their holsters—on the night table beside the bed. But all the mags for the SIG and the Walther have been emptied, my cell's nowhere, there's no phone. And there's no lock on the door.

For a moment my heart rate goes up a few beats. It's involuntary, a reaction to a feeling of vulnerability. I chill. I don't need pistols here, I wouldn't want to call anyone even if I could, and what's it matter if Allison or anyone else can barge in on me anytime they want? Worst case is somebody catches me jerking off, which would embarrass them more than it would me. Fuck it. I take a long shower, towel off, dress in the clothes I started the day in, and lie down on the bed.

I must drift off, because I'm seeing Annie, hearing her say I'm hemorrhaging and she's going to clamp the artery, hearing her say, "Luther? Luther?" and suddenly I'm bolt upright and there's Allison framed in the doorway calling my name.

"Pretty good reflexes for an old guy," she says. She's done something to her hair, ditched the officewear for hip-slung jeans and a ribbed top. "How about some dinner? I was in the mood for expensive French, since Uncle's picking up the tab. But considering your wardrobe? You like ethnic?"

"Thai, Mex, Chinese, Viet, whatever. I'm easy. Just one question. All you mid-twenties chicks shop from the same catalog or what? Those jeans, that top . . ."

"'Chicks'?" She laughs. "That's just so quarter-century-ago, Ewing."

"I know. But it's a lot more polite than right-this-minute cop and military nomenclature."

"Which is all you know, because those guys, and scummy drug dealers, are who you've been hanging out with for years, while the world's been spinning right out from under you. You never noticed?"

"Oh, I noticed all right. Just never found a way to get back on board and still be able to do the job. It's an alternate universe from yours."

"So we'll go to one at least a little more like yours for dinner, okay? You know Adams Morgan?"

"No, can't make him."

"It's a neighborhood, not a guy, for Christ's sake." Allison laughs. "Three-quarters yuppified, which accounts for all the good little restaurants. The other quarter? Not a gangbanger world like Anacostia and South East, but some urban grit. You'll feel right at home, I think. How about we do Mexican? Because pretty soon you'll be eating Far East an awful lot. Las Lobos Cantina has super-hot tomatillo sauce."

I get up and move to the door. "Oh, by the way, you can leave your wallet here," she says. "Actually, you have to."

Right. No ID. Seems like an unnecessary precaution at this stage, but house rules are house rules.

Which seem to have various extensions outside the house. We've got a chaperone, who introduces himself as Rob when we meet in the foyer. Then we're in the Mini, moving along unfamiliar streets to Adams Morgan. I see at once Allison's description was in the X-ring; at the edges of the stream of yuppies I spot at least two dealers on the short walk to this Las Lobos place. They've toned down the gangsta look—it's all about fitting in, for sure—but I'd bet my life they're holding, waiting for customers.

"Two players, small-time. One by that phone booth, the other near the Laundromat, by the alley," I say. "The laundry guy's packing. Probably a new niner, stainless steel. Not used to the weight. He keeps brushing it with his elbow."

"You mean the kid in the black pants? He's a fixture around here," Rob says.

"Sure, must be his office," I say. "You and I go over and hassle him, he might show us his fresh tool."

"Let's skip that," Rob says.

I'm pretty sure Allison and Rob aren't carrying, but he's probably field-trained. Same cohort as Allison. They could be five years out of college, together in their first serious affair after four or five false starts with other partners. They're tuned into each other. But, I'm almost certain, strictly professionally. Westley probably teams them because they look like a pair of lovers, they give off that aura. Except to a trained watcher.

Inside the cantina, I make sure I get a seat with my back to the wall, and note all exits.

"You always on full alert?" Rob asks.

"Auto-reflex." I pause. "Same as you, though you're subtle about it. You scanned the tables, assessed the clientele when we came in. Pretty smooth."

"Chicken enchiladas, with that tomatillo sauce, for me," Allison says, shutting down this little exchange. "Dos Equis all around?"

The beers come, then the food. Poor acoustics, loud mariachi blaring. We can barely hear each other, so forget being overheard. But naturally there's no talk about the job. Allison wants to draw me out, and I let her. Why not? It's all in the dossier Westley has to've given her. She just wants to see how I'll present it.

I do it straight, as she and Rob eat enchiladas with that hot green sauce she recommended and I tuck into beef fajitas. Where did I grow up? All over, military gypsy, never anywhere longer than two years, if you don't put together a couple of separate stays outside Camp Lejeune. Born there, in fact, some time after my father, Gunnery Sergeant Thomas "One Way" Ewing, returned from his last tour in Nam with his Viet bride in tow. Left there when he did some embassy postings, spent two years in Yokohama and two years in Guam later on when he was assigned fleet duty.

"What was that like?" Allison asks.

"Wired off from the world. Very closed community. School, everything, right on the bases. The ethic was dependents didn't mix much with the locals."

"Sounds kind of claustrophobic," Rob says.

"Felt like prison, when I was fourteen in Yokohama," I say, knowing neither of them can comprehend. CIA newbies don't come from military families. They're mainly middle-, upper-middle class, they've got bachelor's and maybe advanced degrees from Stanford and Georgetown and MIT in computer science or Middle East Studies, they're likely to be fluent in Mandarin or Farsi or Arabic as well as one or more of the major European languages. Junior year abroad, some postgrad studies in St. Petersburg or Beijing. Their passports are nearly full of visa stamps before they set foot on the Farm.

I laugh, give them something as we're finishing the meal that maybe isn't in the dossier. "You know how it is at fourteen, hormones doing a number on you. I was off-base in Yokohama as much as I could manage. Wanted some action, wanted some weed or speed. No luck. Not a lot of drugs on the streets in Japan. It was easier to score on base. Lots of supply sergeants' pencils weren't real sharp about certain crates that came in.

"Anyway, that left girls. Not much luck there, either. Supply sergeants' daughters were easier than the wildest Japanese girls. Tended toward ugly, though. But I did make it with one lovely local. Miko Yamaguchi. God, I still remember that."

"At fourteen? No way I'm believing you. This is a brag story, Luther," Allison says.

"Oh, it's true," I say, pulling up the sleeve of my waffle shirt, showing them a six-inch scar on my left forearm. "Problem was, Miko had a boyfriend. Who happened to be the son of a local Yakuza underboss. The boyfriend and two of his pals jump me one night. But I'm big for my age. I hammer them. I pay extra attention to the boyfriend's face. Radically rearrange his features, specially the nose and his dental work. Next time I'm in the neighborhood, two of the Yak's men grab me, hold me down, give me this cut on the arm, tell me they see me around again, it'll be my balls."

Rob and Allison stay slick. They're grinning. I don't have even ten years on them, and they're humoring me like an old man. "So. You have to go back to the base hospital, get maybe twenty stitches, your father finds out, of course, and whips your butt. Bye-bye, sweet Miko," Allison says.

"Affirmative. And then one night my papa and five or six of his buddies go down to the Yak's bar, kick the shit out of him, the two cutters, and miscellaneous personnel. They then procede to totally trash the bar. Anything that could be broken got broken. Hoo-ah!"

"Sounds like an international incident of serious proportions," Rob says lightly, as if he's being bullshitted and wants it clear he knows it. "Wicked repercussions."

"Zero repercussions, Rob," I say, hard-eyed and holding. "This guy's a gangster, a walking billboard of criminality with Yak tattoos covering his chest, back, and arms. Minus his left little finger, too, which means he lost face with his boss over some earlier fuck-up and had to atone in the traditional way. Is he likely to go to the police? Is he going to lodge a complaint with the American base commander? Worst of all, what if his boss finds out what he ordered done to me? He'd lose his other little finger."

"Colorful! I think he's got you, Rob," Allison says. "Hey, one more beer for the road, guys?"

"No thanks," I say. "I sense I'll be getting an early wake-up call tomorrow."

"Prescient, Luther," Allison says. "Can you tell fortunes, too?"

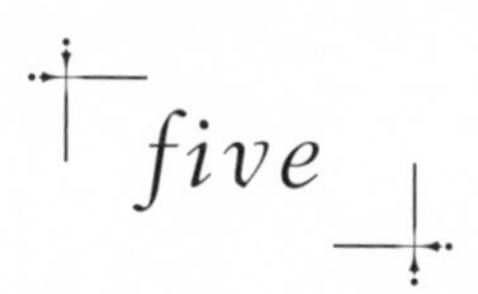

five

NO CALL NECESSARY. I'M UP BEFORE SUNRISE, PULLING ON SWEATpants and a hoody to go for a run, which is something I've skipped way too often these past years.

I'm in the foyer, my hand on the door latch when a guy I haven't met grasps my wrist. I start to spin into a kick, pure reflex, when Westley materializes between us.

"You can't, Luther," he says.

"Can't go for a run?" There's no hand on my wrist now. In fact there's no sight of whoever it was grabbed me. A cold bolt streaks up my spine, stops at the base of my neck.

"Leave the house alone," Westley says. Early as it is, he's already in suit and tie. His tone is easy, like he's trying to soothe a dog that's bared its fangs. "You want to run mornings, do it all you want. But let me know first. I'll have a partner for you."

"I like to run alone."

"House rules. You're never out by yourself. Put off the run for a half hour or so. Let's have some breakfast, talk about your program."

For a moment I consider telling him no, I'm going out. Very dumb, to permit any such notion to even flicker. No question I'd be stopped. No real surprise, that door guard. But I'm jolted when Westley leads me into an office done up like an English parlor with nailed leather Chesterfields and paintings of horses on the walls, and I see two cups on saucers beside a silver coffeepot, a creamer, and a sugar bowl on a round mahogany table.

It clicks. Sensors or cameras in my room. Somebody watching over me in my sleep, somebody knowing the moment I get out of bed, somebody aware if I'm just up for a quick piss or getting dressed and leaving. And Westley knows I never eat anything in the morning. Always get started with nothing but strong coffee, heavy on the cream and sugar, and cigarettes.

There's an open pack of Camel Wides, a Bic lighter, an ashtray next to one of the cups. I don't need to be told where to sit. I do need to start keeping who I'm working with front and center in my mind. Need to light that up bright and keep it lit. And shuck the habits and attitudes of Dugal's narc squad.

"So," Westley says, pouring coffee for me. "Room suit you? You getting on okay with Allison? So far, so good?"

"So far," I say.

"So, good enough. All right. As we discussed, this is going to be easy duty, no strain, no stress. But maybe you need to get back up to speed in a couple of ways. Your weapons skills are as sharp as ever, I hear. What about the rest?"

"Not as good with my hands as I used to be," I admit. "Haven't had much use for that in a long time."

"No problem. I'll bring in a sparring partner every day. There's a place here where you can work out."

"Okay."

"Next. As we discussed, some Russian practice every day. And you're going to need some Korean, too. Just enough to get by in a pinch. Plus some style things. Manners, behavior, gestures. You know the drill."

"Sure. Fit in, don't stand out, don't give offense. Unless you mean to."

"Exactly. Now let's talk weapons. Nothing heavy, no military-type tools. Your role will be purely, absolutely defensive. What you brought with you would be perfect, except they're yours. You'll need things just as concealable under a suit, but no serial numbers, no history, no discoverable source. Make a list of what you want, give it to Allison today."

"So when do I get the exact who, where, and what? In detail?"

"Closer to the fact. Right now, let's just take care of these few basics."

"Fine. But how close to the fact?"

Westley laughs. "I won't wait until five minutes before your plane takes off, you can count on that. You'll know everything you'll need to know to fulfill your task in plenty of time to digest, analyze, plan for various scenarios."

"Who decides what I don't need to know?"

"I do."

There's no perceptible change in Westley's voice, but I feel absolute confidence, absolute authority behind it. At the same moment, there's the sense that I'm seeing the man for the first time. He must be in his sixties. Even features, thin lips, skin still fairly taut but bearing the fine furrows and creases of age. No distinguishing marks, nothing anybody would remember. His gray eyes seem cold and soulless as the steel rims of his glasses, but in my trade half the people you run into have eyes like that.

"And if I decide there's something vital missing, some blank that could blow the op and me away, what about that?"

"There won't be that sort of blank," Westley says. "But you can ask me. I might even answer. Unlikely, but I might."

"Ghosts playing a game with ghost rules."

"That's just occurring to you? I don't think so. You've always known we're called 'spooks' for good reason," Westley says.

Allison's waiting in the foyer, wearing sweats and doing straight-leg stretches, her heel on the staircase's banister. "How long do you usually like to go?" she says, not looking at me, bending at the waist until her chin is almost touching a knee. "One K, max, am I right?"

"Wrong. Five minimum. Under thirty minutes."

"Really?" She gives me a look that says she knows I'm full of shit, moves past me to the door, sniffs. "Smoker, too! I don't think I'm going to get up to aerobic level if I pace you."

There's no place near we can go except Dupont Circle, which starts out looking really small but gets bigger and bigger with each labored lap. Labored for me. I hardly ever work out in any way, but in my head I've retained the cracked illusion that physically I'm still the eighteen-year-old who charged right through Special Forces training. Just how cracked that is gets demonstrated conclusively when, by the tenth lap, Allison starts running backward and stays side by side with me. She's even laughing, while I'm starting to pant.

"Hey, don't let me crash into anything that isn't really soft, okay?" she says. "Hate having to keep turning my head to see if my way's clear."

"How 'bout a bus? That soft enough?"

"Don't get bitter."

"Oh, never. That'd be so inappropriate." I have to gulp two or three breaths before I can even get that out. Goddamn Westley. He knows I've spent most of my time sitting on my skinny ass in a car with Ice Box for too many years. Knows it's going to take a hard and concentrated effort to get back into the shape I'll need to be. And uses humiliation as an incentive to get me on that road.

It's working, too. When we're finished, I'm determined I'll run every morning, put myself through whatever PT torture it takes to get back to speed. Westley's got me taped to the millimeter.

Lunch is in-house. An invisible kitchen, an invisible cook, but a steam table in the dining room, first floor rear, overlooking a fenced-in patio. The food's standard government agency cafeteria for grades GS-13 and below: choice of mediocre meat loaf or breaded, fried fish patties, plus oversteamed peas and carrots, broccoli, mashed potatoes. Or the mini–salad bar, mainly a big bowl of nearly frozen iceberg lettuce with canned chickpeas, shredded carrots, croutons and bacon bits for add-ons.

Westley doesn't eat this, and not because he's GS-15. I've seem him scarf MREs and unnamable local specialties I'd want my dog to test first before I tried them, in that bad place we'd spent a year in. He's out somewhere, doing whatever he does. It's just Allison, Rob, and the semi-phantom that seized my wrist at the door this morning, who turns out to be a fairly small but lithe-looking guy called Terry.

"Yum yum. Sometimes you eat the bear, sometimes the bear eats you," Allison says, her plate heavy with meat loaf, mashers, and a load of gravy.

"Not a bad James Earl Jones," I say.

"God. Movie-referential again. She's always doing this," Rob says. He's a salad-only eater. "Okay, I'll play. The film was, uh, *Gardens of Stone*, right? James Earl Jones, top sergeant. James Caan, next sergeant. Some actress with a short neck. Director . . . I give up."

"Anjelica Huston, and her neck's not so short. Coppola directed. How could you not know Coppola directed?" Allison says.

"Why not? Obscure film, a week in theaters, then straight to video," Rob says. "*You* know it was Coppola, Luther?"

"Sure," I say, experiencing a definitely gummy aftertaste of meat loaf. "Jones and Caan, they're two-tour Vietnam lifers now running the infantry company that does all the formal military burials at Arlington. Caan hates it, wants out. But he's got this real dick of a CO, played by that weird dude who was as likely to show up in David Lynch flicks as Dennis Hopper, what's his name? Dean Stockwell."

"Bingo," Allison says. "So you spend some serious VCR time, too, Luther?"

"Nah, gotta be DVD. To get the full experience."

"Limiting, limiting," Allison says, shaking her head. "Lots of the greatest movies, the older ones, haven't made it to DVD. I mean, think about it. Real classics, like *Best Years of Our Lives*, *The Lion in Winter*, *The Conformist*, *The Night Porter*, almost all of Garbo and Bergman."

"You're not buying any of this, I hope, Luther," Rob says. "Her favorite all-time great, the one she's watched six times, is, get this: *Gladiator*! You can't imagine the depth of her interest in Russell Crowe. She cries when he slices the SPQR tattoo off his arm. Her big dream is that one day they'll somehow meet and Crowe'll be hit by the love-at-first-sight phenomenon."

"Wrong," Allison says.

"Wrong what?" Rob says.

"I don't cry when he cuts the tattoo."

Terry giggles. That's it. He looks sideways at her and giggles.

"I only cry with rage when that spineless bitch stands over his dead body in the Colosseum and says, 'He was a soldier of Rome.' It's her fault he got killed, dammit. She should be taken out and shot."

"Oh, okay, just jump a whole bunch of centuries. 'Taken out and shot.' Little cognitive continuity problem here, Allison?" Rob's smiling big-time.

"Oh, blow me, Rob."

"Hey. Another little cognitive hitch."

And it's all kind of fun, watching these kids perform. They're very good, they're improvising around the script, which calls for drawing the outsider—me—into the group, making him feel he's a welcome part of a tight crew. Smart and competent on duty, but open, relaxed folks off, the kind he'll like and trust and maybe believe are his friends. Every contact—the Mex dinner, the jogging, now lunch—has had that object, and they haven't fluffed many lines.

"Hey, you've got a free half hour before your next task, Luther," Allison says as we're finishing up. "Rob and I have some stuff to take care of, so do what you like. We'll catch you later."

What I'd like is more of a sense of the place that features, apparently, 24/7 surveillance in my room. What else have they got in place? How hardened is this house? This is definitely need-to-know for me, though nobody else seems to think so.

I decide I'll try the back patio the dining room overlooks. It seems fenced no differently than every other house on the block I can see from the window. I find some stairs going down a level, a short corridor that ends at a steel door. There's a Terry clone sitting in a wooden chair there. I make a gesture, he nods, punches some keys on a numeric electronic lock. Interior bolts pull back with a heavy click, the door swings open, and I'm out on the flagstones, flickering patterns of light and dark from the sun peering through the leaves of trees. The door stays open, the Terry clone seems preoccupied with his fingernails, but I act as if someone's watching me. I check out the flower beds built up against the fence, with is ordinary eight-foot cedar planking, I amble to the far end of the patio and look back at the house. The security's damned near invisible, but after a few minutes I finally spot some telltales. Tucked under a couple of windowsills are small cubes

I'm pretty sure are motion sensors, though they're cased in wood painted the same off-white as the sills. Where the rain gutter meets the downspouts at each corner of the house, I spot a glint when the breeze shifts the leaves and sun hits glass. Surveillance cameras, but smaller than any I've seen before. My eyes track the downspouts. About a meter above the fence, I see the first of what look like copper rivets spaced evenly about six inches apart. Turning, I see the four-by-fours at the fence corners are about a meter taller than the planking and feature the same copper circles: infrared, or maybe the latest laser system. The ordinary-looking fence may as well be topped with coils of razor wire; nobody's coming over unseen or unheard.

Tight. I'm walking back toward the steel door, which has to be four inches thick, hinges set inside so they can't be popped, when I glimpse a bit of insulated wire poking through the moss between the flagstones. I take a little skip, feel the stone I come down on give just a fraction. Pressure pads under the flags, wired to the interior alarm system?

Christ! I'd thought this was prep house, but if the rear security is representative, it's been as hardened as a safe house for defectors or high-value sources some bad guys with lots of skills and resources very badly want to kill. That's a nasty surprise.

But soon after I'm back inside, the armored steel door thunking solidly shut as I head upstairs, I run into an unexpectedly sweet one.

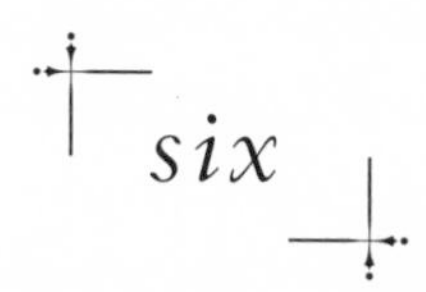

six

SHE'S STANDING BY THE WINDOW AND HALF-TURNS QUICKLY WHEN I walk into my lockless room: large, slightly canted eyes the pale blue of a Siberian husky's, almost black hair with perfect bangs and a sharp cut at the jawline, and a smile that almost cracks my heart. She's wearing a tight black turtleneck over a short, russet suede skirt and matching suede ankle boots. She says hello, tells me her name is Nadya. In perfect Russian, slight Moscow accent.

Nadya. Not something real but unappealing to the American ear, like Ludmilla or Svetlana. Not tutor-prim, plain, stiff. The damned profile again.

Nadya's smile is a sham, she's brisk, all business. But that's okay; the devious bastards knew it would be, since she's stunning—not per the general American standard, but exactly the way I can never resist. Maybe they don't know it would still have been okay if she wasn't, so long as she was as bright and quick as she soon proves to be.

She suggests we go to the library, which turns out to be on the second floor and fully equipped with walls of books, plus a complete suite of high-end video and audio gear. None of this interests her. We sit on a sofa, a meter apart, she curls her legs under her and faces me. Then she begins an I'd-like-to-get-to-know-you-better conversation, like a girl you just met in a bar who's maybe a little intrigued but wary, too: What do I do? Is my work interesting? She guessed so. Hers is sometimes a bit boring, but a couple of evenings a week she goes out dancing, though most of the men she meets in Washington are also a bit boring. New York must be more interesting, she's sure. Am I married? No? Do I mean never, or just not at the moment? Never? Why not? So what do I do for fun? Really? And your girlfriend doesn't mind? There isn't one? Ah. You mean they don't know about each other, don't you? You're wicked, a real dog. I wouldn't stand for that. Not for a minute.

All in Russian. A game develops. She wins. I can't lure or trick her into speaking a single word of English. We go back and forth in Russian, drinking coffee and smoking, for almost three hours. I learn a lot about her: born in Moscow, raised in the U.K., came to the States after Cambridge, hasn't had a regular boyfriend in almost a year, sometimes feels she's wasting her youth, spending too many nights alone just surfing the Web. None of it true, I'm sure, except maybe the Moscow bit. She pounces like a cat every time I skitter on pronunciation, syntax, or preferred current usage.

"Not nearly as creaky as I expected. A bit old-fashioned, a bit stiff here and there. Not to worry," she says in English—BBC, not American, so maybe the U.K. bit at least is true—as she's leaving, putting on that beautiful smile she was wearing when she first looked at me across my room. "Tomorrow then, Luther? Super."

Oh yes, super. They've punched the right button, sending me little Nadya. I like this girl, this game. It's a shame, I find myself thinking, about the circumstances. I'm wishing we'd met in the real world, as real people. I'm missing her alluring presense already. But my mood rises from its slump when I go back to my room, sit at the desk, and begin that list Westley told me to make. I start thinking of all the weapons I've used, how they felt in the hand, how they performed. I circle in on a few things I've handled but never owned. It's a wish list and Westley's buying, so what the hell. Pretty soon I've filled a small mental box with what I consider the very finest tools in the world. Gives me a kind of Christmasy feeling, just as the encounter with Nadya did. Can't wait to unwrap those packages.

Defense only, not offense, Westley said. So. Primary: Wilson SDS, a small, supertuned and absolutely reliable custom version of the old classic 1911 .45 ACP. With a custom Mitch Rosen shoulder holster to carry it unseen and safely under my left armpit even in condition one, cocked and locked, and a double mag case on the offside. Secondary: a Springfield XD in .357 SIG; it out-Glocks a Glock, it's lighter yet holds twice the rounds of a SIG 239. A Kramer horsehide small-of-the-back holster for it, plus a belt-clip double mag holder that'll also carry a SureFire Z2 combat flashlight. For my pants pocket, I want a Boker folder with a four-inch ceramic spearpoint; no steel knife made can cut as surgically as a properly sharp ceramic blade.

Now the backup, in case some little incident turns into a true goat-fuck. I'll want a very nice leather attaché case, custom-made with Kevlar armor forming the hard-sides, and custom-pocketed inside to hold the ultimate revolver, a .357 Magnum Korth, Swiss-made, each by a single gunsmith, and as perfectly smooth and precise as the finest Swiss chronometer available. Worth every penny of the $6,000 it'll cost. Plus three full speedloaders for the Korth, two full spare mags for both the Wilson and the XD, and four grenades: one smoke, one stun, one gas, one frag.

Perfect, I'm thinking as I survey the list. The finest gear there is, in a neat, unobtrusive carry mode. Not at all what I'd choose for a night assault on a military target, but ideal for a protection job. Even Westley, though, with all his resources, will have some trouble putting my package together in time for me to work out with everything, break the pistols in by putting a few hundred rounds through them and so forth. The only items readily available are the XD and the ammo: has to be Hornady XTP.

"Scribble, scribble, scribble," I hear from the doorway behind me.

"Love letter to Nadya, Allison," I say, not turning. "Amazing how fast it happens sometimes, isn't it? What do the French call it? *Coup de foudre?*"

"How about coup de takeout dinner in front of a couple of DVDs?" she says.

Shit. Just like Helen, the girl I had until—Christ, it wasn't even a month ago that I left her. Or she left me. Graduated from her fancy college in Baltimore, went back to her parents in Connecticut for the summer, probably getting ready now to move to California, grad school at Stanford. This is getting beyond psych profile. This is getting really personal, really spooky. Can Westley know everything? Is there a thing inside my head or outside in my whole life he isn't conscious of, down to the smallest detail?

Cancel that, Luther. The emotional bonds with Helen were tissue thin, and I'm utterly indifferent to Allison as a woman. But assume everything is known, accept it. Get into the role, say something in character. Every word you utter is being recorded, either electronically or in somebody's head.

I swivel, watch Allison walk over, hand her my list.

"I'll deliver your love letter later. I won't even read it first. Well, maybe a quick glance in private," she says, pocketing the paper. "So, you're cool with takeout?"

"Oh yeah, I'm very cool with takeout and a movie."

"Okay! You pick the food, I'll choose the movies. Chinese, Thai, or pizza? Really excellent pizza, very thin crust, crispy."

"You've convinced me. Pizza. This place, they deliver everything-you-can-think-of-type pies?"

"Sure. I go for everything, too."

"Extra anchovies, then?"

"Double extra, since neither of us have dates tonight. So, in the library? Say forty-five, fifty minutes if I go call right now?"

"Nineteen hundred ten, sharp. The library."

"Military time, European airport time. Still always have to translate in my head," she says, heading out. "Um, eighteen hundred hours is . . . right, so you mean ten after seven? You do."

"I'll be on aroma alert."

Her laughs disappears with her down the corridor.

Westley's nowhere, Rob's out somewhere, and Terry's probably clocked out, replaced by another Terry type who'll do nightwatch on the first-floor front.

So it's just Allison and me. Pizza's great, movies not. Allison's so rapt during the first, *Proof of Life* or something with Meg Ryan, the dreadfully implausible hippy wife of an oil company executive who's been kidnapped by Colombian rebels, that she dribbles sauce down her front and doesn't notice. When I groan for the third or fourth time over some idiocy or other that comes out of Ryan's mouth, she says, "Oh, give her a break. She didn't write this."

"She didn't bother acting it, either."

"Who cares? Look at him. He's unbelievable. Cool beyond belief."

Him, naturally, is Russell Crowe. Rob did warn me. But at least a decent military adviser choreographed the big scene in which Crowe and a squad of mercs hit the rebel camp and snatch the hostage. "Not bad," I say when the firefight ends.

"So it's like that? Actual action?"

"Close enough, in terms of fire and maneuver. The way Crowe's rifle jams on him. What's missing is certain details."

"Such as?"

"Oh, like your hands are shaking, you're shaking all over, you're white with fear and your mouth's so dry you can't speak, or you're screaming and drooling like a lunatic. And very frequently there's piss running down your legs and you don't even know it."

"Despite all the training? Like his SAS-type training. Aren't you on autopilot, sort of? Kind of like a machine?"

"There is no training in the world that approximates the way a firefight rattles your bones. All the training does is maybe keep you from total freeze-up or panicked dirt-chewing when the noise, the confusion, the terror hit you like a hurricane."

"Shit."

"That's right. A very loud, very disorienting storm of it," I say.

She doesn't respond, just keeps on watching the screen.

"Even the best books, written by very experienced guys who've seen it all, done it all, are crap," I say.

"Why's that, do you think?" She glances at me, a hint of appraisal in her eyes.

"Because there is no way at all of conveying how it feels. Gotta live through it once or twice to know."

And instantly I'm thinking why the fuck am I ranting? What am I trying to prove to this young thing here? That I'm merely another testosterone-overloaded asshole? Annie once told me that just because I'm a jarhead brat doesn't mean I have to keep acting like a jarhead. "Look at your father, for instance," she'd said.

My father. Right. Old-school Marine lifer, total believer in Semper Fi legend, been in shit so deep so many times it's a miracle he survived. Just a classic jarhead gunnery sergeant, scruffed and tough and foul-mouthed—on the surface. Only better read in tactics, strategy, and military history than most of the officers he served under—most of whom got dead and One Way Ewing didn't 'cause he was also smarter in the fight. Smarter with people, too. He'd have just patted Allison's hand, said something like fuckin' A, that's just the way it is, this movie's real as real. And dropped it there, not another word, smiling a big smile. He'd have been that cool about it.

Pizza's long gone, she's on her second beer and I'm still nursing my first and only, when movie number two rolls. It's some tired thing with Pitt as a CIA contractor and Robert Redford, who looks like his makeup's been slathered on by an inept mortician, as his field officer. Allison's laughing and chuckling from the first scene, becomes more and more amused as the plot congeals. She's practically howling during the final stretch.

"Watch a lot of CIA movies, do you?" I ask.

"Sure! They're always such a hoot. The poor bastards try so hard, but they never get anything right. Same with you and cop movies, I expect."

"Yeah. When I want some laughs I give the comedy section of the video rental place a big miss, head straight for the action/adventure section. Love the jokes, like guys shooting their pistols sideways, ejection port up, actually hitting their targets and never getting their eyes put out by hot flying brass."

"Wait a sec. You can so shoot like that, if you have to."

"Really? They teach you that at the Farm?"

"You keep making this agricultural reference. I'd love to know what you're talking about."

"Got it from a movie."

"Figures!" She laughs. "I think I even know which one. But no, I haven't shot like that. I don't shoot. But maybe when you go the range I'll tag along, give it a try?"

"Okay. Just make sure you're at least two lanes to my right. And wearing heavy-duty goggles, not regular shooting glasses."

"Yeah, yeah, yeah. You know much better than me. Well, naturally. But big deal. You don't have to be so damned superior and professorial about it."

"No one's ever used that term to describe me before."

"It's a wonder. If that's true. Which I deeply doubt. I'll bet at least a few of your girlfriends have. Patronizing lectures about warrior stuff. Probably it works on some girls."

"Hey, I assumed I was having an exhange of views with a colleague, not talking to a slightly kinky student."

"And I think you're absolutely style-consistent, when it comes to women, anyway."

"Ow. That hurts."

"Hurts? Hah!" Allison laughs at me now. "If you have any tender spot at all—and it's looking to me as if you do not—it certainly isn't in that area."

And that's the first time, I'm thinking, this girl's been wrong.

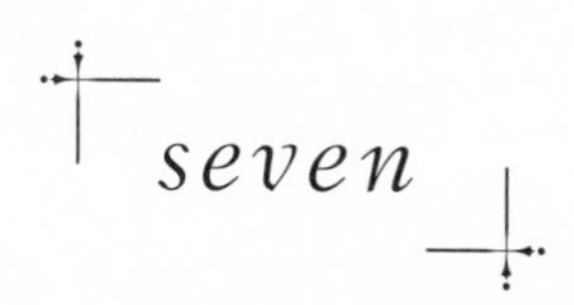

seven

THE GODDAMN BED'S TOO SOFT. THEN IT'S TOO HARD. I TRY THIS POSItion, that one. No good.

I lie very still, systematically tensing and then relaxing every muscle group from my feet on up. Still no good. There's a riot in my head, a mad crowd of images pushing and shoving that I can't control at all.

Fucking Westley.

It's nearly midnight when the movie ends, Allison's headed off to her room and I'm on my way to mine when a stiff finger taps me once on the shoulder. I spin, jolted, and there's Westley, eyes blank as ever behind those steel-rimmed glasses.

"I have something on my mind," he says. "Discuss?"

We go down to that pseudo-Brit drawing room. Coffee is already on the table, just as before. He waits until I've lit a cigarette, taken a sip.

"You're a quick study, Luther," he says. "Is Allison handling everything properly? Is she up to this?"

"Hasn't been much to handle yet. She's fine."

"You're wondering why I'm asking. It's quite simple. She hasn't done a major operation before. I have very high hopes for her. So I'm concerned she does well, doesn't make any missteps the first time out. I'd like you to keep an eye on her. No intervention. Just report back to me from time to time as the op progresses. Keep me informed of her progress, or any mistakes you see developing."

"Spy on a spy? Not really my game."

"Oh, but it is, in a way. Eyes and ears, that's all I'm asking."

"Hard to report anything to a man who keeps your kind of office hours."

Westley smiles. "Not too hard. Not much different from Sarajevo—except we won't be in a combat zone."

Yeah, Sarajevo. Worst place on earth—at the time. Those of us in Westley's little private army (several dozen ex–Special Forces guys, ex-SAS, ex–French Foreign Legion, ex-Spetsnaz) call him "The Man Who Isn't There," pretending a bitter irony. The truth's that phrase is a sort of verbal crossing of fingers, or knocking on wood. He's always there—materializing when you least expect or want him, fading away like a phantom, without a trace.

Most of the force are assigned to train Bosnian combat troops; I draw sniping, teamed with a Muslim girl named Mikla whose hopes of shooting for the Yugoslav Olympic team were shattered by the war. I'm armed with a .50-caliber Barrett and I'm taking out Serbs easily with that weapon, sometimes at ranges of a mile or more. The fucks just explode for no apparent reason, which must terrorize the shit out of any Serbs nearby. Because at those kinds of distances, the boom of the rifle isn't heard until several seconds after the bullet hits.

I get high on that, really juked.

Off hours, I gravitate toward the Spetsnaz guys, who welcome me because I speak Russian. We hang at cafés, getting drunk on the local brandy, trading stories. They're leading small Bosnian units in night assaults on Serb positions in the mountains. They ask me if I want to go along on a couple. I'm young and stupid, so I do. I dig it, hosing Serbs up close with an MP5, tossing white phospherous grenades into bunkers.

One day, hidden in the ruins of a shelled apartment building with Mikla, I turn two Serb artillary officers way up the mountain into pink mist with one shot. Lucky angle, lucky hit.

"Perfect," I hear. I turn, there's Westley, big binoculars to his eyes. No idea how he knew where we'd be that day, or how he got into the room without me or Mikla noticing. "Call it a day, Luther," he says. "Come with me."

Westley's concerned with his Russian guys; calls it a Cold War reflex of his, never trusting Russians. He says he knows I'm tight with them, asks me to keep him informed about what they're up to, especially if they're straying beyond the rules of engagement he's set up. Which seems weird to me, because those rules are loose as rubber bands. But I do what he wants—whenever he appears, since I can never find him.

Then, a few months later, something so weird happens I still can't be sure it wasn't a hallucination. The top Russian—a guy called Vassily who did three straight years in Afghanistan—wants to take his Bosnians on a silent raid of a Serb outpost that's been giving us some mortar trouble. Invites me along.

A moonless night, but clear skies, stars like diamonds on black velvet. Vassily, two other Russians, a dozen Muslims, and me are all wearing white parkas and overpants. We've got MP5s and shorty AK-74s, but Vassily's orders are that they are not to be used unless we're counterattacked from another position. We'll hit our target like ghosts, using knives, sharpened trench shovels, those short, heavy, brutally hooked Spetsnaz machetes. Takes us two hours to make the thousand-yard crawl through dry, powdery snow from our start point up to the Serb mortar post. We're up against their sandbags, unseen and unheard, when Vassily hand-signals a stop. I can hear a couple of Serb sentries cursing the cold, smell the pungent smoke of their cigarettes. The clock's ticking quarter-speed, it seems. Then Vassily hand-signals and we're over and into the trench almost as one man. No screams, no shouts. Just the thunk of shovel blades splitting skulls, the wet hiss of knives plunging up under rib cages and spitting hearts, the soft crunch of steel cutting through thoraxes. It's mainly a visual blur, a white blizzard covering green-uniformed Serbs. I slash the throat of a huge Serb with my K-bar Warthog, then power-cut from sternum to navel. Turn, see Vassily decapitate a Serb with a powerful backhand sweep of his Spetsnaz machete. Turn again, and freeze.

There's Westley, leaning over the sandbag parapet. Apparently unarmed, or at least not using anything. Just looking down, scanning as we clean the trench. His eyes seem to stop on me, hold for a second or two, then sweep on.

It's finished in two, maybe three minutes. At least thirty Serbs dead, inch-thick blood on the trench floor looking black in the starlight, streaks of it black on our white snowsuits. Vassily hand-signals, we're out of there, sliding down the snowy slope fast as we can, like human luges. I try to spot Westley, can't find him anywhere. And he isn't there when we all regroup at the start line.

Three nights later, Vassily and I are getting drunk in a café when Westley appears at our table. He doesn't join us for a drink. He simply says, "I understand your unit sent a lot of Serbs to Allah with cold steel recently. Nice. Well executed." Then he leaves.

Vassily empties his glass, looks at me. "Him, I saw there too, little brother. Watching us," he says. "But I don't let myself believe it."

"Scribble, scribble, scribble." That's my wake-up next morning, though I'm not really asleep, but still pondering if it was really me who did and felt what some madman did and felt in Sarajevo. No knock, no hello. Allison just walks right over, puts an inch-thick stack of—what?—postcards on my night table, then heads back to the door. Her ponytail swings as she swivels her head toward me.

"Westley wants all those addressed to your friend Annie in Baltimore. Says you'll be able to figure out plausible dates for each place. The road trip story you told Westley you fed your friends, remember? They'll get mailed from each place on the right dates. He also requests you try for something a bit more personal than the usual 'wish you were here.' Throw in at least a couple of credible details, but don't overdo it, sentiment-wise.

"Oh, one more thing. Your checkbook and some forms will be on your desk later. You've got to set up automatic withdrawls to cover your monthly condo maintenance payments, utility bills, car loan, all that. But let's run first."

We do twenty laps around the Circle. Allison doesn't pace me backward this time. But I'm breathing a hell of a lot harder than she is at the end. Back at the house, she goes to her room, I go to mine. By the time I'm finished showering, my heart rate is back to normal. It's scary how long that took. Age? Or is my physical condition poorer than I ever imagined?

I slip into my cargoes, pull on a black Oriole T, head downstairs, needing caffeine bad. Follow my nose to the kitchen, which turns out to be just below that rear dining room. Allison's not there, but I get grins from Rob and Terry—until I pour myself a mug of coffee and, ignoring the array of muffins, croissants, two kinds of granola, and a bowl of oranges, light a Camel.

"That is so unhealthy, man," Terry says, his spoonful of granola halting midway between the bowl and his mouth.

"Yeah. No wonder Allison waxes you when you run," Rob says. "And she only runs when she has to. Once a month, usually."

I add cream and sugar to my coffee, take a long drag and a big sip. Not bad; probably Panama La Fiorentina. "Patches don't work. Tried nicotine inhalers, till I realized I was overdosing."

"How did that become apparent?" Rob asks.

"Started noticing I was only putting seven out of ten rounds into the X-ring at twenty-five meters, instead of all ten. Shakey hand, Rob. You know?"

"Could have been all that caffeine."

"Oh no. Had the caffeine level taped. Same way I learned how many army-issue stay-awakes I could safely down on missions without bringing on the jitters. Only variable was the puffer."

"All that stuff will kill you. You're committing suicide. Glad I'm not addicted to anything," Terry says, rising from the table and putting his half-finished bowl of granola into the stainless-steel sink.

"You are, man," I say.

"To what?"

"Endorphins. Why the hell else do you feel so shitty when you don't get your full daily workout?" Just guessing here, but an educated one. "Because you didn't get your endo high."

"Gotcha, Terry," Rob says, chuckling. He looks at me. "Allison calls it NoExS, days Terry misses. His version of PMS. He gets kind of cranky."

Terry shrugs, leaves the kitchen, no doubt headed for wherever it is he mostly lurks during his shift. I finish the Camel and my coffee, go for seconds on both.

"So, Luther. Busy day for you. Allison's arranged lots of surprises.

"Already got one."

"I hate writing postcards, myself. But your day is definitely going to get better."

"What about yours? Looking forward to it, are you?"

"Frankly, no," Rob says. "First part, anyway. I have to drive to

Langley, put in some quality face time with a few people. People who actually like meetings, and feel depressed if there aren't at least three long ones on their daily agenda. I get depressed if there's any at all."

"Comes with being on staff. With any agency."

"That it does, Luther. The price we pay for the good stuff."

"And that would be?"

"Oh, this and that. Closer to your field of endeavor than you might have imagined. Anyway, gotta go. Langley calls. Maybe catch you at dinner."

Rob gone, I pour a third mug of coffee, take it up to my room, spread Allison's little present over my desk. It's like a photo map of the route I told Annie and everyone else at my suspension party I'd be taking. First stop Biloxi and the Redneck Riviera, where I might have run into college girls getting some last beach time before the fall semester started. Then New Orleans, Galveston, Padre Island, and into Mexico: Tampico, Vera Cruz, Mérida, the Yucatán coast. Finally Belize. She's included a tourist brochure for each place, from which I'm supposed to crib those one or two authentic details.

Big help. I can estimate drive time, and how long I might stay in a particular place, so dates are no problem. I date them all. But after "Hey, Annie" on the very first, my pen—one of several different ballpoints and rollerballs, since I can be expected to lose pens—just hovers in the air. I've never written to Annie. Never written much of anything to anyone, anytime or anywhere.

I'm stuck. I stay stuck. Not a word down, when Allison comes in what has to be hours later, looks over my shoulder.

"That's pathetic," she says. "Postcards, Luther! Not an essay for *Foreign Affairs*, or an op-ed piece for the *New York Times*. Come on."

"Been trying."

"Not hard enough, that's clear. I can't believe this. It's more than pathetic. I mean, you're fine in converation, you're smooth enough, sometimes funny. Even witty."

"Talking's different."

"No, it isn't." She sighs, picks up the Biloxi card, holds the photo side in front of my face. "You've been here. You want to amuse me, make me smile, also maybe impress me a little with your cynical acuity. So you say, 'Hey, Allison, what a waste of perfectly good sand. College brats with daddy-bought BMW convertibles staying in sleazy motels side by side with seriously overfed families with vans. All of them chugging beer and shoveling down tons of barbecue. Soundtrack to this movie's by Dwight Yoakam, about twenty decibels above the threshold of permanent hearing loss. Dominant skin color, lobster red. Most memorable scene: beautiful blonde (Ole Miss cheerleader for sure) cross-eyed drunk and puking repeatedly on the leather seat of a new Boxster.' I'm grinning, despite the clichés. So will Annie, right?"

"Probably. Sounds close enough to my idiom."

"So talk your way through the rest of these." Allison sweeps her hand over the card layout. "Pronto. Lunch at twelve hundred hours, then a pretty crowded afternoon for you."

I copy down as much as I can remember of Allison's words on the Biloxi card, find myself unstuck, and actually have a little fun with most of the rest. Akumal's a snag. It's the one place I've actually been—with Helen. We spent a very sweet couple of days there. I drift into intimate memories, savor them more deeply than I should. Lose all sense of how I might "talk" to Annie about the place, since I'm half-wishing all that sweetness had been shared with her—or, semi-guilty thought, with Nadya—and not Helen. In the end, I have to go strictly flora and fauna: the iguana, looking like a minature dinosaur but chomping down brilliantly red hibiscus flowers I fed him, the sea life—parrot fish, grenadiers in tight formation, the dark wings of angelfish, the missile rush of silver barracuda after prey, all in a jungle of staghorn, fan, and brain coral. Floating for hours over it all, conscious of each regular breath through the snorkle but free of time or care.

Lame, I know, but it'll have to do. The rest? Easiest to fake is a brief encounter with a machete-wielding mugger in scummy Belize City. Annie won't like it, but she'll believe my description of the puzzled look on the mugger's face when he realizes both his arms suddenly don't work anymore.

Allison smiles when I hand her the cards across the lunch table. Nadya, who's eating with us, smiles as she leads me up to the library afterward and starts a series of Russian "encounters." She's by turns an inquisitive customs agent, a cheating taxi driver, a suspicious militiaman, a very aggressive hooker. She critiques my responses: I inadvertently made the customs agent uneasy with my tone in a couple of phrases, almost got arrested for a single disrespectful word to the militiaman, and am bound to get my wallet and passport ripped off by the prostitute because I was way too light and flirty.

"Hard not to be, when a girl as attractive as you is talking dirty to me."

"Rather you'd keep it businesslike, thanks very much. The hooker certainly would," Nadya says in that upper-class English drawl of hers. But she can't stop a flicker of a grin.

Which widens when her twin—well, almost, except this girl's eyes are black, and aren't just canted but also lack the lid fold—breezes into the room. Korean, I guess.

"Well, hi, Nadya! This one has to be your latest squeeze, right?" Make that Korean-American. Her accent is one hundred percent Southern California. "Hi, you. I'm Eunkyong and we're going to do some Korean stuff, okay?"

"Hi, Yunk-jong," I say.

"No way. It's Eunkyong."

"Uke-yung."

"Hello? Slowly now. Eunkyong, okay?" she says. She rolls her eyes at Nadya. "How come I get the hopeless ones? Is he this awful in Russian, too?"

"Almost," Nadya says.

"Wait a minute," I start, but Nadya's already up and leaving.

"Same time tomorrow, Luther?" she says.

"Really," Eunkyong sighs, settling into the dent Nadya's left behind in the overstuffed sofa, but doing nothing that counters the odd hollow I feel now that Nadya's no longer with me. "God, I guess I have to start at the start. Do you know anything at all about Korea?"

"There's two of them, and we don't like one of them," I say.

She mutters something in Korean—curses, no doubt—then moves without a hitch into educated Valley-girl lecture mode, minus the "So I'm, like, totally bummed" she's no doubt thinking. Her face is broad but neatly arranged, her smile is sweet the few times it appears, she's a bit stocky but still lithe when she moves. Which is fairly often—getting up from the sofa, pacing around the room, sitting back down again—over the next two hours. At the end of which I can say to her satisfaction the Korean versions of "Hello"; "How are you?"; "I'm pleased to meet you"; "Yes, sir"; "Of course, sir, I will do it immediately"; "My pleasure"; "thank you very much"; and a few other phrases beyond the usual tourist's "How much does this cost?" and "Where is the toilet?"

She also makes me conscious of some key points of behavior and etiquette: always take your shoes off before entering anyone's house; never blow your nose in public; avoid the number four (it's unlucky, sounds like the word for death, and buildings skip from three to five in floor number); it's polite to bow slightly at introductions and when saying good-bye, as it is in Japan; it's impolite to point at anyone; and it's "totally grotty" to write anything in red ink, or leave your chopsticks sticking vertically from your bowl—death signs, both.

I get the impression Eunkyong wouldn't mind drumming even more into my head, but she leaves without a word when Allison appears bearing two big mugs and nods Eunkyong out.

"You're about to have caffeine withdrawl symptoms, right?" she says, handing me one of the mugs. I sip. Exactly the way I like my coffee: almost as strong as espresso but cut generously with half-and-half, one spoon of sugar. I smile gratefully at her, light a Camel.

"That is so unhealthy, man," she says, then instantly bursts into what seems like genuine laughter. "Heard you left Terry slightly miffed this morning."

"Miffed? Yeah, well, now that I think about it. Nothing major. But, hey, you already know that."

"So how's it going up here? With Nadya and Eunkyong?" Her Korean pronunciation's much better than mine.

"It's going. Had some fun with Nadya, anyway."

"Let me guess. When she did her whore number, right? She's so good at that one."

"Had me convinced," I say, and Allison laughs again, mid-sip from her mug of what smells like chamomile tea. "Tried my best to convince her we ought to go up to my room, remove some of our clothes, make it more realistic."

"One-track mind, Luther. No, make that two-track in your case. Sex and violence. Just think of all the things in between you're missing."

She's off. Should be violence, full stop. Sex, full stop. Those are the true priorities of my life so far, but always and utterly separate. "Only one track playing here," I say. "Pretty Nadya."

"If you can't damp down your hopeless little fantasies, or

whatever, think you could at least keep quiet about them?" Allison says. "If you can't, what about pretty Eunkyong, too?"

"She's a piece of work."

"Is she? Imagine how you must seem to her."

"Hard labor?"

"Right. And you have some more to do. Westley says you need workouts. So, we've got maybe a ten-minute break here. There's one of those white martial arts costumes laid out on your bed. After your fix, go up and put it on, then go down to the basement, mix it up a little. Suit you?"

"Sure. Not sure how far out of my usual zone I've slipped. Be nice to find out, do what I have to do to get back into it."

"Positive attitude. Just what we love about you, Luther," she says. But something's going on in her eyes she can't quite mask. "Drinks out later on, so we don't feel too housebound? If you're up to it?"

The basement's a dojo, padded walls and floor, full-fledged but compact. I'm standing there alone, feeling kind of awkward in my stiff whites, when a panel on the far side of the room slides open and my sparring partner backs in. Isn't till she turns, bows, and assumes an attack posture that I realize it's Eunkyong.

Shit. That Allison has a kinked sense of humor.

I shake loose, then slide into a position, figuring I'll go fairly easy on the girl. I don't know much about the formal oriental martial arts, the gliding gracefulness of it. All I know is close-combat moves, Special Forces version. Which by design are choppy, brutal, short, and deadly. Maximum violence to end it fast. Nothing like the ritualistic duels of the dojo.

Still, the SF way must have borrowed some things, because I find myself instinctively matching Eunkyong's moves—just much too slowly.

She's all over me, arms and legs a blur. In less than a minute my forearms are sore from blocking a few strikes, my ribs bruising from those I fail to block. Which are many, especially from her feet.

I get serious, fewer strikes land, but I'm still scarcely getting past her blocks. Eunkyong's cleaning my clock. Can't let that happen; losing face, she'd explained earlier, in teacher mode, is as important in Korean culture as it is in Chinese. So I come on harder, feeling forgotten skills starting to come back as they should: automatic, without thought. She's in retreat, I ease up just a bit, which is a stupid mistake because next thing I know I'm flat on my back, never feeling the flip she's thrown me into. She steps back, I get up, we bow, begin again. Standard repertoire of strikes and blocks, a fairly even match. Then I play dirty, swing into some combat moves that I wasn't sure I still had. But I do. She's down, and maybe she'd be about to die if this was real.

"Pussy!" Eunkyong says.

She's right; shitty thing for me to do in a workout. Fuck this face nonsense. I apologize, tell her I was getting desperate, she's that good. Offer my hand to help her up. She takes it, smiles in what I take to be a forgiving way, starts to rise. Next instant I'm sailing head over heels and land with a thud on the mat. And her foot's on my thorax. Real world, I'd be dead.

"Accept a surrender?" I manage.

She grins. "See you tomorrow. Library first," she says.

Standing under the hot spray of my shower, I touch a few spots here and there, and wince. There are at least a dozen light purple bruises on my arms and chest, and they're growing deeper in color, and larger. It's a job putting on some clothes, and I'm moving kind of stiffly when I go downstairs and meet Nadya and Allison in the foyer.

"You're going out dressed like that?" is all Allison says.

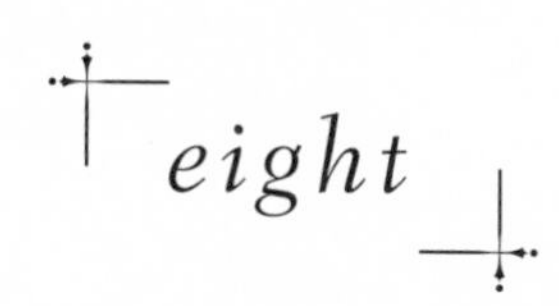

eight

"EVER NOTICE HOW ORANGE THIS CITY IS?" I ASK AS ALLISON DOWN-shifts and slides onto one of the spokes that radiate from Dupont Circle. Nadya's in the backseat.

"What? Oh, the streetlights. Crime deterrent, right? But we're heading into a cool neon zone. You like neon, don't you?"

"Not especially," I say. "Hey, when are you going to let me take this tin-pot for a spin?"

"You'll never touch my baby," Allison says.

"Quite attached to it, she is," Nadya says.

"True. And it's not meant to be crudely handled by middle-aged men in crisis. That's the group market research identifies as the primary buyers of Audi TTs."

"The Mini requires subtle handling," Nadya says. "Rather like its owner."

"Very witty, Nadya," Allison says.

"It's a finely tuned rally machine, though a bit high-strung. Rather like its—"

"Oh shut up, Nadya."

"The original Mini was tough," I say. "Don't know about this replica. I'd like to see if there's any Cooper left in it."

"Over my cold, dead body."

"She means that, I'm sure," Nadya says. "She's so tough."

"Enough," Allison says. She's driving almost tenderly, turning easily here, easily there. But pretty soon I'm completely disoriented, and give up trying a back-trace to the spook house. Somehow we're purring past Jefferson's monument, the ghost of it gleaming on the dark Tidal Basin, and very quickly we've left white-marble Washington entirely, entered a neighborhood of row houses, bars, restaurants that could be Baltimore or Philly or any other city I've been in. The neon display's average only.

The bar doesn't have any. It's more like a lounge than a saloon, lots of modern sofas and upholstered chairs, some banquette nooks. Very designer, very upscale, nearly empty. We settle into the rear-most nook, Nadya next to me on the banquette, Allison sprawling in a big chair, a small round chrome table between us.

"You have to try the mango daiquiris," Allison says. "They chop up fresh ripe mangoes, turn them into juice with a blender, add great rum. The best. Better than the straight Stoly you usuallly shoot, Nadya."

"I am not convinced. Do you trust her, Luther?" Nadya asks.

"Absolutely. Without reservation."

"How I doubt that!" Nadya says. "No one else does."

"Now, why would that be?"

"Ah, I've the sense I've gotten rather too often into her bad books lately to honestly answer that one."

"Your name has been written down, Nadya. There will be consequences." Allison laughs. "Anyway, Luther knows you lie. He's a detective, after all. People lie to him all the time. Don't they, Luther?"

"Constantly," I say.

Allison tells the waiter to bring three mango daiquiris. When they arrive, at least they aren't sporting little paper-and-stick umbrellas. I take a sip. Nice. Too bad a few sips is all I can have.

"Luther likes it. Look at his face," Allison says to Nadya. Then she turns her eyes to me. "So. What's it like, being a narc?"

"Nothing you'd particularly enjoy. Except the role-playing. You get to dress up in funny clothes—"

"So we've noticed," Nadya says dryly.

"—like mall rat, biker, gangbanger," I go on, ignoring her, "and pretend that's the real you. The interesting moments are mostly physical. Drug dealers tend to be clever, the way rats are, but not real intelligent. The cerebral challenges would be too minor for your taste, Allison."

"Cerebral challenges? Are you trying a little psy-op thing on me? Isn't that what they called it in your late, lamented SOG posting? Or could you be just a bit insecure, even bitter that your formal education ended with high school?"

Her shift of tone blind-sides me for an instant. Friendly chat suddenly gone mean, nasty. Why? She's pushing, wants to see how I'll react. I decide to push back a little, see where that takes us.

"While you, after learning to walk like a lady at Miss Porter's, went on to ace a master's from the Fletcher School of Law and Diplomacy," I say. "Asian studies for sure. First in your class, probably."

"And that's somehow a negative?"

Nadya's concentrating on her drink, staying clear of this.

"No. Good for you. Just wondering if you have a wall anywhere you can hang that nicely framed diploma?"

"If it was about that, I'd have joined the State Department. Those suits all have walls perfect for that sort of thing. As well as photos of themselves with various muckety-mucks of whatever administration happens to be in at the moment, plus distinguished ambassadors, foreign heads of state."

"So what is it all about for you, Allison?"

"Don't go there."

"Because we're in public? Because Nadya isn't cleared? Or—just guessing here—because you don't really know?"

"I'm cleared from top to toe, but I don't want any part of this aggro, thank you," Nadya butts in.

"I'm as self-aware as I need to be," Allison says.

"Now, that sounds a bit defensive. Or is it some of that psy-ops stuff you mentioned earlier?"

"Simple confusion. Where's all this sudden hostility coming from, Luther? Any one of us offended you in any way?"

I laugh, then shake my head, decide against reminding her that she started the static, with that thing about high school. Just another test. I decide I'll pass. "Sorry about all this," I say. "Everyone's been great. Just that I'm used to doing ops, not prepping for them. And I'm also feeling way out of the loop."

"Sure. That's a natural reaction to any sudden transition from what you're used to. Confined, never without handlers—though most men wouldn't complain about the close company of women like us. Would they, Nadya?"

"Not straight men, at least." Nadya leans into me, smiling.

"There it goes again," I say, hoping almost desperately the girl hasn't fully sensed how deeply I'm attracted to her.

"Come on, Luther," Allison says. "You enjoy a little light teasing. You know you do, 'cause you tease back. That's all this is. And you are not being kept out of the loop. You're being eased into it. Standard prep. In a little while you'll probably know more than you really want to."

"From Westley? Or from you?"

"From the team. Which you are a new but integral part of, okay?"

"You are our true heart-of-hearts," Nadya says. "Eunkyong didn't actually mean to thrash you so."

Now I'm laughing for real. What else can I do? I know when I'm being outmaneuvered. But my riposte just pops out from somewhere deep, surprising and embarrassing me.

"Nadya, I know this is kind of sudden," I say. "But would you marry me? We'd have such beautiful babies."

"Oh dear. Bit of a shock. Of course I'm in love with you, darling. But this would change the course of our entire lives. Might I have some time to think on it?"

"Disgusting, the both of you," Allison says. The atmosphere's completely cleared. "Especially you, Russki slut. Remember, I saw him first. Thief."

Nadya goes pure innocent. Protests even as she slips a hand on my forearm. I'm feeling very vulnerable, until I realize they're taking my remark as pure joke, untainted by any sudden welling up of genuine emotion. Emotion is not in my profile. So my mood's fine—except for puzzlement about my feelings—when we leave the bar, after they've had two more drinks each and I've had three more sips of my daiquiri.

Nadya disappears down the street with a wave as Allison lets us into the house. We're heading upstairs when she pulls me into the library, closes the door, stands so close I can smell the faint fragrance of whatever shampoo she favors.

"Time for a little reality check," she whispers. "How unhappy are you, Luther? It's important."

Christ! Now it's tests within tests. "Not unhappy at all," I say. "Just restless. I want to get moving."

"That's it? You're sure?"

"Would I lie?"

"Every which way. But this isn't tease time. I need to know the truth. Right now."

"As I said. I'm used to action. Long time since I've had to train. For anything."

"But you do realize how far you've got to go, physically? You're very clear there are some new things you've yet to learn? This isn't like any job you've ever done before."

"Yeah, you're right, I do know. Maybe that's what's frustrating. I'm working hard and not getting as far as fast as I'd like. My physical condition is a disgrace. But I'll deal with it. As long as it takes is fine by me."

"You're certain?"

"Yes. Unqualified yes."

"Good," Allison says. "You'll get into super physical shape once you pass this initial plateau. And there are some cool new things coming up. I think time is going to pass faster than it seems to right now."

A bright voice calling, then a tremendous flash that turns my shut eyelids red, jerks me out of sleep. I sit up, blurrily spot Allison, looking like a page from a J. Crew catalog, one of those that suggests the morning after a sleepover: men's boxers, sloppy top, thick socks. She's holding what appears to be a big Nikon, professional grade with strobe, and she's laughing.

"Professional? Fuck me," I snap. "This is a sorority house. What am I doing in a goddamn sorority house?"

"What I need you to do," Allison says, "is wash your face, comb your hair, put on a shirt—one of your new ones, any color you like as long as it's white—a tie, and a suit coat."

"Too big. Your little man hasn't altered 'em yet."

"Won't matter. I just need some head shots, Terry."

"Knew it. You got the wrong fucking guy."

"Not. From later on today, you're Terry. Might as well start getting used to it." Allison laughs again. She closes my door as she leaves.

The armoire doors are open. Someone's sent all those button-downs to the laundry. They've come back heavily starched, folded, boxed. I tear one open. I see the name Prentice has been laundry-printed on the inside collar of all the shirts.

Five minutes later I slop down to the library, correctly attired but cranky as hell. Allison's dressed in office-wear, but that Nikon's hanging from her neck. Before I can start bitching, she hands me a cigarette, already lit.

"Get your fix. Then some pics. He'll have it set up in a minute," she says, nodding toward the real Terry. He's raising what looks like one of those rickety old home-movie screens, except it's matte white instead of silvery. "Christ, who taught you to knot a tie? I thought they were meticulous about details like that in the military."

"Not my branch. Ever seen a camo tie?" I mutter, raising my chin so Allison can redo the silk at my neck. Then she manhandles me onto my mark, about a meter in front of the screen.

"Try to look amiable. That's your best? Oh, go finish your cigarette, gulp some coffee, think pleasant thoughts. Then step back on the mark."

I do as she says, feel half-human by the time I take a last sip and butt out the Camel. "What are these for?" I ask.

"Passports, driver's license, visas. What else?" She's two meters away, twisting the Nikon's lens into focus. She snaps a few, the motor drive advancing a frame each time, the strobe leaving spots before my eyes. "Try a little smile, businessman-type. No, you look like a ladies' shoe salesman. Tone it down a bit. Hey, that's it. Perfect."

Click and whir, click and whir, click and whir. I lose count. I'm almost blind when she says, "That'll do it. Now please go up and put on some street clothes. Meet me down in the foyer."

Then Allison starts delivering on the cool stuff.

We drive to an area of abandoned warehouses and small factories near the river, but well out of sight of the manicured, official showplace center of town. Dirty brick, busted panes of glass in the windows, a musky, mousey smell when she pushes open a rusted steel door and we enter. It's a single huge room, no trace at all of what it once was. I see some crack vials and a few needles littering the concrete floor. Feels off, like a stage set, but it could be a junkie shooting gallery the Company appropriates every once in a while.

And I see three cars and at least eight guys in suits waiting for us. No names, no introductions, but one suit with the broken nose of an ex-pug immediately starts giving orders in a voice so harsh it sounds like somebody did a job on his vocal cords with a rasp file. Nobody needs to mention he's the chief instructor here. Two guys join me as security, and five play bad guys. Rob's one of them. The package I'm supposed to protect is Nadya. I know some basics from hostage rescue training, but this is nothing like tossing stun grenades, storming into a building and taking down terrorists. It's more Secret Service VIP protection drill. When the bad guys pop out from various positions, my sole role is to bundle Nadya out of any fields of fire, screened by my two colleagues, who're supposed to be my friendly shooters. We do several scenarios; I get critiqued by the instructor after each go. He isn't subtle about it.

"Goddammit, you started to move *into* the fight, dickhead!" he growls after the first. "Never, ever do that. You are *not* a shooter, get it! You take even a half-step into it, you'll lose your package." We continue.

"Pathetic. You were way too slow securing the package. You *thought* about taking a half-step into the fight, lost a second before you reversed. You gotta kill that instinct, understand?" he says after the second.

"That was just goddamn stupid!" he shouts after the third. "You steered yourself and your package through one of the fields of fire, not out of them. You're both dead."

Every scenario is slightly different. Sometimes I'm supposed to get Nadya out the building's door in less than five seconds, other times I've got to shove her into the rear seat of one of the cars in less than two. In another I have to grab her, swing her down to the floor, lie on top of her, my body her shield. She squirms under me and I'm supposed to pin her.

"The fucking package will often panic, go berserk trying to run," the instructor says. "Never let that happen. Never lose body contact. Pin that fucking package."

That's the drill I'm worst at, this first day. Nadya gets away and runs the first time. "You some kind of pussy?" the instructor rasps in disgust. "Do I have to fucking show you how to hold a woman down?" I glance over where Allison's leaning against a wall, hoping for a grin or something. "Gentle is nice, Terry," Nadya says, strolling back. "But not in this situation. You do need to do a full-body press. I won't hold it against you."

I'm able to keep her down a bit longer the second and third times, but she manages to wiggle at least partly up and out from behind my body shield. The instructor's abusing me like a Special Forces drill master, comparing me to insects and other puny things that live in the earth. I glance at Allison, see Westley has appeared beside her. They're looking at each other, and I'm pretty sure they're talking about me. I try to ignore the chill I feel from that, concentrate on my task.

I take Nadya down fast and hard the fourth go, pressing my groin down on her wriggling ass, hands locked on her wrists. "Do not for a moment entertain any wicked notions," she says, small giggle following. As if. I have to let her get away again. The cost in verbal abuse is higher than ever. But I pay it gladly, because all through this drill I've felt so strangely shy, almost unbearably awkward and strange, body to body with Nadya.

The session lasts until past noon. "Tomorrow? Here?" Allison asks.

"Yeah. And every day for a while," the instructor barks. "Then we'll take it out to other places once I judge your man's got the speed and the moves. He's got a fuck of a long way to go yet. All these former special-ops shooters need their instincts rewired for this work."

I don't even feel miffed, let alone insulted. Any time with Nadya is fine time for me. Usually. But I'm baffled by how powerfully I felt like a scared schoolboy every time we wound up in a rough embrace.

We go back to the spook house, Nadya up front and me crammed in the tiny rear of the Mini. Allison starts to make some remark about the pin-the-package drill, but Nadya cuts her off with "I don't mind at all being groped by Terry, but you, snotty bitch, can take your turn lying on that filthy, scratchy concrete tomorrow, or I'm resigning." She sounds like she means it, and there isn't a lot of conversation over lunch. Afterward, during our Russian session, Nadya's more businesslike and stiff than I've ever seen her. But a couple of times I catch a glint of that smile I'm starting to love so much, and there's a hint of a new light in those arctic-blue eyes. I feel she's on the verge of something I'd very much like, but our time runs out before she gets there.

I'm sorry to see her go when Eunkyong comes in, and not at full attention during our Korean lesson. She has to rebuke me several times. But I try to be fully focused during our tussle in the dojo. It doesn't help much. I'm not sure which gets more battered, my ego or my body.

"Didn't you say you weren't field?" I ask Eunkyong when the session ends with me on my back again.

"I'm not," she says. "But my father, who's not real traditional, was very scared of American cities when he first came here and opened his little convenience store. In Korea, they don't have anything like the robberies, the street crime that goes on in L.A. He got worried. Tae Kwon Do lessons for me, three times a week, starting when I was five."

"Yeah?"

"Yeah, and I liked it. I got into the competition circuit for a while. I've kept it up ever since. Actually I do a fair amount of instructing. Training new field agents. Contractors, we expect them to come fully equipped with the entire range of skills."

"I'm beginning to wonder what happened to mine," I say, touching a couple of fresh bruises.

"Oh, you've still got them. You just need a tune-up. I think once you were very, very good. Fast, instinctual."

"That why I'm lying down and you're still standing?" I laugh.

"Took all I had to keep you from killing me," Eunkyong says. "Another week or so of this, I'm reporting you ready and asking for an immediate transfer out of this job. Before I do get killed. Because I think once you're tuned and into it, you won't be able to stop yourself."

A few bad flashes hit me then. I work through them on the light bag in the room off the dojo, ignoring the heavy bag and the weights. What I need is more speed, not power or strength. I go through every combination of strikes I know, turning the bag into a blur of leather that's never where I expect it to be when I start the next set of blows. Which is the point. I put everything I've got into it, end up exhausted, drenched in sweat, and still wondering if I've got some glitch that causes me to overestimate threat levels, react with excessive force. But surely Westley's factored that. And surely I wouldn't be here if my profile didn't show I'd never turned on my own, always stayed on target, on the enemy.

So far. Westley must believe I'll remain consistent that way. I'm not so sure. Sometimes I think somebody ought to take me out and kill me in the head.

I laugh. That's been tried. Didn't work. My contract in Sarajevo ended slightly early because a Serb countersniper got lucky one day when I was spotting for Mikla. A second after she'd canceled a guy's ticket permanently at six hundred yards, I took a love tap from a 7.65 x 54mm Dragunov upside the head. A few millimeters lower and to the right and I would have been as gone as Mikla's target. The Swiss surgeons found only a bit of skull too shattered to repair, so they picked out the bits of bone, sliced away a sliver of shredded brain tissue, patched the hole with a thin silver plate, and sewed flaps of scalp over it. Whatever that tissue controlled, it appeared to have nothing to do with cognitive function or physical coordination. One bad aftereffect, true, but with the Klonopin, I was good to go within a year.

Not back to a war zone; I swore off that. And as a narc my personal body count was, naturally, nowhere near as high as Sarajevo or Desert Storm. Yet it was sufficient. More than sufficient; I seemed to have to take down drugistas and other bad guys at least ten times more often than any other cop I knew, or heard of.

So for the last year or so, usually late at night in bed, my pulse suddenly throbs, my muscles tense till they ache, and I find myself scared and seriously wondering if there's any active principle of reciprocity in this world or whatever (if anything) comes after. X body count over Y skipped mercies equals X^2 times pain. If that's the equation, I hope it's completed here in life, comes in types of pain I know I can handle. Not some nightmare that never, ever ends.

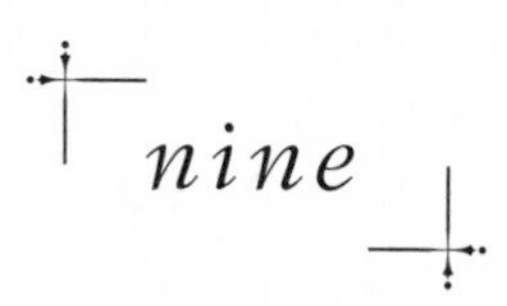

nine

THE ROUTINES DON'T VARY: I RUN WITH ALLISON EVERY MORNING before breakfast, adding a few more laps each time. We go through the package-protection drills in that grubby warehouse for several hours; Allison even takes a few turns being pinned to the concrete, Nadya laughing quietly as she watches. I find I have no trouble at all keeping Allison down, even through she struggles much more than Nadya. And I'm scarcely aware the abuse from that broken-nosed, raspy-voiced instructor is diminishing until it's almost gone, replaced by a few words of grudging, rough praise when my moves and timing hit his mark.

The best part of each day remains my hours alone with Nadya, sparring in the dojo with Eunkyong, and working myself to sweaty exhaustion on the light bag, adding kick practice on the heavy bag and some weight work as well. Most evenings I'm tired as hell but feeling satistified, having dinner with Allison and Nadya, sometimes in-house, Chinese or Thai or pizza with a couple of movies, or out somewhere.

The shadows fall only when Westley materializes, always when I least expect it. He's never unpleasant, he behaves, on the surface, as if I'm his equal. But I'm always left feeling I've been visited by some presense from beyond the grave.

Maybe a week—or even two, as my time concept is changing—after I spotted him with Allison during that first day at the warehouse, I feel bony fingers grip my bicep the moment I enter the spook house after a morning run. Westley leads me into that parlor. Coffee and cigarettes are on the table as usual, but I skip the smokes; been cutting down. Westley sits next to me on the Chesterfield instead of in one of the chairs.

"Enjoying yourself a bit more now, Luther? Things becoming more interesting for you? Allison performing?" he asks easily. Yet it feels like the ambient temperature has suddenly dropped ten degrees, this close to the man.

"None of us have gone for anyone else's throat yet," I say. "So her management style must be adequate."

Westley seems to consider this for a moment. Eventually he nods. "Has she spoken with you about the operation, filled you in at all?"

"Oh yeah. In some detail," I say, watching for reaction. No change in his face, not even a blink. "Paraphrased, she's said I'm too old, still too slow, too out of condition for rent-a-cop duty at a VIP wedding, let alone to go out on a field op."

"Sounds like her." Westley smiles. "You haven't been able to pry out anything more than that? Hints or clues of places, schedules, personalities?"

"Nothing," I say. "If it weren't totally implausible, I'd be thinking she actually doesn't know any of that. Because you haven't told her yet."

"She's supposed to give that impression, Luther. She knows as much as I do," Westley says, standing up to leave.

"Give her an A-plus, then," I say to his back. He raises his right hand in a sort of wave, not looking back.

* * *

There's an acceleration, an unmistakable quickening. I can feel it, see it, though no one else remarks on it or gives any sign they notice. The routines are changing, becoming more intense.

The package-protection drills move out of the factory, go live-action. In a huge, deserted mall parking lot before a dozen dawns, we do simulated car ambushes, with the vehicles moving thirty miles per hour or more, fishtailing with tires squealing when the trap's sprung. Then, on maybe a dozen noons, we do a sort of mime of snatch attempts in front of a big downtown hotel, in full view of hundreds of passersby; almost no civilians seem to notice something odd is happening, the action's so fast and subtle. I lose track of the mornings we spend at an airstrip in rural Virginia, where we're hit by bad guys spraying loud AK blanks, my guys returning fire with MP5s. I'm given a SIG 220 but I never pull the trigger. Just throw Nadya into the rear seat of a big Merc, quickly lob a smoke grenade into the firefight before I jump in, and drop another out the car window as I bark at the driver to put the pedal to the floor and keep it there until we run out of tarmac.

It's getting interesting.

The Nadya sessions are, too. We practice business-type negotiations, deal persuasions, rising tempers and threat levels, deal-gone-bad hostility, back-away diversion talk. She introduces me to current Russian military verbal slang code, too. Eunkyong presses hard on basic conversation way beyond standard experienced tourist stuff. Close to what Nadya's doing, though naturally I'm not expected to get anywhere near fluent, just understand the basic flow and respond halfway appropriately. Plus a couple of sessions that approximate a police interrogation, the objective being for me to understand the drift of questions but answer as if I understand nothing.

And she raises the violence level in the dojo, rachets it up day by day until the day I'm in the zone so deeply I don't even realize I'm about to snap her neck until she screams at me to stop. When I get clear, I see her sitting slumped, rubbing her neck.

"God, I'm so sorry," I say. "You're okay? Sure you're okay?"

She looks at me, fear palpable in her eyes. But she says, "Don't apologize. I was supposed to get you there. Job well done, yeah?"

Through this stage, things begin appearing in my room, small surprises always placed there when I'm somewhere else. Shortly after Allison's photo shoot, I come sweating from a session with Eunkyong to find a passport and driver's license—Canadian, my face but in the name of Prentice, Terence—on my desk. Also a few valid credit cards, with varying expiration dates, naturally. I leaf through the passport. There are current multiple-entry visas for Japan, Korea, China, Russia amid some entry and exit stamps from Seattle, Vancouver, Taipei, Hong Kong, Manila, and other places, dating back as far as three years. Everybody in the spook house is calling me Terry, except for the real Terry. He looks annoyed the few times he hears me addressed with his name.

Other things show up at random: the new underwear and socks, laundered. A first-class suitcase, new shaving gear, assorted toiletries, hair brush, nail clippers, a dop kit to carry all that stuff in. A Tag Heuer chronometer with a crocodile strap. Also, one day, some electronics I see no need for, unless they have sub rosa functions not yet revealed to me: a pager, like every kid crack dealer wears, an Olympus micro digital memo recorder, a battery-powered coded car-key holder with no key attached.

Finally, after the last Eunkyong session, I come back to my room shaken and unhappy, and see the bed heaped with boxes all wrapped in plain brown kraft paper. I grab one at random, I'm tearing it open when Allison and Rob walk in.

"Hey, Christmas come earlier for you than the rest of us, Terry?" she says.

"Told you Terry was connected, didn't I?" Rob says to her. "If I asked for all this stuff, any chance I'd get it?"

"No way. Switches and coal, best case. You haven't been a good boy like Terry this year," Allison says.

First out of the box is the Wilson SDS, and it's a beauty. Tapered-cone four-inch barrel, ultra-light hammer, and crisp light trigger, completely dehorned for smooth draw, everything hand-fitted and polished. Tight, but so very slick.

Allison grabs it from my palm, racks the slide, sights on the bed-side lamp, squeezes off. "Ooh, smooth. Super-clean trigger break."

"Hey, don't dry-fire it," I protest, grabbing it back. So she doesn't shoot? My ass.

"Can't hurt, Terry, you possessive bastard," she says. "Stop playing with it and let's see what else is here, okay?"

Everything's here. I hesitate to lift the Korth out of its case, the gun's so pretty. But I do. I feel the perfect balance, look down the sights, examine the muzzle crown, swing out the cylinder and check the chamfering before spinning it, flipping it shut. "A work of art," I say.

"Better be, at that price," Rob says.

"Hey, Rob, know what?" Allison says. "Some guys—you, right now—really do get a greenish tinge when they're envious."

I give the Springfield XD and the Boker folder a faster once-over; fine utilitarian tools, wouldn't pain you to scuff them up with heavy use. The briefcase looks utilitarian, too; nice enough leather but not overly showy for a mid-level executive to carry. The inside's the neat part, and whoever designed it must be some genius. The grenades, speedloaders, and spare mags are already in secure but easily accessible pockets. I slip the Korth into its suede-lined place, find it's angled for the fastest draw with the case only partly open. Then I slowly close the case, peering at the crack till the edges meet. Brilliant! No metal touches metal. Latch it, shake it, just to be certain. Nothing inside shifts, no click of metal on metal. Open it, tap the sides. Sounds like Kevlar under that leather.

I'm a little worried about the holsters. Custom leather is always so tight, hand-boned to the exact contours of the particular gun it was made for. It takes a few hundred practice draws before there's no hitching or hanging up. I put on the Rosen shoulder rig, then the small-of-the-back, holster the Wilson and the XD, figure I'll start the process right now. Both pistols come out like they're greased, though they ride tight. Some gnome's already done all those hundred draws for me. Very thoughtful touch.

I'm grinning like a fool. Which is certainly how I'm behaving. I catch Allison regarding me closely. There's something in her eyes that says she knows this, has always known it. But she smiles, makes whatever I thought I saw vanish.

"I'll need range time. Lots," I say. "To break the guns in."

"Already arranged. Starting tomorrow afternoon," Rob says.

"But that's Eunkyong time."

"She won't mind, Terry," Allison says. "Actually, she won't be coming around anymore. At all."

The pleasure I'd been feeling over my new acquisitions feels truly crass, idiotic. I liked that girl. Now the last image I'm going to have of her is scared eyes. Worse, her last image of me is . . . shit. I don't want to think of that.

"Hold on. That can't happen. I need more practice."

"She doesn't think so, Terry." Allison smiles. "She says you're ready. We trust her judgment. So should you."

The peeling away, the vanishing, begins. People and things. One day it's my wallet, all ID with Luther Ewing's name on it. A few days later it's every item of clothing—except a pair of jeans, a couple of shirts, socks, and boots—I brought to this spook house in my duffel—what was it . . . five, six, maybe even eight weeks ago? I realize I've lost all sense of time.

Worse, I've lost sense of my life. When's the last time I thought of Annie or Helen, Dog or Ice Box? They seem a world away, maybe two worlds, not quite real, figures from a distant past, or an imagined one. Am I seeming as far from them as they're seeming to me? Can I bear that big a loss?

Then Terry stops appearing at breakfast, not that I care, since I never connected with that cipher anyway. But it is another manifestation of the process. Whoever's guard-dogging the house in his place—there has to be a crew, working shifts—stays invisible. Yet there's an increase in the comings and goings—people I don't know and am not introduced to, huddling with Allison or Rob in rooms I've never entered. I feel like the house ghost; visitors look straight through me, don't seem to see me at all.

Thank God for the shooting, out at the FBI range in Maryland. The instructor's a tall, thin guy, maybe forty, with the slightly hooded eyes of a raptor. He doesn't say much. He doesn't need to. I feel in my zone from the start, which is simply putting two hundred rounds through each gun into steel silhouettes at ranges from seven to thirty yards. I don't miss much.

Feel even better when we move on to combat town. It's a block of buildings made of plywood and two-by-fours, like a Hollywood set minus any period details. The game is simple: as you move along the block, life-size photos on plywood cutouts pop up unpredictably at windows, come through doors, flash out from behind corners and jerk rapidly back. Most of the photo targets are bad guys with guns aimed at you, but every so often one of a young mother holding an infant appears. You fire at a mom, you lose major points and have to start over, even if you miss.

The instructor wants to begin with the most basic drill: pistol unholstered, cocked, and held at low ready with both hands, just as you would enter a known hot zone, real-world. The first time I move fast in a slight crouch, cold and clear, doing nothing fancy with the Wilson. When I'm through, the instructor reads the talley: fourteen of fourteen bad guys with one bullet each in the kill zone, no shot taken at three moms. I go twice more, once with the XD and once with the Korth. The place and timing of the targets' appearance changes with each run. Same score, same time with the Springfield, same score but six seconds slower with the Korth, because it takes longer to reload a revolver.

The instructor manipulates the target control panel and we go through as a team. He uses a SIG 226, fifteen rounds of 9mm in his mags. We cover each other; I take out a bad guy who jumps up behind him, he does the same for me. Our scores match: twelve of twelve shooters dead, no shots at four moms, each.

"Hey, can we give this a try?" Rob asks the instructor.

"Solo or team?" he asks.

"Team. Okay, Rob?" Allison says. Rob nods.

"Give me a minute," the instructor says, flicking some switches on the control panel, then disappearing for a little while behind the buildings. He comes back grinning.

"On my signal," the instructor says. He pauses. *"Go!"*

They move into the block, looking pretty good, Rob holding an HK USP and Allison gripping her SIG 229 in the approved fashion. The targets and their pistols start popping early but, it seems to me, at a slightly slower pace than before.

"They look like they can shoot, they think they can shoot, but ten bucks says they're going to be real surprised," the instructor says to me.

"Won't take that bet," I say.

"Wise man."

After they come back to the start and the instructor goes out to score, he waves us up about midway on his return. "Allison, eight of twelve dead, two moms wounded. Rob, seven of twelve, and one great shot." He leads us to the corner of a building, pulls the spring on a target. It's a mom, "Allison" printed in red Magic Marker at the bottom, and a hole right in the center of the infant's head, which is positioned just in front of the mom's heart.

"A two-for-one, Rob," the instructor says.

"Aw, shit. *Shit*!" Rob says, face coloring a little. We start laughing, but it takes a beat for Rob to join in, and he manages to sound both pissed and embarrassed.

Next day, I go down the block with the Wilson and the XD holstered. First run I draw the Wilson and use a two-hand grip, but double-tap targets. Same score as before: fourteen kills, no moms. The instructor asks for a repeat. The results are identical.

"Can you go both ways?" he asks me.

"If I have to, yeah," I say.

"Let's try one that way," he says.

So it's down the block again, pulling the Wilson from under my armpit with my right hand, the XD from behind my back with my left when the first target appears. It gets tricky quick; at a couple of places, two targets pop out simultaneously at awkward angles. I pop the left one with the Wilson, swing toward the right and fire just as I put a second round into the left with the XD.

The instructor checks the targets, reports. "Slight fall-off in accuracy, but not nearly as much as I expected. Twelve instant kills, five more so close to instant they'd be down, no threat. No misses," he says. "And no Allisons."

Rob's smile is lame.

"Where did you learn to shoot?" the instructor asks.

"Army," I say. "Brigade pistol team, not all-Army."

"Real-world experience?"

A couple of years ago, I'd have snapped back that I'd capped, greased, hammered, taken down, smoked, or any other euphemism you like for shot to death probably five times as many human beings as the photo targets I'd holed here. Now I just say, "Enough."

He nods, turns to Allison. "There's no work here for me. Your man's one of the best shooters to come through in a long time. I'll tell the guy at the gate to let you all pass if you want to use the place. But there's no point to my presense."

"Okay," Allison says. "Thanks for your help."

"No problem," he says. Then he shakes my hand. "Nice watching you work. Good luck."

It's a useless vanity, I know, but during the ride home to the spook house I find myself expecting Allison or Rob to say something—even a couple of words—praising my performance. They do not. Apparently shooting isn't a high-value item on their scale of skills. When I insist to Allison later I need shooting time at least twice a week, she agrees. But it's Nadya who takes me to the range. She at least seems interested in what I do there.

And thank God for Nadya. I was worried she'd be next to disappear. But she still comes around every day after lunch, comes over most evenings for dinner or drinks, too. She's changing, but in a way that eases me. The stiff drills slip almost unnoticeably into casual conversations, boy-girl stuff again, but between people who're long past the first meeting stage, are good friends, maybe lovers or on the verge of being that.

Nadya's my comfort, until I realize that's one more illusion, in which I'm an eager collaborator. Then I hate it, knowing how well they know me on some levels. And how wrong they can be about others. That damned psych profile badly needs updating. Yes, I once was a hound, in the worst ways. That changed a long time ago. Does the profile reflect the fact that I now play the foul-mouthed, swinging-dick role because I have to? That my bonds with men are a survival tactic, necessary to my trade? That men bore the hell out of me, unless we share certain very narrow professional experience and expertise. And even then I can only take so much before their company feels stale, stagnant? That my interest in women, on the other hand, is only sometimes sexual and more often mental? Is there any indication that I genuinely believe women in general are sharper, smarter, and much more intriguing to talk to than any male friends I've ever had? That I find the subtle shifts their minds can make, the differences in the ways they perceive the world, endlessly fascinating? That my flirting is generally only cover for another interest?

No. And they absolutely can't know the feelings I'm developing for Nadya, because I scarcely understand how this could be happening myself, in such a fucked, false, and strained situation.

Allison's a pro, but she can't mask the strain entirely. I begin to notice nervy gestures she never made before: tugging her ponytail absently in the middle of a conversation is the most obvious. There's also a faint brittle quality to the mutual teasing. And the sorority-house silliness isn't fully present when she wakes me one morning, even though she's in her Crew catalog sleepover mode, wearing the boxers, the sloppy top, the loopy smile as she shakes my shoulder. "God, you're the lazy one. Up! Skivvies, a shirt and tie, suit pants and coat, shoes. And put on your holsters, holding. Alteration time."

Right, I'm thinking as I get dressed. Had to wait until my gear arrived, so the suits can be nipped and tucked just so. They have to hang naturally, no telltale bulges or lumps anywhere, no printing. No hint I'm heavily armed.

The tailor, a fat bald guy who never lost his Italian accent, starts complaining the moment he comes in with Allison and sees me standing there, coat swimming from the shoulders down, pants folded at the too-large waists, inches of fabric bunched over my shoes.

"Too skinny, too skinny," he mumbles, walking around me, looking me up and down. He has to mumble—lots of pins held in his mouth—but the chalk and tape measure in his hands don't keep him from making the palms-up gesture of dismay.

It takes a half hour to do the pinning and chalking. No fun being a dummy, so I'm relieved as hell when he's finished. Until he insists—and convinces Allison—that he has to repeat the process on the other four suits, since each is cut slightly differently.

That kills the entire morning. I'm tired and cranky when at last that fat obsessive-compulsive says "*Finito*," carefully packs everything up, and leaves. Allison closes the green folder she's been studying for the past two hours. She looks at me vaguely, as if she's still mainly concentrated on what she read. Then she focuses. "Hey! Free day today. We'll go out, wherever you want. Nice lunch, relaxing afternoon?"

"Sounds good."

"Uh, one condition. Forget the jeans and boots. Wear a polo, khakis, those new loafers."

"Sure."

"Not much to ask, is it? Anyway, you've got to get used to this stuff. Have to feel easy and natural in it. In fact, from now on, it's all you'll be wearing. Suits, too, when they come back." She grins. "If you behave, I might even let you touch my Mini. For a block or two. Okay?"

"The gardens of stone? That really where you want to go?" Allison says when we're out and moving in her Cooper.

"It is."

"Are you feeling a little morbid or anything? Arlington National Cemetery isn't generally a favored destination for guys who've been cooped up with us. Now that I think of it, it's never been a destination. You have somebody there? Family, friends?"

"No." She knows I'm lying. Has to be in my dossier that there is a friend there all right. From the first Gulf War. One of the unlucky few. But I've no intention of staring at his grave.

"Care to share why, then?"

"No."

Allison makes a few turns, we're crossing a bridge over the Potomac, almost blue today under the cloudless sky. I get a partial view of white splendor: Lincoln's place, Washington's obelisk, the green mall, and rising green to the white Capitol. Another illusion; ten blocks southeast of where congressmen, senators, Supreme Court justices pursue their particular interests, it's a war zone, black gangbangers with no future and nothing to lose. So they're rolling every night, trying to make their dime, capping anyone who gets in the way. D.C. has one of the highest murder rates in the nation. Southeast—and a couple of other 'hoods—is where it goes down. And nobody woke up to it even when a congressman got robbed and shot on the Capitol grounds a few years back. Nobody wants to admit it's hopeless, endless. Like the civil wars in Africa.

Just a glimpse, a fleeting thought too straight on to resonate. Pretty soon we're cruising a pretty Virgina parkway, turning into Arlington, parking. I stretch, suck in some breaths deep as I can. Not quite autumn yet, but the monsoon humidity's gone, the air seems clean and crisp.

"Well, where to?" Allison asks.

"Kennedy's first."

The eternal flame's not much, most certainly not eternal, so it's hard to know why the expressions on the faces gazing at it look so awed and reverent. The white stones around it, bearing chiseled words, interest me. "We will bear any burden, pay any price," I read out loud.

"You a closet patriot, Terry?" Allison asks. I'm thinking she sounds just a bit spooked.

"No," I say. "Just considering that ruthless, ambitious bastard sure knew great speechwriters when he read them." I pause. "Let's walk."

I take point, aiming for quieter, less trafficked precincts. The gardens are beautiful, white marble crosses bright against the clipped grass, flowing along the contours of the rolling terrain, parting gracefully as a brook around copses of well-tended mature oaks and maples and pines. It's artfully arranged so you can see straight lines only obliquely, though the spacing is perfect. I can't find an angle of view that reveals the graves are as rigidly positioned as an elite division in full-dress formation on some vast parade ground—which is a brute demonstration that no man's an individual, just an easily replaceable part. The designers worked hard to make sure no one ever sees it quite that way.

"You know what this really is, Allison," I say. "This beautiful ground is nothing but a junkyard for broken pieces of the machine."

"I could say that's cheap nihilism," she says. "Or I could spin it once, say this is the real land of the free, home of the brave. Sure, most of those here weren't combat heroes. But they served, they didn't shirk it. And now they're free."

"Free?"

"Of this fucked world, they are."

I stop under a broad-spreading oak on a little knoll, the familiar pleasant scent of newly mown grass in the air. Allison moves up near me. So near our shoulders are almost touching.

"What are we going into?" I ask.

"What you and Westley discussed. We have an interest in a certain package that'll be moving. From Busan to Vladivostok to Pyongyang. Sensitive, but not hot, not high intensity. We've got our Russian connections, the package has the North Korean ones.

All you have to do is keep the package secure. We think it will be about as straightforward as it ever gets. We do not anticipate trouble. But, as usual, we want to be geared up for anything, no matter how unlikely."

"Oh, that clears up a lot." My tone's sarcastic but my mind's racing. All Westley'd said was North Asia. Now I've got actual places, a hint of the actual players. Did she slip up, or was she told it was time? "Listen, I know you're wired. But here's a question I'm sure your handlers won't mind you answering. Why me?"

"I'm not wired, and you already asked Westley that. You're still wondering why you were picked for something outside your specialty, when we must have a dozen contractors who do specialize in baby-sitting? And this apparent anomaly's giving you a slightly paranoid sensation?"

"Come on, Allison. Do you really think I'm just another no-brain shooter? Yeah, probably you do. I behave like one, so maybe that *is* all I am. But I am not, repeat not, prone to paranoia. So, why me?"

"As you were told, we're stretched and busy. Some attrition these past few years, too. Some burnouts, some too compromised to use again. A couple of casualties we're sure of. A few more just missing. That shouldn't come as startling news to you."

"It doesn't. But it isn't an answer, either. Come on, Allison."

"I don't actually know. Partly your Russian fluency. Partly the military stuff," she says. "But I'm guessing. Because I didn't ask for you. Westley gave you to me, Luther."

"Luther? So I'm myself again. Terry sure did a fast fade."

Allison won't meet my eyes.

"And of course Westley did," I go on. "The man's running the op, he picks the team. Standard."

"Actually, it isn't. Because he isn't." Allison pauses. "I'm running this, Luther. Westley's contributing."

This is fucked beyond belief. I cannot buy it. "Don't you mean 'controlling'?"

"Hey, use whatever word you're comfortable with," she says.

"I'm real careful with words. Subtle little bastards. The wrong one at the wrong time, in some places, will get you killed."

"Then hear this: I will be giving all the orders on this op. Nobody is going to even get bruised. I am in charge. Completely. Trust me."

Either Allison's deluded, or I've been had. Instantly every instinct I've been stupidly ignoring or deliberately burying since Westley appeared at Flannery's begins strobing. I have got to get some hard intelligence on Westley, on Allison, on this whole deal. The problem: Who can provide, and how? I'm in virtual lockdown. No phone, no computer I've seen with Internet connections in the spook house. Never out alone, so I can't even drop a quarter in a pay phone. And who to call? I've got no one inside the Company, no contacts at the DEA—not since the Francesca Russo incident—who might have CIA friends, nobody at NSA or the Pentagon.

I'm obsessed with this the rest of the day and all through a pizza dinner in the library with Allison, Nadya, and Rob. My pre-occupation is impossible to miss, but they ignore it. I hardly pay attention when Westley strolls in, says, "Well, shall we watch some movies?" even though this seems completely bizarre.

But I snap to, the moment the tape starts to roll.

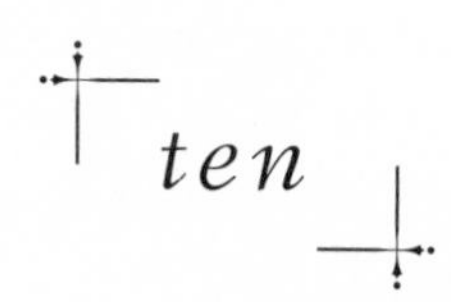

ten

NADYA NARRATES, STILL CURLED IN HER CHAIR. SHE'S THE ONLY ONE who hasn't straightened up, turned slightly tense, since Westley appeared.

"Thug on the right, that's Bolgakov. Delicate villain left rear is Tchitcherine. Amazing they're still in business. Almost chopped by Gorbachev, slipped under Yeltsin's scythe, and so far seem to have escaped Putin's notice."

"Tell us why, Nadya," Allison says.

"Swaying reeds, I imagine, no matter the breeze." She laughs. "They've not been good boys, but they've groveled and fawned and spoken out of school about others less discreet. And of course their commands are no longer so sensitive as they were in tenser days. Siberian missile regiments. Been twiddling their thumbs for ages now."

The video's a combination of official coverage of what seem to be ceremonial meetings with Chinese and American figures, plus some clandestine stuff of Bolgakov and Tchitcherine's private comings and goings. It's been digitally enhanced or the technology has made a quantum leap in a decade, which is how long it's been since I last saw this kind of surveillance.

"Take a good look, Terry," Allison says. "The generals are our new Russian assets. These"—the video cuts to lower-rez short scenes, all crowded, but four faces that appear in every one—"are our package's North Korean friends."

"They have names?"

"Sure. They're in the dossier you'll be getting. Hope you can pronounce them better than you managed Eunkyong's."

Allison's dig draws a chuckle from everyone. Except Westley. Westley just glances at me, shrugs, as if to say "Kids. What can you do?" It reminds me of a meet we'd had in '99, during which he invited me to take a brief holiday in Kosovo, exercise my long-range termination skills on some Serb commanders. Which I politely declined.

"And this," Allison says as the video switches to perfect clarity, the subject clearly conscious of the camera's presense, even smiling and waving, "is the package. Kim Chung-hee. Mister Kim. Chairman of one of the ROK's most progressive *jaebeols*. Very forward-looking businessman."

"*Jaebeol*?" I say.

"Korea's got about thirty of them, their version of the Dow Jones Industrials. Only they're not public corporations. They're huge conglomerates, family-controlled, thick as thieves with the government. Modeled somewhat on Japanese *zaibatsu*, like Honda, Sony. You know some of the Korean ones: Samsung, Daewoo, Hyundai."

"Jesus."

"Kim's is one of the smallest. Think Apple compared with Microsoft. Family control and government alliances, though, have an exponential effect. The Kim wealth is hard to imagine. But that's not important. You know North Korea's a rogue state, paranoid, sealed off. Kim's forward-looking, as I said. He had business feelers out to Pyongyang before the 2000 meeting between the ROK president and the North's maximum leader, Kim Jong Il. After that, he got more active, started trading with the North through its two back doors, China and Russia. He's very welcome in Pyongyang now.

"The cool part is this: he loves us. He has a house in Big Sur, comes over maybe once a month, and talks for hours about everything he's seen, heard, and been doing in the North. About two months ago, he told us about a possible deal, buying something from our Russian generals, selling it to North Koreans. Asked if we wanted to go along for the ride. Absolutely! We want the North to have what the Russians are offering, so we want to protect the deal."

"I think it would be useful to point out that money does not move Kim in this," Westley says, his tone calm, knowing, almost paternal. "The man's an idealist. He keeps asking why the thirty-eighth parallel exists anywhere except on maps? Why is there a DMZ there? Koreans are one people, south and north, he says. As the Germans are one people, west and east. The Germans tore down the Wall, turned off the death strip separating them. Why shouldn't Koreans do the same?"

"He's being a bit naïve, of course, for such a smart man," Nadya says. "He doesn't seem to understand how change bubbled up from below in Germany, until the DDR leaders couldn't keep the lid on. Nothing bubbling at all in the Democratic People's Republic of Korea."

"I don't think he's even entertained the notion that the famine in the DPRK may be artificial, deliberately created as a means of control by Chairman Kim, who's taken a leaf direct from Stalin's book," Allison says.

"None of this," Westley says, "lessens our Mister Kim's value.

He has access to the North. Access we otherwise would not have."

I'm looking hard at the videos. I'm seeing a man still in his thirties, very corporate, very at ease and seemingly jovial. I'm also seeing his eyes change suddenly while his smile stays the same, and people in his entourage snap to when he utters a few words. Like young staff captains hearing the voice of God in the person of the Joint Chiefs head: with eagerness, obvious deference, and terror. I also see he's got a personal security team around him, not in-your-face but obvious to anyone who knows what to look for, in every situation. From the ways they move, they appear to know their trade.

"So why not insert an intelligence agent into his entourage? He's got his own protection team," I say.

"Going forward, we might," Allison says. "On this particular outing, the intel will be obvious in the deal. But Mister Kim's a little nervous about the Russians. He doesn't quite trust them. Also, he's a bit worried someone might get to someone on his own team. So he asked for security assistance."

"And I'm it? That's crazy."

Westley laughs. But this time he's the only one.

"No," Allison says. "We'll have people on the ground in each place Kim goes. Including a former colleague of yours. He's already out there. You can have a big reunion."

"That is so reassuring." I wonder who she's talking about, knowing by now she wouldn't tell me if I asked.

"It should be," Allison says. "One foreigner—with one task—is all we can put into Kim's entourage without arousing suspicion. What did you expect? A bunch of Secret Service types with badges on their lapels and little ear mikes hovering around him? Come on, Terry."

"And it's only a business exchange, not an espionage mission," Rob says. Another country heard from.

"My task, in full?"

"Stick close to Kim, protect the package. As you've been told." It's Westley now, in command tone. "Any little thing goes wrong, you will be well covered. You will be picked up by friendlies within minutes after you've got clear and signaled."

I look at Allison. She's looking at Westley.

"Package. Right. Kim. But what are we talking about in terms of merchandise, since I assume you want me to get it out with him? Small, light? Bulky, heavy?" I ask.

"Easily portable. Kim can slip it into his coat pocket. Once we obtain it from the Russians," Westley answers. His next words are not those of a mere contributor, as Allison termed him. "Oh. If you do have to move, and anyone appears even vaguely to be in your way—theirs or ours—just kill them, okay?"

"Well," Allison says when the video stops, the lights go up, and Westley's disappeared. "Let's have a drink. Shot of Barbancourt Rhum, souvenir from my last trip to Haiti?"

Rob and Nadya say yes. "Make mine a Cuba Libre, hold the rum," I say. Allison produces her bottle from a nook near the video/audio system, pours three shots of rum. She takes a can of Coke from the mini-fridge I never knew lurked there behind the cabinet doors, hands it to me.

"Tell me something," I say, when everyone's had a sip. "You guys work with Westley before?"

"You have," Rob replies, taking a swig of rum, swirling what's left around his glass.

"Brilliant," Nadya says. "Rob, you're amazing."

"Yeah, he's super," I say. "But he didn't answer the question."

"Ah, no. I mean we have, but not this way," Allison says. "The three of us have teamed on lots of things. Westley delivered a contractor for some of them. Here, to the house. Then he went away.

One or another of three guys from the Langley operations unit was always the officer in charge."

"So this is the first time Westley's actively engaging in an op?"

"With us," Nadya says.

"Couldn't possibly be his first, though," Allison says. "He's way too senior. We assume he's run plenty. Just not in our area."

"Assume?" I say. They don't know as much about where Westley's been on the ground and in the shit as I do, and I don't know even half. Serious lapse here. "You check with any of those three Langley officers on this?"

"Who do you imagine told us Westley would be in on this one?" Rob says. "Jesus."

"And did they say why?" I ask.

"Terry, Westley didn't just bring *you* to us," Allison says, seemingly a little anxious to chill the static that's developing between Rob and me. "He brought the Russians. And the package."

"What?"

"Kim is Westley's find," Allison says.

Rob and Nadya look at her as if they're thinking maybe Allison's gone too far, given up something she shouldn't have. Then Nadya must decide it's okay.

"One might," she says, "call Mister Kim Westley's man, actually."

"Hey," Rob says.

"No reason Terry can't know this, Rob," Allison says, a bit more sharply than I've heard her speak before. God, I'm getting slow. This is deliberate, building a little creative tension between me and Rob. Supposed to push me closer to Allison. "He's Westley's too, for God's sake. Terry's going to be so close to Kim they'll almost be touching. And that's what Westley wants, right?"

Rob just looks at her. "A contractor," he says. The tone's nasty. A tone of voice, wrong time, wrong place. Once that would've been sufficient provocation for me to radically rearrange some guy's facial features, but I'd reckoned I was past that now. So I'm juked when the old demon starts rising fast. My muscles tense, my stance shifts. If that prick Rob says one more word, he's meat.

"So the relationships should be clear, before people start tripping each other," Allison goes on. "We all slide smoothly, as a team. No friction, no bumps or stumbles. Understood?"

The demon vanishes, just like that. Rob's a cipher again. I'm busy thinking Allison had better get clear on her role relative to Westley's.

Rob drains his glass. "Got a refill left in your souvenir?"

"Sure," Allison says, drawing Rob back to the cabinet.

Nadya snuggles into the sofa next to me, not close enough to mean anything, starts talking lowly in Russian.

"Rob's such a shit sometimes," she tells me. "Here's something useful. Kim has no Russian. One of his executives has some, does all the translating, but rather poorly. So. Best not to let on you're fluent unless one of two things happen: the executive is making dangerous mistakes, or our beloved Generals Bolgakov and Tchitcherine start playing games he's not getting. *Da*?"

"Paws off, Russki," Allison calls cheerfully across the room. "Poaching's against house rules, remember?"

"No wicked intentions on my part, I'm sure." Nadya laughs. "You'll want to watch this one closely, though. I doubt Terry's the faithful type."

Rob snorts, as if disgusted by our lack of seriousness. "I'm out of here," he says, and leaves.

"Why's he wrapped so tight?" I say when Allison flops on the sofa next to Nadya, deciding it's best to pretend I haven't spotted their game. "Fucking asshole."

"Can't you be more colorful, Terry?" Nadya grins.

"It's territorial," Allison says. "He wanted to do your job. Rob's very good at lots of things, but Westley felt he needed someone with more real-world experience. And someone who's off the books. Just in case. Anyway, Rob feels somewhat slighted. Maybe envious as well."

"Then he's an even bigger asshole than I thought," I say.

"The atmosphere's getting rather thick in here," Nadya says. "Fancy a stroll, Terry? Turn or two around the block before bed?"

"Love it," I say.

"It'll have to be a threesome, then," Allison says, rising. "No way I'm letting you two wander off into the night on your own."

"Bitch," Nadya says, laughing.

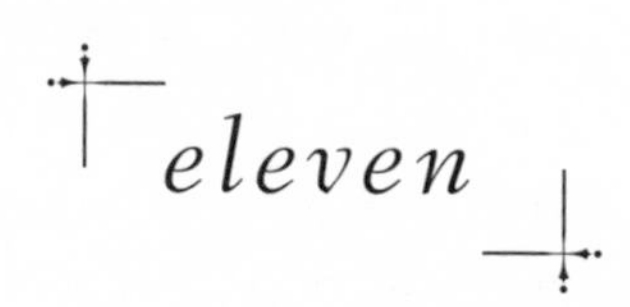

eleven

I'M STALKING SLEEP THAT NIGHT, BUT SLEEP STAYS OUT OF RANGE. I lie there, face feeling flushed and forehead hot, as if I've got a fever. Yet my hands and feet are cold.

I'm voodooed. Partly it's the situation. Mainly it's the way I was so ready to hurt Rob bad over a word. If it had been a street or bar encounter, I'd have done it without hesitation. If he'd flashed a weapon, I'd have capped him and walked away without feeling a thing.

No. I would have felt everything. Which is why, these past few years, I've tried to chill out edgy situations, remake them, manipulate whatever players are involved. So there'd be no bang-bang, no bodies but live ones, no brass shell casings gleaming in the dark red wet. So much for resolve, good resolutions. I can handle street punks with words usually, no need for my hands. Yet I didn't say a thing tonight. Just clicked up to attack mode. Because of a nobody's fucking tone.

What if the training—when they get you young enough, malleable enough—can never be truly undone? What if they get it in so deep it becomes all of what you are?

There's more. An acute episode of free-floating anxiety, Annie would explain to me. This is not necessarily bad; keeps you sharp, if there's some genuine reason for it; if you're sure something's out there—unknown but real—you may need to counter. Bad, though, if you cannot identify any threat beyond the phantoms in your head.

I'm sure there's at least one real thing: the elaborate charade about who's really running this mission. Why? It cannot be a delusion of Allision's. Either she's been ordered for reasons unknown to claim command, or she's being duped by higher-ups at Langley into believing she has it. Both seem so doubtful, going against everything I know about the Company, about Westley. But there's clearly a game in play, though I don't know the goal, or what the rules are. Only that my role seems to be shaking out as some sort of pawn, low-value and expendable.

Chess! It hits me who I can go to. Rhino, the only person I've ever met who knew absolutely his opponent's intentions four or five moves before the attempt. Not just on a chessboard, but in the field, in combat.

Rhino. I was his star pupil, his protégé, when I was a green eighteen-year-old and he was in charge of Special Forces training. He wouldn't speak to me for two years after I went berserk at twenty-two during Desert Storm and slaughtered two dozen cringing Iraqi soldiers who were begging to surrender after a short firefight. That little move cost me my army career. I'd called Rhino as soon as I got back to the States. He wouldn't let me say a word. "Discipline, asshole. The difference between a warrior and a psycho-killer," he'd barked. "I busted my chops teaching you discipline. I was sure you aced the lesson. You let me down bad, maggot. Fuck you very much." He'd slammed the phone down then.

But he finally got back in touch, and we'd stayed in touch pretty regularly—the only gap being my time in Sarajevo and the

Swiss hospital. Five years ago, having done his thirty in Special Forces, he took a job offer from the Defense Intelligence Agency. Rhino was a legend in the special-ops world, and he had friends in every agency that ever mounted clandestine actions, because he was so often called in to consult, even by the CIA.

If Rhino can't find out what I need to know, the information does not exist. Problem is, how to get him on the case, with no phone, no e-mail, no access to any sort of secure communication? My little balloon of hope starts to deflate fast. Until I recall one of Rhino's maxims, delivered over and over in a roar to thousands of green kids who came under his tutelage: The simplest way to your objective is always—always—the best way, you stupid fucks."

Simplest? The U.S. Postal Service.

I'm out of bed and rummaging through the little desk almost before I finish the thought. Somebody will know I'm moving, but not what I'm doing; I gave my room a total toss after that first morning, and I'm monitored only by motion sensors, no cameras. I find a small set of stationery and one of the pens Allison had me use to write all those postcards to Annie. I'm about to scribble, scribble, scribble as she liked to say, when I freeze. It's unlikely, but they might count the sheets, not like finding a couple missing.

But I still have one personal thing I'd brought to the spook house that never was confiscated: a little pocket notebook. I take it and the pen and go sit on the toilet. I spend the next half hour laying out my situation for Rhino, and what I urgently want to learn about Westley, Allison, and this op. Then I make an envelope out of two pages from the notebook and a couple of strips of Scotch tape. I insert the letter, seal the envelope, slip it into one of my running shoes.

Still revved, I pick up the Kim dossier Allison had given me, slip into bed, and read it for the third time, looking hard for misinformation, omissions, any subtext that might alert me to things I should be concerned about.

Kim took over the family concern on the death of his father, five years ago. It was a planned succession of the first son, he'd been groomed for it. Bachelor's in mathematics from Berkeley, a year as an analyst with Bear Stearns in New York, then an M.B.A. at Wharton. Excellent student, hard worker, partied hard, too, but not to excess. No overt displays of excess wealth, either; drove a 300-series BMW, shared a Manhattan apartment with two pals from Berkeley for that year at Bear Stearns, never flaunted his family fortune. Left a normal string of girlfriends in his wake when he went back to Busan.

There he worked one year at each of the various sectors of the conglomerate, always as assistant to the division chief: light manufacturing, heavy manufacturing, export, marketing, finance and currency. Five years, then a transfer to headquarters staff. Not as his father's number two, either. Started as assistant to the CFO, moved on to assistant to the COO, with the plain title of vice president. Kim's old man apparently followed the American corporate model, with himself as CEO and chairman of the board. Kim wasn't appointed to the board until his second year as assistant to the COO—eight years after he started work.

Patient young man, it seems to me. If he chafed at the slow pace, he kept it to himself. Didn't vent any frustration in his personal life, either. According to the dossier, he lived pretty much as any salaried executive at his level would. Nice apartment in Busan, nice country house down south on the coast. No pleasure palaces, no flashy cars, no wild behavior. Quiet social life, dinners out and small parties in with good friends. One big interest outside business: flying. Began taking lessons as soon as he arrived at Berkeley and continued when he returned home from the U.S., working his way up the qualification ladder from single-engine prop to multi-engine prop to corporate-size jets. Got his pilot's license for jets. Occasionally takes controls of a corporate plane on business trips, but not known to have taken one out joyriding. Ever.

My profile of Kim shakes out simply:

Heterosexual male, serial monogamist, no kinks at all.

Generally gregarious and easygoing, values friendships, socially adept and active, moderate alcohol consumption, occasional recreational drug use: weed and coke in the States, some opium in Korea, always in the company of close friends.

Even temperament, collegial attitude with employees, fair, strict when they make business missteps but always gives second chances. No tendencies to outbursts of rage, irrational decision-making, emotional volatilty.

Americanized to a large degree but retains strong sense of certain traditional Korean values, including a strict structure of relationships based on age, education, and socioeconomic status, and the concept of *gibun*, which is similar to the Chinese concept of face: i.e., every effort is made to avoid situations or confrontations in which one party or the other may suffer embarrassment by having to back down.

Miscellanous: good sense of humor, sometimes plays mischievious jokes on close associates, business and personal. Generous and hospitable. Currently romantically involved with a twenty-six-year-old girl, Korean, graduate of Stanford, employed as a junior executive in a bank. She lives in her own apartment, spends several nights a week with Kim in his Busan compound. She has no strong domestic political ties, no known connections with agents of any foreign government.

As for the *jaebeol*, Kim's father ran it aggressively but honestly, no evidence of shady financial or other dealings. On Kim's ascension, he retained his father's CFO and COO, but appointed two trusted contemporaries from within the company as their assistants and presumed successors. He worked to build the *jaebeol* by friendly acquisitions, mainly in electronics and computer-related businesses. Took large stakes in some small, very edgy U.S. software start-ups. He made only one initiative his father would never have permitted: the development of trading ties with the North.

Christ. The man seems as decent as any big industrialist can be. He's got no vices or bad habits that might make him vulnerable to pressure. He believes in democracy and free trade and America's global role. His political views are moderate.

What's not to like here? Anyway, all I've got to do is help keep him safe, so it wouldn't really matter to me if he was kinked or perverted or a completely nasty fuck—so long as I knew about it, since you have to be extra-vigilant when your man is busy indulging vices.

It's my own team that's got me anxious, not Kim or any bent Russian generals.

Maybe I finally drift into sleep. Maybe I don't. All I know is that at some point I'm aware of early light flowing through the window in my room, I'm up and getting dressed. I head down four minutes earlier than usual, which gives me time to find and score a stamp in the library, stick it on the Rhino letter, put the letter into the kangaroo pocket of my hoodie. Allison seems a little down when I meet her in the foyer, but I don't ask any questions. We go for our run. When Allison calls last lap, it's no great trick to let her pull ahead a few yards and slip the letter into that one friendly blue mailbox on our circuit.

Subdued. That's the way I feel over the next few days. That's the atmosphere in the spook house. Only Nadya seems usually cheerful and sassy, gives me some genuine smiles now and then.

Mostly we discuss. Thoroughly, seriously. Not much about movement, logistics, who'll be where when, but about personalities. Kim's dossier and profile are the most complete, so Westley, like a professsor leading a seminar, steers us in other directions. Kim's two chief business advisers, for instance. His chief security heavy. His girlfriend—she's a screamer during sex, and Kim digs that. He sometimes tells her more than he ought to about what he does up North. She's being watched.

Allison gives a report on the Pyongyang Four. It's fairly thin, naturally. They're contemporaries of the young maximum leader, not of his dead father's generation. They seem to act as a team—or a cabal. They're the leader's inner cabinet, the ones with the most access, the most influence over a dictator as isolated as the worst Byzantine emperor. No hard intelligence on their personal lives, beyond the fact that they're all married, all have a couple of kids. Believed to be loyal to their boss—so long as he comes around to their point of view, according to some sources. When he doesn't, they bow in unison, remain patient and agreeable, but subtly keep up the pressure. There are some indicators they'd do whatever it takes to stop the boss doing anything insane—like invading the ROK, shooting down Chinese, Russian, or American planes. But they let him rattle his saber as much as he likes.

Most of it's boring and gets more tedious by the day. All this stuff may be important to Company careerists, who have a longer view, but it's got little relevance to my task; all I want to know is who might be likely to try a burn on Kim, and how good they are.

Meanwhile, the clock's ticking on my SOS to Rhino. On morning runs with Allison, I feel a little hope bleed away each time I pass the mailbox where I dropped the letter to him four, five, six days ago. Every afternoon when discussions finish, I go down to the dojo and punish the hell out of the small bag, the heavy bag, until my arms and legs are leaden with exhaustion.

Twice a week Nadya takes me out to the range, usually has to drag me away from combat town because the groove I get into there is the only place my mind burns clear and concentrated. But it isn't enough. My sleep each night becomes shallower, patchy, dream-tossed. Nasty dreams.

One evening, though, Nadya gives a rundown on her Russians, and that at least is entertaining.

"Bolgakov's quite old school," she says. "Married twenty-five years to a woman who wears the trousers. He comes right to heel whenever she calls. Terrified of her, absolutely. Can't blame him, really. She looks like she was on the Soviet Olympic weight lifting team in her youth, gone a bit to fat now of course but still formidable."

It's "for-*mid*-able" in Nadya's Brit-speak. The girl has no idea how erotic her smoky voice is.

"Little Tchitcherine—now, he's a rogue. Rogering here, rogering there. Also married twenty-five years to a quite slim and lovely woman, who has a quite slim and lovely younger sister who has a stunning seventeen-year-old daughter. The dog's defiling his innocent flower of a niece as often as he can. The amount of his Viagra bills defies imagination."

There's a blurt of laughter from Westley. Rob and Allison stay buttoned up. They always stiffen in Westley's presense.

"Bolgakov's all stuffy and puritanical about this," Nadya goes on, clearly enjoying herself. "Probably envy, I should think. He'd love nothing more than a nubile beauty of his own. But professionally they are in harmony. Shamelessly venal. Bolgakov's under pressure now because his wife has developed expensive tastes. In any case, they started in a quite small way, post-Gorbachev. Diverting food and fuel alotted to their units onto the black market. Soon they were approached by a mafia composed mainly of ex-KGB types. And they've been handsomely rewarded for favors, such as arranging for heroin and cocaine shipped into Vlad by the KGB mob to be transported in military trucks and trains, that sort of thing. Not much more than simply turning a blind eye, that was all our generals had to do. Envelopes fat with cash got slipped to them under tables in restaurants. Their appetites whetted, they did not say no when the favors asked escalated to spare parts for vehicles, vehicles entire, ultimately, spare parts for weapons, which the mafia laddies were transhipping to former Soviet clients such as Iraq.

"They were quite clever about it, actually. Amassed fortunes, the two of them, never once coming under suspicion. They grew so bold they decided they could do business on their own, eliminating the mafia middlemen. Naturally the ex-KGB laddies disapproved. Naturally they made some threatening gestures. But Bolgakov and Tchitcherine well and truly slipped the leash. They had Spetsnaz squads attached to their regiments for security. It cost them almost nothing to get some of these boyos to eliminate most of the KGBers. They were then in position to present themselves directly to interested businessmen. So when our own Mister Kim happens along—"

"I think that should wrap it up, Nadya," Westley interrupts. If he's decided she was about to go too far, he keeps it well hidden. If she's wondering why she's been cut off, she doesn't let it show. But I get this sudden sense that everyone at the briefing is focused on me, wondering if this contract wetboy has the brains to make certain connections he was never supposed to make. Concerning Kim, and what exactly he might be getting from the Russians and selling to the Pyongyang gang. I try to look as bored and stupid as possible.

Westley moves briskly on to the big picture.

"Possible threats this trip. Number one, the Russians. Bolgakov and Tchitcherine may double-cross Kim. Or other Russians—

unknown at the moment, but we're looking into it—may want to screw our generals, and Mister Kim may be caught in the cross fire," he says.

"Number two, radical right-wing South Koreans who oppose any dealings with the North. Two separate groups of these, groups with the capabilities and motivation to strike at Mister Kim, have been ID'd and are under our scrutiny.

"There is the Chinese government. Very fluid situation with them. They've been alarmed that North Korea's crashing economy could make the state dangerously unstable, which is why they've allowed Kim and others to deal through China. On the other hand, they fear a strong North. They want a dependent client state as their neighbor. So they're watching every North-South connection very carefully. But only watching at this point.

"Finally, the Pyongyang Four. They may turn on Kim, though it would not be in their self-interest to do so.

"So my conclusion is this: A strike at Kim is possible in Busan, by the right-wingers. But being Kim's home turf, that's also where security is easiest and best. In Pyongyang, worst case is they aren't satisfied with Kim's product and send him home. Vladivostok is the hot zone. If anything is going to happen, it will be in Vlad. Any of the threats could strike in Vlad. We must be most alert there."

No shit, you empty suit.

twelve

"HEY! BIRDBONES, THERE! YOU THE INFAMOUS LUTHER EWING, OR some goddamned impersonator?" comes booming across the Dupont Circle park, a boot-camp voice but unique as a fingerprint.

"Who the hell is that?" Allison mutters hurriedly as we stop our run and watch the massive, slope-shouldered figure of Rhino moving toward us in his distinctive rolling walk.

"Christ! My former Special Forces boss. Now with Defense Intelligence. How do we play it?"

"By ear, I guess, but straight as we can," she says.

"It *is* the infamous Ewing, by God," Rhino bellows from ten meters off and closing fast. "What the hell you doing here, off the reservation?"

"Uh, jogging, Rhino. What's it look like?" I say. "What the hell are *you* doing here? In a suit? With a briefcase?"

"You damned well know. Going to my goddamn office. They make you put the uniform in mothballs after thirty years. And the DIA has a dress code."

"Great to see you, Rhino. Been too many years. But you

haven't changed at all. Well, maybe some gut expansion, but what the hell."

"You're the same, too, you skinny little low-life," he says, nodding toward Allison. "You still have no clue about basic social graces."

"Oh, right. Allison, this is Colonel Clarke. Colonel, this is my friend Allison."

"Glad to meet you, Allison," Rhino says, burying her hand in his for a moment. "I can see why Luther comes down here from Baltimore to visit you. But, if you'll pardon my bluntness, why would a lovely young woman like yourself want him to?"

"Low blow!" I say. Allison laughs.

"So, I guess I don't need to ask how you're keeping, judging from your fine company here," Rhino says. "You still playing cop or what?"

"Sure."

"Too bad. A gross misuse of natural talents."

"Speaking of gross misuse, you still playing spook?"

"Semi-spook. Mainly I'm a fat bureaucrat, deskbound, drinking bad coffee out of paper cups. I'm too old, too slow for the field. So they say."

"Must be true, if 'they' say it."

"True believers never need facts, Luther. They hate 'em. Facts are nasty, troublesome little bastards. You of all people know about that."

"Guess I do, Rhino. Hey, hear much from any of the team?"

"People keep in touch. Some are still in, mainly doing their thing east of Suez," he says, glancing at Allison. "Uh, how detailed can I get here, Luther?"

"Allison?"

"Whatever you're comfortable with, Colonel," she says. "I'm in your line of work. Different branch, but highest clearance."

"Yeah, it's true, Rhino. Gives her the perfect excuse to say, 'That's classified,' when I ask 'How was your day, honey?' So what about Rat, Klein, Rudy, any of that bunch?"

"Rat and Rudy are in northern Iraq, Kurdling. Those two, they always loved going native. Klein, the scumbag, didn't re-up when his last enlistment ran out. He went into private security, Blackwell's or some outfit. I hear he's in Iraq, too, baby-sitting Haliburton execs. Some useless shit like that."

"Must be big bucks in useless, then."

"Bigger than we'll ever see, that's certain."

"Whatever happened to Gassel and Cardello? You got a line on them?"

"Gassel" is Westley and "Cardello" is Allison in the crude code I laid out in my letter to Rhino more than two weeks ago, the letter that begged for this meeting in this place—because it would appear so unexpected and open Allison wouldn't clue to the fact that it was arranged.

"They're still the odd couple, still perfecting the love-hate thing, still inseparable. But we don't want to bore the lady, do we?"

"Go right ahead, Colonel," Allison says. "I've developed a tolerance, hanging out with Luther."

"Outstanding." Rhino laughs. "Okay. It's funny you should mention those two in particular, Luther, because one of my guys just came back from Colombia and damned if he didn't run into them. They sent regards. Then just yesterday I heard from someone else that Gassel's out on the hairy edge again. He's actually made solid connections with a couple of FARC narco-revolutionary *jefes*."

That's the code for the Russian generals. "Neat coup," I say. "Good for him."

"Maybe not," Rhino says, shaking his head. "This is hearsay.

Pretty solid source, but still hearsay. On the surface, it's a simple, sanctioned, mutually beneficial arrangement. But hiding behind that, Gassel's stepping outside the usual chain of command. And Cardello doesn't know it. Worse, it's rumored he's using Cardello as a cutout for an unsanctioned side agenda. Any goat-fuck develops, Cardello takes the heat. And some other players may fall hard."

"Oh man, Gassel wouldn't do that. Not to Cardello. He couldn't. It's too shitty even for him."

"Deeply and truly shitty. That's my thought, too. Gassel's long service, lives and dies by the rule book. But my guy seemed pretty certain. And I gotta admit, Gassel's take on the rules was always very, say, elastic?"

"Like big rubber bands. He's lucky none ever snapped back, took out an eye or something. But he never put a buddy in jeopardy, and this sounds like a super-stretch. Hope this is a misread by your source."

"Who knows? If I was certain, I'd have to rat Gassel out, old teammate or not. Guess we'll have to wait and see," Rhino says. Then he looks at his watch. "Shit, Luther, I got a clock to punch, can you believe that? But listen up. If you don't call me next time you're here and let me buy you the decent dinner you sure look like you could use, I'm gonna hunt you down and kill you."

"Hoo-ah, Colonel Rhino, sir. Sergeant Ewing will phone the colonel as ordered," I say, shaking hands.

"See that you do. Meantime, watch your step and make sure your back is covered."

"Always do."

"So long, then, Luther. Nice meeting you, Allison. Maybe you'll join us for that dinner if Luther and I swear to God we won't fall into miserable, maudlin reminisence?"

"Could be. Bye, Colonel," she says. We watch Rhino roll off in his too-tight suit, looking nothing like the smartest, toughest special operator I ever encountered. Then I turn and resume running. Allison's by my side in two strides. "So that was really your commander?" she asks.

"Yeah, and my mentor. He invested a lot in me. Kept saying I'd make major by thirty. Then Desert Storm breaks just before I'm due to ship out to OCS. My ticket gets punched for Kuwait instead. Hurt him a lot when I fucked up in Iraq and got discharged. Hurts me to remember that. So we stay in touch, but never mention it. But it's been two, maybe three years since I've seen him in the flesh. Is Massachusetts Avenue near here?"

"Yeah, it runs right into the Circle. Why?"

"He lives on Massachusetts. Moved there when he left the army, joined the DIA. We send each other Christmas cards, phone every once in while. It felt kind of strange, bumping into him now. But since he lives nearby, hey. It happens."

"It's almost stranger it hasn't happened before, Terry," Allison says. "Considering we've been circling this park every morning for months."

"That long? God, I've lost track."

"That long."

The address is for real, in case Allison decides to check it out. But I don't think she will. And I doubt she'll ever know Rhino's tip, vague as it seemed, is something I can use to protect my ass. And maybe hers too. If I decide to.

Another week of discussions drags by, the only new thing being that Westley stops attending midway. There's a lightening of the atmosphere in the spook house once he's gone, as if someone opened all the windows. But I still feel we're overpreparing, dulling our edge instead of honing it. Everybody's tensing, tempers are shortening.

Allison must feel something similar, because she starts thinking like a leader whose team is showing some stress fissures. She decides we need some R&R. All together, to get back together. She decides this shortly after Westley's vanished.

"Dinner? Then some clubbing? I really feel like going dancing," she says late one afternoon. Sounds like a suggestion, but I know it's not the sort anyone can decline. "Let's say we break now, leave at seven, okay?"

"Super," Nadya says.

"One condition," Rob says. I think he's going to be a jerk about this, but he fools me.

"What's that?" Allison says. Just a faint brittle note, as if the same thought flashed across her mind.

"We go in my car, not your Mini," Rob says. "It hurts, squeezing into those child-size backseats, you know? No, you wouldn't. You never have to."

"Not sure I want to be seen in that machine of yours, actually," Nadya says. "Notice I'm too polite to mention your driving technique."

They laugh, the three of them.

"Right, right," Allison says. "Your car, Rob. We'll probably have to taxi it back, though. Unless you're willing to be the designated driver and skip all the drinking?"

"Let's see how it goes," Rob says. "If I get polluted, Terry can always drive. He never has more than a beer."

"I think we should try to get Terry really drunk." Nadya smiles at me. "Make him babble all his secrets. He's full of secrets, I *know* it."

All I'm full of is some mild curiosity about what sorts of clubs these kids can possibly have in mind. Not the sort I'm used to, I'm thinking, as I go up to my room, strip, shower. And then some consternation, when I look in the armoire. All the Ecko, Quicksilver,

Billabong stuff I'm used to wearing is gone. I mean, *what*? I'm going for a night out in a junior executive suit? Or, worse, Ralph Lauren chinos? I do what I can: mess my hair up, wear a black T under the darkest gray suit, black suede loafers, put my earring back on.

I make a quick study in the mirror, see I look okay, and feel instantly like a fool. What does any of it matter? I'm going out with three spooks, in buttoned-up Washington, not to some 'hood hip-hop club with metal detectors at the entrance. I don't have to be credible to anyone, and there isn't anyone to look good for. I really ought to grow up.

That's brought home when I hit the foyer at seven. Rob's wearing baggy jeans with Hyde bowling shoes, a T over a long-sleeve waffle-weave. Allison's wearing red suede flares and a top that leaves about an inch of her belly bare.

"Terry! Love the mob hit-man costume," Nadya laughs. She's looking great, super-short spandex dress that shimmers like mercury, a gold chain around her neck that loops just where her cleavage starts.

"People'll think we're rock stars or something, with our own security man," Allison says.

"Ignore 'em, Terry," Rob says. "They live to bust balls."

They're all in on this. They've decided I'm the disaffected one, the wayward one they've got to bring back on board. I shouldn't be surprised, but I am a little, anyway. Rob did nice work, making it seem he was the one going off-team. God, I'm getting tired of this.

Rob's ride is a deep blue Volvo S60. Common, anonymous in this town. Unless you check the low-profile performance tires. Unless you notice when he keys it, lets out the clutch and winds it up a bit in first gear that some serious engine work's been done. He's smooth, using the car's quickness subtly, darting through traffic without drawing attention to the maneuvers.

First stop is Miss Lucy's, a joint on Capitol Hill that specializes in Deep South food: three kinds of barbecue, fried chicken with mashed potatoes and red-eye gravy, baby back ribs, greens, yams, corn bread. The crowd's split about fifty-fifty, race-wise, but no split at all in economic status. The prices on the menu would keep me from being a regular on my cop's salary. Off limits entirely on military pay. Little Nadya turns out to be the chow-hound, even lets out a burp when she's swallowed the last forkful of pecan pie.

Then Rob hustles us across town to a place on the edge of commercial Georgetown called Matrix. Failed New York imitation: fake velvet ropes channeling a line of people who want in, a white guy with a long ponytail flanked by two big black dudes picking who gets that privilege. Nadya just leads us straight up to the door, does a little eye and smile thing with Ponytail, and we're in.

It's dead, despite the black kid DJ working turntables hard. We take a table up on a tier around the dance floor. Nadya orders a bottle of Stoly; it comes encased in a block of ice—an actual fucking block of ice. There are four shot glasses. I take mine, turn it upside down in front of me, ask the waitress for a Rolling Rock, check out the place. Don't spot anybody I'd make for a player, not even a resident small-time coke merchant hawking a night's high for fifty bucks. Don't see a soul who isn't post-college or grad school but under thirty. The bouncers are pure window-dressing; the kinds of people I'm seeing never get into it, mix it up, tussle. Too respectable, too career-centered to risk any static. Like yuppies, only they're the generation after gen-X and I don't know if there's a name for them yet. Maybe there won't be.

X-squared. That'll do.

They're trying hard. They're churning on the dance floor, doing their best to get loose, get revved. They aren't making it, though. Too intense, approaching fun like they approach work. Nobody's letting go, gliding.

Until Nadya, after three quick shots of Stoly, grabs Rob by the arm and leads him down into the crowd. She stands there a sec, cocks her head to catch the beat, then goes mobile, sleek as a seal. Rob's playing catch-up, always a stuttering step or spin behind. I laugh.

"Russki slut," Allison says. "You dance, Terry?"

"Usually just watch," I say. "Usually on the job when I'm in clubs."

"That's past tense. You're not on the job tonight."

"But *you* are, aren't you?"

"Partly," she says. "But I could put it down, if you'd meet me halfway."

"Yeah? Let's just check that out." I stand up, take her hand, lead her down to the floor. She's the insecure kind, the type who reins herself in, tries to make up for it by flipping her hair and catching my eyes once in a while. My style's minimalist. I know I look just as awkward, but in a few minutes I let go, allow the sound to take me where it wants to. I'm down with it, pretty much dancing by myself, Allison sort of recoiling when our bodies happen to brush. Next thing I know Nadya's slipped in between us, her face close to mine, and Allison's spinning with Rob. Nadya locks those arctic-blue eyes of hers on mine, we get into sync, she smiles and slides a palm across my cheek. For a while I'm tight with her, though we're not touching. I'm feeling the connection, jamming on it. When the DJ cranks down, segues into a slowly pounding rhthym, Nadya presses close so my hands find her hips and hers lock around the back of my neck. I don't even care if this is part of the game. I'm just feeling the girl, liking her moves and her smile and her smell.

Then Nadya's lips graze my ear, and I hear, "One time only. That interest you, Terry?"

I lose the rhythm instantly, but manage to paste a huge smile on my face. A couple of years ago, I'd have been panting at an offer special as that from a girl special as the one looking up at me, taking her wrist and leading her somewhere—a booth in the ladies' room, the backseat of a car, anywhere we could get right down to it.

Not now. Not with Nadya.

It all breaks over me, like a rogue wave. The quick lurch of my heart when I walked into my room and saw her for the first time, the sense of deep contentment I've felt ever since just being near her, hearing her voice. The pulse-quickening but always suppressed feeling that this woman is my match, my mate, that we were born for each other—a range of emotion I've had only once or twice before in my life.

"No," I say. "Don't think it would be a good idea, pretty."

"Just once, Terry? See how we feel about replays after this mission?"

"No, Nadya." My smile's still fixed, but my eyes slide away from hers. I'm afraid of what she might see in them.

"Whoops!" Nadya cries, pulling back and spinning as the tempo revs again. "We're being watched."

I glance at our table. Rob and Allison are there, looking.

"I don't give up so easily," Nadya says, when her spin brings her near me again. "Soon, Terry."

"It's impossible. You're so lovely, but it's impossible."

"I'll find a way." She moves in as close as seems natural, dancing. "I'm a spy, remember?"

I laugh. So does Nadya. But for different reasons.

"And you claimed you didn't dance, Terry," Allison says when Nadya and I return to the table. The Stoli bottle's more than half empty. Nadya picks it up, iceblock and all, takes a long swallow. Then she starts mussing up Rob's hair. He ducks away, grinning.

"Hey, you got me up and moving," I say to Allison.

"Up, maybe. But somebody else got you going."

"Don't be bitchy, dear," Nadya says. "Hardly my fault Rob's a spaz, is it?"

"Now you've really hurt me, Nadya," Rob says.

"Oh, don't be a twit, mate. Come try again, I'm just getting into form," Nadya says, tugging Rob out of his chair and leading him back down to the floor.

Allison's looking at me, not them.

"What?"

"Nothing much," she says, sipping her vodka. "Having fun? Feeling good?"

"Are you?"

"Sure. Absolutely."

"Not real convincing, Allison."

"Now don't go all cop on me, Terry. Do you always see shadows behind shadows? Can't things sometimes be nothing beyond what they seem?"

"I think you have it reversed here. You're the one trained to assume absolutely nothing is what it seems."

"You are, too."

"Wrong. And you know it. Christ, I'm not even a very good detective. I'm only a walking weapons system. You're the one who'll aim and fire me, if necessary."

"Is that how you see all this?"

"Is there any other way of seeing it?"

"Shit, Terry. This is going the wrong way. I just wanted us to relax, have a good time."

"I am. Nadya sure is. Don't know about that Rob, but he could be. Just isn't real demonstrative about it. But you?"

"Yeah? Well—"

"Let's dance."

We do. There's less self-conscious hair-tossing this time. She doesn't recoil when our bodies connect. She giggles when she makes a misstep. It's almost genuine.

We leave two empty bottles of Stoly behind when we exit Matrix around two in the morning. I make Rob try to walk straight along the curb. He wobbles, falls after four steps. So I take the keys, drive his Volvo back to the spook house, following Allison's slurred directions. Have to pull over once so Nadya can lean out the rear door and puke.

"She always does that," Rob says, then sort of passes out. We have to help him into the house, stuff him into bed in one of the extra rooms. Nadya weaves her way into another.

"Stay tight, Terry. We're almost good to go," Allison says to me as she closes the door of her room. I hear the deadbolt click.

Three evenings after club night. Pizza in the library and a viewing of *Snatch*. The whole crew minus Westley. Then Allison drops the hammer.

"Pack tomorrow. We'll take two cars to the Sheraton near Baltimore-Washington International about five in the afternoon. Rooms are reserved in your work names. Wake-up call at three forty-five in the morning. We're going to California."

thirteen

ALLISON'S SITTING CROSS-LEGGED IN THE VERY MIDDLE OF MY BED, watching me pack. She doesn't seem to care that I'm fresh from a shower, wearing only my skivvies.

"Unusual set of scars," she says.

"The best ones are invisible."

She laughs. "God, Terry. What movie did you steal that line from? It had to be one where the girl instantly falls for the tough guy's unexpected sensitivity. Straight to video."

"Tough? I'm a pussy, everybody knows that."

"Hey! Careful with the pants," she says. "Alternate each pair, cuffs to waist, then fold all of them over the coats. We don't want a lot of creases and wrinkles, do we?"

"Think I've got the method. You did demonstrate, remember?"

"Right. So look over here for a moment and I'll demonstrate something else."

"Nothing I'm likely to get off on," I say, but I see her hold up a titanium wafer about the size of a Camel pack.

"You might. You cross-trained in communications as well as

weapons specialist, no?" she says. In her other hand is the little Olympus digital memo recorder.

"I've been pondering possible memos ever since that thing showed up in my room, weeks and weeks ago," I say.

"You wasted your time, then. Pay attention now," she says. "This Olympus is a burst-transmitter. Yes, it will do memos, though I doubt you'll use it that way. But if you have an urgent message, say it plainly into the recorder. No code necessary. Then press the play button twice, quick. It'll send your message to a satellite in, oh, maybe a nanosecond. Too fast to be unscrambled in transit. Mostly never even detected. Satellite hides it, unscrambles, codes, microbursts it to one of our ground stations, which patches it through to my cool little magic box here."

She puts the Olympus on the bed, holds up the key holder, which now seems to have acquired a key to a car I don't have. "The center pad, the blue one, that's the panic button. If it looks like you cannot get the package away, just tap it twice and keep on moving if you can. Some people will show up fast at your location, wherever you wind up, 'cause it's a finder beacon, too."

"And where will you be, Allison?"

"Oh, out there somewhere. Out of sight, out of mind. Unless you send a message or tap the panic button. What you should be asking is battery life, where the spares are."

She gets up, comes over to where I'm packing. Takes a look at my efforts.

"It would save some space if you stuff a couple of pairs of socks into each shoe," she says. "Batteries, the little round watch type, are in the heels, by the way."

"Blown before I start, then. Won't get past airport security shoe checks."

"There won't be any. We don't fly commercial."

* * *

We do take a commercial airport limo from the spook house, out along New York Avenue to the B-W Parkway. Rob and Nadya must have other arrangements, and Allison won't say a word as we cruise up one of those lovely, old-fashioned highways built long before the six- and eight-lane interstates. Two lanes north, and you can't see southbound traffic because the median's a meticulously maintained park maybe a hundred meters wide, thick with poplars, oaks, pines, and maples planted to plan at least sixty years ago. The lanes follow the terrain, sinuous as a snake. Reminds me, in the gathering dusk, of so many roads taken so many times, me in the backseat of Papa's big Chevy station wagon, cached amid suitcases, duffels, cardboard boxes that overflow the cargo space into the rear bench. Heading toward a new post, Papa always cheerful, teasing Mama, singing along when he finds a radio station that plays Motown sounds. And me glum and silent, for reasons I can't explain. It was never as if I was leaving good friends behind—never made any, on any base. Still, there was always a vague sense of loss, of saddening departure. Papa looked forward to destinations; I looked back to places I hadn't even liked much when I lived there.

Not this trip, though. I pull out of memory and into a pleasant anticipation; I want to go, go faster, go now. I want the action to hurry up and happen. I want to get into it, deep as I can.

The ride, the Sheraton check-in, watching my Terry Prentice Amex card swiped through the slot, being given a card key by the smiling redhead in a blue blazer and skirt—it's all too slow.

Allison senses it. "Soon," she says as we ride the elevator up to our rooms. "Pick you up in five minutes, we'll go down for dinner, okay?"

It's okay. I love airport hotel restaurants. Done by the numbers, always the same, no surprises. No ambient visual noise, a sort of blank in which the only thing that might matter—who's there—stands out clearly. I order prime rib, usually as dependable as the decor, and quarter the room. A couple of middle-aged suits, worn-out salesmen is my guess, dining alone. A few couples in what still passes for flight uniform even now: upscale sweatsuits with brand names prominent, upscale runners. A couple of families in varied states of disarray and uproar, depending on how many kids, and how old. Small people going to small places, or they'd have had direct connections from their incoming and wouldn't have to overnight it here, waiting for tomorrow's flight.

When an old couple already dressed for Florida clear away from the salad bar, I spot Rob at the far side of the room. Alone. He's done up like a photojournalist who's never been in a war zone, pressed khaki safari jacket and olive cotton shirt, probably the kind with epaulets and two pockets too many. He's concentrated on devouring a drumstick and thigh of fried chicken.

To my right, on our side of the salad bar, which is the epicenter of the room, I glimpse Nadya. Dressed rich urchin, sipping from a glass of wine, intent on conversation with a mousy-looking, fifty-something guy in a tweed sports coat and knit tie. An intelligence wonk, or maybe one of those fierce desk heroes who bay for war—so long as they're safely ten thousand miles from the front.

"Like that pussy Wolfowitz," I mutter.

"Stop looking at them. Look at me. Or that raw slab of heart attack fodder on your plate," Allison says. "Feel free to keep muttering, though."

"There ought to be a rule that civilian national security guys got to go in with the first wave on at least one major action before they're allowed to bend the president's ear," I say. "So they can get sprayed with blood and brains when some kid grunt takes a round through the head. So they can see and hear and smell the troop whose abdominal wall has been sliced open by shrapnel, yards of intestines spilling out on the ground."

"Jesus, Terry! I'm trying to eat here."

"They always try to grab 'em, stuff 'em back in."

"What?"

"The intestines. Dust and dirt all over them, but the guy tries to shove them back inside. Never works. Too slippery. But they try. Must be some kind of instinct."

"Do *not* feel free to keep muttering," Allison says, pushing her plate two inches away from her. "Just shut up, okay? I understand your dislike of the desk warriors, but must you share combat details over dinner?"

"I apologize. Sorry."

"It's all right. Some other time, if you care to tell me some things, I'll be a good listener. I just have this small problem when I'm eating."

"I think I've pretty much killed my own appetite."

"Hey, you notice anything a little weird here?"

"No."

"The Muzak? Somebody's slipped in some Dave Matthews. God, he'd die if he knew."

"No wonder you didn't dig Matrix," I say. "Dave Matthews fan! Should have guessed. Though his first CD's the only one worth listening to more than once. Reminds you of college, does it?"

"Grad school. I've got some sweet memories, with the Matthews Band as background music."

"Cryptic. How about providing some detail?"

"Hell no. My romantic interludes aren't something I'd care to have you leer and drool over. You tell me about yours, instead."

"Don't know that I've had any."

Allison practically hoots. "You are so full of it, Terry! I know every one of those poor girl's names."

"Close encounters only. Thought 'romantic' was the operative word here."

"Poor you, then. If that's true. But I don't believe it."

"Why not? You know so much about me, what I am. Can you feature any woman being in love with me? Or me with her?"

"Sure. There's types and types. Like finds like. That's how the world stays populated, isn't it?"

"Haven't done my share of that work, then," I say.

"Slacker. After this is over, go back to Annie and get busy." She grins at me like I'm a kid who's misbehaved in some slightly amusing way. I'm stung. Badly. Try hard not to let anything show.

I look around when the waitress brings our coffee. Rob's gone. Nadya's still sipping wine with guy in tweed. Businesslike expressions on both their faces.

"So, Dave in the background," I say, "singing that one where he asks the gravedigger to make his shallow, so he can feel the rain. Cheap nihilism you'd call it, if I said anything like that. But it's okay, it's a beautiful metaphor, from Dave. And I ask, 'Allison, why are we really doing this job?' And Allison looks into my eyes, truth on the tip of her tongue, and says . . . ?"

"Sorry. Details are still need-to-know. You want the broader view, for lots of jobs? It's pretty obvious. We got a new mandate, post-9/11. Go proactive again in major ways, after being reactive only after Vietnam and Iran and even Desert Storm. And not just us. All the agencies. We're going to sucker-punch anybody who even looks at us funny, not just sit there and take a hit first."

"So you're pulling in and using every guy like me you can dredge up."

"For the moment. We've got more newbies than we've ever had, and training classes are twice, three times the size they were a few years ago, when I went through. Covert, black, even what they used to call 'termination with extreme prejudice,' all mandated again. The old guys are saying it's like the sixties, pre-Carter seventies all over. They're only pissed that they're too creaky for the field now."

"And that's why kids like you are in charge of ops."

"Kids? I've got six years in. Which is more than your military time, on or off the books."

"God, I'm practically a rookie."

"Yeah. So go get some rack time," Allison says, signing the check Amanda something or other I can't read upside down.

"Army jargon doesn't suit you," I say. "And it's barely nine."

"Who cares?" she says. "Wake-up's at three forty-five, be down in the lobby ready to go at four-fifteen. Oh, and you might as well wear your tools."

I hang up my suit and shirt, wallet and passport and money still in the pockets. Loosen the noose of my tie just enough to slip over my head and hang it too; don't want to have to fumble around knotting it in the middle of the night. Don't want to mess up my neat packing job either. So I leave the suitcase locked, figure I'll wear what I came in. Take off my T and jockies, pull down the bed covers. Why do they always put too many blankets, comforters, and shams or whatever they call them on hotel beds? Dump most of them on the carpet. I lie there in the dark, smoking, feeling more than hearing the occasional roar and rumble of big jets lifting off, beginning their climb.

What I hear, after two or three more Camels, is a quiet but sharp click as the door lock snaps to open. The XD's in my right hand quick, and I flash the brilliant Z2 on the moment the door swings and someone slips in.

Nadya, jacklighted like a doe, freezes.

"Oh bugger, Terry. Turn that off and turn on the room lights. You bloody blinded me with that thing," she says.

"How'd you get in?" I ask, doing what she's asked.

"This." She's got one hand over her eyes. The other's holding up a clear plastic wafer, credit-card size, that seems veined with copper circuitry. "It'll open any card lock in any hotel in the world. Didn't they give you one?"

"Guess they don't trust me with one. What are you doing here?"

"Just wanted to ask what I asked when we danced: One time only? This is the last unbugged room we're likely to be in for quite a while."

Her eyes are bright under those black bangs.

"Nadya, please go back to your room. I don't think I can do this."

"Just relax, Terry, and let me do the thinking."

"What about feelings? Can you feel for me, too? Please go now," I say, moving to switch off the bedside lamp.

"Don't, darling," she smiles, swaying up to me, kicking off her shoes, slipping out of her skirt, pulling her top over her head. "I like to watch. I like to be watched."

She bends, face close, her nose lightly brushing one cheek, pulling away a little, brushing the other, pulling away, brushing my lips, pulling away. Her incredible eyes wide and locked to mine all the while. I'm gone, incapable of resistance. Then her lips, sweet and soft, meet mine lightly, withdraw, meet mine again and stay.

So very, very slow. So very, very sweet. I lose all sense of time. Her eyes never leave mine.

It's like nothing I've known. It goes on forever.

fourteen

COLD LIGHT, TOO BRIGHT, IN THE LOBBY BEFORE DAWN, AND A NIGHT manager handling our checkout too cheerfully for the hour. Everybody must have had the same idea I did. Everybody's wearing the clothes they arrived in. The only difference for me is the weight of the shoulder-holstered Wilson, the Springfield at the small of my back. In a day or two, I know, I won't be conscious of this at all. Which is important. A man who feels he's carrying shows he's carrying—in small ways, but always.

We board a white van, unmarked except for a small yin-yang circle bisected horizontally by a wave, red on the top, blue on the bottom. The Korean symbol, it's even on their flag. What was it Eunkyong told me? The red's for male, day, heat, action, the blue symbolizes female, night, cold, passivity.

A Taoist sign. Totally wrong, like most mystic shit. What do monks know about anything real? But I'm suddenly aware my own grasp on that is pretty weak at the moment. Last night, for instance. Maybe I only dreamed it.

I must scowl or something at that notion.

"I think Terry here is deep in caffeine withdrawl, needs a fix bad," Allison says as the van hums away from the hotel.

"He's not alone," Rob mutters. He's yawning as the van bypasses the main road to the passenger terminal—still dark, empty, not open for business—and turns onto a broad expanse of tarmac. Up ahead, maybe half a klick from the sleeping airliners flocked around the commercial terminal, there's a neat row of corporate Hawkers, Falcons, Challengers, a few little Lears. The private aviation sector, three or four hangars, only one of which is lit up. We stop there.

I step out of the van, look up at a Gulfstream, the G IV, I think. All pristine white, no markings beyond the standard FAA-required numbers. Except on the tail. There's a discreet circle, no bigger than a basketball, divided by a horizontal wave, red on top, blue on bottom. I see men in the green glow of the cockpit. The engines are already whirring lowly, the gangway's down. A couple of guys in white jumpsuits are transferring our luggage from the van to the plane's belly.

"KimAir, flight one, nonstop from BWI to Monterey, California, is now boarding. Have your passes ready, please," Allison calls out, mounting the gangway.

"You miss your true calling or what?" Rob says. "'Hello, my name is Allison and I'll be your cabin attendant.'"

"Just board, Rob," Allison says, disappearing into the plane.

Rob climbs the few steps, Nadya follows, I bring up the rear. We pass a curtained cubicle that must be the galley, enter the cabin. No rows of seats. It looks like a small cocktail lounge, half a dozen fat leather easy chairs around a low table, a couple more chairs against the rear bulkhead on either side of a brushed-aluminum door. Plush carpet, the same shade of blue as the yin-yang circle. A slim table flush against side of the hull, three slim brushed aluminum laptops on it, one under each porthole. Three tiny silver cell phones, one next to each computer. A slight girl in a kimono appears from the galley, inquires in a whisper if I'd like coffee, then pads around to Allison, Rob, and Nadya, asking what they require. Then she retires behind the curtains.

"Pick your spot," Allison says, flopping into one of the leather chairs that faces more or less forward. I guess I'm the only one who doesn't mind flying backward—lots of chopper time—because Rob and Nadya flank her. The kimono girl returns with a tray, serves each of us with a bow. A couple of gulps of the coffee and I'm feeling sharper.

"What did I say about Terry needing his fix?" Allison says. "Look at him. It's like his switch has been flipped on."

"I think it's Nadya who needs to pop a stay-awake, or whatever flicks her switch," Rob says. "Did you sleep at all, Nadya?"

Uh-oh, I'm thinking.

"Up your bum, mate," Nadya snaps. "You didn't have the longest, most tedious dinner of your life with the senior Russia analyst from Langley. It could have been over twice as fast, if the old lech had focused mostly on business instead of mostly on my tits. Gave me bad dreams."

She leans a little forward, looks over at Allison, and laughs. "Now Rob's doing it, too. This is covert harassment. I'm filing a complaint with Human Resources."

She doesn't look at me. Her attitude's perfect—treat Terry like you've always treated Terry. "At least that one's not sexist," she says, nodding in my direction.

None of us even notice the plane's taxiing, until the pilot's voice comes over the intercom, announcing we're cleared for takeoff in Korean-accented English.

"Hey, where's Westley?" I ask, more than a little late.

"He's already been out there for a few days, playing golf with Mister Kim," Allison says. "Korean businessmen have picked up bad habits like that from their Nipponese counterparts."

"A nice walk, spoiled," I say.

"Where'd that come from?" Rob asks.

"Some rabid anti-golfer. Read it someplace," I say.

Then we're accelerating a whole lot faster than any jet I've been on, and the lift-up's much more sudden, the climb so steep it's disconcerting. My hands squeeze the chair arms hard. Feel embarrassed when I notice my white knuckles. Hope the others didn't see. I deliberately relax my hands. I'm used to the long, slow lumbering of C-130s, which always feel like they're never going to get airborne.

Allison's up and booting one of the laptops as soon as we level out. She types a few words, taps one key, waits a second, then shuts down. Must be an e-mail.

"Cool plane. Kim's done it right," I say. "But you said noncommercial all the way. This can't have the range to cross the Pacific."

"It might. But he doesn't use it for that," Allison says. "He keeps this stateside, for local hops here and there. He's got something a bit bigger for intercontinental."

"Oh, it's huge," Nadya says. "Enormous."

"Nadya's phallic obsession," Allison says. "You wouldn't believe what she did when we saw an ICBM in North Dakota once."

"I missed that one," Rob says.

"She stroked it!"

"Cow!" Nadya says. She can't stop herself from giggling then.

Fucking sorority house again. The mood's too flip, too light. It's making me uneasy. But then I remember we're just going to California, hang out with Mister Kim and his people for a week or so, everybody getting comfortable with everybody. And then Busan, the man's hometown. The mission won't get serious until Vlad. I relax a little. Too used to the raw, rough ways my team eased tension on the way into a hot LZ. Or on the way up for a HALO—high-altitude, low-opening parachute drop. Training or real world, never mattered which. One felt the same as the other. That was the fucking point, wasn't it?

And I miss that shit, I realize. It's insane, of course. Nobody should miss live fire, or jumping out of a perfectly airworthy plane at thirty-five thousand feet in the dead of night, free-falling for thirty-two thou, then popping a chute so you can float right into the kill zone of dudes who're just dying to smoke you.

And I can't wait, I'm thinking, to get to Vlad. Tried for years now to put that jones for adrenaline dumps behind me. But even a whiff of action, I want into it.

"Terry's going all pensive on us," Allison says. "Thinking deep thoughts, are you?"

"Terry's taking a nap," I say, settling deeper into my chair, shutting my eyes, and hoping I'll see only Nadya in my dreams.

No such luck.

The bone-dry, bone-chilling desert night. No moon. No wind, no sound except the bass vibe of our well-muffled dune buggy easing up a little rise, poking its snout over the edge. Below us, maybe a thousand meters off on flats dull gray against the black night sky, we see the ominous silhouette of what's got to be a T-55 tank, laagered up with three APCs. A company of Iraqi soldiers, still and featureless as logs, lying close around a small fire. Nobody's up and walking, nobody's on sentry duty. Assholes. No discipline at all. Or maybe they figure they're so far behind the front line they can relax.

Allahu akbar, you poor bastards. God's scourge has a visual.

JoeBoy whispers to his radio. The radio hisses back. White teeth gleam out from his camo-smeared face. I figure it's a grin.

"That big fucker. Light it up, Luther!" JoeBoy says. Snake's behind the twin 50s mounted on the roll bar. "Yeah, man," he says. "Light the fucker up."

I shoulder a LAW, brace myself against the roll-bar, center the tank in the glowing green reticle of the sight. The sight image jitters. I take a deep breath, steady down, half exhale.

"Rock the ragheads, man," Snake says.

One press of one finger.

I'm rocked hard when the missile whooses off, then blinded by the brilliant white flash as it whangs into the tank and explodes. Half-blind as JoeBoy slams the buggy, revved to the max, over the ridge and redlines across the flats straight toward the pillar of flame. Snake's loosing shattering bursts of armor-piercing and incendiary rounds from the 50s, screaming "Fry! Fry, motherfuckers!"

White flash and red flare bypass my eyes, go straight into my brain as the APCs erupt, one after the other. A few dark figures flicker behind this scrim for a second. I hose them down, emptying two mags with my MP5 on full auto. Then there's nothing moving but heavy waves of smoke breaking over the flames in slow motion. Until it's Fourth of July again as Iraqi ammo cooks off into the sky. I try to blink away the awful glare. Doesn't work. Too bright.

It's daylight coming strong and straight in my face through the Gulfstream's portholes I'm blinking away, waking. We're racing the sun, the sun's winning as it always does. Allison and Rob are dozing. Nadya's reading a paperback. She glances up, sees my eyes are open, gives me a small smile of complicity. Then she goes back to her book, whatever it is. I stare at her a while to wipe the dream away, then watch the terrain appear through the cloud cover as the plane descends. Allison and Rob stir, stretch.

The pilot's good. He brings us down very steep but so smoothly the Gulfstream's tires barely squeal. Allison and Rob unbuckle. Nadya puts her book into her shoulder bag. The little kimono bows us out of the plane.

Nobody's waiting for us at the plane's hangar, which is as far from the main terminal as the dimensions of this small airport allow. There's a black Land Cruiser parked beside it. One of two guys in white jumpsuits hands Allison a key as she steps off the gangway, then joins his mate in off-loading our bags and wheeling them to the vehicle. Allison drives, Rob's riding shotgun, Nadya and I are in the rear seat. Feels like a chunk of time went missing. The early sun's slanting sharply over the wooded mountains to the east. It's only around eight in the morning, local, though my watch says eleven.

As we wind up into the hills, I catch a glimpse of the Pacific. Then we get to Carmel, and I feel low-rent despite the suit and the Cruiser. We park and head off for breakfast. I see a couple of Hummers, a $150,000 Mercedes Gelandewagen, one hand-built Morgan among the BMWs, Porsches, and Lexus SUVs. Lots of folks dressed like rich lumberjacks: plaid shirt-jacs, more likely cashmere or alpaca than cotton flannel. Same style idiom in Jake Moon's, a pancake house disguised as a Gold Rush saloon. Cappuccino's five bucks a pop, and fifteen gets you a short stack of Jake's rugged flapjacks—your choice of mango, passion fruit, kiwi, papaya, or organic whole-wheat blueberry. We're crammed around a small table with a tin top, in the rear. I order blueberry.

"I believe, no, I'm *sure* that is Clint Eastwood," Nadya says, pointing at the take-out counter up front, where a tall, lean guy is buying a bag of muffins. "He's not still the mayor, is he?"

Allison glances over. "Old," she says. "Ancient."

"Not so," Rob says. "Hope I look that good when I'm his age."

Nadya snorts. "Highly unlikely. You don't look that good now."

"Could we possibly take a banter break? For once?" Allison says, picking at some unrecognizable fruit in her pancakes. "So, Terry, a little parting of the ways coming up."

"How's that?"

"Westley's staying with Kim. You'll be staying on the compound with Kim's security guys. Rob and Nadya and I are camping out about a mile away. You could call it a motel, but it's a dozen little log cabins around a main cabin. Very fancy cabins, actually. Four-star accommodations."

"And what am I going to doing, exactly?"

"Well, first you'll meet Mister Kim. See if he approves of you. If he does, you and one of his guys will team up, do what security always does."

"If Kim doesn't approve?"

"Oh, he will. He knows all about you."

"And if I don't approve of him?"

"You'll have to deal with it. Prep's over. As of today, you're on the job."

fifteen

"HELLO, MISTER PRENTICE," KIM SAYS, SHAKING MY HAND, SMILING. "Are you by chance Native American?"

We're standing on the redwood deck partly cantilevered out over the Pacific, Kim's house set back maybe a hundred meters, and Westley's just made the introduction. He's hovering at my elbow now. Allison, Rob, and Nadya are just behind. They've already been presented; that hierarchy thing Eunkyong was so firm about. I'm not surprised by my ranking, but Kim's idea of an opening line is something else.

"I believe there's Lakota, perhaps some Comanche in my bloodline, sir," I say, bowing very slightly, a little less than I've been instructed to. Fuck the truth.

"I hope you don't think me blunt, Mister Prentice," Kim says. Damn, I was sure I'd kept all feeling masked. "Only a bit of pretty outdated Korean culture, this interest in physiognomy. You're not offended?"

"Offended? Not at all, sir. I'm proud of my ancestry."

"Yes, I share that. So when I first came to America as a student,

I'd get angry as hell when people almost automatically assumed I was Chinese. Or, worse, Japanese."

Westley laughs softly. "You know Americans, Mister Kim."

"Oh, I do now. Now I know very well that those who haven't spent time in Asia simply lack an eye for the differences. And I understand those differences even seem quite subtle to those more well traveled, though they're far from subtle to us."

"The attendant on your plane, Mister Kim, was clearly Japanese. The pilot was Korean. But the copilot was probably Cantonese, or at least his grandparents were," I say.

"An experienced eye, Mister Prentice," Kim says. "And what did you see in the face of the man at the front gate?"

"A mix of Manchu and Mongol, I think. His grandparents would've likely arrived in Korea during or just after World War Two."

"Your Mister Prentice is very sharp," Kim says to Westley.

"Our team members are always experienced, and professional," Westley says.

"Mister Prentice, let me introduce you to my assistant, Mister Park," Kim says. A Buddha steps forward, six-two and maybe 240 pounds of him, face expressionless. He was not presented to Allison and the rest. Hierarchy again. "What do you make of Mister Park?"

"South Korean by name, but from the far north by blood," I say.

"Ha-ha!" Kim smiles at Park, who bobs his head. Then Park and I shake hands, and I say, "Always a pleasure to meet a colleague," in passable Korean. He grins.

Kim gestures toward the house, which appears to be an enormous plate of glass framed by redwood logs at the corners, and leads the way. Park sticks close to him, which gives Nadya the chance to slide by me, ram an elbow into my ribs and mutter, "Bloody show-off." Inside, Kim suggests coffee and a chat to

Westley and the others. "Perhaps," he says, "Mister Prentice would like Mister Park to show him our arrangements?"

Westley nods at me, and I go off with Park on a tour. "How much you know, Mistah Prentice?" he asks as soon as we're out of earshot, heading down a corridor lined with celadon porcelain vases—probably priceless antiques, plain-looking as they are—on wooden pedestals.

"Enough," I say.

"I already figured that. I mean Korean talk."

I laugh. "Memorized a few phrases, like the one I used with you. That's all."

"Pretty good trick, Mistah Prentice. You gotta a lot of those? You some kind of tricky fella?"

"Usual tricks of the trade."

This brings on a Buddha smile, narrows the hard black slits of his eyes. Then we're outside, moving along the compound's perimeter in bright California sun. Park slips on shades. "Goddamn bright. Most days, fog, lotsa clouds, like at home," he says.

He doesn't say much else for a while. We just walk. Everything's a test, I'm thinking. Thanks, Allison.

The side of the house that faces the road has no glass; it's all wood with a kind of gull-wing tiled roof that's traditionally Korean, according to the photos in the books Eunkyong made me study. The grounds look wild, nature undisturbed for the most part. But there's some telltales here and there. Little humps in the ground that don't look quite right, for instance.

"You got motion sensors in the ground, and you got infrared beams on those," I say, pointing to the posts of the slatted wood fence anyone could climb. Park just grunts.

I start scanning more intently. In some of the wind-bent, torturously twisted coastal pines I see boxes no bigger than cigarette packs, almost but not quite perfectly camo'd, like the cameras serious deer hunters place along likely buck trails. "Smile, Mister Park," I say. "We're on TV right now, aren't we?"

"Hunh," he mutters, keeps walking. I stop.

"Seen enough," I say. "The place is taped. You got a guy in a room somewhere twenty-four seven, watching monitors. Also watching a computer screen with an image of the fence perimeter. The line'll start strobing exactly where anybody or anything breaks the beams. I'd have to see a schematic to tell if the system has any video shadows. But it wouldn't matter much, would it? Because there's multiple beams along the fence top, since a single can be stepped over by guys who figure there is one. And nobody can come under cleanly because the motion sensors'll give them away."

"Right so far, Mistah Prentice," Park says.

"Power goes down, you got a generator that kicks in automatically. But there's a second or two delay before the monitors go back on. Somebody really clever could take advantage of that, get pretty close to the house. But then they'd fry. Because you've got every possible entrance wired, instant battery backup."

"Goddamn right." He's grinning.

"If I want to take this place out, it goes out, though."

"How you do that, Mistah Prentice?"

"Roll up in a van, forget stealth, just stand on the roof and send about six RPGs into the place. Then a couple of LAWs, just 'cause I like fireworks with big booms."

Now the Buddha laughs. "You musta spent a lot of time in crazy places. This is California, Mistah Prentice. No craziness like that here."

"Nah, nothing like that here. Never happen, Mister Park."

"California. So hey, you call me Sonny, okay?" he says, leading me to the left side of the house and down some steps to the entrance of a wing that's less than half aboveground. Inside, there's the room I expected: a bank of monitors, a computer, and intercom, radio and phone setups. A Korean sitting on a swivel chair turns, glances without much curiosity at me for a second, then turns back to the screens. I see not only the outside is covered; on one screen the corridor with the celadon vases appears, on others other rooms, and on one the great glass-walled room overlooking the pool, deck, and ocean, Kim and Westley and the rest sitting around talking. There's no sound.

We move along a short corridor lined with doors. Sonny opens one. "Yours," he says, gesturing into a room that could be one lifted whole from a decent airport hotel, except it has no windows. It does have a big bed, a desk with a laptop, a TV, a mini–stereo system on it, an overstuffed easy chair, big closet set in one wall, and a full bathroom, complete with white hotel towels. My suitcase is already on the luggage rack.

"Good enough," I say.

"Damn bunker," Sonny says. "Me, I'm in the next room. Don't like being underground."

So, this Buddha's a little claustrophobic. I'll remember that.

"Let's get outside, Mistah Prentice," he says, and then we're through another door, up another set of steps and onto the deck around the pool, salty sea-taste in the wind. Sonny sucks in a deep breath.

"Ahh. Good, good. This I'm liking. Mistah Kim, he love this, too. We got places like this in Korea," he says, sweeping his arm toward the gnarled trees, the cliff, the glittery heaving expanse of ocean.

"You work for Mister Kim long?"

"Ah, six, seven years."

"Professional question?"

"Sure thing, Mistah Prentice."

"You ever have to take out anyone coming at Mister Kim?"

The Buddha stops his raptuous comtemplation of the sea, looks obliquely at me. "No," he says, after a moment.

"You ever have to defend him at all from an assault, a snatch attempt?"

"No."

"Security always this heavy?"

"Heavy? Nothing heavy here, Mistah Prentice."

"Don't think most of the neighbors have more than standard burglar alarms. Which makes motion sensors, guys like you, and the video watcher in the bunker kind of heavy by local standards. Like you said, this is California, not some crazy place."

"You got some kinda point here, Mistah Prentice? Some kinda problem or something?"

"No. Just a little curious how long things have been this way."

"Long time, just me with Mistah Kim."

"Good enough," I say. "So when did it ratchet up?"

"Ratchet?"

"When did the electronics, the extra men get added?"

Sonny looks at me fully now. Can't tell exactly what's going on behind those black slits. Could be suspicion, could be some quick calculation of how much he ought to reveal.

"Little while after Mistah Kim start going up to the North, that Mistah Westley start coming around a lot. That Mistah Westley, he start telling Mistah Kim I'm not enough anymore."

"Mister Westley, he's kind of nervous," I say. "Sees ghosts, I think."

"Hah!" Sonny barks. "That's exactly what I think. Sees a damned lot of ghosts. Everywhere, all the time. Keeps telling Mistah Kim ghost stories. Mistah Kim, he don't believe in ghosts. But pretty soon I got a lot of assistants anyhow. Pretty soon we got motion sensors, all kinda shit. Military-type shit."

"And no ghosts ever show up?" I say.

"Fuck no. Any do, they probably belong to Mistah Westley, damn straight."

I can't tell if he means me or not.

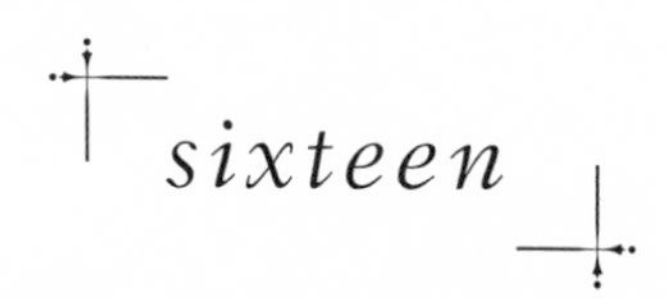

sixteen

SO I'M ON THE JOB, BUT NOT FULL-TIME. AND NOT EXACTLY CONCENTRATED, either, because just what the job is remains as grayly opaque as the billows of fog that rise up and roll over the cliff before every dawn, shrouding the house and grounds. Figures move through it, shapes waver in it, like images in dreams. The sun soon burns that away, everything material becomes sharp and precise.

There is a clear routine. I breakfast with Sonny and his three assistants; Sonny's a cigarette-first man like me, while the others—Lee, Lee, and Park, no further ID given—chow on some kind of gruel, except for whichever one had night duty in the monitor room. That one gets a stew and rice and a beer. The assistants are silent in my presense. Sonny gives them a few orders my Korean's not limber enough to follow, then he and I go off and give the house a quick patrol. After, we do the same on the grounds. Sonny always takes a huge, deep breath, sniffs, and shakes himself like a wet retriever the moment we're out the door.

Mostly we orbit around Kim, once he's up and about, but at a distance, always eliptical. Mostly we're outside by the pool, watching Kim and Westley and Allison and Nadya and Rob sitting around inside, talking. They move anywhere, we trail them, closer but always out of earshot. I feel like a rookie patrolman, walking the smallest beat in the precinct, measureable in meters instead of blocks.

"This is boring me to fucking death," I mutter on maybe the third morning.

"Ah, you get used to it, Mistah Prentice," Sonny says. "Easy life, this. Or you one of those crazies, like to be in some goddamn firefight all the time?"

"Say half-crazy, maybe."

"Firefights even half the time? Oh, that is full crazy, Mistah Prentice. Completely."

He's right, of course. But I see no advantage in adjusting his attitude toward me by agreeing with him. Let him think I'm some kind of juked-up maniac, under control for the moment but unpredictably explosive.

Then I get a little hit of mind-gaming, which is something at least. It's midafternoon, mare's tales streaming in the Pacific sky, me smoking out on the overlook where I was introduced to Kim, Sonny off taking a piss or something. There must be some kind of lull in the daily players' huddle inside, because suddenly Allison's beside me, forearms resting on the redwood rail, shoulder brushing mine.

"Hey, boss," I say, not much enthusiasm evident.

She hears the flatness, but stays silent for a moment, looking out to sea. No usual clever Allison comeback. She's still looking there when she says, "What's your read so far, Terry?"

"No read at all, since I'm not in the loop," I say. "Some impressions from the periphery, that's it."

"I'm always interested in impressions."

"Are you? That's never been my impression of you."

"Lame, Terry. I liked it better when you were smart-assed and sharp. Have we left you alone with that Buddha too long? Are you losing your edge a little? Going contemplative?"

"You amaze me, Allison. So perceptive."

"Poor Terry, feeling left out," she says, glancing at me, smiling, then turning back toward the water. "Those impressions you mentioned. Care to cut to them?"

"Okay. Sonny's a little disaffected. Thinks Westley's probably bad news for his Mistah Kim."

She faces me now, eyes to eyes. "He told you that?"

"Not in those exact words. But, yeah, he said it."

"Any sense why?"

"He was Kim's only security until the trips to the North started and Westley came around. Said Westley sees ghosts everywhere. Convinced Kim to ramp up his security. You know, I imagine, the extent of it here?"

"Three guys, the usual alarm system?"

"Take it higher, Allison. Take it up to spook-house level. Complete video coverage all the time, inside and out. I can sit in the monitor room and watch all your meetings. Plus perimeter defenses up to in-ground motion sensors. That I know for sure. Shit, there may even be claymores. Sonny said it was military-grade."

"Jesus."

"Yeah, and feature this: Sonny's been baby-sitting Kim for seven years. Never once faced a threat, let alone had to take one out. He says if any damn ghosts do show up, they'll be brought by Westley. And he doesn't dig that. At all."

"Not good," Allison says. "Is he a threat? Could he turn on Kim?"

"Don't you get it? He's exactly the opposite. He'd take a bullet for Kim. Secret Service presidential protection detail–style. But he'd be smiling as he smoked Westley. On a nod from Kim. Or any of us, on his own hook, if he decides we're endangering Kim."

"Is this instinct only, Terry? Or do you have something more?" She's at full attention now.

"Nothing more. Except I've known guys like Sonny all my life, zones cold and hot. Shit, I'm like Sonny. So I generally trust my instincts, even if you don't. I'd likely be dead by now if I didn't."

"Trust isn't the issue, Terry. It's real-world possibilities based on hard intel I need."

"Can't help you out there, Allison. I'm just a contractor, on the wrong side of that big glass wall."

Allison has a moment of what feels like intense internal debate. Her fists are clenched tight as they go, and she's not even aware of it. She looks out at the waves, the hypnotic way they come on, line after line, to suicide at the cliff base. She looks back at me, searching my face and eyes.

"I think . . ." she starts, then pauses. "I'm thinking maybe it's time you do need to know some things."

"Yeah?" We both feel more than hear Sonny's heavy tread on the planks behind us.

"Soon," she says quickly, then turns, waves at Sonny as they pass, heads back to the house.

"Hey, she pretty good-looking. How come I don't notice that before?" he says when he reaches me. Then he nudges me with a heavy elbow, laughs. "You got something going with her, Mistah Prentice? You bouncing her good or something?"

"I keep trying," I say. "She keeps turning me down."

"Ah, hate when they do that. Make a man crazy. You and me, we don't get some soon, we probably pop!" He clutches his balls, laughs louder. "Me, I can't wait to get back to Busan. Damned straight. Promise you, Mistah Prentice, you and me gonna have a lot of fun in Busan. Plenty girls never turn you down, Busan-side."

"Believe it when it happens."

"You can believe. No damn ghosts I'm talking about."

Twenty-four, plus or minus one, Sonny off taking care of personal business again, me smoking on the overlook, and it's Westley's forearms resting on the rail. Quick work, Allison, I'm thinking, before the man even opens his mouth.

"Better view than the one you had last time we worked together, eh?" So says The Man Who Isn't There. But he is. He was. He'd appear at every unlikely place in Sarajevo, this faint weird glow about him, as if he could stroll down Sniper Alley with complete confidence no bullet would ever touch him.

Have to credit Westley for wading through the shit, when he probably could have stayed comfortably behind a desk at Langley, or one of our embassies, punching our buttons by remote control. He was full field, all the way. Maybe I only dislike him because he's smarter than me.

"Fuckin' A," I say now. "I could get to really dig this kind of life."

"Don't get too comfortable, too settled, Luther." He's the only one who's never bothered with that Terry bullshit. "You satisfied with the security arrangements? You comfortable with your new Korean teammate?"

"Everything's tight. This place is tight. We're tight. Though I won't know that absolutely until there's some action. And I can't even speculate because nobody's telling me shit about that."

"Nothing's coming, here," Westley says. He sounds genuinely convinced of this, his tone has a superior surety I don't trust. It feels too absolute. Or artfully deceptive. Experience says scratch overconfidence. "You may take this whole ride without even drawing once. Then you'll owe me for an all-expenses-paid luxury tour of the Far East."

"Such exotic destinations, too," I say. "Why think of Phuket or Kota Kinabalu when you can have Pyongyang and the stunning beauty of Vladivostok, Russia's sub-arctic Riviera?"

Westley makes small barks—his version of mild laughter. Now he's going to give me some need-to-know, I'm thinking, when the barks stop suddenly as they started.

"I know you're restless, bored. But we'll be moving soon," he says. "You're off tonight. Why don't you go out to dinner with Nadya and Allison?"

"Their idea? Or yours?" So where's the information, I'm thinking.

"Luther, you think I'm getting slow, losing my touch?" Short, sharp barks again. "Nadya's been radiating since that night at BWI. Give the girl a break, won't you? I want her content, relaxed, happy. Keep her so. Not exactly rough duty, I imagine. If she didn't regard me as a fossilized fart, I'd gladly fill in for you."

"No idea what you're talking about. We're all business, total professionals."

"Our teams are always professional." He's mocking himself a little. That's a new one. "Anyway, she's made reservations. And tonight's the night. Tomorrow night Mister Kim is throwing a party for his local friends. He always does this when he's about to head back home, some sense of social obligation, I suppose. You and your big Korean colleague will be on duty. But out of sight. Invisible. You know the drill."

"Right. No problem."

"Good. Stay sharp tomorrow. Be any way you want tonight," Westley says. He turns, walks quickly away.

Damn! He gave up nothing. Just neatly deflected me by revealing he's conscious of that airport night with Nadya. The man's uncanny. He knew about Mikla too, though we kept it as secret as we could—her parents were fairly strict Muslims—appearing together only when we were working. So now he throws up a little screen to take my mind off the fact that he decided Allison was wrong, that I have sufficient information for the task at hand. Pure Westley, devious bastard.

Suddenly I'm juked.

Allison did not tell Westley about Sonny. He'd have made at least an oblique pass on the matter, if he knew what I'd said. He'd want more. He'd need more. It was his nature, it was hardwired into him, he had the skills to get it from me. But he never even tried.

Allison did not tell him. I'm certain of this, down to the bone.

And I'm certain something's off. Something major. An operational protocol's been broken. Allison would never have held something like that back without powerful reasons.

But I don't have any idea—not even enough data to speculate—what those reasons could be.

It's Nadya who picks me up at Kim's front gate around nineteen hundred hours. Just Nadya, who's taken some trouble over her hair and dress, smiling like a Siamese cat who's pleased as hell with herself.

"Where's our chaperone? Where's Comrade Allison?" I ask as I slide into the car.

"Our commissar?" Nadya laughs. Those canted blue eyes seem luminous in the dimming light. "Purged! She slandered a trusted apparatchik."

"Yeah? Who would that be?"

"Why, me, actually. She called me a Trotskyite tart. It was my duty to denounce her to the Chekists. As any good Bolsheviki would."

"Okay, Russki. That's the *Pravda* version. What's the truth?"

"Terry, darling! I'd thought you'd be rather pleased to have me to yourself. Your concern is beginning to make me rather jealous."

"As a highly trained operative, I can't wait to see you naked again. But deviation from norms concerns me."

"Dialectics! And from a proletarian! Shocking, I must say." Nadya huffs, then giggles. "Our oh-so-ambitious Allison, if you must know, begged off. She claimed she absoutely must work tonight."

"And you believe that?"

"Well, of course! Allison would never allow a Russki slut like me to go out alone with you unless she had matters of highest urgency concerning national security to attend to. Quite dedicated, she is. As you know."

I lean over, find her lips, give her the deepest kiss. "And I was so sad thinking there'd only be that one night."

"Aren't we the lucky couple, then?"

"For sure. Where are we going to eat?"

"Intimate little place. Nothing much in the way of food, but the atmosphere's quite special." She grins. "My cabin? Will that suit?"

It does, perfectly. Nadya's a gift, her lithe little ballerina's body a treasure. I'm really into her way of keeping her eyes wide open and fixed on mine. It feels like a kind of superintimacy.

"Confess. Confess, you," she murmurs.

"Anything," I say.

"Then admit I'm the best. The best ever."

"Yes. It's true."

"And say this is better than any fantasy you're ever had about that Annie woman or any other girl in the wide, wide world."

"You've erased all fantasies. Gone. Never had them. You are my whole world."

"Hah! I do not believe this. You're a revisionist dog. You need correction. I'm going to give you more correction. I am going to be very strict with you."

And she is. I'm loving it, even if a nasty, naggy little suspicion that Nadya might only be on the job won't vanish like every other thought or sense except the pure physical sensations she's creating.

But even that bad thought's reduced to the barest outline by her corrective methods. When she drives me back to Kim's just past midnight—my Cinderella hour—I'm a wasted man. Who has the poor luck to bump into Sonny in the corridor just moments before I can reach my room and collapse onto my bed.

He looks me up and down, shakes his head in mock digust. "You some kind of disgrace, Mistah Prentice. No trusting you at all. Turn my back one minute, you sneaking off to bounce around that Allison girl. What you got to say for yourself?"

"I'm about incapable of speech right now."

Sonny almost howls. "Skinny piece like her beat you up too much? Me, I'm disgusted. She really jump your bones, huh? You bettah get lots of sleep tonight. 'Cause you and me, we got a late night tomorrow."

"Oh, yeah," I manage. "The party. No problem."

"Never been a problem before," Sonny says. "But never had that Mistah Westley around before. Eyes sharp tomorrow, you hearing that? No more bouncy-bouncy for you, I think."

seventeen

THE HITTERS COME JUST PAST MIDNIGHT. FUCKERS THINK THEY'RE ninjas or something. But they're amateurs, watched too many movies.

Sonny and I have finished a circuit, half-finished coffees in the monitor room, when the watcher hisses through his teeth. Our eyes go to the screens. The steady green lines of the infrared perimeter are strobing in two separate places. Then the motion sensors in those areas buzz. Intruders over the fence. I don't hesitate; I ease back the slide of the HK SOG .45 with the long, tubular supressor screwed to its muzzle, confirm there's a round in the chamber. Then slip the night-vision goggles I've felt like a fool carrying around all evening over my head. Shadows flick on the video monitors. I turn toward Sonny, laugh. We look like a couple of giant insects in business suits.

"Crazy guys, Mistah Prentice," he says. "We go commit some mayhem, okay?"

We slip out the rear door of our wing like we're greased. No moon, no mist. Lights from the main house dancing on the surface of the pool seem bright as lightning flashes through the goggles, but wisely Sonny's had no floods illuminating the grounds. We pause where two tightly clipped hedges of cypress form a straight path to that nice redwood deck on the edge of the sea cliff. Only sound's the breakers bashing the cliff base. Sonny listens a second to what's coming over his earphone from the watcher in the monitor room, holds up three thick fingers, points right, then holds up two, points left. Before he's even finished the gesture I'm moving right, hugging the outside of the hedge, then moving crouched but fast over the needled ground from one low, twisted pine to another. Scan the terrain, everything that weird wavery pale green night-eyes make the world, every object and feature clear but somehow not quite real.

Gets real, real fast. An idiot all in black with a black hood, carrying a suppressed MP5, emerges from behind a tree fifteen meters off. My HK pop-pops softly as I double-tap. A can't-miss situation, no challenge at all. Asshole never even sees who sent 200-grain XTPs slamming into his belly, his upper chest. Just goes down, doesn't even twitch.

I cut an arc around behind the body, moving from tree to tree, cliff at my back. See my other two targets moving together toward the house, zigging and zagging on the far side of the pool. I'm behind them now, maybe twenty-five meters. Looks like one's got an M4 with a grenade launcher under the barrel, the other's carrying a Steyr AUG assault rifle. They pause behind the last stunted pine before a stretch of open grass. From there they've got a clear, short shot at the glass wall of the main house. Bad mistake, that pause; they should have zigged apart. I'm zeroed on them, kneeling, with the HK held in both hands. The M4 ninja slides sideways a foot, ready to send a grenade arcing through glass into the main room. I cap him, aiming for a head shot but hitting him in the back of his neck, just where it meets his shoulders. He sprawls foward, flat on his face. The Steyr guy fucks up worse. He freezes, head swiveling wildly, no doubt wondering where the hell that pop came from. I double-tap him in the back. Down. Then I sprint up, put one in each of their heads, just in case they're wearing body armor.

I think I hear a couple of pops on the other side of the house. Must be Sonny committing mayhem. I move fast toward the first hitter, head-shoot him once. Just in case. Fuck cover then. I run back to the hedge, go left. See Sonny strolling back, pistol pointed to the ground. I lower mine.

"You take them down okay, no problem, Mistah Prentice?" he calls.

"Three. No problem at all."

"Ah, that good, Mistah Prentice." Sonny removes his goggles. "Yeah, watcher telling me they down, no movement. Good mayhem. But now I gotta inform Mistah Kim, goddamn. You like to walk around the house once, twice? Double-check?"

"Roger that." Sonny's hitters are sprawled awkward in death, one on either side of the gravel walk about ten meters from the front door. I keep circling, take off my goggles when I reach the swimming pool. I can see perfectly into the main room. There's the party in full swing, a few couples dancing, Nadya about to give some white-haired coot in a blue blazer cardiac arrest, Allison pretending she's not bored shitless by a white-haired woman with a black cardigan draped over the shoulders of her garishly flowered dress. A couple nice pieces of imported eye candy walk around hipshot, like runway models. Giving Rob and a few strangers who look like him neck strain as they try to watch and keep their conversation going at the same time. Kim's off to one side, into it with Westley and two CEO-types closer to Westley's age than his. Kim's grinning big time. Trace of music, mostly bass notes, leaks through the double-paned glass.

Nobody in there ever heard a thing. Nobody there had any idea the party was seconds away from getting juiced and jolted by a 40mm grenade, followed by a lot of full-auto spray.

Anybody in there still alive after the grenade would have heard that pretty clear.

I see Sonny sidle up to Kim, suit unmussed and weapon either left in the monitor room or perfectly concealed. He mouths a couple of words. Kim bobs at the two CEOs, takes Westley by the arm, and they follow Sonny out of the room. Nobody seems to notice. Except Allison, whose eyes track them. A Rob-type, likely some software start-up's starter Kim has invested in, is dancing so close with one of the imported sweeties that their bodies look like they've been glued together. They're moving toward the wall. I see the girl's ass pressed against the glass, see her partner's hands creep round, start pulling up her skirt. She isn't wearing anything under.

That's enough. I cross the pool terrace, enter the back door, go straight to the monitor room. Sonny, Kim, Westley, and the watcher are all scanning the bank of monitors. Most just show landscapes. Three show still lifes, with corpses.

Kim's face is tight, skin gone sallow. "Terrible, terrible. How can this be?" he's saying, flicking a hand at the screens as if the gesture will make the images vanish. "How can this be, Westley?"

"As we discussed, Mister Kim," Westley says. "The very reason we agreed to take certain measures."

Kim's right leg starts to tremble. "People murdered outside my house. No, no, no. This can't be. We did not discuss killing. We did not."

"I must remind you we spoke at length of threats from ultra-rightist Korean groups bitterly opposed to your connection with the North," Westley says. "Someone—perhaps one of those groups—sent these men to kill you tonight, Mister Kim. They had to be eliminated. I assumed you understood the possibility of such an event. Why else would you have accepted my suggestion that we increase your security arrangements?"

"You assume too much! I never wanted anything like this. It's horrible!"

Kim's voice rises half an octave, both hands flapping now. Suddenly he notices my presence. He makes a visible efffort to calm himself, shoving those hands into his jacket pockets. Face. He doesn't want to lose face. He may also be realizing at last that he was very close to being assassinated a few minutes ago. But his eyes recoil from the HK he spots in my hand.

"Mister Prentice," Kim says. "Mister Prentice, I . . . yes, thank you for dealing with this so efficiently."

"I realize this is very unpleasant, Mister Kim," Westley says. "Extremely upsetting for everyone. But I believe it would be instructive if we reviewed the incident. To put it into proper perspective, so to speak. May we?"

Kim looks at Sonny, glances at me, stares at Westley. Then his gaze seems to drift down to his leg. It's still trembling. But he nods to the watcher at the console, who rewinds and plays the tapes on two monitors. I see some alien insectoid in a suit with an HK, see some muzzle flashes, see the alien cut an arc. More muzzle flashes as he shoots two ninjas from behind. First time I've ever seen myself kill after the fact. I'm juked, a little dizzy.

"Those men were heavily armed, Mister Kim. Their intentions were evil. Mister Park and Mister Prentice did only what was necessary to prevent a tragedy," Westley says. Kim's face is tighter, his color worse.

"Yes. Of course," Kim says.

"I'd appreciate it if those tapes were erased. Right now, please," I say.

I'm ignored.

"Be assured, Mister Kim, there will be no trace of tonight's unfortunate incident," Westley says. "We will identify the bodies. And we will find whoever might have sent these people here."

"The, eh, bodies will of course be removed quickly? Before my guests begin to depart?" Kim asks.

"Absolutely, sir," Westley says. "No need to ruin anyone's evening. No need anyone outside this room should ever know a thing about this."

Fucking Westley. This kind of shit was not supposed to happen. Not here, for sure.

In the little staff lounge next to the monitor room, Sonny pops a beer and I pour myself a coffee from the Thermos. I sit, light a cigarette. He stands, shifting his weight leg to leg, drains half the bottle in one pull. "You some pretty slick guy, Mistah Prentice." He kills the bottle, tosses it into a plastic trashcan. "Long time since I commit any mayhem."

"Looked to me like you've kept your edge," I say.

Sonny laughs, pops a second beer; the sound's only marginally less than an HK firing. He drains half the bottle, sets it down smartly on the table. The adrenaline dump does a fast fade. So does his smile.

"That Mistah Westley! All his fault, damn straight."

"How's that?" I ask.

"What I tell you before? Six, seven years, never troubles. None. Westley come around, I'm thinking here troubles coming up, for sure."

"Not quite following you on this."

"Listen, Mistah Prentice. Seen this lotsa times before. Before I work for Mistah Kim, I'm in ROK Army—special unit, all I can say. We train hard, nothing ever happen, though. Then three, four times American guys like Westley show up, hang around a little. Next thing, crisscross DMZ, shitload of fireworks or sneak around slitting throats, what's the difference?"

Sonny retrieves his beer, sips. "First time, I think oh, special mission. Second, I think, what's the damn word, coincidence? Third time I get it. CIA guys just draw trouble like shit draw flies. Fourth time, know I'm wrong. Shit just lies there, don't do nothing, flies come automatic, understand? CIA guys, they don't just lie there. They run around, make lotsa noise, invite the bad guys for party. Only they never stay to party. Leave us to do it. Fuckers!"

"You got a point," I say.

"Hunh!" Sonny grunts. "You one of them, Mistah Prentice."

"No, I'm not. Ex-Special Forces, never CIA. Just got a job offer from Westley, short-term, and took it. Needed the work."

"Hunh!" Sonny interlocks his fingers, pushes out. His knuckles pop. "Maybe yeah, maybe no. You do pretty good work. I got no problem working with you. Got big problem that we got to do it. Why those men come over the fence? Why they want to get Mistah Kim?"

"Westley said it: somebody doesn't appreciate Mister Kim's business with the North. Not so hard to imagine, is it?"

"Nobody bother Mistah Kim about that before. Just a little business, so what? Me, I think fucker Westley, he leaving shit all around Mistah Kim, so flies come. They don't, so Westley running around now, making lotsa noise, invite bad guys to Mistah Kim's party."

"You ever suggested this to Mister Kim?"

Sonny looks shocked. Dumb mistake on my part. Of course he'd never dream of saying anything to Kim. That hierarchy thing. It'd be rude. It'd be regarded as an insult, and cost Sonny his job.

"Sorry. That was stupid. You can't, can you?" I say. "I got a person I can talk to, though."

"You shut up!" Sonny's suddenly near rage. "You keeping your mouth shut tight, understand? Understand?"

Dumber and dumber, Luther, I'm thinking. "Yeah, absolutely. All this—all of it, every word—stays between you and me."

"Better had, damn straight," Sonny says, heavy threat in those black slits for a moment. Then he eases off. "Me, you, we take care of our business. Like we did tonight. Okay, Mistah Prentice?"

"We're on the same page."

"What that mean?"

"A saying. Means we have an agreement."

"Oh. That's good, Mistah Prentice. I like you okay. Make me unhappy if I got to mayhem you, too."

Too? Does this Buddha already have something in mind for Westley? Allison, Nadya, Rob? Can I talk to Allison and be certain she'll again keep it from Westley? Who do I trust now?

Nobody. That's what I conclude. Nobody but myself.

Westley catches me early next morning as I'm coming up the stairs from my quarters, squared away in shirt and tie but missing the suitcoat, mug of coffee in one hand.

Oh shit, I'm thinking, there goes a nice start to what looks like a beautiful Northern California day, sun and cool sea air and sky the deepest blue it can manage. Because the dick's first words are "Let's discuss."

He looks fresh, rested, unperturbed. But maybe he is slowing down, slipping. He's got to know how those particular words resonate. But he gives no sign, just leads the way to a couple of chaises near the end of the pool. I look around as we go.

"First-rate cleaners," I say. "Nobody'd ever guess what went down last night."

"Not a shell casing, not a blood drop on a pine needle. That is why we have cleaners. Self-evident, no? No one is supposed to have any reason at all to even speculate," Westley says as we recline.

"Self-evident that no one speculated we'd get hitters," I say.

Westley laughs. "You mean my remarks about no situations

here? You do. And you're partly right. I did not expect such a thing. On the other hand, I was prepared."

"Yeah," I admit. "I understand the enhanced perimeter security is a fairly recent addition. And then there's the brand-new addition. Me."

"Actually, Sonny and his longer-time colleagues could have dealt with last night adequately. That's not to say you didn't do very well. You performed to expectations. But your presence wasn't the decisive factor."

"Whatever." I try to blow some smoke-rings, but they're whisked away before they're formed by the light sea breeze. "Know who they were yet?"

"Yes. And I don't think you're going to appreciate it very much," Westley says. "All members of a Korean-American street gang in San Francisco. All with arrest records. Aged nineteen, eighteen, eighteen, eighteen, and seventeen."

"Bangers would have no reason to try what they did. Bangers don't usually have access to the kinds of weapons they had," I say, coolly as I can. Won't give him the pleasure of seeing me even slightly unsettled over killing three kids.

"That is so obvious I'm surprised you bothered saying it, Luther."

"Somebody hired and armed them."

"Again, why are you stating the obvious?"

"One of those two groups I believe you mentioned?" I ask. "The far-right ones who hate Kim for going up North?"

"That, I do not know yet. We're still looking into that. It had to be one of them. What's puzzling is the stupidity of method. Neither group is composed of amateurs. I'm leaning toward the idea those kids were pawns, sent on a suicide mission designed only to deliver a warning."

"No speculation of a third force?"

"Luther!" Westley laughs. "What did you do, read *The Quiet American* on the flight here?"

"No, I slept through the flight, dreaming peacefully," I say. What I'm thinking is that Westley knows very well the reference was to him, his circle. Wouldn't put it past him to stage a very controllable incident—and last night was so easy, so controllable—just to frighten Kim, herd him closer. And if he doesn't know I can think this, he really is getting slow and sloppy.

"A word of advice, Luther," he replies. "Don't start looking for conspiracies where none exist. And please don't skip the first step and jump straight to looking for conspiracies within conspiracies. Not everything we do is as straightforward as the Sarajevo operation, true. But this operation is. What you see, what you've been told, is all there is."

"Then there's pretty much nothing to it. Since I haven't been told shit."

"That's what I wanted to discuss." Neat segue by Westley here. "In a few days you'll leave for Busan. You'll spend perhaps a week there, much as you've spent it here."

"How much like here? Taking out another three people or so?"

"No. Some steps to ensure against that are already being taken there. You'll have a pleasant stay. A very quiet one. Then you'll accompany Kim to Vladivostok, to his meetings with the Russian generals. That deal done, on to Pyongyang. Two days there at most. Then back to Busan for a few more days. Finally, back to the States."

"Who's going with me?"

"Openly, Allison, Rob, Nadya to Busan. I'd like you to do me a favor. Observe how Allison makes the final arrangements in Busan, give me a heads-up if any little thing appears off, all right?"

"Okay."

"Good. Then, openly, you and Nadya move on to Vladivostock,

Allison preceding you by a day or two. It will be just you, with Kim's people, to Pyongyang, naturally."

"What about you?"

"Me? I'm leaving." Westley consults his wristwatch. "In about forty-five minutes."

eighteen

WESTLEY GONE—NOBODY MENTIONS WHERE—AND SONNY PLEASED about it, but still sulky because he knows it isn't permanent. Some of his CIA hate splashed over me, but didn't seem to stain, maybe because Taoists or Buddho-Confucians or whatever he is don't have a pollution concept like Hindus and some others. Probably we could still go back-to-back in a situation and trust our backs were well covered.

But soon enough I'm feeling real uncovered in other ways. Allison triggers it.

She catches me early afternoon, the day after Westley bolts. I'm out at the spot I like so much, cantilevered over the cliff, when she comes up wearing a black Speedo, towel draped around her neck, ponytail swinging.

"Hey, Terry, are you too old and tired to pace me on some laps?" she says.

I look her up and down, then point my thumb at the pool. "What? In a circle? Round and round like seals in a zoo?"

She feigns surprise. "Boy, am I dumb or what," she says. Then she laughs. "There's a four-lane, twenty-five-meter one in the basement. You never checked the basement? What kind of security guy are you?"

"Very insecure, I guess." And getting worse.

"Well, too old and tired? Or not?"

I flick my cigarette into a long floating fall I don't bother to watch, follow her back to the house, down some stairs, and into the pool room. Off to one side's a gym full of the latest workout machines. On the other there's what seems to be a row of very large closets. "Try the last door left," Allison says. "There's a bunch of men's Speedos in there. One ought to fit you."

I'm stripped, tanked, and walking toward her end of the long, narrow blue rectangle. She looks like a serious swimmer, slim, long-muscled, but minus the overdeveloped shoulders female competitors get.

"Interesting set of scars, Terry," she says when I'm next to her on the concrete lip of the pool.

"Exactly what you said in the spook house when I was standing around in my underpants one morning," I say. "You might want to consider acquiring some fresh lines, Allison."

"But I like my usual ones. How about 'I don't think I'll even get to my aerobic level pacing you'?"

"Great tone, Allison. Your body, I mean. Tight and toned. I wouldn't mind—"

"Lap time," she says, race-diving.

I'm after her in a blink, and we settle into an easy freestyle, flip-turning at the end of each lap. My arms are starting to feel leaden after about ten, I'm breathing on every stroke instead of every other. After twenty, I'm gulping air hard. I start my flip too far from the wall, get a noseful of water, and Allison turns it all on for the last lap, beating me by at least five meters. She's already up and sitting on the edge, grinning, when my hands touch it.

"Think he caught something from Terry Uno," she says, me

still in the water, chest heaving. I check out where she's looking. Rob's in the gym, pumping iron as if his life depended on it, almost as wet with sweat as I am in the pool. I heave myself out, twist and sit, then give that up and lie down. The concrete's rough as sandpaper on the skin of my back. Couldn't care less.

"Jesus, Terry! You're a disgrace," she says, looking down over her shoulder at me. "Smoked you again!"

"Who cares? Laps isn't real-world. Party night was real-world."

Puzzled little crease appears on her forehead. "What's that supposed to mean?"

"The smoked guys on the ground, what else? Dead is real," I say.

The crease deepens, her eyes change fractionally, too.

"Uh, Terry? You getting enough oxygen to your brain? Because you're kind of babbling, you know? Bodies on the ground, stuff like that?"

For a moment I simply cannot believe it. Westley wasn't being literal when he said nobody outside the monitor room would know. Couldn't have been. Major protocol violation, not informing your team's leader of something like that. No, I definitely don't believe it. She's got to be playing with me. Everything's a test, right? But it's way late to be testing. It pisses me off.

"Get fucked, Allison. I'm tired of these games."

"There you go again. You all right, Terry? You aware you're not making sense?" She actually looks worried now.

That's it. I stand, grab her bicep, tug her up. Then I switch my grip to her wrist and lead her, both of us still dripping, down a few corridors to the monitor room. The guy on duty—Lee or Park or Lee, I don't know which—looks at us like we've dropped from heaven or some shit. I tell him to run the party-night tape, cueing up around midnight; I'm betting Westley did not have it wiped. Lee or Park or Lee just stares, mainly at Allison's puckered nipples pressing the thin nylon of her tank, judging by the trajectory of his gaze. I tell him again.

"Ho, Mistah Prentice. You up to some kind of no good, right?" It's Sonny behind me, but he's chuckling, not serious. And probably he's staring at Allison's ass. "What I tell you after the other night? No more bouncy for you."

"What the hell is going on here, Terry?" Allison snaps, wrenching her wrist from my grasp, crossing her arms over her chest.

"Hey, Sonny, can you get your colleague here to show us the tape? You know which one," I say.

"Aw, Mistah Prentice. In front of the lady? You sure?"

"Yeah, I'm sure."

Sonny says a few words in Korean, Lee or Park or Lee flips through the tape rack, finds one, slips it into the player. He fast forwards, the digits in the lower right of the frame blurring time, slows a bit so they're readable, goes to standard speed.

Allison doesn't say a word, and neither do I, during the three minutes the action lasts, including a very long thirty seconds of still life with corpses.

"Want a replay?" I ask.

"No. I want out of here right now. And you come with me. Understood? Now."

I nod. "Thanks, Sonny," I say as we depart.

"Hey, no problem, Mistah Prentice. For me, anyhow." I can hear him and Lee or Park or Lee laughing as Allison power-walks down the corridor, takes the stairs up to the outside deck two at a time, and turns on me like she's going to strike.

"Westley knows," she says. But her voice is taut, strained in a way I haven't heard before. It's difficult to tell if she's making a statement or asking a question. Come down on question, respond appropriately.

"He had no clue as it went down. Just like every other punk

inside partying," I say, keeping my suspicion that Westley may have organized the incident himself locked well away. "But of course he fucking knows. Sonny reported soon as we finished, Westley and Kim came right to the monitor room, watched the show. Then Westley celled for cleaners."

"That's it." Again, hard to be sure if Allison's confirming or asking.

"You didn't know? You weren't told?" I say.

"I did. I was."

It doesn't feel convincing.

"So, what? Too trivial to 'discuss' with the security man who did the job?"

"No reason to discuss," she snaps.

"Big-time reasons, Allison. We're on what's been billed all along as a low-risk op. We're not even in the operational zone and I gotta kill three kids before they waste Kim, you, Westley, and every other other live body having a swell time behind that glass wall. Seems worth a word or two, at least. If you knew."

"I knew."

"Yeah? Then what was all that shit at the pool? About lack of oxygen making me babble nonsense? What was that 'what the fuck is he talking about' look on your face?"

"Christ, Terry. You stay too intense way past the point you need to be."

"Hey, Allison, you, uh, getting enough oxygen to *your* brain?"

"Do I have to spell it out for you? I suppose I do. I was hinting to you then, Terry, that it would be wise to shut up. That sitting there poolside was not the time or the place."

"Oh, Rob isn't supposed to know? Excuse me. But he was too deep into his muscles to hear anything but his own breathing."

"Mikes are more sensitive. How smart would it be to have a conversation we don't want on tape in a place where it would go straight to tape? Hence, the hints. Which obviously went over your head."

"Hey, if you say so, Allison." I'm getting anxious now. Very edgy. Westley never told her about the hitters. The tape was a total surprise.

"Yeah, and I also say it was a dumb move dragging me out to see the video in front of Kim's boys. That certainly must have really filled Sonny and his pal with confidence in our professionalism."

"He doesn't have any. I already told you that."

"You told me he does not like Westley. That is not the same thing as doubting our team. Not the same at all."

"No? You really missing the subtext or just pretending, so you don't have to face it? Kim's chief security doesn't like Westley. Doesn't trust Westley. Therefore, he doesn't much like or trust Westley's people."

"If that's what you read, then you should be trying to correct his impression, not reinforce it by making us look as foolish as you just did, Terry."

"That's part of my job now, is it? I'm no longer just a contractor hired to protect a package? I'm supposed to do *your* job, too?" I say. "Well, fine. I reckon somebody has to, since you've disengaged. But how about telling me what your job is, so I can do it?"

"I haven't disengaged, asshole. But that's obviously over your head too," Allison says.

I turn to go but Allison moves faster, elbowing me aside and going down the steps three at a time. When I get back to the pool, dump the Speedo and get dressed, she's nowhere.

Bad static. Bad enough to postpone, even scratch a mission if timing was discretionary. Timing is not. Green light's on, so Westley told me. No choice now but to make the jump. What he did not tell Allison—and almost certainly others who very much needed to know—means I'm likely in serious jeopardy. It means Rhino's rumor about Westley possibly having a side agenda, possibly setting up Allison to take the fall if anything goes wrong, about side players like me being expendable as those five kids who tried to assault Kim's party, may not be just hearsay, but fact. Or it could be a reverse: Allison's the bad actor here, and Westley's trying to counter her. Either way, I'm in the middle, first to go down if cross fire erupts. I have to reduce my personal risk level somehow.

First, I make sure I run into Sonny, so we can trade some coarse banter about "bouncy bouncy," about Allison's sexual performance and preferences. I make it colorful as I can. Raw and raunchy. At the end I feel he's seeing me well outside the Westley-crew box, which is the whole point, and that we're tight as we were in those moments after we capped the intruders. The way guys who've just teamed in battle always feel bonded.

Next task is harder, and I'm cursing myself for not doing it from the start. Got to get into cop mode, start an investigative jacket. Not on the key players: Kim and those Russian generals. Nadya's done good work there. What I need to decipher is the message Westley's sent me; he had to know I'd discover he'd cut Allison and the team out of the loop on the hit attempt. What I also need to know is precisely what Westley thinks I should not. Specifically, what Kim's buying and selling, how high-value it is, and how likely someone will go to extremes to take it.

The start point seems to be one simple question: What would North Koreans want very badly? If I'd had the sense to search this out back at the Washington spook house, I might have found at least approximate answers in the *Post*. Or the *New York Times*. We only get the *San Francisco Chronicle* here, I've looked at it, it's just a rag that must be edited by reader focus groups instead of news professionals. No serious international coverage, lots of LOCAL

MAN MAULS ROTTWEILER–type stories, plus lots of garbage about entertainment, restaurants, even a TV critic's column. I guess a few tube junkies, eyes glazed and brains mushed, might take a break once in a while to read a sixth-grade opinion of what's glazing their eyes and mushing their brains.

I'm drifting, dammit. Stay focused. Got to stay focused.

Okay. The basics I know. They're in the air, accessible to anyone who bothers to pay attention. North Korea's one of those countries the Bush Two adminstration has designated a rogue terrorist state. It's got some nuclear capabilities—unless that's as inaccurate intel as the stuff about Saddam's WMDs. There's no negotiation with the North, maybe because they're paranoid, feel targeted, or simply watched what we did in Talibanstan or what the Fourth Infantry and some Brits did to Iraq on CNN and Al Jazeera.

The laptop in my room's got DSL net connections. Quick and easy to search the *NY Times* site. Find a nice analysis piece there. Says U.S. intelligence believes the North already has one, maybe two nuclear weapons. Also opines that maximum leader Kim Jong Il has drawn a different conclusion from seeing Saddam dragged out of his spider hole by U.S. troops than Qaddafi, who scurried to inform the world that Libya had already abandoned its weapons of mass destruction program, and would welcome U.N. inspection to prove that was no bullshit. Chairman Kim is speculated to now believe his best chance of avoiding a Saddam-like fate is to hurry the fuck up building a bigger and better nuclear shield.

And another, earlier story says North Korea has sucessfully test-fired medium-range missiles. Very tough luck for Seoul or Busan if the shit comes down, but Tokyo doesn't have to worry yet; it's too far away. Even so, China and Russia and particularly the U.S. are getting extremely edgy about Chairman Kim.

And what do Bolgakov and Tchitcherine presumably have

access to? God, I've been dumb. Nadya said clearly they'd moved well past spare parts, fuel, petty stuff like that. And would Kim Jong Il's gang of four bother dealing personally with our Mister Kim over anything less than really serious shit—say, plutonium? Possession of a bit of that would save the North years of troublesome transformation of uranium into its weapons-grade derivative.

Then I realize I've gone down, in cop mode, one of those speculative blind alleys. No motive. No possible fucking motive. It's insane to entertain the notion that our Mister Kim would want to increase the power of what's already the biggest threat to the ROK and his *jaebeol*. An idealist, Westley called him. His goal is some sort of rapprochement with the North through peaceful trade, he's dreaming of eventual reunification. Even if Westley lied, I do not read Mister Kim as any kind of fanatic with a crazed secret agenda. Not for a minute. It's also insane to think of the CIA actively assisting a regime the U.S. wants to cut the balls off. Not that the CIA hasn't acted rogue or failed miserably or gone off half-cocked in a dozen different places around the world. But something like this? Even the most obsessed and blinkered conspiracy addict would reject it out of hand.

So I'm missing something. It may be right before my eyes, something quite simple and clear. But I am not seeing it. In a normal investigation, time and motion would eventually solve that.

I'm fucked. Already in motion, time all but run out.

nineteen

MAINTAIN. DOG'S WISE ADVICE. GAVE IT TO ME DURING A PARTY, AT Annie's. I remember it. But I seem too far from it, space and time. Dog, Annie, IB—they real people I was tight with? Difficult to feel it, believe in it, just now. I'm out on the sharp edge, all by myself. Losing all sense of whatever life I was living before I discussed with Westley.

Westley? How real is he? "Off prepping the ground," Nadya says when I ask about him. So how real is she?

Maintain, Luther. Stay in the fight.

It gets harder and harder, after Allison's fit, after my futile tries at figuring out what this mission's truly all about. What's most scary is that no one else seems perturbed about anything. Not Nadya, not Rob, not even Mister Kim, despite the jolt he got. There's a man who knows how to maintain. Baby-sitting him's a non-job, mostly. Every day before the assault, he rose around dawn, spent almost exactly four hours wired to his Busan headquarters by Internet instant messaging, phone, fax. He'd check in again for an hour or two before dinner. Poor fucks who work for him. He operates on his time, never considers all the zones, never mind the International Dateline and people's sleep cycles, between here and there. Some functionary is expected to jerk awake at two A.M. on a Sunday and instantly spiel off any facts, figures or news he demands. I don't think it's a deliberate arrogance on Kim's part; it's something beneath his radar.

After that, he sat through meetings with Westley and the crew, lunched with them. Every other afternoon, he played eighteen holes at a country-club course with one or another of his local cronies. Insisted on one-man coverage only, usually Sonny but sometimes Lee or Park or Lee.

Post-asault? Same-same, detail and timing, except Westley's soon absent from the daily meetings and lunches. Kim stays so regular, so unwavering, that if I were a hitter instead of a guard, he'd be the easiest kill I ever made. I checked out the course with Sonny once. Piece of cake to clip Kim teeing off at the eleventh hole. One shot from a copse of pines three hundred meters east with a suppressed M-24. A leisurely stroll maybe fifty meters, out to a car waiting on the verge of a nice two-lane blacktop. All over in less than a minute.

I'd be gone before anybody even figured what the hell dropped Kim. Heart attack? But what's all this blood leaking on the grass?

Just one more contradiction that's fucking with my head. Kim's real protected and extremely vulnerable at the same time. Anybody wants him, they can have him on any golf day they care to. How come nobody on our team is concerned about this? How come the assholes on the other team sent five punks over the fence into our kill zone, instead of a single sniper into the pines at the golf course?

Nobody to ask, really. An oblique mention to Sonny reveals he at least is aware of the eleventh tee. Says he's always glassing that copse with his Steiners when Kim moves up to make his drive. But he shrugs his heavy shoulders as he says it. Which I take as his way of letting me know he knows it's idiotic, he'd never spot any decent sniper before he got off his shot, but there's nothing else he's allowed to do—like station Lee or Park or Lee in those pines as out-of-sight interdictors.

If it wasn't for the still life with corpses I've viewed twice now, I'd be convinced there was no security issue at all. I'd be wondering lots about why Westley ever paid good money for my unnecessary services. I might even come to the notion that maybe I'm being set up—in ways and for reasons I can't comprehend.

Fuck the still life. I am at that notion. Feels like something that's gonna balloon into an obsession if no explanations appear damn soon.

I don't see Allison for two, three days, except through the glass wall of the main room at Kim's, when she meets with him, Nadya, and Rob. No private time with Nadya, either, though I'm sure in her case it isn't a deliberate shunning. Couple of times I catch her searching me out from behind the glass, flashing me a nice smile when she sees I see her.

What I get a couple hours after lunch on the third day is Rob, coming up from the gym, pumped and sweating in his brand-name exercise shorts and guinea T, arms held out a bit from normal vertical like most muscle-heads. Sonny starts chuckling before Rob's halfway to where we're smoking, out on the redwood overhang.

"You pals with this guy, anything like that?" Sonny mutters.

"We're acquainted."

"That's good. Otherwise I think I gotta throw this asshole over the edge. Ho!"

"Don't let my being acquainted with him stop you. Feel free to toss."

Sonny gives Rob his Buddha smile, but fades it fast.

"Hey, Terry," Rob says. Then to Sonny, extending his hand: "We've seen each other around but never actually met. I'm Rob. You're Mister Park, right?"

Sonny nods, waits a beat, takes Rob's hand. Just grips it briefly, no shake, then drops it. I see white pressure marks on the skin of Rob's hand, though he manages not to wince. Instead he gets real occupied with the vista.

"Hey, I see why you guys hang out here so much. Spectacular. What's the drop, fifty meters?"

"Sixty-two," Sonny says.

"Jesus, how'd you measure it?"

"Real simple, Mistah Rob. Drop something over, time how long it take to bust on the rocks."

No veiled threat in Sonny's voice, not even any edge to it, but I swear I can see some of that overconfidence Rob liked to display back in spook-house days leaking out of him.

"Thirty-two feet per second per second, clock the seconds, do the math on a calculator," Rob says. "Pretty neat."

"Ho! Not pretty," Sonny says. "You don't see what I drop. Make a real mess. Low tide, low waves. Take a while, till tide high, to wash away."

Rob's quicker than I usually give him credit for, does the right thing—laughs. And makes it sound genuine. "Oh yeah, but then that strong northward current must have swept any big pieces pretty damned fast," he says.

"Sure thing, Mistah Rob. Seen that lotsa times," Sonny says, deadpan.

"Well." Rob steps back from the rail. "Guess I won't get that chance, since we're pulling out of here soon."

"Maybe you get one, Mistah Rob. Mistah Kim, he got a place like this south of Busan. Maybe we go there, before we go to that stinkin' Russia."

"I'd have thought Vlad was your kind of place, Sonny," I say. "All those tall Natashas working hard for the dollar."

"Hunh. You dreaming, Mistah Prentice." I've asked him half a dozen times to drop that "Mister" crap, call me Terry, but though he's agreed, he can't seem to break his habits. "Russki whores, they don't even let you get your finger wet, less than a hundred dollars. You want any real fun, maybe three. Bad inflation in Vlad. Anyway, those girls so cold your dick freezes, snap like an icicle."

"I'll keep that in mind," Rob says, trying on a grin for size, finding it maybe a size too large, since he won't be seeing Vlad.

"You do that, Mistah Rob. And stay away from dockside. Go down there, somebody gonna have to fish your body out of that stinkin' harbor. No current in that harbor."

"I guess I can take care of myself," Rob says.

"Oh sure," Sonny says. "I can see that okay."

"Hey, Terry," Rob says, "you hear from Westley yet?"

"Yeah, he phones in every other hour. What kind of question is that, Rob? Christ. You need to study subtlety before you go fishing."

"I was just wondering where he went. He left quick, without telling me."

"And you suppose *I* know? You can't be serious."

"Well, you worked with him before."

"Just a contractor then, as now. Think he bothers to keep contractors fully informed of his comings and goings?"

"Uh, maybe you got tight in Sarajevo, something like that. I thought it was worth a shot at least."

"His absense concerns you so much, Rob?"

"Okay, okay. I'm kind of compulsive about being in the circuit at all times. I admit it. And, yeah, I should study subtlety."

"Don't bother," I say. "Ask Nadya about Westley. She knows."

"Right." Rob looks doubtful. Then he makes a show of checking his watch. "Shit. Gotta bolt. I have to check in with people in

Virginia, before those nine-to-five desk warriors quit for the day. Let's all have a beer one night before we leave."

"Anytime, Mistah Rob," Sonny says. "I never say no to a beer."

As Rob goes back down the deck, arms a little less held out from his sides than when he arrived, Sonny says, "Where they find that pussy?"

"Not a complete pussy. Got the training, got some skills, just never had to use them for real," I say. "Maybe if he gets the chance, he'll come out of it less of an asshole. If he comes out of it."

"So what's he want, coming to talk with us, have a beer shit?"

"I think," I say, "he's got a sudden case of premission nerves. Anxious to make some friends before we go in. Understandable."

"Sure. Only pretty late, and pretty stupid, too. What, he thinks me and you gonna watch his ass for him, he offer us a beer?"

"Not totally stupid, just shaky and inept. You know how guys are, when they're trained but never been in the shit."

"You right, Mistah Prentice." Sonny shakes his head. "Poor sorry-ass bastards."

Never occurs to me to mention he and I were poor sorry-ass bastards our first times, when we were young. Laughed at by men of experience, who didn't even want to know your name because they reckoned you wouldn't last long enough to matter. The concept gets erased from your brain once you've gone in, done your job, and come out more or less in one piece. After that, you get to join in the laughing.

I'm the completely stupid one. That's driven home, wiping any grin I might have had right off my face, by this sequence: note from Nadya waiting in my room, says "Fancy dinner? Front gate, 1900 hours? All yours, N." Front gate, right on time, the black Land Cruiser pulls up. Nadya's driving. I'm already in the seat, leaning toward kissing her, when I clue to her eyes. I fasten my seat belt instead, look in the rearview mirror. Allison's in back.

"Hi, Terry. The reservation's not till eight, so we're going to just drive around a while and talk," she says. Nadya's already pulling out onto the blacktop, accelerating.

"Looks like I don't have any choice."

"Terry, first of all I have to say I'm sorry I blew up the other day. It was unprofessional. I'm embarrassed by it. Won't even try to make up some excuse. There is no excuse."

"Stuff happens sometimes. Forget about it," I say. "I have."

"You have?"

"Of course he has," Nadya says. "A gentleman, Terry is. Quite gallant. I told you so."

"Well, it's bothering me anyway," Allison says. "I'm not very tolerant of mistakes, least of all my own."

"Look, Allison. I provoked you. Did it deliberately," I say. "I expected a reaction. I needed to know some things."

"And did you learn them?"

"No."

"Then here's some information. Maybe it's what you wanted. If not, say so."

"Sounds good."

"Oh," Nadya says, "I'm sure I wouldn't be so quick to put a value on it."

"Okay, Terry. Westley gave you our approximate itinerary before he left," Allison says. "That still stands, and the specifics are these: we fly out of here for Busan day after tomorrow, which is Thursday. All of us. In Busan, you'll stay at Kim's with your counterpart, while Nadya, Rob, and I take a hotel. The following Tuesday, you and Nadya will fly with Kim to Vladivostok. I'll already be there, but you won't see me. The evening you arrive, Kim's having dinner with our generals. If that goes well, there'll be a meeting and an exchange two nights later. Immediately upon exchange, you'll accompany Kim to the airport and fly to Pyongyang. We don't know yet how long he'll need to stay there."

"You and Nadya?" I ask.

"When we've seen Kim and you take off from Vlad, we'll go commercial to Busan, wait for you there."

"Where's Westley in this picture?"

"Here and there. He likes to move by himself. Langley gives him a long leash. I'll be in touch with him, but, honestly, I will not know his location at all times."

"Okay. I'm cool with all this. I stay teamed with Sonny throughout, anything nasty develops during or after the exhange, I run with the package, get back to Busan. Troubles, I clue you with the burst transmitter. Need help, same drill. Real bad, panic button. Anything else?"

"Yeah," Allison says, leaning forward and handing me a very small cell phone. "There's a new protocol. If certain things go a certain way, I'm authorized to give you a certain order."

"Sounds like a lot of uncertainty to me." I mean this as a joke, I'm feeling better now that I'm clearer on where I'll be and what I'll be up to. But no reaction from Allison. Even Nadya looks serious, extra-intent on driving.

"A termination order," Allison says. "Are you prepared for that?"

Why's she so solemn? She knows my history as well as I do. "Sure, why not?" I say. It's the answer she needs to hear, in just that tone. But it takes major effort to keep surprise and, yes, deep despair out of my voice. I can still rationalize killing someone in a fight or in combat, though I never feel as cold and guiltless about it as I once did. I cannot excuse or reconcile assassination. A dark, powerful dread that feels almost physical seizes my mind, squeezes hard. And all the suspicions and uncertainties turn fearsome.

"The phone vibrates, no ring. You hear me say 'Bright,' you terminate the name that follows."

"Bright? That's the go code? Kind of lame, Allison." I'm maintaining, but just barely. The pressure—the fear—in my head increases.

"Bright, then a name. That's it," she says.

"So who'll be giving this order, if certain things go a certain way?" I ask, trying desperately to relieve a very bad reality by turning it into a simple mechanical problem. "And are these certain things going to be visible to me, on the spot?"

"They will not be visible to you. I will be giving the order based on information I receive," Allison says.

"And who," I say, twisting in my seat to look her in the face, "are you exactly? In the chain of command? Because that's been real unclear lately."

"I'm team leader," she says. "I am operationally in charge."

"Oh? Really? Sort of had the impression there was a guy named Westley in charge."

"It's still as I told you at the start, during the prep," Allison says. "I'm in charge, under Westley's supervision. Supervision, understand? Not command. Back channel, I report directly to Langley."

"Don't mind me if I feel a bit skeptical about arrangements at this point," I say, still working hard to sound purely professional. "You're in command, Westley supervises you, but you get to give a kill order if some ghost at Langley says so."

"That sums it up."

"It sums up to a goat-fuck, Allison. I'm in some dark, dank corner of Vlad with the package, it's about to go hot, Westley pops in and tells me one thing, you cell me telling me another. Who the fuck do I believe? Whose order do I follow? I'm getting set up here. The guy who takes the stroke if anything goes wrong, if we lose the package."

"Wrong," Allison says. "It is my order that counts. Westley or no Westley, 'Bright' overrides anything else. That's an absolute. He won't show, anyway. If anything goes wrong, the blame falls only on me."

"Great. Real reassuring." Westley won't show? She's underestimating the man, big time. "Then I've only got to worry about being the one who gets blown away."

"But you never do, Terry. It's your métier," Nadya says. I notice we've pulled into a parking lot outside what looks like an extra-long log cabin. "We're here, our table's likely waiting for us. If you two have finished your natter?"

It's a unique experience, even for me: a civilized dinner with two attractive women, one of whom has fucked me silly. And the other trying to flirt as if she'd like to, all of it theater masking the fact that she just did, in one nasty way, turning me into something like a walking smart bomb. So many high-value targets to choose from, too. Maybe the only reason I don't explode then and there is because something manages to force its way through all the dread and despair: I know something certain Allison does not.

The final decision, if the order comes, remains all mine. Not hers. Not anyone else's. I choose.

twenty

NOW. GOING LOUD.

Just as the sun begins gilding the vast quilt of cloud we've been cruising above all night, the 747 lumbers down away from the nascent golden day, through the cover and into the dull-brown fug of Busan airspace. Maybe thirty-five minutes to touchdown. My guess, anyway. No voice comes over the cabin speakers announcing a "final descent." Weird, how commericial airlines always use "final." You'd think they'd adopt a more optimistic word, one that doesn't hint of possible wind shear, missed runways, collisions, a huge fireball.

Sonny comes awake—wide awake, completely alert—at the first sensation of dropping. No yawns, no stretches, not even a blink. He grabs his suitcoat, slips it on, and adjusts it just so. The table's clear, cleanly wiped. Sonny checks me out, from neatly knotted tie to well-polished shoes. He nods, gives me the Buddha smile.

The Japanese attendant lilts in my ear like a songbird: Would Prentice-san like coffee? Yes, he would, thank you. She only bows slightly to Sonny, who ignores her. He's standing now, smoothing his hair, smoothing creases in the light wool of his pants, tugging lightly on his lapels. His suit's custom-made, I figure. Extra room just under each arm, because there's no bulge at all where the Uzis rest. He's just sitting down again when the attendant reappears, bows as she hands him a celadon cup of green tea, then turns to me and places a silver tray bearing a white porcelain cup, a small silver coffeepot, silver creamer, silver sugar bowl, silver spoon, and white linen napkin on the table before me. She pours the first cup, then bows away.

Fresh-brewed, dark and powerful. Tastes like Sulawesi or New Caledonian. I'm dying for a cigarette, but Mister Kim doesn't allow smoking on his plane.

"How you drink that stuff first thing in the morning, Mistah Prentice?" Sonny says, holding his cup with both hands and sipping delicately. "After lunch, after dinner, okay, I like it. But first thing, waking up? I gotta run and take a big crap, two sips only."

"Years of practice, Sonny," I say. "Hey, you ever going to call me Terry, like I've asked?"

Sonny grins. There's a brief flash of gold near the back of his mouth; his front teeth are whatever the latest dental technology has done to make them look real. "Too many years of practice, Terry. Mistah Kim, he likes us all to be Mistah. I'm Mistah Park, you Mistah Prentice, everybody Mistah."

"Ah, your grandmother was a Korean pleasure-girl, got knocked up by a sumo wrestler drafted into the Imperial Nipponese Army. Sonny."

"Very good, damn straight." Sonny laughs. "Never heard that one before. Funny guy, Mistah Prentice. But time to get serious. Duty."

"Noted," I say, making a little toasting gesture with my cup. "The tiger's second assistant trembles and obeys."

"You some funny guy, like I say." Sonny laughs again, then squelches himself when there's a "bing" and the seat-belt sign comes on. The quiet, delicate girl reappears and makes the silver coffee set, the celadon teacup, and herself vanish. I buckle up and gaze out the window.

Busan. Long time coming.

But it's just like coming into L.A. on the smoggiest day of the year. Huge urban sprawl lapping at jagged hills, topping some of the nearer ones. Traffic already bumper to bumper on the expressways. Any green space looks wilted and dull, like it's been dusted with fine gray soot.

"Too bad, too bad," Sonny says, pulling his face away from the porthole. Still, he's obviously pleased to be home. "Air here usually damn clear, city looks very nice, very shiny."

The pilot brings Dumbo the Flying Elephant—always think of 747s like that, have since I was a kid, first saw the size and awkward shape and didn't believe anything so clumsy-looking could get airborne—down on a main runway without much bounce or tire-scream, taxis fast away from the huge commercial terminal to what seems to be Mister Kim's own reserved area in the private aviation section of the airport. Not another corporate plane within two hundred meters of the hangar we halt before. Sonny's already unbuckled and on his feet, gesturing to me.

"Okay, now we go to work, Mistah Prentice," he says, moving toward the plane's door. "Anything I do, you do, right?"

Then we're outside on the gangway, Sonny to the right, me to the left, looking down at the tarmac. I scan: two guys who could be Sonny's twin brothers at the foot of the steps, other guys holding open the rear doors of three identical black cars in line. God. Lincoln Town Cars. Kim could have any marque in the world, he picks the favored vehicle of Manhattan car-service drivers. A stretch Mercedes limo would be less conspicuous; I see at least six next to other hangars in the private aviation sector. "We follow Mistah Kim down gangway. You and me, first car," Sonny says.

Got it. Three-car convoy, Kim rides the middle, sandwiched between point car and follower. Pretty standard medium-threat security. Except for one thing: a twelve-man squad of South Korean troops form a perimeter between the rest of the vast airfield and our cars, backs to us, Daewoo 5.56mm assault rifles slung combat-style, butts near the shoulder. Just know those Daewoos are off-safety and hot.

Sonny hisses.

Nadya, Allison, and Rob emerge, descend. Nadya to the first car, Allison to Kim's, Rob to the last.

"Good morning, Mister Park," I hear. There's Kim, slim and spruce in a charcoal suit on the gangway between us, shaking Sonny's hand. Then he turns to me, offering his hand. I take it. His handshake's firm. "Mister Prentice. Good morning. Trust the flight was satisfactory."

"Very pleasant, Mister Kim," I say. He's smiling, his black eyes are in neutral, not scanning or appraising.

"Good, good," he says. "Well, welcome to Busan. First time here, isn't it?"

"Yes sir, it is," I say.

"I think you'll find it's an enjoyable city, not at all as ugly as it appears from the air. And not at all like Vladisvostok and the others business will be taking us to. Am I right on that, Mister Park?" he says, still looking easily at me.

"You bet, Mistah Kim," Sonny says.

"Well then, gentlemen. Let's go, shall we?" Kim starts down the gangway, Sonny on his heels, me on Sonny's. We walk him, flank rear, to the middle car. There's a driver and a guy riding shotgun who gives me a hard look. The moment Kim slips into the rear seat next to Allison, Sonny and I trot to the first car, climb in the back, Nadya sandwiched between us. Sonny says something short and fast in Korean to our driver, who just grunts and goes.

The convoy rolls around behind the hangar Dumbo's parked in front of, then down a one-lane road and through a gate in heavy chain-link fence topped by coils of razor wire. Looks like a private exit, except there are four ROK army troopers with Daewoos manning it.

"Pretty heavy," I say.

"You see the crazy driving in Busan, pretty soon you wishing we riding in tanks, Mistah Prentice," Sonny says. "Betcha we pass two, maybe three-four crashes. Big mess. Dead bodies. Same thing, every rush hour. Lotsa crankedpots on the roads these days, damn straight."

"Cranked pots?" Nadya giggles.

"You betcha."

I'm a little puzzled. Why's Sonny pretending he doesn't understand I'm talking about the ROKs, the hot Daewoos? I know he knows. What's the deal? Little embarrassed maybe, doing some Korean thing to cover that. I push.

"Mister Kim must have important friends," I say, once we've gone a klick along the one-laner and are swinging onto a public highway. Sonny grunts, unbuttons his suitcoat and, cross-armed, loosens the Uzis slightly in their holsters before he answers. Nadya's pushed tight to me in the process.

"Man like Mistah Kim got a lota friends. Some surprise or something for you, Mistah Prentice?" He isn't grinning.

"Small one. In the States, businessmen don't usually rate regular troops like that perimeter squad and the gate guards."

"Nothing special, this place. You a long way from America now, Mistah Prentice."

"Yeah, I should keep that in mind."

Really ugly urban sprawl, this Busan. Somewhere out there Westley may be installed with whatever team he requires. Or he may be roaming, not even in-country at all. Exactly where, I do not know. And I will not know for the duration, which is, what, maybe seven days? Unless there's a situation. And for a moment I'm doubtful he'll emerge in that bad case. He'll probably send people, but he may not be among them, especially since Allison added that serious addition to my job description a few nights ago. Then I remember that The Man Who Isn't There loves materializing in the hottest zones. Only problem is, you never know when or where.

So I decide I've got to adjust my visualization. Got to reboot my psych prep, tune it to this: I cannot count on assistance from anyone. I'm going to be on my own, in hostile territory.

Well, not alone. There's Nadya to Vlad with me, which actually worries more than reassures me; on the job I'm cold, focused totally. But can I hold that necessary concentration, feeling what I feel for her? Not even glance her way if any troubles come? Allison'll be there, too, but out of sight, which is better. There's Sonny, his crew, reliability factor unknown. Sonny and I seem tight, been acting tight, but we both understand that's provisional. Shit, even Kim has doubts about his own people, though I think he'd be very wrong if he's including Sonny in that. Yet doubt is why he asked Westley for someone like me. If Kim *did* ask, it suddenly occurs to me. That's only Westley's version.

Our route turns unmappable. The freeways and tunnels and bridges blur into a maze. Best I can do is clock the trip from the airport to Kim's place. Which turns out to be a fairly small compound in a neighborhood of compounds a couple of economic steps below Kim's true level, perched high up on a ridge commanding a sweeping view of the downtown high-rises, the sprawl, the freeway spiderweb, and the huge bulk of wharves and ships, harborside. Exactly forty-nine minutes from the airport. Big iron gate swings open when our driver presses a button on the Lincoln's dash, the convoy pulls into a circular drive. Standing there on the low entrance porch of the house are two guys, mid- to late fifties, dressed in what appear to be identical dark blue suits, each holding indentical black attaché cases in their left hands.

"Ah, Mistah Roh, Mistah Yoon," Sonny murmurs. "Mistah Kim's top assistants running business."

"Which, may I ask, is which?" Nadya says.

"Guy with black-rim glasses, that Mistah Roh. No glasses, that Mistah Yoon. Both numbah two under old Mistah Kim, same under my Mistah Kim."

Flanking Roh and Yoon, right rear, are a couple of Lees or Parks or Lees, unmistakably security boys, at attention military-style, thumbs aligned with the seams of their suit trousers, already bowing their heads. Except the last guy in the line, who isn't Korean, who's making a bad job of being serious. I blink. His hair isn't high and tight, he's a lot tanner than I remember, he's added maybe ten to fifteen pounds, too. Nice suit, not dusty BDUs, and no shades. But I know that face almost as well as I know my own.

Fucking Westley. He'd said I'd be seeing one of my old Storm teammates in Busan. I'd pretty much blown it off as recruitment bullshit, promptly forgot all about it. And never would have thought it might be this particular one, even if I'd thought hard about it.

We make eye contact soon as I'm out of that car, but maintain parade-type decorum until Kim and his corporate men, trailed by Allison, Rob, and Nadya, go inside. Once Sonny starts talking to his Korean security boys, he sidles over to me.

"You don't deserve what you're going to get here, you worthless bag of shit," JoeBoy says. He punches me on the shoulder. "But hey, what the fuck! Neither do I."

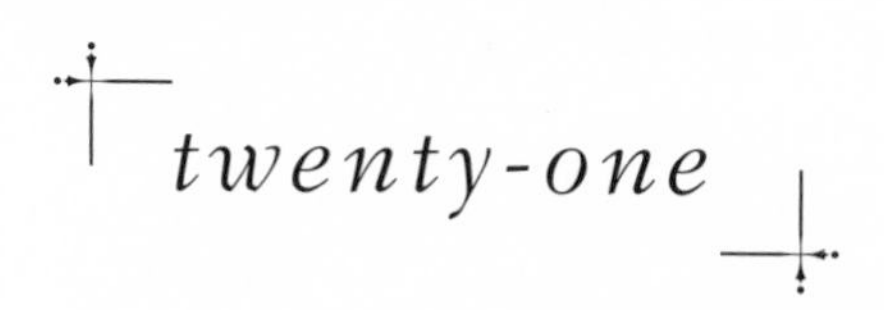

twenty-one

"PROB'LY YOU DON'T DESERVE AIR YOU BREATHING."

It's Sonny. He's dismissed his crew to their posts, slipped up beside me and JoeBoy.

"Maybe we take it away," he says to JoeBoy. "This day, that day, who knows? Pretty damn soon, no shit."

"Hoo-ah!" JoeBoy says. "Sonny, man! I'm real pleased to see your pretty face again too."

"Hunh."

"So it seems you guys," I say, "are longtime best buddies. How in hell did that happen?"

"Hunh. Bad luck for me, damn straight. Mistah Boy, he show up here with that Mistah Westley, maybe week, two weeks before we go to California. Very bad. Got no manners, don't know shit. Me, I gotta teach him everything, real quick. Hardest job I do in long time."

"Yeah," I say. "It would be. Mister Boy, he's some kind of animal."

"How come you know some kind of animal like him, Mistah Prentice? You see him in some zoo, Stateside, sometimes?"

"Much worse than that. He was my driver, a long time ago,

when I was touring the desert around Kuwait. Behind Iraqi lines," I say. "He was so bad at his job I had to fire him."

"Ungrateful fuck never even gave me a tip, either," JoeBoy says.

"Mistah Boy, you pretty lucky Mistah Prentice didn't drop hammer on you, what I think," Sonny says.

"I was going to," I say, "but I decided to kill my tour instead, just leave the sorry bastard driving around in circles till he ran out of gas and died."

"Too bad this don't work so well," Sonny says.

"Aw, man, he's just frontin'. Some kinda Korean thing, know what I'm saying? He loves me, can't show it," JoeBoy says, throwing an arm around Sonny's shoulders. *"Ay, compadre?"*

Sonny shrugs off JoeBoy's arm, spits. "Hey, Mistah Boy, think you can show Mistah Prentice where we stay, how we got things set up here? You still got map I gotta draw for you first time?"

JoeBoy taps his temple with a forefinger, nods.

"Very sorry to do this to you, Mistah Prentice. Mistah Kim, he wants to talk to me 'bout this and that. So I gotta leave you with this animal, little while. I see you later, okay?"

Soon as Sonny goes inside, JoeBoy says, "Let's do it backward, just to fuck with him. Stroll around the grounds first? Not a good idea to talk anywhere inside, unless you like your voice on tape, 'Mistah Prentice.' You got some kind of first name to go with that handle?"

"Terry," I say. I don't ask about who he's supposed to be. But I don't need to.

"Me, I'm Carlos Bolívar Martinez, merchant seaman out of Costa Rica, dude. It must be true, 'cause I got a passport that says so," JoeBoy says as we start walking the compound's perimeter. "Fuckin' good to see you again, dog. I knew somebody was coming, didn't know who, though. He wouldn't say."

"He being a real spooky guy, calls himself Westley, right?"

"Shit yeah. I see we're moving in the same circles again, Terry man."

"What did you do so bad in life that got you mixed up with him? I thought you'd be teamed with the Kurds, fucking up Iraqis again."

I hadn't seen the man—real name José Jesus Rodriguez, born in Chicago to illegal Mex immigrants, tagged first "José Jimenez" in training camp, which morphed to JoeBoy soon because that was quicker to say—since Desert Storm. Hard to feature that was more than a decade ago. But we'd kept in touch over the years. Last I heard he was still in Special Forces. And that was just after 9/11.

"Passed up that opportunity. Me and Snake and some new guys you never met were with the Northern Alliance, hammering Taliban ragheads. We're kickin' ass pretty good when a cluster-fuck of CIA assholes show, start telling us how to do our jobs. Dig this: one of those stupid *cabrones* has a beard, arrives wearing a turban, starts talking in Pashto with a fuckin' Alabama accent. Our ragheads are laughing their asses off, but he don't notice. He thinks they like him!"

"Oh, I believe it. But you aren't answering."

"Okay, Luther, okay. Dig: this older guy, who don't bother trying to disguise what he is or any other dumb shit—such as tellin' us we ain't handlin' our ragheads efficiently—he hangs for a while. Just watching, know where I'm at?"

"That's Westley, all right."

"Anyway, when we're just about finished cleaning the Taliban clocks, he asks me if I'm interested in another line of work. Something, he says, that would broaden my scope. No more military chickenshit. Mucho travel, mucho adventure. It's sounding real fine, since I ain't much lookin' forward to going back to the States and the fuckin' training routine at base camp again."

"So? You discussed options with Westley?"

"*Discuss*, yeah. That's the exact fuckin' word the man used. My enlistment's running out in a few months—which he already knows somehow. He's discussing some better pay, too. Better? Shit! Talkin' four times what I'm getting from the army. So I don't re-up, I sign on with Westley. Since then, a couple of neat jobs in the Philippines, a couple down Colombia way.

"Poor career move, JoeBoy."

"Poor my ass, motherfucker! Best thing that ever happened to me. Snake, Tark, Radar, Tony Ducks from the old crew, they go into Kurdland. Fuckin' Snake. That little sideshow against the Iranians who'd staked a claim in Iraqi Kurd territory? Medium-intensity assault, the fucks all surrender? Maybe three KIAs our side? Well, Snake's one. Smoked, man. Figure that. No more."

"Aw shit. Not Snake. That really sucks."

"Yeah. So now all Professor JoeBoy does is drop into some jungle from time to time, show the locals my moves, take 'em into a little bang-bang, chopper out. Got a nice apartment in Panama City, another in Davao. Got the sweetest pussy ever, one living in each place. When I gotta work, I work for a while, maybe four-five weeks straight. But average it out, figure I'm on the job about five days a month. Spend the rest of my time fuckin', suckin', going to the beach, going out to eat, going dancing. Whole lot better than barracks life. Come to that, whole lot easier than bein' a narc. Which you were, last time we talked. What're you doing here, Luther?"

"Got suspended for six months. Broke a little rule," I say. "And instead of taking a nice road trip to Mexico, I fucked up again, discussed with Westley, signed on for a short-time-only gig, baby-sitting Mister Kim. And since this is damn far from Panama, Colombia, or Mindanao, and there's no jungle but a concrete one, what the fuck are you doing here?"

"Short-time gig only. Covering some bitch's ass in Vladivostok.

Name's Allison. You know her? Got a sweet ass? Am I gonna like pushing up against it?"

"Affirmative, both counts. Thinking love at first sight, you two. She really digs hairy-ape types, JoeBoy."

Fucking Westley. Poor, sorry-ass JoeBoy. But at least Allison will have competent backup in Vlad, because he's real good with his tools, and the same with his hands.

We cover the grounds, talking biz instead of bullshitting. Security's pretty much the same deal as the Big Sur place, except there are a few more men. I'd noticed most of the neighboring places are modern, but Kim must really love big wood beams and columns and gull-winged tile roofs. Silla architecture, I think that's what Eunk-yong called it. Very old Korean vernacular. This place isn't old, of course. And inside it's kind of schizoid. A large room where Kim might entertain, for instance, looks like a museum, everything very traditional, very antique. Other parts of the house are right-this-minute, one room with a huge plasma TV screen dominating a wall, Samsung's latest video array, Bang & Olufsen sound system, leather Saporiti chairs and sofas. Same as the California place. Two underground levels here instead of one, though. First has the pool, the gym, the monitor room. Second's staff quarters. Nice touch I notice when I'm shown my room: a big rice-paper window streaming light. Bulb light, yeah, and if you slid the window open you'd see a bare concrete wall with a fixture, but it dispels most of the feeling of being in an underground bunker. Nice staff lounge down there too, done up with the same plasma TV, the same audio and video systems I'd seen upstairs.

JoeBoy's showing all this off as if he owns it. We finish in that lounge. Nobody else is around. I settle into a chair, he goes to a kitchen off to one side, returns with beers.

"Ahh," he sighs, settling into the cushions of the sofa. "Easy duty, man. Everything a man could want. You want a girl? Tell one of Sonny's guys, a girl shows up in your room. Nice young Korean girl, unless you specify Thai or Jap. I sampled, came out favoring Korean. Toned, strong bodies, amigo. Give you a hot workout."

"Sounds like Allison," I say. May as well jerk JoeBoy's chain a little, just for the hell of it.

"Hoo-ah! Then I won't be so sorry to leave."

"Say what? You jumping ship already?"

"Jumping on one—tomorrow. I'm Carlos Martinez, going into Vlad as a Costa Rican deckhand. *No habla* Russki, what the fuck. It's a sailors' town. Nobody bothers you, long as you stay down in the docks district. The female-type ass I'm gonna enjoy coverin', she flying in the day I dock. She finds me, I stick to her butt. That's what Westley said."

"And where'll she find you?" Handy thing to know, just in case.

"Some seamen's hotel called, shit, what's the name? 'Dumb' something. Nah. Dom Pokrovsky, yeah. Westley said four, five days max, Allison flies away. And so do I. Back to Busan, don't even leave the airport, make a connection to Manila. And then home to Davao. You oughta come down there when you're done doin' what you do. Nice beaches, great food. And my little friend knows some sizzlin' Filipinas just dying to meet a man like you. You ain't done the juicy with a Filipina, you ain't lived yet, amigo."

"Might do that," I say, sure I never will.

"Good to go, motherfucker! Taxi from the airport to the Hotel Insular outside town, on the beach. Drivers all know it. Funny fuckin' sign at the lobby entrance. Says 'Check guns, please. NO DURIAN.' Ask the desk guy where Big José stays. He'll get you there. Real good times. Guarantee it, bro."

Dinner's in-house with JoeBoy, Sonny, a couple of Lees and Parks and one Kim, unrelated, plus a Chun. They don't have a lot of surnames in Korea, Eunkyong had told me, and about thirty-five percent of the whole population is either a Kim or a Lee. Chun's a wild card. But it's as before: Sonny's boys don't want to—or can't, because they have no English—talk. They shovel up chow, concentrated as hungry dogs, then slink off to wherever. So afterward, it's just Sonny and JoeBoy and me in the lounge.

I last about one slow beer. In the service, JoeBoy was my brother, we were that tight. We lived tight, fought tight. But now he gets deep into the remember game. "Remember that time we choppered in . . . Remember how we smoked . . . Remember how Snake was rattlin' those fifties . . ." War stories, big and braggy and mostly bullshit. I guess I talked that way once, too. But it was a long, long time ago. I was a kid, we all were kids. I'm not anymore. And pretty soon, though I feel bad for thinking it, I am thinking JoeBoy's a loud-mouthed asshole, a guy stuck in a time warp, drunk on the past and babbling. It's boring, then it's irritating, JoeBoy's jive. But he doesn't get it, just stays in the same groove. Clear why Sonny's down on him; I'm heading that way, even if I don't want to. So I start yawning, complaining about super-bad jet lag, promise I'll catch him before he leaves, and go hit my rack. I don't take advantage of the room services that night. I crash.

JoeBoy goes. When I wake up next morning, shower, dress and go out to the lounge, Sonny's waiting for me with a pot of coffee. Hands me a note: "Post-op, haul to Davao, pronto. J."

"You sleep okay, Mistah Prentice. You feeling pretty good." It's a statement more than question.

"Very fine. Even better when I've had coffee and one of these," I say, lighting a Camel.

"Miss Allison, Miss Russki Girl, they want to see you pretty soon," Sonny says. "Hey, maybe Miss Allison, she missing bouncy."

"Don't think so. She's a serious woman. Sure she wants to talk business."

"Hunh. Women got no business in our business, for sure. You guys making big mistakes, with women." Sonny shakes his head. Whether it's sorrow or pity, I can't read.

"Ask you one thing?" Sonny doesn't wait for a reply, just goes ahead. "How come you friends with some low-life like Mistah Boy?"

"We did some combat together. Think you must've heard too much about it, last night."

The Buddha grin appears. "Yeah, know how that is. You don't like a guy before, you like him plenty after. He's your brother. If he's any good. This Mistah Boy, he any good?"

"Oh yeah. You want a target lighted up, he really lights it. Never have to worry about your back either, if he's watching it. But you don't like him much. Any reason?"

"Yeah, that fella make too much noise in my head, someways."

"Mine too, last night. He's picked up some bad habits somewhere. Might change your opinion if you go into a hot zone with him, though."

"Might. Might. But I like to feel sure before." Sonny laughs then. "Don't need to say it, Mistah Prentice. I know pretty good you can never be sure, before."

"Good thing, then, those guys dropped in on us in California. Now you and me, we know, right?"

"Damn straight. You and me, good to go, okay?"

"Okay by me. Any time, any place." Big-time lie, but one I really want him to believe. So I make it sound solid, straight.

"Pretty soon, pretty soon. Meantime, you and me got not much to do. Mistah Kim, he want to stay home, private. Miss his girlfriend pretty much," Sonny says. "Guess you better go see your women. But I tell one story first. My father, he got the same job as me, with Mistah Kim's father. Just my father, no more assistants, those days. Senior Mistah Kim, he die natural, some kinda cancer, old guy, you know? My Mistah Kim, he gonna die same way. Natural. Long, long time from now. Old age. I make damn sure of that, understand? No Westley, no nobody stop me."

"Roger that," I say. "Mister Kim, you, me, we're all going to live to be ninety. Won't vouch for Westley, though."

"Nobody care much, that one go down," Sonny says.

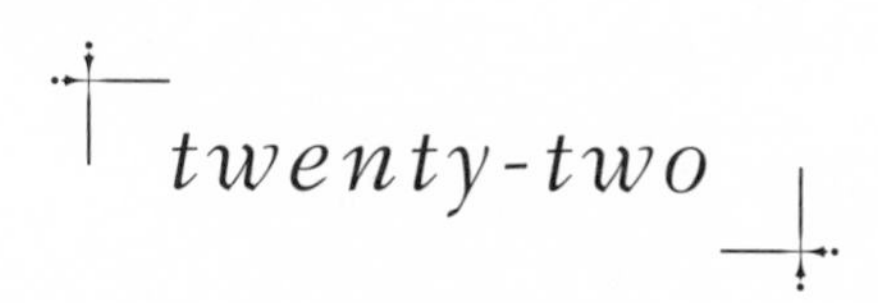

twenty-two

THERE'S A CAR—NOT ONE OF THE LINCOLNS, BECAUSE I DON'T RATE and anyway I'm supposed to keep a low profile—idling quietly in the driveway when Sonny and I emerge from the house. Hyundai's biggest sedan, a sort of seaweed green they don't export, driver dressed casual, like it's a taxi. "One of my guys, Mistah Prentice," Sonny says. "He take you to where your women are, wait, bring you back whenever."

"Whenever," I say, getting in. "What about that good time you promised me?"

"Ho. Maybe tonight, maybe tomorrow night, we do just like I say." Sonny chuckles. JoeBoy's departure has cheered him, I guess. "Unless that Miss Allison, she put you on leash like some dog or what not."

"In your dreams, Mistah Park," I say.

"Not mine, you bet, Mistah Prentice. That kinda woman, she's not my type one bit. She like some kinda man with tits."

Wrong about that, Sonny. That's what I'm thinking as I'm driven down into the gut of Busan, not bothering to say a word to the driver because I'm sure he won't answer with anything but a grunt even if I use my bit of Korean. Sonny hasn't learned—never will, the kind of life he leads—what I did in the hard school: women are a different species, so many of them smarter and more ruthless than us. Allison's shown a portion of her smarts, not all; she's keeping some in reserve. Ruthless? Almost certainly. To what degree I won't find out till Vlad. And likely not then, unless she says "Bright" and I have to hammer someone. Curious to see how she handles ordering an assassination. How she maintains, once it's done. Too bad it'll be arm's length; I'd know for sure if she watched while the XTPs blast flesh and bone into hamburger, smelled the smell of it.

Wipe all that crap, I tell myself. Stay in the now. Futures always come to you out of the blank. Ugly, beautiful, any gradation in between, they find you, brand you, slip into your accumulated past. Happens real fast. No point or purpose, trying to see 'em coming.

I try zeroing on what's framed by the car window instead. And register some stuff I hadn't on the way in, though none of it seems worth saving and storing. Where Kim's place is must be the only area in this jammed city where there are any private houses left. The narrow defiles that run down from the mountains to the water are crammed to overflowing with tall apartment blocks, some clearly luxury ones, some middle-class, some pretty shitty, but they're lower down, mainly hidden. Feels like a sort of hive, or ant colony. Traffic's a bitch everywhere, and real aggressive; if it was like this in any city I know in the States, you'd see cars stopped in the middle of streets, guys punching each other's lights out, pumped on road rage and cheered on by a huge chorus of honking horns. None of that here. Must be a game—all this dangerous cutting off, scraping past, bulling ahead—that Koreans enjoy playing.

It's no more decorous when my driver squeals to a stop almost perpendicular to the curb, completely blocking a big limo about to pull out from the entrance of the Lotte Hotel, a double-slab glass tower maybe forty stories tall. He ignores the limo driver's harried gestures, turns off his engine, apparently considers he's satisfactorily parked. I walk into the lobby through doors held open by kids in white sailor suits and caps, other people heading out without acknowledging their existence. The multinational five-star deluxe world, part of a constellation where it's impossible—and unimportant, mostly—to know if it's Hong Kong, Singapore, Kuala Lumpur, Jakarta, or Tokyo pulsing outside. Rich locals, Texas "awl boys," coveys of ranking *zaibatsu* Japs and lone American CEOs outpacing their small entourages, all in a quiet swirl but never colliding, never mixing. All under the discreet observation of hotel staffers, ready to glide up to anyone who appears to require something and inquire, in English, if they may be of assistance. I see Nadya sitting catlike in one of a couple dozen big, cushy chairs, cup of tea on the little table before her, looking like the house's pampered pet. She smiles, waves me over as she rises to her feet.

"Terry darling. Seems like ages. Want you up in my suite chop-chop," she says, linking an arm to one of mine, leading me into a manned elevator, saying, "Thirty-four," to the operator, who bobs his head and obeys.

Her spike heels don't make a sound as we go down a thickly carpeted corridor to its end, where there's a single door. She dips a card into the lock slot, gently nudges me inside, secures the door behind her. Instinctual scan: lounge with twin sofas, center, facing each other across a glass-topped coffee table; straight on, a wall of glass, panorama of the harbor. Ninety left, a half-open door, flash of Allison pulling a sweater over her head. Ninety right, door wide, Rob hunched at a desk flush to a window, twin black laptops and drab-green mil-spec communications box lit up, neat little satellite dish stuck to the glass with suction cups. Must stash the box and the dish whenever the maids come to make up the room. Butt of his SIG's peeking out from an inside-waistband holster.

"Hey, Terry," Allison says, emerging from the room I figure she's sharing with Nadya.

"Thought you GS people had a per diem, traveling. Never cover even a quarter of this," I say.

"Special allowance for hardship postings," Allison says, motioning me to have a seat on the sofa where Nadya's already assumed her catlike curl. I sit. Allison doesn't. She paces awhile by the big window.

"Are you okay up at Kim's?" she asks. "The situation is good? All secure?"

"It's fine. Sonny's a pro. Got it organized," I say.

"Is he still feeling kind of hostile toward us? Toward what we're going into?"

"He's all right with it." I don't feel like mentioning what he said about ensuring Mister Kim's life expectancy. "Hates Vlad, though. Says the Natashas there turn his dick into an icicle."

Nadya hoots. "Poor dear. He's clearly consorted with the wrong type of Russki."

"Certainly must have. We know some—naming no names—who have just the opposite effect, don't we, Terry?" Allison says, looking at her. Then, facing me, "What about our Mister Kim?"

"Talk's getting kind of loose, isn't it?" I say. "This place swept?"

"Before we even unpacked. We added our counterbugs, too. It's standard procedure. You know that," Allison says. She seems wrapped maybe one turn tighter than I'm used to. "Kim?"

"Haven't seen him. Been in his quarters. Presumably with his girlfriend. Sonny said he's been missing her."

"That checks out," Allison says. "We knew she was there waiting for him to arrive."

"So you summon me down here to ask questions you already know the answers to? Or just because you've missed me?"

"Of course we've missed you," Nadya says. "Twenty-four hours without seeing you is about as much as we can bear."

"Can we stay focused here, Nadya?" Allison says. "There's been a development, Terry. Westley got in touch. Nadya's generals have become impatient all of a sudden. They want to move everything up a couple of days. That means we go to Vlad tomorrow."

"No way. No fucking way," I say, standing up. "What kind of ops have you been on? Rule number one for this type is never change the plan. Never. Guys you're dealing with want to change, it means they're under pressure from somewhere. That means big danger. Or they want to rip you off. That's good-as-dead danger. You with that?"

Allison gazes at me as if I'm some newbie who's only supposed to speak when asked to. "I don't see your problem, Terry. We're ready. What's a day or two?"

"Didn't you hear?" I'm talking louder than I like to. "Problem one is that Carlos, the guy who's supposed to watch your back, won't have even reached Vlad before the deal goes down. So you maybe get capped, but hey, no big deal, to me. The big deal is what I said: the generals are either in trouble and need to move fast—or else they're planning to smoke Mister Kim and the rest of us, take the money, and keep the merchandise."

"Oh, your thinking's stuck with drug deals, and—" she starts.

"Never change the plan. Never. There's no fuckin' difference between a multimillion-dollar coke or smack buy and this, except maybe weight, or political shit. A buy's a buy. Anywhere, anytime. The rule holds. Fuck! Can't you comprehend that, Allison?"

"Westley wants to do it."

"So *fuck* him. You're in charge, right? Or was that bullshit? If you are in charge, tell Westley we stick to plan. Tell him to tell the generals no changes in schedule. Otherwise, this thing's aborted."

"You don't have any say in that, Terry." Icy. She's not liking this one bit.

"What? You think I'm frontin'? Dig it: I tell Sonny what I just told you. Sonny goes postal. He knows how we play. And he makes sure his Mister Kim stays right here in his 'hood. Vlad's a no-go. Guaran-fuckin'-teed." I *am* frontin', big. I don't have a choice, though. I only hope Allison's not conscious of the fact that Sonny wouldn't dare to tell Kim not to go, wouldn't presume to even suggest any such thing.

"You had better stand down, Terry. I don't respond well to threats." Harder voice. Now she's wrapped two turns too tight.

"No threat. Just truth. What? Can't take it? I'll lay it out again, large: sellers try changing, they got serious reasons. Gotta cover their asses, or wanna be fucking yours. Maybe you're willing to take it up your sweet butt, but you really down with jeopardizing your package, your entire op?"

"Do you want to make some kind of intelligent point, Mister Prentice? Offer some advice from your vast experience—which right about now is coming across as real overrated, just a lot of narc-type jive?"

"Okay. Plain and simple. You tell Westley—or you go through that back channel you claimed you have with Langley and get Langley to tell him—absolute negative on any change. You or Langley tell Westley to turn bitch, suck the generals' cocks if that's what it takes to make them stick to schedule. Or don't you have the stones for that?"

"Wow! Terry sounds quite nonnegotiable, doesn't he?" Nadya says. I sense rather than see Rob slip into the lounge from his communications center. I turn a little so my back's to a wall and all three of them are in my sight zone. Escalation's seeming like a possibility here. You never know, with Company people.

"Everything's negotiable at some level," Allison says. She paces before the window, stops, stares out at the view for what feels like too long. I know she's hating everything I've said, especially my last line. I hope she's pro enough to get beyond it, see the real point.

"Allison?" Nadya says softly.

"Goddammit," she says, not turning. "Goddamn! Right, then. All right. I'm telling Westley we stick to plan."

"But Westley said—" Rob starts.

"Don't you dare, Rob!" Allison spins and snaps. "Don't even think of going there. The decision's mine. I've taken it. Clear?"

"As crystal, love," Nadya says. "No worries. Right, Terry?"

"I'm on board. Totally. We'll make it happen, the whole deal," I say. Then I shrug slightly, let my arm muscles go down a notch from combat-ready level, but keep my mind cold, focused. Bad sign, this bullshit about change. Even worse, how high the tension torqued up over it.

Nadya must feel it, too. She moves to damp things down. "Well, that's that, then, I suppose. I'm famished. How about you, Terry? Yes, of course you are. Allison, may Terry and I be excused for lunch, please?"

Allison makes a small smile. It's costing her, that's plain, but she does it. Then she nods assent.

"Now that was brilliant!" Nadya says. We're in one of the Lotte's restaurants—there's fourteen, count 'em, she picked the Korean one—and chowing on some kind of tasty seafood dumplings.

"What?"

"Well, from the audience's view. Picture as we set our scene: attractive, ambitious young woman entrepreneur in conference about the largest deal of her career with one of her slightly older assistants. He's businesslike, quite attractive in his nicely tailored suit. And suddenly he's shouting like a gangster rapper. 'Smoke yuh ass, bitch! Goin' postal, holy ghostal!' " She giggles.

"You think I was acting?"

"Oh, the contrast was amazing. Perfectly played."

"And the content?"

"Would've been quite staggering," she says, "if I wasn't in complete agreement. Have been since the moment Allison mentioned her brief communication with Westley this morning. I'd said my little piece before you arrived. She wasn't having any. Thought it best to let you go it alone."

"So you understand something's wrong here?"

"Well, of course! But absolutely not surprised. It's the nature of these things, I suppose. There are always a few bumps, a bit of rough road, on any op. It would be a bit boring, otherwise, don't you think?"

I laugh. Little Nadya's tough enough. I ask her if she thinks Allison will stick with the plan or cave for Westley.

"Stick. She has to now. Matter of pride, all that rubbish. You made it impossible for her to back down. But of course you know that."

"I know nothing's ever sure, that's what I know. What do you think the generals are up to? They're your boys."

"Nothing terribly sinister, I'm thinking. I doubt they have—what was that colorful expression you used?—oh yes, 'the stones' to try any radical actions with a serious personage such as Mister Kim. Additionally, they're very interested in repeat business. They're probably testing their leverage. And they do like to bark orders just to see which way people will jump, and how fast. A military thing, I imagine."

"Not running scared, then? Not feeling heat from somewhere?"

"Anything's possible. But it's unlikely in this case. They have, after all, very brutally expelled the local mafia from their sphere of interests. I can't imagine anyone else who might be in a position to threaten them."

"Not big guys in Moscow? Government or mob?"

"If either were fully aware of what Bolgy and Tchitch have been up to, I think the stroke would have been applied well before now."

Far from hard intel, but somehow I feel eased by what she says. Nadya, light and sassy as she acts, is probably the most professional member of this team. Certainly the brightest.

"Darling," I say, "I know the timing's awkward, but when all this is over . . . if I come back . . . will you marry me? Be the mother of my child?"

"Oh, Terry! This is so sort of . . . bad World War Two film. But you don't look a bit like David Niven in an RAF uniform, your accent's deplorable. Worse, you've used that exact line before. You're gifted, but your repertoire is, well, limited."

"Even in the love scenes?"

"We won't speak of those. It simply isn't done," she says, so fake prim she makes herself chuckle. "And how's a girl to know, when her experience is so limited?"

"Easy enough to broaden it, if the girl was inclined to."

"You tease! You flirt! Offering what you can't deliver."

"I can't?"

"Time, darling. We have so little now. But when all this is over . . . if you come back . . ."

I'm a sucker for mocking from the Nadyas of the world, and this one knows it, keeps it up awhile, temporarily driving away any lingering bad vibes from the scene in the suite. Whether for my benefit or her own isn't clear and doesn't matter.

Eventually she segues gracefully into tales of Vlad, strictly travelogue, nothing mission-related. Says I'll feel depressed there at first, but not to worry; everybody always finds Russian cities depressing. With reason, as I'll see. Something not easily defined, a mix of decay and new money spent tastelessly and wastefully. Exudes a very Third World feeling.

"How Third World, you're wondering?" she says. "Well, it's rather late in the season, but if you have an urge to walk barefoot on the sands of lovely Sportivnaya Beach, do not!"

"Why not?" I ask.

"Absolutely infested with larvae of intestinal worms, so tiny they burrow in through the pores of your skin. Ah, but once they reach your gut, they grow and grow. Half a meter or more!"

"Right. That gives me the picture. Third World."

After we've eaten, she links her arm through mine, walks me out between the sailor-suited boys at the doors.

"I know what's part of the hospitality package at Mister Kim's," she says, not mockingly but certainly mock-serious only. "Don't you dare touch one of those dirty shamless sluts, Terry. It would break my fragile heart if you proved untrue."

She's laughing as I get into the car, still parked at that blocking angle to the curb, though the limo somehow managed to get away. And so am I. If Nadya's got a heart, it's probably at least part stone. But her mind, yeah, her mind is one I could love madly, truly. In fact, I already do, dammit.

I try emptying my mind on the long drive back to Kim's. Manage to jettison a couple of doubts, a file of suspicions, a few desires and memories and some other junk that's been piling up there lately. Don't pay any attention to the traffic snarl, the snaking crowds of pedestrians downtown, the massive waves of apartment buildings that flow up the valleys between hills. Soon I'm in a calm, clear zone, the kind I frequently seek but don't reach as often as I'd like. I'm barely aware when the car stops. I look out. It's a moment or two before I realize we've reached Kim's place.

Guess that's why Sonny's able to blindside me soon as I go in through the staff entrance.

"Why you people trying to mess with Mistah Kim, huh?" he barks, gripping my left bicep. "What shit you people pulling?"

"Let go of me, Mister Park. Right now, please," I say. "Do that, and I will answer any questions I have answers for."

"You better have answers, Mistah Prentice, or people goin' down pretty soon," Sonny says. But he releases my arm. "Mistah Kim, he's very disturbed. That Westley, he call him here, say we gotta go Vlad right away. Don't know why, Mistah Kim don't tell me, just say get ready, we going tomorrow morning."

Oh fuck, I'm thinking. Allison caved. But I take too long for Sonny.

"What's this hurry-up shit? Bad, bad. Better stick to plan. Always better, stick to plan. Answer, Mistah Prentice."

"I don't know anything about Westley calling here."

"You better know something. 'Cause it gets worse. Short time after Westley phone, that Miss Allison call. She say to Mistah Kim she talk to Westley, plan stays same-same. Mistah Kim, he don't like any of this. Wants to know how come you people say one thing, then say another. Not the way Mistah Kim like to do business. Not the way I like, either. Bad, bad. Some kinda troubles for sure."

"Listen, Sonny, it's a misunderstanding." I give him a slanted description of the scene with Allison, casting it as Westley hearing from the Russians they'd like to push up the meeting a couple of days, then asking Allison if that would be possible. She decides it is not possible. She decides we stay on the original schedule. And she's in charge.

"That woman in charge? Not Westley?" Sonny's voice is heavily doubtful. "First I hear about that. Here's Mistah Kim's message. You get that Westley to tell him what's going on. And you get that fuckin' woman up here to explain everything pretty quick. Better be good. Or Mistah Kim, he say he don't go nowhere with you people. Nowhere. Never."

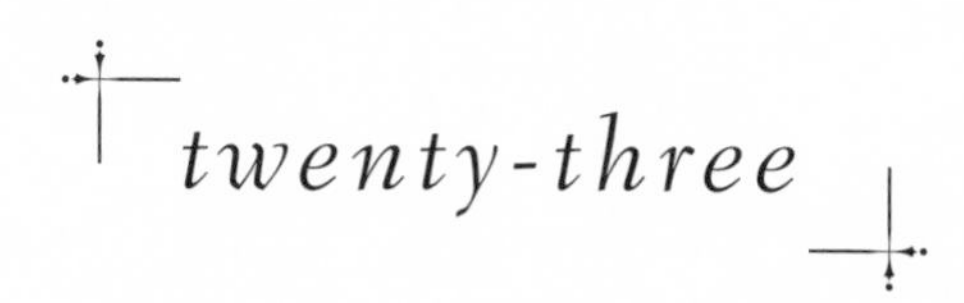

twenty-three

I PHONE IN THE MESSAGE TO NADYA, NOT ALLISON. I FIGURE I'VE already pushed that one within an eyelash of kill-the-messenger mode; any more from me might be seen as active coconspiracy, provoke a strong, wrong reaction. "Oh dear. Very messy," Nadya says, not bothering to ask why I picked her. She knows why. She'll pass it on.

All I can do, meantime, is wait.

That gets spooky, fast. I expect some faint buzz, some hint of random static, at least that almost imperceptible tightening of the air you somehow sense before a big thunderstorm.

But there's nothing. Kim's place feels as tranquil as a Zen monastary. I sit there in the staff lounge for a long time. Don't see Sonny, don't see any Lees or Parks or Lees, don't hear any phones ringing, any doors slamming, any Lincolns pulling into the drive, or pulling away.

I begin to believe everyone's vanished, that I'm the only live body in the place.

I go into the staff kitchen, make myself a pot of coffee, take it back to the lounge, sip on the first cup while I check out the DVD library. A couple of shelves of martial-arts thrillers from the Far East's Hollywood—Hong Kong. Not up for that, even though they always have a large laugh factor, fighters soaring impossibly through the air courtesy of special effects. Tucked away behind one set of discs, I find a porno cache, Thai-made. Definitely not in the mood for watching exquisite Thai girls, maybe fourteen years old, maybe a lot younger, pretending to enjoy humiliating sex acts with grown men, probably dogs and other animals, too. Even thinking about what's on those DVDs makes me feel disgusted, angry.

Zero interest in the CD racks. And there aren't any books in sight.

I go up one level. Nobody in the pool, nobody using the exercise machines. Feels like nobody ever does, maybe never has. The place doesn't want me.

So I go down to my room, unholster the Wilson and the XD, remove the Korth from my special briefcase. Unload, check chambers, start carefully wiping down the Wilson with a silicon cloth. And stop abruptly; my tools are already free of dust, oily fingerprints, any blemishes at all. As clean as if they'd just come from the box. Reload, reholster, shut the Korth away. Kick off my shoes, lie down on the bed, hands clasped behind my head. Tense, then relax every muscle group I've got, starting with my feet and working up to my neck.

When I'm loose enough, I decide to try eyelid movies. Usually a pleasant enough way of filling empty time, especially if I begin with something sweet and recent. Like that night with Nadya, her eyes on mine as we made love. Cue up the mental tape, start. But something's off, it won't track. Damn. Nothing but gray horizontal bands, not even scrolling but jerking fast from bottom to top. No sound, either. Just an aroma, some mix of wild honeysuckle and musk. Or the idea of such a scent; you cannot really ever recall smells, reexperience them the way you sometimes do touches and sights and voices.

Voices especially. Now, those you can frequently hear almost as clearly as if they'd been digitally recorded in your brain, even without a visual. I let go as much as I can, wait to see what voices might come.

That starts random, fractured, does a quick devolve to disorienting, then nightmarish.

"Any bored troubles just hanging out with nothing to do, they say, 'Hey, there's always Luther. Let's go see him. He likes it.' "

"Wake up every morning, nothin' but a blank facing you. Dead hours. Lot's of 'em."

"Pink mist! No head no more, Serb pig."

"You're a lying son of a bitch, Luther. You're going on a job."

"No one available I trust not to dump or waste the package if there's an incident."

Each distinct, the real thing in tone, timbre, pitch. Then here comes some devil's chorus, everybody trying to shout everybody else down, demanding to tell of the terrible, soul-sickening things Luther Ewing's seen and done: Light the fuckers up! I piss on your grave, little brother. C'mon, rock the fuckin' casbah. No son of mine who goes merc can expect to be welcome in my house. Gunny numbah ten, Luther numbah one.

Orchestra starts roaring up out the background, no melody, raw noise: AKs sounding like corn popping extraloud in the microwave, timpani boom of my .45 as I cap someone, high laughter of a little kid dashing across the street, the heartbreaking, soggy slap of a bullet sprawling the kid into a blood pool, crack of the Serb sniper's Dragunov that did it. Huge crescendo of RPG explosions, fast sort of snip-snip-snip of M4s doing three-round bursts into flesh, a man's girly scream squelched to a gargle as a piano-wire garotte tightens around his neck, the flat pop-pop-pop-pop-pop-pop-pop-pop of my

MP5 on full auto, hosing a dozen kneeling, wailing Iraqi soldiers. AK corn-popping mixes with snare-drum reply from M16s. Howls and shouts, some hoarse and urgent, some agonized. Screams, wails, a thousand screams at once. And then a smell, a real smell, sickening-sweet blood mixed with burnt powder and hot grease.

Lying there, my whole being twists with regret and shame and horror at what I was, things I did. My stomach revolts, sharp pains stab up and down my chest, the overpowering sour burn as I swallow my own vomit before it can spew.

All at once I'm sitting up, drenched in something, eyes stinging and blurred. Barrel of the Wilson's pointing at a figure of a man silhouetted by a door frame. Pull or not? Don't know.

"Mistah Prentice? Hey, Mistah Prentice. You don't wanna point that this way. Man, you looking sick as hell, Mistah Prentice." It's Sonny. Aw shit. Where the fuck have I been? How long was I there? I lower my pistol.

"That's good, very good, Mistah Prentice. You need a doctor maybe?" Sonny says. I swipe at my face, hand comes away wet and salty. Shirt front's wet, sticking to my chest.

"Nah, not sick. Not sick."

"You sure, Mistah Prentice? Maybe I better get doctor, just check."

"Think I dozed off."

"Hunh." Sonny moves near to the bed, watches as I holster the Wilson. Then he lays the back of one big hand against my forehead for an instant. "No fever. Demon sleep, I think."

"Say what?"

"Me, once in a while, same-same. Take a little nap, all kind of hell hit my brain. Demon shit. Wake up sweaty, shaky."

"How real is it, when it happens to you?"

Sonny grunts. "Too damn real. That's the problem. Realer than real. Demon shit. Gotta be. 'Cause nothing worse than real stuff."

"Oh man," I sigh, shaking my head.

"Hard to believe demons never visit you before, Mistah Prentice."

"Not these kind," I say.

"Me, I get right up, take a real hot shower, put on fresh clothes, pretty soon everything all right, everything normal then. You try that, Mistah Prentice. Okay? You do that, you feeling right after that, come to the lounge. Okay?"

"Yeah. Sure. It's what I'll do."

"Demon sleep, that fucker ambush everybody sometime. Don't mean nothin', Mistah Prentice."

"Nothin'," I say. "Walk on."

"Ho! What my father always sayin'. Long time before I understand. Once I do, I know he's right, damn straight."

The water that sluices the soap off my body somehow sluices the demons from my mind, too. Towel down, put on fresh skivvies, clean starched shirt, different suit. Feel like I'm a new man. But I do not look at my eyes in the mirror. Got a sense I need a longer interval before I'm up to that. So I just go into the lounge, grabbing and popping a bottle of Red Rock on the way.

Sonny's lying on one of the sofas, no suit coat, tie loosened at the neck, sipping his bottle when I come in, sit opposite him.

"You good now, Mistah Prentice?" he asks.

"Never better."

That draws a Buddha smile. "Hunh. Not sure about that 'never.' But maybe everybody, they at least a little better than two, three hours ago."

"Yeah? Something go down I should know about? You sure weren't feeling your usual cheerful self two, three hours ago."

"Had damn good reasons. What goes down? I don't know what, exactly. Guess only. Think maybe that Westley, he call back. Think maybe that Allison thing, she some kind of witch, come up here, meet with Mistah Kim, talk long time. Anyway, Mistah Kim calm down now. He say to me we stayin' with original plan."

"That's good."

"Maybe not, but anyway better than that switch shit." Sonny looks at me awhile. "Tell you somethin', your ears only, right?"

"Nobody else's."

"Me, I never feel happy about this trip. Worries me, Mistah Kim being okay with it."

"Yeah, you've conveyed that before. Maybe you worry too much. What can anyone throw at us in Vlad that you and me can't handle? Who's gonna be dumb enough to try to ride the tiger?"

"Russkis that dumb."

"They are, we eat 'em up. Yum."

"Damn straight. They don't trouble me so much. CIA fucks worry me lots. And then it's just me. Very sorry 'bout that, but you one of them, Mistah Prentice."

"Not one of them. I told you that before. Just working for them."

"Same-same. I work for Mistah Kim, you work for them."

"Not the same at all. You got loyalties to Mistah Kim. Maybe you owe him. Your ears only? I got loyalties only to whoever's a friendly, whoever sticks real tight with me in a situation, understand?"

Sonny nods, but I don't know if he's really getting it.

"I owe Westley and Allison and the rest nothing, least of all loyalty," I say. "Same as the army. One obligation only: absolute total loyalty to the guys holding your flanks in the fight. Stay loyal, stay in the fight no matter what, until the enemy's dead, or you are. Fuck anything else."

"Some kind of philosopher, Mistah Prentice. Pretty good words. Me, I'm hoping we don't have to find any hard way how true."

Difficult to make any credible response to that. He won't

believe a new truth: at this point, he's the person I trust most, suspect least, in the whole damn outfit. Even if it isn't mutual. So I punt.

"My best guess, Sonny? We're going to fly in, Mister Kim's gonna do his business with the Russians, maybe drink a little vodka, eat some Beluga. Then we go see his good friends in Pyongyang. And pretty damn soon you and me will be right back here, laughing and wondering why we even bothered carrying all those guns."

Sonny chuckles. "Yeah, turns out like that, joke's on Sonny, Mistah Prentice. Be one time I'm glad big joke on me, for sure."

"So. We're on schedule. Two nights free. What about your promise?"

"Promise?"

"Yeah, some guy calling himself Sonny, looked a lot like you, was talking real big about how fine Korean girls were, Busan-side. Swore he'd prove it to me. I believed him."

"Big joke on you, for sure," Sonny says seriously. Then he laughs, sits up. "Got some inspiration, Mistah Prentice. Mistah Kim, he staying in tonight with girlfriend. I got the night off. What say you, me, we go get laid? I know this one place, really great."

Sonny hasn't driven more than a half a klick from Kim's when I feel all wrong. I do not want to do this. I cannot do it.

"I've changed my mind, Sonny. No offense, but think we could just go back to Mister Kim's? That be okay with you?"

He looks long at me, something like relief in those dark hard black eyes. "You sure? I make promise, I always keep it."

"I believe that. But I'd be grateful if we gave this one a miss."

"Okay, then," Sonny says, hanging a sudden U-turn that barely misses causing a multicar crash. He is glad to be rid of an obligation he wasn't keen on; he starts humming as we head back toward Kim's, and pretty soon he's cheerfully singing *"Lord lord, lord lord . . . All over the world . . . all over the world . . ."*

"John Lee Hooker addict!" I say. "Who would've thought that?"

Sonny bobs his head, grins. I know which type for sure: he's a little embarrassed I've discovered a secret of his, almost as if it's some kind of vice. "Got every CD the man ever made," he says. "Listen a lot, never make me sad. Why they call music like that 'blues,' Terry? Don't blue me."

"Just the name of a style, tunes all based on three chords," I say, very aware and pleased with his form of addressing me. Good sign. "Lot of 'em are pure love songs. Sad-sounding, if you're in a certain mood. But they got a happy side: the world's rich with women, and there's always a chance you'll get together with a good one."

"Damn straight. Where we be without good women?"

"Wishing we'd never been born," I say. "Lucky for us, we never would be born, without women in the world."

"Some kinda philosopher, that's you for sure. Maybe you oughta change jobs, write some books."

"What? There's too much bullshit all over as it is. And you know you can't believe anything you read. You gotta know the man that's telling the tale, trust him, and hear it from his mouth."

"Ah. Maybe that's why I like John Lee very much. Me, I don't believe he bullshitin' one bit."

"Doesn't even know the meaning of the word," I say.

Pretty soon we pull into Mister Kim's compound, Sonny just waving at the Lee or Park or Lee stationed at the gate. But he doesn't turn off the engine, even after I've climbed out.

I lean back in. "You're not coming? You got someplace else you need to be?"

"Oh yeah, Terry. Home," Sonny says. "Any night, any day I'm off duty, I go home. See my wife, my little boy. Good woman I got. My little boy, he something very special. Very fine son. Pretty soon, very fine daughter, too. Six, eight weeks only, she pop out. My wife, she's patient. Me, I can't wait to see her."

"Hey, good luck," I say, shutting the car door. But Sonny doesn't pull away. Instead, he leans over to the open passenger window, motions me close. "Still early, Terry. Maybe you like to come see my little boy? Meet my wife?" he says.

At that moment, there's nothing I'd like more.

Sonny lives in a new middle-class high-rise not ten minutes from Kim's compound. The moment he swings open his apartment door, a whirling dervish about three feet tall with arms and legs thin as sticks comes hurtling across the living room and leaps up into his father's arms. He's bright-eyed, piping rapid Korean I can't follow. Sonny just beams at the boy, then hoists him onto his shoulders. A pleasant-looking woman, maybe late twenties and as pregnant as can be, waddles out of what must be the kitchen, wearing the broadest grin. Which narrows, turns shy when she spots me. Sonny walks over to her, the boy still on his shoulders, kisses her on the cheek, murmurs something in Korean. She nods, and her smile regains most of its radiance. She bows to me, goes back to the kitchen.

"They don't speak any American," Sonny says, gesturing toward an easy chair, inviting me to sit. He slips down on the sofa, switches the boy from shoulder to lap. The kid keeps stealing glances at me, then turning to Sonny and piping a few words, as if I'm a great curiosity. Which I guess I am. Sonny's tone is so gentle and patient when he replies to what are obviously questions. It's hard for a moment to reconcile the hard-eyed heavy I know with this obviously doting father.

"Tell you something, man," Sonny says. "Wish to God I learn another trade when I was young. 'Cause this"—he makes a sweeping gesture that seems to take in his son, his wife, the neat-as-a-pin apartment—"this is all the world, for me."

"That's the problem. They get us when we're too young and too stupid."

"Hunh. Exactly right," Sonny says. "Okay for some people, they born to it or something. Like that animal Mistah Boy. But big problem, if sometime you see better way, right way to live. I gotta work very, very hard to be somebody else, have this kind of life."

Sonny's wife returns bearing a tray with two bottles of beer and a dozen little bowls of Korean snacks I can't ID. She giggles a little when I say "Thank you very much, Missus Park" in my fractured Korean, then gingerly eases herself onto the sofa, one hand cradling her enormous belly. The boy slips off Sonny's lap, snuggles up between his parents. She ruffles his straight black hair, then gives Sonny a look of complete trust and adoration, which he returns.

A look I've never shared with anyone.

And suddenly I have a flickering image of Nadya and me, in a peaceful home with a child, gazing at each other in that same way. Fucking pipe dream, I know that. But the idea lingers anyway.

I don't overstay, I feel like an intruder whose presense is soiling something delicate and fine. We chat a bit about the boy and the baby to come, Sonny translating. The boy's curiosity eventually gets the better of caution, because he comes over to me, starts talking, touching my hand, trying to bend my fingers to show me how strong he is. Sonny and his wife laugh, a true couple.

When I've finished my beer, made some polite sounds to Missus Park, given the boy a good handshake, Sonny drives me back to Kim's. We don't talk much; he seems to be in some quiet state of grace.

"That was great. Thank you," I say when we stop in Kim's circular drive. "Get home safe, man."

"You betcha," he replies.

Then I shut the car door, watch Sonny pull away. And wonder, just for an instant, if I'll ever have such a place to go.

twenty-four

SAME HYUNDAI, SAME STONE-FACED DRIVER, SAME—THOUGH I CAN'T be sure about the exact route—trip to the Lotte next afternoon. Mister Kim left early for his corporate HQ, Sonny's either with him or at home enjoying a day off. Nadya, same proprietary air, waiting for me in the lobby. She smiles in that way I suddenly realize I'd miss terribly if she ever stopped giving it to me.

Allison's another small shock when I see her in the spook suite. She's deliberately scruffy, hair only finger-combed and yanked into that ponytail, pilled old sweater, patched jeans, hiking boots scarred and dirty. She looks like one of those so-serious Dutch girls backpacking their way through parts of the world they oughtn't even dream of going, not if they knew shit about what could happen to them—or had enough imagination to consider it.

"Uh, they actually let you in the lobby, dressed like that?" I say.

"Skip the lame jokes, Terry," she says, crisp and professional. There's no sign I can recognize that she's pissed over the near fiasco of yesterday, the face-off with Westley she had to've had, the diplomatic visit to Kim later. But she's not the loose, easygoing Allison I like, either. "Let's just get down to it."

Rob's on one of the sofas. Nadya sits on the other. I join her. Allison keeps standing.

"Right, the gang's all here. So let's run through this trip one more time, just to be sure we're all on the same page," she says. "Rob stays here for the duration. Are you all linked, Rob?"

"Yeah. I've established secure communications with our help on the ground in Vlad and Pyongyang. I ran four test messages with each. No problems. I'll run another tonight, and another tomorrow."

"Good. I'll send you a retest from Vlad tomorrow," Allison says. "Your arrangements, Nadya?"

"Arranged. Mister Kim has his usual suite at the Best Eastern Hyundai, on Semenovskaya Street. Sonny will camp in it. Terry's in an adjoining room on one side, and Kim's numbers man, old Mister Yoon, and his assistant have a suite on the other. I'm in a single on the floor above. Directly above."

"Fine," Allison says.

"On arrival, they'll all dawdle in one of the restaurants, Terry and Sonny at the bar, Kim and Yoon at a table. I check in alone, sweep their rooms before they go up, mike Kim's suite. That properly done, I signal Rob, he confirms the link. Then I go down, do my hooker act on Terry."

"Good. If you don't get hit on by our Russki slut, Terry, if she just walks right by like you don't exist, you tell Sonny to get Kim out of there," Allison says. "You do not, remember, speak or understand Russian. If she stops, starts flirting with you in broken English, you let Sonny know it's okay to take Kim to the suite. After they've gone up, you take Nadya to your room. I've explained all this to Kim. Kim's on board. Please arrange an 'all clear' signal with Sonny. A subtle one."

"Will do," I say. "Where'll you be in all this?"

"Moving. A different place each night. But I will be close by always."

"And the dinner with the generals?" I ask.

"Unfortunately, we have to let them arrange that. We don't know where yet. It will definitely be someplace very good, which means very public. We'll know exactly where some hours before, which will give Nadya time to check the place out. You follow Sonny's lead on how to handle security going to, during, and coming back from the dinner. It's important there's no deviation from Kim's normal Vlad pattern. He's got to behave as he's behaved on every previous trip, clear?"

"That bit sounds insecure," I say.

"It has to be. But I'll be near with Carlos. Out of sight to you, but everything will be on our screen. Nadya will be close, too. And you've got the Olympus, the cell phone, right?"

"What cell?" Rob says. "There's nothing in the communications plan about Terry carrying a cell."

"I decided, Rob, it would be a good idea. Just as backup, close quarters," Allison says, voice even but brisk.

"Hell, if he's walking around with it on, his location can be triangulated. Not good," Rob says.

"Only by someone with equipment like yours, who also happens to be looking for him, and who also happens to know the number," Allison says. "Nobody is likely to be looking for him. And it'd fail, anyway. The cell is brand new, no calls made, none received. Nobody knows the number but me. So, as you well know, no triangulation."

That shuts Rob up, but he shifts his position slightly, tenses a little. I know what it is: he hates little surprises like this. Tough shit, pal, I'm thinking. Need-to-know only, and you, not me, didn't have the need this time.

"Anything else?" Allison asks.

"The meet? The exchange?" I ask.

"We won't know that for sure until after the dinner. We'll be flexible. Since it's a small item, there will be no need for skulking around, midnight meet in some waterfront warehouse or anything—as you're no doubt used to and comfortable with. Our generals wouldn't want that any more than we would. Kim will ask for something semipublic, they won't go for it, he'll suggest his suite. I think they'll agree."

"If they don't?"

"We're flexible, as I said, Terry. Carlos and I and Nadya will be in the shadows anywhere Kim goes. It's in the generals' self-interest to do this straight, quick, and clean. And I've got an asset watching their backs, ready to interdict if they've got a local threat behind them. We're covered all around."

Now would be the time for Nadya to say something smart-ass, lighten everything up, the way she always does. She doesn't. She avoids looking back when I try to catch her eye.

"Okay, then," Allison says, "I'm flying out in a few hours, commercial, as per plan. Carlos's ship docks tomorrow. Nadya and Terry go on Kim's plane day after tomorrow, Nadya peels off at the airport. Next time you see her, Terry, she'll be all over you in the Hyundai bar, offering you a special rate to get laid. Sound good?"

"Depends on the rate, and what it includes," I say.

"Oh, the works. You know those Natashas."

Do I? Seems not. Back at Kim's, after I'm sure Allison has gone to catch her flight, I phone Nadya, suggest dinner. She teases around, but she's flat, halfhearted about it, and finally begs off. Maybe tomorrow, she says. But she doesn't say what the maybe might be.

Okay, I figure, we're really on the job now, fun's over, she's behaving professionally. Normal, natural, and about time. After all, she isn't some half-crazed SEAL, juked on adrenaline, ever ready to rock 'n' roll. She knows she's heading into something serious, wants to get herself clear and concentrated, not play. That's what the rational part of my brain transmits, accepts. The more primitive part, where instincts reside, lights up a little, signals something's off, something's not quite as it should be.

Decide I'll ignore it: the light's dim, the signal weak.

And I have forgotten it, though I'm still disappointed and actually missing the girl, when Sonny appears in the staff lounge after dinner. I give him a detailed briefing of the meeting in the spook suite, all the arrangements. He seems satisfied, even appears to admire the thoroughness of Allison's tactical dispositions.

"Hunh. Good idea, some guy on the Russkis' backs. Good idea, exchange in Mistah Kim's suite. Nobody fool with us there. Dinner, I think, no worries. What we gotta watch is moving from hotel to airport after exchange. Anybody want to hit us, they do it then."

"That's when I'd strike, if I was on the other team," I say.

"How you do it, if you a bad guy?"

"Three-car block, somewhere where the airport road leaves the city, enters the suburbs. Have to see the route to be sure, but I'd pick a place where traffic's pretty thin, maybe an exit ramp. One car in front of Kim's stops, two others come up fast, bump his butt and block a turn. Very close, cars touching. Quick snatch, no shooting unless Kim's guys start it. Gone in thirty seconds."

"I think Mistah Kim's guys see anything like that coming, they shoot the shit out of the front blocker, drive real fast around it, and make it to airport okay."

"Sounds like a plan," I say. "One thing. Allison says there's got to be no deviation from Mister Kim's ordinary behavior and methods. *I'm* a deviation. How do we handle that?"

"Two men, always. Me and one of my guys. Two this time, you just a new guy, no big deal."

"So how do we behave?"

"Kind of disappear, you know? Never real close to Mistah Kim. At dinner, we stand at bar, sit at a separate table. At meeting, we're like statues. Don't move, don't talk, don't stare. Act like we don't understand shit. Usually there's a couple of Russkis, acting just like that. Never make eye contact, pretend they don't exist. You sense anything about to happen, you let me know before you act, right? Same-

same for me. We make any moves, we move together, understand?"

"Sure. No problem." And that's half-true. I'll team with Sonny, unless my cell vibrates and Allison gives me a word. Then I'll move so fast it'll be over before Sonny or anyone else can blink twice.

It's what might happen after I'm done, what Sonny might try if he doesn't like it, that troubles me a little. Allison's factored that into the plan, for sure. Which means Allison reckons I'm expendable.

Nothing personal. Just business. Right, Allison? What asshole dreamed up that rationalization? Why do assholes like me go into situations, knowing that's the twisted ethic? Answer: because we think we're so good, so deadly, that nobody can take us down.

Never shows up in any postmortem: inflated ego as cause of death. The actual physical agent—bullet, knife, whatever—never would have found its mark if our fucked delusions hadn't led us into the kill zone in the first place.

Allison and her kind know this, they count on it. I liked her better when she acted as if she had scruples, when she was still pretending—back in D.C., back in California—that I wasn't just a tool she needed to do one thing and would leave behind without thinking twice after the thing was done.

Wonder if she ever worries I realize that? She sure didn't bother acting or pretending today. Wonder if she ever considers I might not dig it, might really escape and evade, then come hard after her?

She should be afraid.

If she isn't, she knows things I never will.

Fine clear morning, crisp air. Busan doesn't look too bad on the way to the airport, from behind the tinted glass of one of Kim's Lincolns. I've seen much worse. ROKs with Daewoos at the gate don't hesitate, just wave our convoy through that single gate to the private aviation sector. A Gulfstream IV with that little Korean magic circle painted on its tail is warming up outside the hangar. The 747 is inside, asleep.

"Oh, he only uses the big one for longish hauls," Nadya says, walking up to me once we're out of the cars and on the tarmac. We didn't get together, didn't even speak, on the single day we could have, but she seems close to her usual cheerful, mocking self. "The big one's for Singapore, Bangalore, Kuala Lumpor, Guangzhou, all the faraway places where our Mister Kim has assembly plants or factories or offices."

"Sure," I say.

"Vlad's a shortish haul, relative to those. Anyway, Mister Kim doesn't consider the airport there adequate for his 747. Something about runway length, careless air traffic controllers, poor ground crews," she chatters on.

I watch Kim and Yoon, his numbers man, head up the gangway into the Gulfstream. Trailing Yoon is a stranger, tall Korean in maybe his late twenties carrying a big aluminum Halliburton.

"So who's the new guy? Baggage handler?" I ask.

"Oh, that's Tommy. Some kind of MIT genius, a wizard with computers. Whatever you do, don't go near that case of his. He has guard-dog reflexes about that case," Nadya says.

"What's so special about a laptop?"

"It's Tommy's special laptop. He never lets anyone around it. Not even Mister Kim," Nadya says. "NEC's most powerful model. But Tommy, I'm told, has tweaked and supertuned it. Way beyond anything that comes from the factory. MIT Media Lab special. That's why he's so proprietary."

"Don't see any need for a guy like that and his gear. On a simple merchandise purchase."

"Ah, think chemist doing a purity test on a cocaine buy," Nadya says, then walks to the gangway, goes on up.

Damn! The item the Russians are selling is computer-related. Hardware of some type? Software's more likely. I'm racing through the thousands of possibilities when Sonny waves me over, we board the Gulfstream. Soon as we're in, the little Japanese flight attendant—she has that lifeless porcelain-doll face, but I can't be certain she's the same one we've flown with before—levers the door shut, bows, points toward some empty seats.

Sonny and I sit, buckle up. The setup's like Kim's U.S. Gulfstream: no rows, just a lounge with big leather chairs. Kim, Yoon, and the wizard are at the far end, facing forward. Nadya's a couple of seats forward, her back to the portholes. Sonny and I will be flying backward. Doesn't bother me, though Sonny'd prefer another arrangement, judging from the way he fidgets.

"Comfortable, Mister Prentice?" Kim calls. "Looking foward to the trip?"

"Absolutely, Mister Kim," I say.

"Your first visit to Vladivostok, I believe?"

"Yessir, it will be."

"Well, to be frank, it is one of those places that could be pleasant, should be interesting at least, but manages to be neither. In fact, it's pretty damned nasty."

This draws smiles from Yoon, Nadya and Sonny.

"But, then, we can't always choose our venues in business," Kim says. "Or with whom we do business, regrettably."

"I understand, sir," I say. "In my position, though, unpleasant, uninteresting, and nasty are actually an advantage."

"How is that, Mister Prentice?"

"Encourages total concentration, total focus on my particular task," I say. And maybe pushing it a little, I add: "Also provides an ideal environment for judicious application of my particular skills."

No reaction for a moment. I have gone too far.

Then Kim laughs, and everybody else smiles. "Very aptly put, Mister Prentice. Truthful, too, I imagine," he says. "I'm very much hoping, however, that you won't have to apply any of your particular skills on this trip."

"I'm sure it won't be necessary, sir."

twenty-five

VLAD. FADED NORTHERN COLORS IN THIN NORTHERN LIGHT. RUST-streaked steel, mold-stained concrete, cracked bricks and pitted mortar, peeling paint.

It could have been beautiful. Maybe it was once, little more than a century ago, when energy and money began turning a frontier outpost into a permanent city, rising on low, terraced hills from a fan of bays and inlets ribbed by peninsulas.

I can see this as we make our approach, angling in from the seaward side. The heart of the town is compact, buildings of three, maybe five stories, lots of decorative work around windows and entrances, reminds me a lot of places I've seen in old Austrian parts of Central Europe, down to the pastel stucco facades. But gaps have been torn in the rows, featureless concrete boxes crammed in. Also a lot of new work rising here and there, international corporate style: steel and glass. The working harbor—wharves, cranes, warehouses, a web of railroad tracks—is the usual wasteland. And so is everything surrounding the old center. Hard-worn blocks of classic Stalinist-style apartment slabs, a monotony of poured-concrete warrrens nine to twelve floors high, and more still being added, probably using fifty-year-old blueprints.

I look away and catch Nadya's eye as the Gulfstream banks and drops. She makes a sour face, points with her thumb toward the porthole. We're passing fast over a huge, bleak, nearly deserted square. There's a monumental bronze statue in the middle, the figure's limbs too heavy, awkward. One very tall monolith flanks one edge of the square, dominating the smaller, older buildings around the other three sides.

"Square of the Fighters for the Soviet Power in the Far East," Nadya says when I look back.

"Is that a leftover slogan? Too ridiculous to be anything else," I say.

"The name," Nadya says. "Even now. The ugly white box is the government building. People call it the White House."

"Gimme a break," I say.

"Well, this is still Russia, Terry, not one of the independents like the Baltic states or Kazakhstan. There is one rather large difference now, though."

"What's that?"

"People here can laugh at such names without fearing arrest for slandering the state." Nadya smiles.

"People here can't get arrested for nothing," Sonny offers. "Any kinda crime you like, here you can do it. Police? Hunh. Criminals are laughing, damn straight, 'cause nobody knows who's a crook and who's a cop. Both behave same."

I'd thought Kim was absorbed in quiet discussion with Yoon and the wizard, but apparently he's aware of us. "Very different from Busan, isn't that right, Mister Park?" he says.

"Good order in Busan, Mistah Kim. Everything top-class. Everything kept clean. New subways, big highways. And no street crime," Sonny says.

"Exactly. It really makes you wonder about the Russians. How on earth did they become a superpower, develop a nuclear arsenal, orbit space stations?" Kim shakes his head, looks at me. "I'm not referring to the crime problem, of course, Mister Prentice. That's a natural corollary of the collapse of any police state. It takes a while for order to reassert itself in a positive way. No, you'll see what I mean when we're on the ground."

"How so, sir?"

"All the best new buildings, all the decent reconstructions and renovations of the old ones, were done by Korean, Chinese, and Italian construction workers, financed by foreign corporations setting up to do business here. Not by the Russians. Everything shoddy, shabby, recently made but already deteriorating, you can be sure it was done by Russians. You don't find that careless sloth in Korea, any more than you do in Japan or Singapore. And that's why I often wonder about missiles and space stations."

"And that is the prime reason there is no more Soviet Union," Nadya says. A Korean of Kim's father's generation would bristle at a woman asserting herself, but Kim doesn't seem to mind at all. He seems to like it.

"The Soviets spent all their money on weapons tech, employed all their best minds on military matters, and rewarded them handsomely, by their standards," Nadya says. "It drove the state bankrupt, being so single-minded, so paranoid. Moscow did not believe in tears. Nor in dangerously wired electrical systems in cheap apartment blocks, faulty plumbing and heating systems, inadequate food supplies, any of that. Because the *nomenklatura* never had to endure any of that. No wonder the people got fed up, restless, and slipped the leash soon as it loosened a little."

"I believe that's correct," Kim says. "But, you know, I think there's also something self-destructive in the Russian soul. An inheritance of history, nothing to do with ethnicity or genetics."

"They do often seem that way, don't they?" Nadya says. Is there more than a little irony in her voice? Kim doesn't acknowledge it.

"Yes. That's why they trouble me," he says. "I'd much rather deal with the Chinese. They're devious and duplicitous, of course. But self-interest, self-preservation is always paramount. They never act self-destructively when thwarted. Russians? You can't be so sure."

"In those specific terms, our special Russians are quite sinicized, I'm sure, Mister Kim," Nadya says. "Love themselves madly, the generals do. Self-detonation would never cross their greedy little minds. Nor are they candidates for spontaneous combustion."

Kim laughs. "Thank you for the trenchant analysis, Doctor Zheryova. You have very effectively put me and my generalizations in their place."

"Not by design, Mister Kim."

"But properly, nevertheless, Doctor. I'm aware I have tendencies toward old Korean insularity."

First time I've heard Nadya's last name. False as her first, for sure. But the "doctor" bit, that could be right. Probably she does have a Ph.D. Worked hard to earn it, then winds up going around posing as an expensive prostitute in shitholes like Vlad. But that's just this op, and my own insularity. No doubt she poses as other things, at other levels in other places I'll never know about.

The Best Eastern Hyundai isn't the Lotte. The amenities are international standard, so's the management and desk staff, but the rest of the help is all local: deliberately slow, unsmiling, sullen. Fuck 'em. What I'm thinking about, sitting at the bar having a beer with Sonny, what's pushed the computer question out of mind, is the fifty klicks between the hotel and the airport. An hour and a half, that's how long it took the two new Lada limos that apparently belong to Kim's small Vlad branch office to get us to the hotel, even though the drivers, resident Koreans, drove aggressively, almost suicidally.

The road's just a piece of shit nobody could navigate faster. Narrow, narrow-shouldered, potholed, and half-blocked here and there by heavy equipment generally used to repair and improve highways, but looking like it's simply been abandoned there, nobody at all working. Major cramp in our style, if we have to move quick and slick for the plane. Somebody better have a fallback plan. A chopper'd be best, but I'm not counting on one.

Nadya, at least, is smooth as a mink. Within twenty minutes after arrival, max, I feel her slink up next to me, warm and sweet-smelling, her rooms sweep obviously accomplished. She's so good. Nobody—not even a professional watcher—would suppose for a minute she was anything but the real thing: a Russian working girl plying her trade in a foreigners' hotel. Just the right mix of hard whore calculation and seduction in her chat and laugh. The perfect calibration of makeup and clothes, down to the shade of red lacquer on the fake nails she's glued over her real ones. I nod to Sonny: good to go. He drains his beer, walks over to the table where Kim, old Yoon, and Tommy the Wizard are sitting, murmurs to Kim, them follows them to the elevator.

"Dollars," I say to Irena, as Nadya's calling herself at the moment for the benefit of any long ears in the vicinity.

"*Nyet, nyet.* Euros only," she insists, but trailing her fingers down my arm, eyes bright and inviting. We engage in a little more friendly negotiation. Maybe three minutes after Kim and company have left, she puts on her biggest smile, says, "*Da. Da.* Is okay." We go up to my room.

"Christ!" she says, once we're inside, pulling off one false eyelash set. "Feel like such a bloody tart, done up like this."

"Well, you look a perfect bloody tart," I say. "You go down to the bar alone, little Jap *sararimen* in blue suits will be patting Irena's sweet ass, offering many, many yen for your services."

"Bloody nuisance, that. Well, I'm dragging you with me as much as I can, since I have to stay done up like this," she says. "Ouch. Bloody underwire push-up bras! I'd like to torture the man who invented them."

"Think his name was Howard Hughes. And he's already dead." I say.

"Strange fact for you to know, Terry. Or are you having me on?"

"What do you think?"

"Well . . . I think perhaps our Terry, crypto-clandestine warrior, has a bit of a kinky flip side. Dress up in women's clothing sometimes, do we, love? Ever wear, say, pantyhose, Terry?"

"Sure. Black nylon."

"Balls." Nadya snorts.

"Exactly. Helps keep those snug and warm, as well as legs. We all wore pantyhose under our camo. Gets real cold at night in the desert."

Nadya tilts her head, regards me with her slightly canted eyes. Big doubts visible in them. Then she replaces the eyelash set. "What did we agree on, darling, down at the bar?"

"I believe you said, 'Super time, you can't believe.' Or something to that effect."

"Ah, light moment's over, Terry. Work, remember? Did I say thirty minutes? An hour?"

"Thirty."

"Then that means"—she looks at her wristwatch—"I can leave in twenty-seven. I'll go up to my room, contact Allison, see if she's located the dinner spot. You go over to Kim's, check in with Sonny, familiarize yourself with the layout. Kim's suite is quite clean, except for my mike. And don't dare make any snide remarks about the delicious Irena to Sonny or anyone else. You will pay dearly for them later, I promise."

"Wouldn't dream of it, Irena. Work, remember?"

"Stay with Kim for an hour. Then meet me back here."

"How'll you get in?"

She holds up a thin plastic wafer. "I believe you've seen me use one of these before. You do remember, don't you?"

"Vaguely. But wait a minute, wasn't it Allison who broke into my room at the airport hotel that night? And kind of assaulted me?"

"Oh bugger off, you delinquent." Then she laughs. "Well, at least you're not one of those tensed-up types. Hell to work with, they are. I much prefer relaxed."

"Relaxed, but very, very alert, Doctor Zheryova. Count on it."

"Absolutely. Oh, just as point of fact, that doctorate is the only true thing in my current persona."

"I believe it," I say. "I am wondering, though, why you bother to mention it?"

"It is a bit silly of me, I suppose. But having one true thing out in the open seems to help me with my various impersonations. An aide-mémoire, so to speak? So I don't forget completely who I actually am?"

"I try to forget entirely. Helps on the job, helps you endure the first few sessions of hostile interrogation, if you fuck up."

"The Company preaches a different tactic," Nadya says. "Don't get—"

"Caught. I know. Very catchy. But operationally realistic? Desk warriors' dream, only."

"Why can't you be more cynical, Terry? It's so great for morale."

"Yours seems fine to me. One of the relaxed ones. It is hell to work with those tense types. Their trigger-pull's too light, tend to go off under too little pressure. ADs."

"Yet another baffling idiom."

"Accidental discharge," I say. "Firearms term. Think of it as, oh, premature ejaculation. But instead of just being embarrassing for one party and frustrating for the other, it's goddamn dangerous."

She laughs, really laughs. "Lovely metaphor, Terry. Think I'll incorporate it into my personal vocabulary."

"For any Rob types you might intersect with in your private life?"

"Rob?"

"The boy definitely has AD tendencies. Easy enough to see. Tightens up too much, too fast. Can't stay cool, gets testy and aggressive when he should be chill. Bet he's an AD-er."

"That's it? Quite a relief. For a moment there I thought you were going to share a rather sordid personal experience. Like your pantyhose fetish."

"If I had that particular secret, I'd certainly keep it secret. From you especially."

"Because we've, ah, intersected, and you'd hate to lose my good opinion?"

"Nah. Because you're maliciously mischievous. You'd run around telling anybody and everybody—'Hard to credit, but our Terry's a poofter. Shocking, isn't it? But true. Told me so himself.' "

"I never would," Nadya protests. "On the other hand, that would create wonderful cover. If I decided it might be lovely to intersect with you again. I am leaning that way rather strongly."

"Ah, go cruise the bar, Irena. Make a few hundred euros. You're wasting your time here."

"Righty-o. Time I intersected with Allison. God, I do hope she's not in AD mode."

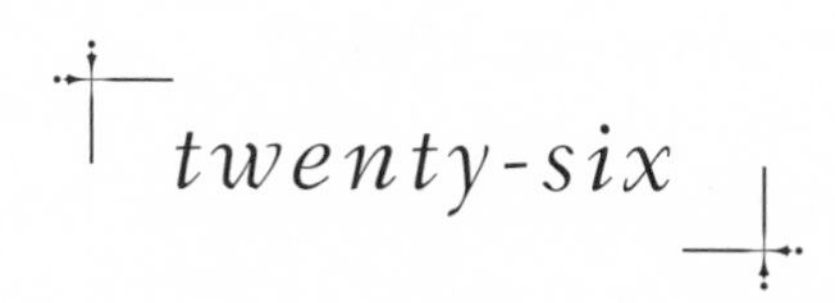

twenty-six

"YOU WILL BE DINING AT THE VERSAILLES HOTEL," NADYA SAYS. SHE'S lounging on my bed when I return from Mister Kim's suite.

This is good, she tells me. Pretty turn-of-the-century building, burned out once years ago, luxury renovation in 1995. On the corner of Svetlanskaya Street, downtown. Easy access, egress. Just four stories and forty rooms. But always busy: locals with money like to take their mistresses there for assignations, and there's a casino as well. The restaurant has two small private rooms for parties of eight or more. We've got one.

"I'm going down there presently, do a bit of a recce," she says. "Should I find anything dicey, I'll be back. If all's nice, perhaps I'll have an early dinner, then try my luck at the casino while you dine. You may not see me until after, in that case."

"Right here? Same general arrangement would suit me."

"Right here, but no arrangement, just a debrief."

"Double meaning in that?"

"Well, of course, darling. You talk, I listen. By the bye, my generals will be ringing Kim in about an hour, to tell him the where and when. Best if you don't let on you knew in advance."

So nothing Sonny tells me is news when I'm called back to Mister Kim's suite about a half hour before we're due to leave, though I act as if it is. I'm packing, per standard, also carrying my briefcase. Tommy the Wizard's staying home with his. Room-service dinner on his agenda, I suppose.

There's a soft breeze, damp and salty, rising up when we step outside the hotel. But it's got teeth. The chill goes right through my black cashmere overcoat. Vlad's a so-called warm-water port, doesn't lock up with ice in winter. But it is late October—Christ, hard to believe where the months have gone. It does get frigid at this latitude, and I'm used to more serious protection than a fine-wool business suit and topcoat in chilly weather.

We move in just one of Kim's Lada limos, me up front, and Mister Kim in the back between Sonny and old Yoon. No cramping: the rear bench in these relics is wide as a fifties Cadillac. The second Lada tails us, nobody in it but the driver. It won't park at the Versailles, but slow-circle the short block around the hotel all during dinner. Sonny's touch.

"We come out, flat tire or something"—he'd grinned when he'd told me—"don't have to worry about finding no cab, right, Mistah Prentice? Me, I hate hanging out with my butt in the cold, trying to wave down taxi."

"Never a good idea to depend on getting a cab when you gotta go," I'd said. "Hunh," he'd said.

Sonny and I are in sync. We stay that way, flank rear of Kim and Yoon when we enter the Versailles. A Chinese majordomo in a tux leads us through a tall arched doorway off the lobby, past the entrance to the casino room and into the restaurant. We don't stand out at all. Every big spender in the place has a heavy close to his side, and not one seems as concerned as Kim that his muscle look executive. The heavies are as blatant as the swarms of Natashas trying to make their dime.

The place is Russian luxe: too much red brocade, too much red velvet, too many gold fringes and tassels, too much crystal chandelier hanging from the elaborate plasterwork of the ceiling. Judging from the dull glint, the crystals are more likely molded plastic than cut glass. Heavy red-brocade drapes, not doors, screen the private room, which looks like the main dining room scaled down. There's a fairly large table set for four in the center; I recognize Bolgakov and Tchitcherine standing before it like proper hosts, open arms and big smiles for Kim and Yoon. I slide off, following Sonny, to a smaller table against one wall, where two other Russians are standing. Cheap suits, bad shoes. No open arms, no smiling. The blond one risks a quick glance at my briefcase. I see one rather like it on the floor near his chair. Once the generals and Kim and Yoon have been seated, we four nod and sit, too. The blond Russian shifts the position of his briefcase slightly with his foot.

"New guy," he mutters to his skinheaded partner, in Russian. "Sure as hell isn't a slant. I wonder where they brought him in from? Darkie, like some damned Chechen."

"Excuse me, what are you?" the skinhead says to me.

I look at him blankly. "Sorry, pal, I only speak English," I say.

"Must be British or Canadian," the questioner says to his partner.

"They got darkies? You're shitting me."

"Sure, up north, Scots or something. Immigrants also. In Canada, immigrants and wild Indians. Bad as Chechens, both." He grins at me, says "Angliski? Ang-land?"

"Tried and true, mate," I say. "Russki? Commie dog?"

That brings a mean laugh from both of them. And ends any more attempts at conversation. Sonny manages to lean back slightly while the food we never ordered is served and we begin to eat. Sonny regards them steadily through those hard black slits of his. The Russians don't punish the vodka bottle on the table in the typical way, limiting their shots. After a while, the skinhead says to his partner, "The big slant, I think, is trying to frighten us."

"Oh, he scares me so much I'm maybe going to piss in my pants or something," the blond Russian says. "Damn fool. He know where he is?"

"They both can go to hell."

Ignorant thugs, and ignorable for now, I figure. I concentrate on what I can overhear from Kim's table. It's kind of alarming. Yoon's very rusty, or never was much good; his translation is bad. Well, slow and halting, anyway. Can't judge the accuracy, because he's putting it into Korean. Sonny can monitor that. I'll take the generals.

That gets easy quick, because Tchitch starts doing all the talking once the polite chitchat's finished. Life is good and it's a perfect world, he's happy to report. He and his esteemed partner have obtained precisely the product Mister Kim specified. Even better, not a secondhand Russian model or a Chinese knockoff. No indeed. Through a colleague who, until the unfortunate dissolution of the U.S.S.R. worked in East Germany and retains trusted contacts there, they have in hand the latest generation, absolutely state-of-the-art German version! Wonderful news, no? Tchitch beams.

Kim digests Yoon's translation, looking steadily at Tchitch. He permits himself a small smile, but his eyes are flat and the smile's almost the same as the one Sonny wears when he thinks he's hearing bullshit.

Bolgy scarcely looks up from his meal as Tchitch plunges on. A small change in the orginal proposal, almost beneath notice, has become necessary, regretfully. Our colleague was forced, by the quality of the product and certain additional costs and risks of obtaining it, to raise his price. We, feeling certain that Mister Kim would want only the very best, covered the increase out of our own pockets. We will, sad to say, require reimbursement.

Kim frowns slightly, snaps a question to Yoon, who says, "How much?"

Next to nothing, as a percentage of the original proposed cost, Tchitch says. Shall we say a new total of seven point five million?

Dollars or rubles? Stupid—these guys would never deal in rubles. So how big's the rip here? I wonder.

Kim listens to Yoon, shakes his head. Yoon says, "That is nearly a million more than the original price. Hardly a small percentage. A most unpleasant surprise."

For them as well . . . until they examined the merchandise, Tchitch says, getting oilier by the moment. Your clients will be overwhelmed when they see what you've brought them. This we guarantee.

Yoon, parroting Kim, says, "Our clients will be shocked at this change of terms. We will be deeply embarrassed to even suggest such an increase."

I understand your position, of course, Tchitch says. Please understand ours. We wished to provide you with the best in the world, because we are anxious to forge a long-term and mutually beneficial relationship with you. Regretfully, as I have said, the best proved more costly than any of us expected. It is, after all, a product with no price standard because it never appears in commercial markets. But because we are so confident your clients will be happy, and as a token of good faith toward a continuing relationship, we are prepared to absorb half of the increase, should your client, after examining the product, continue to insist on paying only the original price.

Kim remains quiet for some moments after this concession is explained. Then he has Yoon ask what guarantees exist that the generals will in fact absorb that half?

Because your reputation inspires trust, Mister Kim, and because we also possess a reputation with which you may not be fully aware, Tchitch says, the simplest guarantee: no payment of half the increase at the exchange. Simply keep the funds at your office here, and we will accept a note for it from you. When you have successfully sold the product to your clients at a price that meets your margin requirements, we ask only that you then instruct your office here to honor the note. That is how confident we are in the product. That is our confidence in you.

Kim ponders this, then has Yoon say they have an agreement in principle on those terms. But, naturally, the remainder of the original agreement stands intact: there will be no payment of any sort if the product fails the examination of our expert at the time of the exchange.

Tchitch smiles brilliantly, says he's absolutely confident the item will impress, even amaze the expert, and the deal with be concluded with complete mutual satisfaction.

But what the fuck is Tommy the Wizard going to test with his super-lap? I've been pondering this off and on from the moment Nadya said think of a chemist testing purity at a coke buy. What kind of computerware could possibly be worth $7.5 million? I don't know enough tech to take more than wild guesses at that.

The talk moves on to where and when the exhange will take place. Kim's suite is ruled out by mutual agreement; a bit too public for the generals, but more important, absolutely inadequate for proper testing of the product. Tchitch has a perfect location: a small office building, PrimorEx or something, half a block from the Versailles. Front company for the generals, newly renovated, wired by Japanese technicians for the latest highest-speed Internet access and other electronic conveniences.

I know Sonny's catching all of this in Yoon's translation, so half my mind goes back to the merchandise. Could there be any hardware so valuable that's small and portable? One man cannot carry a Cray. It has to be software, I decide. Military maybe, at that price. But Kim doesn't do military. And the Germans don't possess anything military worth having; their entire establishment, tanks to warplanes, is obsolete. Industrial, then? Heavy industry, metals? No, nothing special German there. Chemicals? Good possibility. Pharmaceuticals? Even better. New proprietary pharmaceuticals, thickly iced by German patents? Highest value, so highest probability. But I just don't know.

I snap to when I feel Sonny, next to me, rise from his chair. Blondie and the skinhead are standing already. I see Kim shaking hands with the generals in turn, see Tchitch usher them out like an unctuous maître d' who's just been lavishly tipped. Fall in with Sonny, flank rear of Kim and Yoon. Hear a laugh that sounds familiar as we pass the little casino. I see Nadya, leaning on the shoulder of a weasely little guy at the roulette wheel. His fingers linger too long when he slips a chip down her cleavage. Sonny's first out the front door, blocks it, scans right and left, then moves quickly to the Lada, opens the doors. Kim and Yoon slide in the back, followed by Sonny. I make a fast scan, slip in next to the driver.

The trailing Lada picks up our back before we've gone a hundred meters, stays at our back all the way to the Lotte.

Once he checks in on Tommy the Wizard, once we've tucked Mister Kim safely in, Sonny and I go down to the bar. There's a large party of *sararimen*, drunk already and likely to keep on until they pass out, raising a ruckus in Japanese. Sonny takes one look, picks a spot as far away from them as he can find, orders two beers.

Then he says, "This thing, day after tomorrow, what you think? Look okay to you?"

"About as good as it could. Those two dogs tonight, if they're the best the generals got, the generals ought to be nervous."

"Yeah, they nothing."

"And our backup is on the job."

"How you know that?"

"Saw Nadya in the casino on the way out. She was right there for the whole dinner."

"No shit?"

"Didn't see Allison or Carlos, but I'll bet they were within shooting distance of us."

"Ho! Pretty slick, damn straight. Maybe I had a wrong feeling about this before."

"Before we go into that PrimorEx place—what time was set?"

"Five-thirty, day after tomorrow. But Mistah Kim gotta call those guys around three that day, say it's still okay."

"Yeah, five-thirty. Well, that gives our crew a full day and full night to check and tape the place solid. Any tricky bits there, we'll know in advance. Shit, we'll probably have a floor plan of the place, every camera and other security measure marked. My feeling is we'll walk in, stare at that same pair of ugly Russkis while Tommy the Wizard tickles his keyboard, then walk out real relaxed. I'm loose."

"Most likely you exactly right. But I think I carry maybe six extra clips for my Uzis," Sonny says. "Case some fools try to mug us on the street afterward, some shit like that."

"Why, Irena! What a lovely surprise," I say, seeing Nadya on my bed exactly as I'd seen her that afternoon.

"Oh bugger off, you. Had a miserable evening," she almost snarls.

"What? Too many chips stuffed down your bra by a guy with greasy fingers?"

"Haven't a clue what you're going on about. I'm cross because I lost at vingt-et-un."

"A lot?"

"Over a thousand, dammit."

"Rubles. So what's that in real money? Maybe seventy-five dollars?"

"Doesn't matter how much. What matters is I hate losing. Especially when I'm cheating," she says, sitting up. "Now I'm tired as well as cross. So hurry up and tell me all, so I can go intersect with that bitch Allison and get some sleep."

"Bitch?"

"Well, she seemed rather in one of your AD modes this afternoon. I did not appreciate it one bit. She'd better be nicer tonight. Now give."

"In a minute," I say, taking off my suitcoat, draping it over a chair. Then I shuck the shoulder holster, loosen my tie, take a Coke from the frigibar, and lie down next to her, flat on my back.

"Minute's up, Prentice," she says. "I'm waiting."

I try a little imitation of Tchitcherine, in Russian, which is at least good enough to get her smiling. "Oh, they always pull that stunt," she says when I get to the price increase, the Tchitch concession. "How'd Kim take it?"

"About as gracefully as he could, I guess. Have the impression he doesn't give a damn, just looked stern and bargained a bit for face. He wants the item very badly, and very fast, so he can get the hell out of here. Or it seemed so to me."

"Very likely." She stretches. "And?"

I tell her it's a no-go on an exchange in Kim's suite. It's going to be at the PrimorEx building. Her reaction surprises me.

"Ah, the generals overreached themselves on that venture. They're assuming they'll have a going concern for some time to come," she says. "Better and better."

"How's that?"

"Oh, never mind. Just a thought. Main thing is, that building isn't very hard. It's actually better for us there than anyplace else would be."

"You want to clarify that for me?"

"No. Take it on faith. Now, when?"

"Day after tomorrow, five-thirty."

"Brilliant!"

"There's kind of a dissonance here, Nadya," I say. "We're doing a seven-point-five-million deal in the generals' lair, and you think that's brilliant?"

"Oh, relax, Terry darling. It's too complicated for a girl as weary as I am to explain just now. I will sometime. For the moment I'll just say the threat level is quite low in this arrangement."

"Okay. But isn't seven point five a hell of a lot for some software?"

A Cheshire smile. "Ah, figured that one out all on your own, did you? Bright boy, Terry. My one true love."

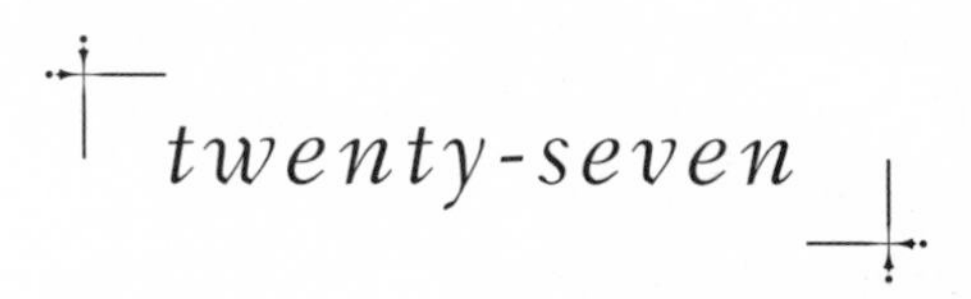

twenty-seven

SONNY COMES INTO MY ROOM EARLY NEXT AFTERNOON LUGGING A black hard-sider bigger than a carry-on and smaller than a suitcase. The bed squeaks when he drops the thing on it.

"Excuse me, Mistah Prentice. Mistah Kim, he got this little quirk. He don't like to watch what I gotta do," he says, popping the latches. I figure he's got all kinds of tools for mayhem inside. I don't get up from my chair, where I'm drinking a Coke, gazing idly out over Vlad. But I hear, as Sonny bends over his case, the familiar crisp riffling of banded stacks of bills. I can't believe it.

"Cash! You're doing a seven-point-five-million deal in fucking cash, man? That's insane. That's begging someone to rob you."

"Think I like this?" Sonny says. "Fucking Russkis, they still in the stone age, like some fellas in New Guinea. Everywhere else we go, even little places in Cambodia, Indonesia, we just plug in laptop and they watch while we make wire transfer. Takes about two minutes, not a dollar changes hands, just numbers move from one account to another.

"Russkis!" Sonny starts to spit, restrains himself. "They never heard of offshore accounts in Caymans, Bahamas, wherever. They don't believe all we gotta do is type in code and numbers, and millions go from Busan to wherever they want. Nah, they gotta see money, feel the bills, count 'em. Ignorance. So I gotta carry this thing to some meeting, waste time watching Russkis count. Feel like I'm carrying a big grenade with the pin already pulled."

"Yeah, well stay away from me, then. Jesus! Stateside, I've seen drug dealers still in their twenties, never even graduated high school, take wire transfers."

"You a long way from home of the free, land of the brave, Mistah Prentice. Like I tell you once before."

"No shit. But I'm learning. Now I understand why you were so damn nervous." Cash raises the possibility of a rip by about a couple hundred percent, minimum. Now I'm getting nervous. I feel like the stakes just red-lined, and I never saw it coming.

"Hunh," Sonny says. "Why you think I tell you I'm carrying six extra clips for my Uzis?"

"No choice? No other way?"

"Cash only way with fuckin' Russkis, Mistah Prentice."

I walk over, take a look at the case, watch Sonny's thick fingers riffling tight bundles of hundreds. The bills aren't green.

"What's this? Why not dollars?" I ask.

"Nobody out here takes hundred-dollar bills anymore, even stone-age Russkis," Sonny says. "These days, fifty-fifty chance any U.S. hundred made in North Korea. Government there, they got great counterfeiters. Use those fake hundreds to buy this, buy that. Fuckers buy too much, people find out they got paid funny money. So now, euros only. North Koreans haven't figured out how to make good euros. Yet."

Getting a fresh bad vibe here. Nobody ever got capped during a wire-transfer deal, as far as I know. Maybe sometime later, usually for cause. But at least not during it. Kill a client who just made an electronic transfer? No, better not. Maybe the transfer will invalidate or something, anything like that happens. Or maybe there'll somehow be a clear trail back to the hitters. Cash? Cash puts whack ideas into people's heads.

Pretty soon I'm almost unaware of Sonny's presense. That's a good sign; it means his particular signal is benign. I start to empty my mind, systematically. Get it clear, get it into combat mode, a state in which the cerebral idles in neutral while the honed reflexes and deep muscle memory embedded by years of training and action shift into high, take care of business all on their own.

I scarcely notice when Sonny finishes, goes back to Kim's suite. I'm about halfway to where I want to be when Nadya cards my lock with her magic wafer, slips in, starts chattering. She's still playing hooker, right down to the fishnet stockings.

Christ! What am I doing? I realize I've started way too early, which is maybe the dumbest thing you can do. Have to stop my process now, at about half-cock. The meet's twenty-four hours off. Best to go straight to condition one, cocked and locked, an hour or less before. Don't want to walk around being an AD about to happen. Like some jittery rookie. That cash surprise rattled me in ways it never should have. I know better than to react that way. What's wrong with me? Getting old? Getting scared?

Or maybe it's that something still won't shake down to any sort of sense. No matter how I figure, even factoring in market ignorance, the price will not click as a match to product value.

Nadya doesn't appear to read any of this. She takes my Coke bottle, drains what's left. "Well, I do feel somewhat recovered from last night's ordeal," she says. The first of her words that actually register meaning as I pull out of my distanced, distracted state.

"Sure. A good sleep usually does the job. Dream of me, maybe?"

"No! When I took off that damned bra, chips worth far more

than I lost at the card table fell out. Made an enormous profit! I fell asleep to the image of a lovely sable hat I might buy."

I laugh. "You on some kind of mood medication? Should you be? Because trying to ride with you is like being on a roller coaster."

"Fine one to talk, you are. One moment there's about a mile of dark emptiness behind your eyes, no Terry anywhere, and the next you're right up front."

Guess she did catch something when she first walked in. Need to divert her. But she makes another swerve.

"I have a few errands to run. Care to come along? It may well be your only chance to have a close look at lovely Vlad. Walking tour. Images for your memory book, that sort of thing."

"I don't keep that sort of thing. Never collect souvenirs, even mental ones. But I wouldn't mind getting out and about. Feeling pretty cooped."

We step out into a gray afternoon, high swept clouds, that devious breeze with teeth. Clears my head, though. Nadya brushes off a couple of taxi hustlers with some crisp invective that leaves them looking sulky. We go along Semenovskaya Street awhile, cut down to the main drag, Svetlanskaya Street. There's a stretch there where the luxe shops cluster, though you have to peer in to see what's on offer, since no retailers seem to believe in big display windows. Hardly worth the effort: imports, the same overpriced international brands, nominally Italian and French, you see in every Asian city with enough business visitors and new local money to support boutique-size operations.

"YSL, Valentino, Gucci Gucci Gucci, and Cardin everything," Nadya says. "Hard to believe people actually pay to be seen in such rubbish."

"No pride. Shocking."

"No taste is more like it. Simply some twisted notions of status."

"By the way, I've been meaning to ask whose fishnets you're wearing. Love the little rhinestone action around the ankles. YSL?"

"Ya ya ya, you yomp." She elbows me.

We head deeper into the city, which means toward the waterfront. The luxe shops give way real fast to purely local commerce, the buildings' maintenance levels decline: rust streaks from rain gutters on peeling stucco, windows that haven't been washed in months. Streets are crowded, Russian faces predominate. Stern, sour, sullen mainly. And alone. But there's lots of Koreans and Chinese walking in small tight groups, chatting and laughing.

Pretty grim, pretty shabby, most of it. But no worse, I guess, then some Rust Belt cities I've passed through—Gary, Indiana, maybe. Or North Philly. Shit, Detroit. Detroit's worse. Here, bright new Audis, BMWs, Mercs almost outnumber the old Ladas and hard-used Toyotas and Nissans clogging the streets.

"Where's all the German metal come from?" I ask.

"Certainly not from your friendly local dealer, you may be sure of that," Nadya says. "No such thing in Russia. These are all stolen in Western Europe, shipped east. Poland's the main entrepot."

"The what?"

"Oh, staging area? Very porous border, you see. Likewise the Polish-Russian. Small gratuities to the guards instead of valid bill of sale, title, and registration. All the new-money people—mafia, government, barely legal businessfolk—have to have their German car. Mark of status they can't seem to resist. And since the trade is a national conspiracy, no risk at all. Another little gratuity duly registers them legally here."

"So everybody's happy."

"Except the West Europe insurance companies. They're bloody furious at the losses. Costs 'em millions to reimburse the victimized owners. Who, being sensible burghers, have insured themselves to the hilt."

"Sounds like a beautiful example of the free-enterprise system working as it should. Exactly what you Washington cold warriors hoped would happen with Russia."

"Excuse me, but I was only starting middle school when the Cold War ended. Just a green girl. Hardly one of that superannuated crowd. Even Westley, old as he is, is a rather junior member."

Somewhere along the way I lose my back-bearings to the Hyundai. All I know is we're in a neighborhood where out-of-towners are seldom seem. I draw a few long looks. Overdressed, I suppose. Damned cashmere overcoat, Church's wing tips. Nadya's errands turn out to be just a weird shopping trip. No sable hat, for sure. Some small six-volt batteries and lengths of thin insulated wire in one place, duct tape and epoxy in another, a couple two-liter plastic jugs and an egg timer in a tiny housewares shop, a kilo of nails in a carpentry place, a little soldering iron and flux in an electrics hobby shop. A kilo of modeling clay at an art supplier's. Three strings of heavy piano wire at a musical-instrument place. Maybe fifty meters of braided nylon rope from a chandler's.

"All you need's some Semtex, or good fertilizer, and you could make yourself a suicide bomber with all this stuff," I say.

"Hardly the type, as you ought to know quite well, Terry," she says. "Just odds and ends for little art projects. I do conceptual constructions. But I doubt you'd know what they are."

"Generally fuzzy-headed little robots that take half a step, fall over, and whirr, right?" Like she has time for her hobby now.

"To the unschooled eye, that might be the vague impression."

We seem to have circumnavigated a small section of downtown Vlad, because all at once we emerge onto what must be the rattail of Svetlanskaya Street. It broadens, becomes more built-up, more trafficked as we move toward the Square of the Fighters for the Soviet Power in the Far East, a couple of klicks off; can't see the square, just the top half of the White House. It's not much past four yet, but street lights are starting to flick on here and there. Maybe half are on strike or something. The air's going blue, an early dusk. Pedestrians seem to be walking slightly faster, yet shop lights cast yellow rectangles on the gray concrete sidewalk. No storekeepers are shutting up, pulling down their steel shutters.

We walk on a few hundred meters. More and more people heading purposefully somewhere: home, dinner, an appointment, whatever. Nobody ever looks at other passersby here, nobody ever makes eye contact.

Don't know what the trigger is, but suddenly I've got the feeling.

"You strapped?" I ask Nadya.

"Pardon me?"

"Carrying," I say. "A weapon."

"Oh," she laughs. "Yet another of your colorful idioms, Terry. Yes. My usual, SIG 239."

"Do not use it."

"On what?"

"The car that's been trailing us for the last few blocks. Don't look around," I say. "And see what's coming down the hill? Christ, the mutts might as well wear big name tags: HELLO, I'M IVAN AND I'M A THUG."

"Mutts?"

"Two guys, a hundred meters up. Usual uniform: black watch caps, black leather jackets, black pants, black boots. Fucking idiots."

"Reckon they want people to know they're thugs, don't you?" Nadya says.

"Sure, intimidation factor. Could be more subtle about what they're up to right now, though."

"Which is?"

"Got us in a sandwich. If something starts, I'll take care of them. You watch the car. For Christ's sake do not use your tool unless whoever's in the car acts bad."

"I had no such intention, naturally."

They close on us. "Don't stop," I say to Nadya in loud English as they block us. We side-step, so do they. One asks Nadya for a light, waving a cigarette. Even as she reaches into her purse, the other says in Russian, "Foreigner? Got yourself a rich foreigner, baby. Good. We'll see how rich."

Nadya says the Russki equivalent of "Fuck off." Her guy laughs, my Ivan moves in close, lets me see the blade of a knife half-hidden in a big hand. They've clearly got ideas.

I don't wait. Spread my arms, say, "Let's tango, shorty." The Ivan, who's at least four inches taller and about twice as broad as me, reads that as an invitation to edge even closer, starts to reach for my pockets. Eyes follow hand. Perfect. Perfectly stupid.

Tensing every muscle from the backs of my thighs on up for maximum leverage, I head-butt the fuck, hear the satisfying crunch as the bridge of his nose fractures, splinters. He reels, both hands moving involuntarily to his nose, which is streaming blood like a faucet. It looks almost black in this light. I stay on him, two-knuckle lefts and rights slamming deep into his diaphragm. He doubles, gasping desperately, and as his head comes down my right knee comes up faster, thudding into his chin like a hammer, snapping his neck back. He goes down.

It's all so fast, a huge adrenaline rush turbocharging my moves. I spin to take down the guy on Nadya. But he's rolling on the sidewalk, rubbing his eyes and wailing. What? Then I see Nadya slip a small can of pepper spray back into her purse. There's a loud squeal of rubber on concrete as the tail car peels away. My Ivan's straining to rise to his hands and knees. I move to kick his lights out, but Nadya grabs my arm.

"Darling, this seems such a bad neighborhood," she says. "Don't you think it would be wise for us to leave? Rather quickly?"

It's weird. Where'd all the people go? How come cars don't

slow down to look, but accelerate hard instead? Hand still on my arm, Nadya leads me in a fast walk to the first side street we hit, then down a long alley. We come out on a street I don't recognize.

In short order, she's waved down a car. Most cars in Vlad are potential taxis, if you offer the right fare. Nadya makes a rapid negotiation with the driver of an old tan Lada. During the five-minute ride she composes herself—not that this seems necessary, since she's been calmer than I have. When we walk into the Hyundai lobby, she's got her big smile on, arm through mine, keeps the pose until we get inside my room.

I completely expect her to crash then. But I underestimate her. She's level, she's cool, she's behaving like a pro.

"You clear on what went down out there?" I say.

She nods. "Of course."

"What's your take, Nadya? Planned, or fucked-luck random?"

"I doubt very much it was the generals' doing," she says. Takes a deep breath, one only. Then goes on. "It's completely counterintuitive. They want this deal done smoothly and quietly. I'm quite unknown to them, I'm sure. You're only one of Kim's bodyguards. No, it had to be gangsters. The only question is, were they working for somebody who wants to hurt the generals? Surely not. A bodyguard—if they even know of you—with his hooker? Quite low value. Utter waste of time and effort, wouldn't you say? It must have been your expensive clothes that drew them, darling."

"Yeah, well, pretty fuckin' sophisticated for ordinary thugs. Street muggers don't usually have a tail car where I come from."

"They do here, sometimes," she says. "Never seen it done, but I have heard of it before. Works rather well even on a street full of people, in broad daylight. A quick snatch, they're into the car and away. No one will call the police. No one will note the license number. People just get out of the way, stay out of the way until it's over. You saw! Then they go on about their business. Like the monkeys."

"What fuckin' monkeys?"

"See no evil, hear no evil, et cetera, et cetera," Nadya says.

"Solid citizens. They deserve to be preyed on."

"They're frightened, Terry. What can they do? The police are useless."

I'm a little juked, I'm pacing. With any luck, Nadya'll write it off to nervous reaction. I don't want her to know I feel good. Real good, that I can still make moves like that.

"What's our status now?" I ask.

"Status? Oh, do you mean will there be any repercussions? Any police nosing around? Of course not."

"How sure are you?"

"Very." She pauses. "I was born here. My grandmother still lives here. Vlad is Vlad."

Vlad is Vlad. Can't help myself. I start to laugh.

I know Nadya's looking at me like I'm insane. "Are you okay, Terry? Your brain a bit rattled?"

"I'm fine. I'll get a headache later. But now, just decompressing," I say.

"You're rather old-fashioned, you know. Using a head butt! I've not seen that since a brawl between two ancient geezers in a London pub, years and years ago."

"Ya, ya, ya." I am feeling kind of embarrassed, not so much by the fight, but by my feelings after. "The situation was too perfect to pass up an admittedly crude but effective technique."

"I suppose I'll have to fetch you aspirin. Perhaps an ice bag? Oh, you've blood on your shirt, by the way."

"I'll throw it away. In fact, right now I'm going to toss all my clothes, take a nice hot shower."

Nadya places a hand on her hip, tilts her head, regards me for a while, a smile playing about her lips. "Would you mind awfully if Irena joined you?" she says at last.

My heart rises in the rarest way as she moves closer, closer, and into a deep, sweet kiss.

After, as we're getting dressed, Nadya says, "Are you going to tell Sonny or Mister Kim?"

I laugh. "Oh yeah. Both. Kim especially would love hearing every delicious detail."

"Yob! I meant our little encounter on the street."

"No, don't think so. Might spook them unnecessarily."

"Indeed," Nadya says. "I'm afraid, though, I really ought to signal Allison. She'll want to know what happened, draw her own conclusions."

She sits on the bed, begins to pull up her fishnets. "Oh, damn! A run. Have to get new ones. And the rhinestone numbers are quite difficult to find."

"A run? In fishnets?"

"Oh, forgot you're a pantyhose expert. Well, a small tear, actually." She laughs. But there seems to be a small hollow pocket in the sound.

Too soon, she leaves, but the sense of her remains deep within me. She's going to her room, going to contact Allison, I suppose. Or maybe not.

twenty-eight

TOMMY THE WIZARD'S FACE IS GLOWING WITH PLASMA LIGHT FROM the screen of his laptop, and deep geek love. His fingers are itching to glide over the keyboard, like it's a synthesizer, he's a rock star, and he's going to dazzle us all with his chops.

But first he's got to angle the disk toward the light. "Yeah, engraved with the Siemens code pattern, but that's easily faked," he says. "I'll scan, do a virus check, make sure it's not a botched bootleg."

Tommy slips the disk into the waiting slot of his computer, lets his fingers do the talking for a while.

Nobody's been listening to him, anyway. Everyone in this spare, clean room that takes up most of the fourth, and top, floor of the PrimorEx building has been concentrating on the quiet riot in his own head. Except maybe Westley, who incited it all.

We'd come from the Hyundai in the two Ladas—Sonny and I with Kim in the first, Tommy and Yoon in the second—and pulled up in front of PrimorEx exactly at five-thirty. One of those turn-of-the-century buildings, newly stuccoed a pale green, decorative stone around the windows and entrance freshly white, new reproductions of the original curly black wrought-iron bars over the windows. Which are, I'm sure, bullet- and blast-resistant glass. No pretense about the entrance door, though. Thick stainless-steel rods fronting that glass, a hardened steel plate with bank-type locks. And a guard inside, armed and wearing the winter camo shirt and pants all the private security at all the currency-exchange offices and hotel entrances seem to favor. Not military, just local fashion, I suppose.

The heavy's turned two knobs and swung the door inward before we even reach it. Small lobby, two doors on the left with no knobs or handles, just locks. I spot two cameras high in corners. He ushers us into the elevator, presses the button for four, steps aside to resume his post as the doors glide shut. Kind of cramped, what with Sonny toting the black hard-sider, Tommy clutching his computer case, me holding my attaché. Only Kim and Yoon carry nothing.

Then the doors glide open and hold. We're facing that one big room, lit by halogens recessed in the ceiling, but dimmed. Walls look like brushed aluminum. No windows, one door in the far rear with a numbered electronic lock pad. I sense Sonny shift his grip on the hard-sider, angle his body slightly sideways. He doesn't like rooms with such limited egress any more than I do.

Dominant feature's an aluminum table, maybe two meters wide and three long, dead center. There's half a dozen leather task chairs around it, two big, flat LCD screens and keyboards at either end, tower processors in carts just underneath each. A flush black strip runs the center of the table, has what looks like lots of power plugs, USB ports, firewire connections, a couple of modems wired in. "Pretty cool," Tommy mutters, breaking etiquette and brushing past Mister Kim toward that table.

Bolgakov and Tchitcherine, standing before the table with arms wide and big smiles, just like at the Versailles, ignore him.

Sonny steps out of the elevator and moves to the left side, back to the wall, Kim and Yoon walk toward the generals. I slide out, keeping tight to the wall on the right. The elevator door closes.

Big Russian hugs from the generals. Kim stiffens visibly. Can't see his face, but I figure he's pasted a smile on it and will keep it there despite his distaste. I bend at the knees, scanning, set my attaché on the floor beside my right foot, withdraw the cell from my suitcoat pocket with my left hand, keep it close to my leg, out of sight. Keep my eyes on the same two Russians who dined with Sonny and me. They're standing at ease on the far side of the table. One's watching Sonny. The other's supposed to be watching me, but Tommy moving about the table, checking out the center strip, opening up his case and revealing his computer, distracts him.

Watching him watching Tommy distracts me, too, goddammit. So I'm juked when I hear that familiar hollow voice: "Very pleased to see you, Mister Kim. I believe you'll find the arrangements excellent in every particular."

Eyes follow ears. And there, partly screened by the generals, the computer table, the two Ivans, are Westley and JoeBoy, no merchant seaman now but suited up like the rest of us. He winks at me. Fuck!

"Mister Westley, a pleasant surprise," Kim says. It has to be costing him to keep an edge off his voice. "I don't seem to recall that we'd planned for you to be here."

"Oh, a last-minute decision, Mister Kim. I thought I should be here, as a sort of facilitator. The generals welcomed my proposal. Unfortunately there was no timely, secure way to consult you. Actually, you see, I'm not in Vladivostok. To anyone's knowledge, at least."

Yeah, the fuckin' Man Who Isn't There. Westley all over. Does that "anyone" include Allison? I'm wondering. Or Nadya?

Kim's maintaining. His pilot's filed a flight plan for tonight.

Our baggage has already been taken out to the Gulfstream. We're cleared to take off at nine-thirty. He likes to stick to plan. He's used to control. I'm sure he's never considered himself Westley's man in this entire deal. I doubt he knew we referred to him as a "package." I suspect he's never understood he's considered an asset as well, that being an asset means you cede a lot of control. Westley's been super-slick in his manipulations. Kim probably never felt the strings Westley attached to him, one by one. Maybe he does now. But Kim's smart and fast. He goes with what he's faced with.

"In any case, I'm pleased, Mister Westley," he says. "Now, if our friends the generals will kindly produce the merchandise, we can get on with the tests."

Yoon repeats that in Russian. Tchitch smiles, reaches back across the table, palm up. The skinhead Ivan takes a matte metal square from his pocket, lays it on Tchitch's palm. Tchitch hands it to Mister Kim. It looks like a CD jewel box, thicker than normal, and made of titanium, not plastic.

"Exactly what we promised, Mister Kim. As your man"—he nods at Tommy, who's practically panting like a dog at the sight of the box—"will soon confirm, I'm certain."

That's when Tommy opens the case, angles the disk, mentions the Siemens code, boots up the disk, starts keyboarding. That's when I go from condition one to red hot, my fingers the only safety.

"Virus-free, okay, you little beauty. Now show me what you got." Tommy's talking to himself. Not murmuring. Talking loud. "Wow! Look at the codes here. Run 'em, run 'em, run 'em. C'mon, get to the good stuff. Okay! Entry made. Holy shit! Beautiful fail-safes, amazing reroutes."

I see Westley smiling at Mister Kim, who's moved closer to Tommy and is gazing, rapt, at intricate columns of scrolling numbers and schematics studded with electrical design symbols, though he can't possibly understand what Tommy sees there. He can feel the enthusiasm, though. Tommy's broadcasting that clear enough.

And suddenly I know absolutely we're safe. Whatever this shit is, Westley badly wants Kim to deliver it to Pyongyang. He needs Kim to get it there. That's his sole goal in this entire op, even if motive remains opaque to me. He's only here to make sure it happens, make sure potential loose cannons like the generals' heavies, me and Sonny, don't go off over some phantom threat. There is no threat. But Westley knows our type, knows the potential for ADs. He's there to keep it chill, see Kim safely away with that software in his pocket.

I'm not sure Sonny's with this. No way for me to clue him. I'll bet the generals' boys, crude as they are, have been briefed to death—shit, probably threatened with death if they make so much as a provocative face.

Nobody here really knows what Tommy's doing, but everybody seems to be drawing closer, wanting a look at his screen.

"Man, this is art," Tommy says. "Put it in the mainframe, all you got to do is plug in the coordinates. Perfect."

Coordinates. Don't like that. Sounds too much like a fire-control system. I move, very slow, very easy, until I'm closer to Kim and Tchitch, only two quick steps from getting between Westley and JoeBoy. It's unconscious. There's no reason. My body just does it.

"You're certain this is fully functional?" Kim asks.

"As sure as I can be with this," Tommy gestures toward his computer. "Let me just put it through our mainframe in Busan for a super-check."

He takes a neon-blue box out of a pocket in his computer case, rewires so the laptop's connected to the box, not the table strip. "Encryption," he mutters. "DSL . . . DSL . . . Ah, there you are." He wires the box to the strip. Removes the disk, lays it tenderly in the jewel case, then sweeps over the keyboard until numbers are scrolling down the screen in a dozen or more columns. Every couple of seconds, a column freezes, one number highlighted. "We're connected. All secure," Tommy says when the last column stops. He slips the disk back into his computer. "Okay, Busan Big Boy. Read this."

Can't look at that screen anymore. The flickers are jolting my brain. Glance at Westley. He's grinning big, for him. Check Sonny. No expression, no Buddha smile, just watching, tight and hard. But he's put his case on the floor, unbuttoned his suit jacket. He's hot as I was. The generals are alternately beaming at each other, at Westley, at Kim, and back again. Nobody notices. Their boys are staring at featureless wall, avoiding eye contact with everybody. JoeBoy's eyes are half-shut. Don't like that. That's his condition-one look. But I remind myself Westley will do anything to get Kim and the package out of here and on to Pyongyang.

"Why are there more disks in the case?" Kim suddenly asks.

"Spares. Originals, just like the one being tested," Westley says. "Best to have original backups. Copies can be faulty. An original can be damaged. So, backups."

"Ohh, ohh, this is looking radically good," Tommy says. "Architecture's perfect, Mister Kim. One sector of the grid approaches blow-out, the program shuts it down. Plus, here's the neat part, the two adjoining sectors as well. Sort of a firewall. Prevents a failure in one sector from cascading down the entire grid until you have total failure in every sector. Which has been a big problem up North. Total grid failure. No electricity in the entire country. Zero. Zilch. Their system's so monolithic and outdated it's amazing they ever have any power."

"Is this a plug-in fix?" Kim asks.

"Almost. If you can get me free access to Pyongyang's system mainframe for a month, I can reconfigure the system into smaller sectors, one by one, and then overlay this control program," the

Wizard says. "The whole North'll have a system then as good as any in the world, at its heart. Of course they're going to have to modernize, replace almost all substations and other infrastructure. But we all knew they'd have to do that anyway, in stages. And they'd still have the cascade problem, without this control system."

"Good, very good," Kim says. "Generals, I believe you have delivered what you promised. I'll buy this product on the agreed terms."

Yoon translates this. Tchitch can hardly contain himself. He's beaming like a lighthouse. Don't think he's even aware he's rubbing his palms together like a little boy on Christmas morning.

"Mister Park, the case please," Kim says, and Sonny brings the hard-sider over to the table, gently lays it down. He's snapping open the latches, lifting up the top, the generals are crowding close, even Westley's craning his neck for a look.

The cell in my palm vibrates.

"Lovely," Tchitch is crooning, stroking the bundled euros with one hand. I hear "Bright Westley. Bright JoeBoy." Fuck. It's Allison's voice. Has to be Allison. But I won't go on that. Not on JoeBoy. What if the voice is digital?

"Shall we?" Tchitch is saying, waving a banded bundle of hundreds like a fan as Bolgakov puts a bill counter next to the case.

"Say again," I whisper to my palm. "Reverse!"

"JoeBoy bright, Westley bright." It is Allison. Live transmission. "Go now!"

Reflex, muscle memory, moves. A practiced hand can pull and fire in less than a second. Take a step forward, drawing the Wilson with my right, the XD with my left, swinging the pistols in a short swift arc until my arms cross with the muzzle of the Wilson almost touching JoeBoy's temple, the XD muzzle millimeters from Westley's. Slap triggers simultaneously. It sounds like one shot.

Spin, back to the wall, Wilson pointed at Sonny and the generals, XD at the two Ivans. Peripheral catches JoeBoy and Westley toppling fast, spray of blood and brains hitting the Wizard, the hard-sider, the cash.

"Don't flinch, cocksuckers," I scream in Russian. In English, "A burn, Sonny! Sonny, Westley burning Kim! Get Kim out of here. Go now! Go! Go!"

Kim's rigid. There's a dangerous second, Sonny fixing me with those glittery black obsidian slits. Oh fuck, Sonny. No! But he slams the case shut, puts an arm around Kim's shoulders, spins him, pushes him toward the elevator, hits the call button. I hear it whir.

God, God, hurry the fuck up. "Tommy! Yoon! Follow Sonny. Now, goddammit! Move now!

The elevator door glides open, Sonny pushes Kim so hard he falls in a corner. The Wizard and Yoon scramble in. The steel panels are almost closed when Sonny turns his head, smiling that Buddha smile, takes one last look at me.

Exactly then the rear-wall door blows into the room with a crack and a blast-wave that lifts me off my feet, shoves violently, drops me flat on the floor.

twenty-nine

"TERRY, DARLING!"

Sounds just like my Nadya, but I'm not hearing so well, I'm kind of concussed. No fucking wonder. And the point's made definitely when I try to roll on my back, point my pistols, and cannot make the move.

I feel hands pry the Wilson and the XD from mine. "Don't want any ADs now, do we, love?" Almost sure it's Nadya. Almost sure it's her hands that roll me over on my back, her lap my head rests on.

See two guys in universal special-ops style—black jumpsuits, black gloves, black gear and weapons, black hoods with eye slits—kneeling on each of the two Ivans, yanking black plastic cuffs tight on their wrists, kicking away the Ivans' unholstered pistols.

Two other guys each on Tchitch and Bolgakov, doing the same.

One black hood, a Krinkov dangling from a tactical sling, carelessly prodding Westley's body with the toe of his boot, calling clipped orders to his men. They can't be anything but special-ops military. They're too precise, too smooth. I hear the leader with the Krinkov and the Nadya voice exchange some phrases in Russian.

"You actually hurt, Terry? Physically? Or just your feelings?" she says to me then. In Russian. Her hands seem to be lightly running up and down my body, little birds, fluttering. "You aren't bleeding. Nothing feels broken. Want to try sitting up?"

She levers me from behind, and I can sit up, though my head feels huge, like an overblown balloon, and my vision's slightly double. Almost topple, but she's kneeling behind me, supporting me. She puts her cheek next to my ear.

"Now, Terry," she says, still in Russian, "the new CIA wants you to meet our recently acquired best friends, the new KGB. Right, Major?"

"Half right," the guy with the Krinkov says, turning and coming over to us. "We prefer not to use those particular initials anymore, however. We prefer to be known as the Federal Security Service."

All I can see of his face is bright blue eyes, almost Nadya's shade, looking at me through slits in that black hood. He crouches, extends his hand. I find I can raise my right arm, give him a limp shake.

"I think we, ah, used a shaped charge a little more powerful than we needed for that particular door," he says. "Sorry."

Then to Nadya: "He hurt? We need a medical team? The generals are bleeding from the ears. They don't know what planet they're on. They're going to be very shocked when they find out."

"Terry's not bleeding. Who are you talking to, Terry?" Nadya says.

"Maybe Irena, sweetest slut in Vlad," I say, and start laughing. My ribs only hurt a little, my head's deflating to normal size. The major's eyes look puzzled. "Private joke," Nadya tells him.

"So what are we up to, Terry?" she asks.

"In a moment, I'm going to secure a package, then escape and evade. Want to join me?"

"Of course. Let's try standing up first, though, shall we?" I bend my legs, push off with my arms, Nadya gives me a boost. I'm up, wobbly for a second. Then a turn. The girl's black-hooded, too. I yank it off. Yeah, there's Nadya, grinning at me.

"You," I say. "Had to be you. Always worth checking, though."

She laughs, keeps holding tight to my left arm. I see two of the major's men dragging one of the cuffed Ivans through the hole where the door used to be. There's a narrow steel staircase there. Down they go, followed pretty close by two guys with the other Ivan. Then Bolgakov, looking like he's had the worst vodka binge of his life, and Tchitch, only semiconscious still.

Four more men come in, snap open two body bags, shove Westley and JoeBoy into them. Fast, neat, and down again.

I walk, carefully and slowly, over to the table, punch a button on the Wizard's laptop, eject the disk, put it in the jewel case. "Package secured," I say to Nadya. "You want to tell me why this had to go so loud?"

"A little later, Terry. When we're clear."

"One small detail before you're that," the major says, taking the jewel case. "Something here belongs to us, I think."

"Nadya?"

She only nods. The Russian opens that titanium box, flicks open a second interior compartment and extracts three disks. He puts them in a leather case, zips the case into the breast pocket of his black jumpsuit.

"As agreed, no? The Siemens disk is yours if you want it."

"Oh, I do," Nadya says.

"And the others go back where they came from."

"As agreed," she says. I retrieve my attaché. The major puts Tommy's laptop into its case, takes that.

We go down four flights of the narrow steel staircase, emerge into an alley behind the PrimorEx building. Two of the ops team are dragging a bagged body. Must be the door guard. They toss it into the back of a drab van. It thuds on the bags holding what used to be Westley and JoeBoy. I can see the two Ivans, hoods with no slits tied over their heads now, facing the two generals, also hooded, all hunched on benches. A couple of the major's men jump in. He slams the door, raps twice on it. The van pulls away. The rest of the assault group is already in an idling SUV with no markings.

"Interesting encounter, but I do hope we don't—what's your word?—ah, 'intersect' again," the major says, shaking Nadya's hand. He nods to me, disappears into the SUV. It goes.

Nadya turns me around. There's a silver Audi S8 sitting there. She eases me into the shotgun seat, goes around the front and settles into the driver's. Engine hums smoothly when she twists the key.

"Where'd the German metal come from?" I say.

"Oh, a very friendly local dealer," Nadya says, putting her foot to the floor hard so I'm pressed back against buttery leather as we squeal off into the Vlad night.

Nadya throttles down, syncs with the traffic flow, as soon we hit a main street. I'm fuzzy on where we are, but it doesn't seem as if we're headed toward the airport, or in any particular hurry to get anywhere at all. And the process starts. Always the same, for me and everyone I know who does my kind of work, that process. The euphoria of coming out alive does a fast fade, and you enter the blank, the big empty. You don't know what just went down, what part you played in whatever it was. You're in a hole of time—no before, no after, not even a recognizable now. You just are, you're breathing and your heart's beating, but that's it.

Then you drop back into the shit. You feel yourself pulling the trigger, see the flashes, hear the booms and the shouts, smell the burn and the blood. You feel a despair so deep you think you'll live in it forever, without hope.

But you rise up out of the pit. Into any one of a number of zones: satisfaction, bewilderment, elation, pride, disgust, anger. That's the only variable in the process, *which* zone it'll be, and there's often no logical connection between the nature of the op and where you wind up.

I rise into anger. Nadya hits another region entirely. That's clear as anything can be. When she breaks the silence we've been in for I don't know how long, she does it in rapid, excited English.

"Rather neat piece of work, I think. Perfect timing, smooth execution, agile departure. Textbook!"

"Goddamn goat-fuck," I say. "The deal was made, we're moments from being out the door with the package, mission accomplished. Clean and quiet. Then I got to waste two men, and you and your Russkis go pyscho-dramatic. For what? For fucking what? I don't mind doing Westley. But *why*? And why JoeBoy? Why's he got to take a bullet in the brain?"

"He was Westley's man, Terry," she says. "He was Westley's insurance against you and Sonny. He'd have done you if things had turned a certain way."

"Turn? Turn? There wasn't gonna *be* a turn. A clean deal, everybody ready to walk away happy. Westley would have done anything to make sure Kim reached Pyongyang with the package. I know it."

"True, absolutely. As far as it goes. But there's a lot you don't know."

"Bullshit, Nadya. Yeah, I don't know the official reason the Company wanted Kim to deliver a power-grid control system to the DPRK, but I can guess. A little stabilization effort, like the food aid against the famine there, to keep Kim Jong Il from maybe going beserk, maybe going nuke, in desperation."

"True again. As far as it goes, Terry. But it goes a great deal further than you comprehend."

"Does it? Or did the Langley cowboys fuck over the Langley suits just for the action rush?"

"Actually, no. The cowboys saved the suits from a major, *major* goat-fuck, as you like call such things."

"Damned if I'm buying that."

"Then I'll be blunt, Terry. It does not matter a wit if you buy it or not. Your contract's completed," Nadya says. She turns the Audi into what seems to be an alley. I look out. It isn't. It's a narrow lane between stacks of shipping containers. We're in the port. She kills the lights, kills the engine, unlocks her seat belt, turns slightly toward me.

Completed, I'm thinking. Or about to be terminated? A little fear chill rises against my will. Aw, no. Please. I do not want to Boker Nadya. But I will, if she's the one.

"I'm not obliged to do this, Terry. But I want to, if you reckon you can actually hear," she says. "I won't even ask you to hand over that knife you're still carrying."

"I'll hear," I say, an unwanted tightness in my voice.

"Kim was going to be burned, definitely. But not as you'd imagine," she starts. "By Westley. No one else. Westley sold the thumbsuckers at Langley a simple proposition. North Korea's about to erupt in chaos, famine raging, Chairman Kim getting desperate. As you surmised. We've got to stabilize, but can't be seen doing it, before the maximum leader goes beserk with his admittedly limited WMDs. Food aid, help with major problems like power supply, usual package. Country's more stable, maximum leader less likely to detonate. As you surmised.

"Only Westley's hard hard-core. Has his own agenda, doesn't

he? Those extra disks the major took? They were long-range missile-guidance programs, Terry. Russia's best. The one thing the North doesn't have, can't seem to develop, can't find on any black market. Westley uses Kim to unknowingly deliver that along with the grid program. Then he plans to rat Kim out. All of a sudden the U.S., China, Russia have got proximate cause to come down on the North. Shock and awe."

"Yeah, real success in Iraq, that shock-and-awe thing."

"Well, of course. Military action on the Korean peninsula is a dooomsday proposition. So. As you may or may not know, our intelligence agencies have been cooperating with their Russian counterparts on matters of mutual interest. Very recently the Russians inform us that they have been closely watching two particular generals whom they believe are up to something bad. What strikes them as peculiar—and irks them immensely—is that said generals seem to have close ties to an American agent. Who turns out to be Westley. The thumbsuckers get quite nervous, quite shaken. Scurry over to operations—never admitting it was their undertaking in the first place—and beg them to stop Westley, if he's operating his own agenda. Clear so far?"

"Reasonably," I say.

"Well, operations look into it. Liaise with the Russians, open the books on the thumbsuckers' brief to Westley. Two days ago, the Russians send Langley a red alert. They strongly believe Bolgakov and Tchitcherine are peddling extremely sensitive missile-guidance programs, with Westley as the middleman. Destination: North Korea. The very last thing anyone wants. Our operations team and their Russian counterparts agree on a joint operation to stop it. I'm ordered to inform that Russian major of the exact time and place of the deal. And to participate in stopping it. So we stopped it. As you saw."

"Persuasive, Nadya. Almost believable. It would account for

your saying 'brilliant' when I gave you the meeting place. But why not just haul Westley home, throw him in a padded cell somewhere with all the other CIA burnouts who got too zealous?"

"Because Westley crossed the one line that cannot be crossed. He was taking a rather large cut of the generals' seven point five. And because the Russians said he was our player, and our responsibility to apply the stroke. If we did not, they would terminate him on the spot, and cease cooperating with us in other touchy places, such as Afghanistan." Nadya sighs, raps something against the Audi's gearshift. It's her SIG. "Now, Terry, please get out of the car."

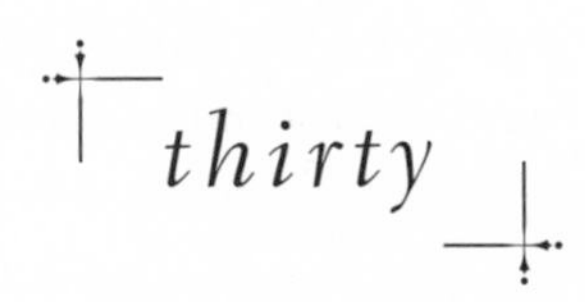

IT'S DANK IN THE CONTAINER CANYON AND DIM, ONLY AMBIENT GLOW from arc lights far off, around the perimeter of the port. Can't recall exactly how we got in here. Did we pass a security checkpoint somehow? I look up. The towering steel stacks seem to be leaning in, narrowing toward the top. Nadya tells me to place my knife and the attaché—which still cradles the Korth and grenades—on the Audi's hood. Very slowly, very gently. Then step forward seven paces, facing away from the car.

She's good. She doesn't give me any kind of opening. There is no move I might make that wouldn't be suicide. I'm feeling skanked and shitty.

"Right, Terry," she says. "Here's the procedure. We're heading for a particular ship. Between here and there will be a few security people. Mobile, except for one fixed post, which we'll give a wide berth. It's to your best advantage to cooperate with me. You will be a good boy, won't you? Do we understand each other?"

"Hard fucking not to, Irena," I say.

"Ah, Terry. There's much you've not considered yet, love. I know you're hardly in the mood, but really you must trust me a little longer."

"Did I ever trust you, bitch?"

"Hard words, Terry. But certainly you did, though you never liked to admit it. You considered it unprofessional or something, I suppose."

We're walking straight down that corridor. More and more I'm getting the sensation that the stacked containers are about to topple over on us. Very faintly, at some distance, there seems to be a whirring of winches, a low rumble of wheeled cranes. But the only distinct sound is the regular click of my wing tips heels striking concrete, echoing. Nadya moves silent as a cat; probably wearing Vibram-soled assault boots, to match her black jumpsuit.

"Hey, Irena, ever make that IED from the stuff you picked up on our shopping trip? You remember that one, and what came after, don't you?"

"Well of course I made it. Would have been a waste not to, surely. In point of fact, it's ticking merrily as we speak in the boot of dear General Tchitcherine's almost new Audi, the lovely machine that brought us here. Should pop off in, oh, an hour or so, long before daylight."

"You stole Tchitch's personal car?"

"We required transport, did we not? It's a well-known vehicle, locally. Special plates, you see. Unlikely anyone would think of stopping it. Likely we'd be waved right through any gates around here."

I'm about to step out from between those oppressive walls when Nadya hisses. "Don't! Tricky bit here. There are clear sightlines five hundred meters right and left. Can't stroll along the middle, can we?"

"So, what? We duck and dodge around these container rows?"

"A bit showy. Also a bit wearing. Look straight ahead fifty meters."

I do. I see a three-meter chain-link topped by coils of concertina, nothing but black on the other side. Then I see lights flick and waver, vanish and reappear on the black. Water. The harbor. Also notice high sedge, both sides of the fence.

Then I hear a sharp, fast snap. Nadya's two meters to my right, heavy-duty wire cutters working in one hand. "Snip a single slit, slip past the fence, go red Indian style through the rushes. To the left. The ship we want is that first one, about five hundred meters off. Our destination."

She tosses me the cutters, I almost fumble the catch. "We hit the fence together, you cut, go through, I follow." She peeps around the container, makes a quick scan. "On my mark. Ready? Go!"

Goes like a training exercise. We're across the open space, into the weeds, slit's cut, and we're through in ten seconds. I trot left in a half-crouch, toeing in like one of her red fucking Indians, silent except for a soft whisping as I brush the rank leafage. Halt, crouch when we reach the concrete wharf. Shabby little freighter, badly scabbed with rust. Longshoremen are working way down at the stern under floods, wharfside, and on board. But the bow's only twenty-five meters from us, unlit. I turn my head. Nadya's scoping the bow with a night-vision monocular.

Now? Fuck. She's got the SIG leveled on my lower spine. No move.

"Rope ladder," she says. "Just past the forward mooring line. We move to the bollard, take a last look round, then it's up the ladder like pirates. Are you feeling piratical, Terry?"

No answer required. We sprint, crouch, scramble up and over. Then we're on the rough steel plates of the fo'c'sle deck, squatting by a big anchor capstan.

"Friendly ship, Terry. Not much to look at, true, but she

sails," Nadya says. "Skipper's our man. Carlos came in on this hulk from Busan. That trouble you at all? Cast any shadows on your soul?"

"All depends on who's going out on her. And how far. Doesn't it?"

A tall, slim figure detaches from the outline of the superstructure, starts walking toward us. Too dark to make out a face.

"Stand up, Terry," Nadya says. "Hallo, Allison. Job's well and truly done. And see who I've brought you."

thirty-one

NIGHTS HERE ARE SOFT AS VELVET, THE AIR ALMOST TOO RICH WITH scents of frangipani and bougainvillea. I sit easily on a sandy patch up among the rocks of a natural little redoubt above the beach, watching the faint lights of slim fishing canoes flicker like fireflies far offshore. That's my reference anyway; fireflies don't exist in these latitudes. When I look up, I see the glimmer of mostly unfamiliar constellations, and that crooked Southern Cross. I can hear the whispering lap of sea against shore when there's a pause in the clatter and whoops of the jungle behind me.

It's almost peaceful. But provisional. Too often I'm back on that tramp freighter. Really back, hi-rez, sight and sound and feeling. Just me on the dark foredeck with a woman I knew as Nadya, one I knew as Allison. A gesture, so fluid yet so very swift and sure. Then it's just me, there on the deck.

Allison coming toward us, Nadya and me moving to her. Allison saying, "Excellent. Great work, really," when we're close enough to touch. "Well, of course!" Nadya replying, something small and silver sliding from her sleeve into her palm, palm flowing toward Allison's neck, the small silver thing just brushing the tender spot behind the jaw. One pop, no louder than a kid's cap. Allison's eyes widening slightly, body toppling as if her legs had been scythed out from under her.

Nadya looking then at me, the small silver thing in her hand a .22 revolver, derringer-size and style, not even a trigger guard. The weapon favored by the best mafia hit men, the ones cold enough to work so close. Little hollow in the forty-grain lead bullet filled with candle wax, it penetrates soft tissue an inch or so, expands and fragments. There's a tiny hole that scarcely bleeds just beneath Allison's ear. But the thing splayed awkwardly on the deck is not Allison anymore. A fist-size piece of her brain has been shredded.

I'm about to die.

Then Nadya tosses the .22 over the bulwark. There's hardly a splash when it hits. She opens my attaché, dumps the Korth and the grenades into the oily harbor waters. She hands the attaché to me.

"I know you've got a Company backup passport. Best not to use it, though," she says. "I'm quite sure you've also got your own emergency one in there, name and nationality known only to you. You should take it now, Terry."

I rip the lining, grab the passport, slip it into the breast pocket of my suit.

"Why? Why Allison?"

Nadya gazes at me with those canted, arctic-blue eyes. "Don't know, actually. Compromised by Westley perhaps? Operation a bit untidy? Too many loose ends? She was in charge, after all." A shrug. "My orders were to clean up."

"And me?"

She laughs silkily. "You, darling, seem to have escaped and evaded. One of your specialties, I gather. They'll expect that of you."

"You, Nadya?"

"Heading home. Long way round, I'm afraid. Via Moscow. Can't be helped. One never goes out the way one came in."

"They teach you that at the Farm?"

"Well of course!" She clicks a plastic buckle, removes a fanny pack. "You'll be put ashore in Fukuoka. If I were Terry, I'd go somewhere by air from there. Though not too far! Then I'd go quite far by other means."

Nadya throws the fanny pack high. When I make the grab and look back, she's gone.

Escape and evade.

Smart enough, I figure, to buy a ticket from Fukuoka to Hong Kong on Cathay Pacific, which keeps first-rate passenger manifests, but fly out four hours earlier to Manila on Garuda, which keeps none. Easy enough, in the pulsing human anthill of Manila's domestic terminal, to secure a first-class seat—under a name I invent but don't have to document—on a Philippines Air island-hopper to Davao City. Simple enough to travel nameless by bus, jitney, and taxi a few hundred klicks of jungle and mountains to Zamboanga.

The hundred thousand euros in the fanny pack Nadya tossed me is only down maybe two thousand, even after I buy a nicely maintained CAR-15 and ten thirty-round magazines from an ancient man with skin like an old shoe, his stubs of teeth stained red from chewing betel, in an airless tin-roofed shack on the Zamboanga waterfront. He seems disappointed I won't take the time to haggle down the price.

Another five hundred and I'm skimming the calm Sulu Sea in an Evinrude-powered outrigger piloted by the ancient man's grandson, who's a part-time pirate and occasional fisherman. Two-fifty at a village built on stilts in the shallows off northeastern Borneo gets me another outrigger ride up to the very tip of Sabah, to this village fronting the Balabac Strait. It's two hundred klics from Kota Kinabalu, heavily jungled four-thousand-meter mountains between the international airport there and here. No roads over that green hell to here, no airstrip. Accessible only by sea.

The headman has heard of European adventure tourists, though none have ever come here before. A hundred euros gets me a bamboo hut with a thatched roof, three meals a day, and honorary membership in his clan for six months. Once every month or so, an old steamer comes by to trade simple goods for dried fish, maybe bring back one of the village's young men who went to Kota looking for work, or take one away. The headman seems proud of this.

He understands I do not want my presence known when the steamer comes. It has to anchor five klicks out, the water's too shoaled, reefed, and shallow for closer approach. The villagers go to it in their outriggers. No one, he promises, will ever mention me. No one wants any attention from the authorities in Kota. Because most of the villagers are smugglers as well as fishermen.

So I live. Some dawns I go with an outrigger and help a man fish. I doze in a hammock most afternoons when the sun's brutal. I swim in the waning day. Evenings, I sit here in my redoubt, the CAR in my lap, watching my imaginary fireflies, my unknown constellations.

I never doubt Nadya made it back. I'm sure Company craftsmen have forged and mailed a postcard or two to Annie, from Honduras or Salvador perhaps. Luther's probably written that he's decided to stay south for a while, to postpone his return to Baltimore. It is not in the Company's interest for a cop named Luther Ewing, who took a road trip to the Yucatán, to be reported missing.

So I'm here. If they want me, they will find me. Six months? A year? Doesn't matter much. If they come hard, they'll get hit hard. That's what the CAR is for.

But for now, I'll just sit quietly. I did the job, I got paid.

Contract completed. Maybe they'll bring me in easy. Maybe one day a little boat will beach and I'll see a small figure walking toward me, shimmering in the heat haze. Hear Nadya, calling clear. "Terry, darling! Ready to come home? Well of course you are!"

Sure. It will be Nadya. Real as the sound of the sea in a shell held against your ear.

II

It may be strange to say this but when I read MacDiarmid's poetry at length I often think of that essay which Eliot wrote on Blake. One might wonder what Blake had to do with MacDiarmid or what the point of the comparison is. Now in this essay Eliot maintained that Blake had been led astray by a hotch-potch of ideas which are completely uninteresting in themselves. It might be interesting for someone to take this comparison between Blake and MacDiarmid further (the present writer doesn't have the detailed knowledge for it).

It is sufficient to say that here are two poets – Blake and MacDiarmid – who both begin with lyrics of a certain kind, that is, lyrics which contain a fusion of the intellect and feeling which is highly unusual and at times hallucinatory. Both poets go on to write long poems based rather insecurely on systems which are fairly private (even MacDiarmid's communism doesn't seem to be all that orthodox). Both have little to do with the classical tradition (it is interesting that MacDiarmid very seldom refers to the Greeks and Trojans from whom so many poems have been quarried but rather goes back to Celtic sources.) Blake too does not seem interested in a classical tradition but goes back to sources found nearer home. Both are radical in their views though they have the basic aristocratic attitude of poets. They write about freedom and the spirit of man in chains.

Another similarity which I wish to stress for a particular reason is that neither had a university training. Now let no-one under any circumstances believe that I consider a university training obligatory for a poet. Nothing could be further from the truth. In fact I would be more likely to believe the contrary. On the other hand I often feel that in comparison for instance with the mind of Eliot the mind of MacDiarmid is untrained, and sometimes it seems to me irresponsible. Eliot's critical work of course is far superior to MacDiarmid's, such as it is. No, what I am saying is this: I cannot see any justification for MacDiarmid's writing most of his later work in verse form. Eliot too had certain things he felt like saying but he developed a prose style for them. I am not saying that all of Eliot's work or indeed much of Eliot's work outside his purely literary criticism is of much value, but at least he made the distinction between the things he could say in prose and the things he could say in poetry. I feel that MacDiarmid might have done better to make the same distinction.

If this comparison with Blake be accepted on a certain level it will be seen that there is a certain progress in the work of each of them.

Now MacDiarmid became a Communist of a particular kind in his career. It may be for all I know that there are signs of Communistic thinking at the end of *To Circumjack Cencrastus* when he attacks his boss on a personal level, and he may well have been forced into it by his later personal sufferings (and here may one say how much one admires the kind of personal integrity that MacDiarmid has shown?) and also by what he saw around him in the 'thirties especially. He wasn't the only one to be attracted by such a system in the 'thirties though I do not think that MacDiarmid could be systematised for long.

However I do not think that MacDiarmid is a Communist in any ordinary sense of the word. True, he writes in approval of certain of Lenin's actions, and in these poems a certain inhumanity emerges. But that MacDiarmid has much in common with the 'masses' I do not believe. How can one prove this, that MacDiarmid is not a Communist? There is only one test. When is his poetry at its best, at its most complex in a good way? MacDiarmid may think he is a Communist but I think on the other hand that his imagination betrays him.

I would suggest that excluding his early work up to the *Drunk Man* the burden of MacDiarmid's imagination does not emerge in his Communist poems nor on the whole do they convince me imaginatively in any way. For after all the poems about Lenin are very often more about himself than they are about Lenin and more about the integrity which will allow him to make good poetry than they are about politics. I would suggest that the burden of MacDiarmid's imagination in his later work can be found where he writes about exclusiveness and not where he writes about involvement with humanity. I am thinking in particular about 'On a Raised Beach' which seems to me his finest achievement after *A Drunk Man*, a poem about stones and an appalling apartness. It is in this kind of conscious loneliness that MacDiarmid is most imaginatively convincing. It could indeed be argued that the progress of MacDiarmid is from the human to a poetry of landscape and stones and language. It is the aristocratic lonely voice in these poems that convinces. (In fact he seems to me to become astonishingly like Yeats in thought if not in style.) The poems about the masses do not really have much resonance.

If Communism among other things means a concern with people, then MacDiarmid is not a Communist. If Communism among other things means the patience of a Lenin – the patience of stones – and a kind of ruthlessness then there are these things in the poems. But on the other hand they are there, as they are in Grassic Gibbon, academically. It is not easy to know how MacDiarmid would have reacted to the turmoil of a real Communist revolution in his own country and to the possible murders and killings. I myself find much of what he says about Lenin distasteful. (This problem of violence is also to be found in Grassic Gibbon and is to be found, academically, in our own time in Gunn and MacBeth for instance.) It is fair enough to say that Lenin had to have a lot of people killed but I do not think that a poet should speak about this without agony for he should try to see people not as faceless masses but as individuals. One should try to imagine what it would mean in the last analysis to oneself. That is why I find MacDiarmid's poems somewhat unreal and rhetorical. The poems of those who have actually suffered in these countries are not like this. And one wonders what happened to Mayakovsky. (Another thought which might enter one's mind is this: if Scotland had had its Easter Rising how would this have affected MacDiarmid's poetry? Yeats saw war close to him and was at times horrified.)

In the later MacDiarmid there is really a great loneliness and coldness. I think his poetry about stones is often magnificent and proud and it convinces me that it is poetry and not propaganda. It is not a question of approving or disapproving of this poetry. The poetry convinces one whether one likes it or not. That is why I often remember a snatch of dialogue between two characters from one of Faulkner's novels. One of them is praising 'Ode to a Nightingale'. The other simply remarks that Keats had to write something, didn't he. And I feel this with the later MacDiarmid that in his latest work he had to write about something and he wrote about Communism and various other ideas. This is not at all a question of saying that MacDiarmid was insincere. It is more profound than that. A man may say that he is a Communist and in the recesses of his imagination not be so. Milton was of the devil's party without knowing it. MacDiarmid's later poetry convinces me when he is at his most aristocratic, a cold eagle, a man in love with stones. This part of him – the truest part of him at this stage – knows that he is not like other people, that they have very little to say to him, that he cannot learn anything from them and that they'll never learn anything anyway.

Again it is not a question of my approving or disapproving of this – and I can see quite clearly how he might have arrived at this position – especially in Scotland – it is merely to say what kind of poetry seems to me to be successful. Whether for instance Eliot says he is Anglo-Catholic, Royalist and classical seems to me to be irrelevant. It has little to do with his most successful poetry, or even with his truest preoccupations in poetry.

III

If I were therefore to pick MacDiarmid's best books I would pick his earlier ones right up to the *Drunk Man.*

The latter I think is a major work on many levels though MacDiarmid finds difficulty with the ending. I am not sure that I completely understand the section about Silence though David Daiches in his introduction to the poem seems quite sure that he understands it. But on balance the image of the thistle and the moonlight does in fact hold the poem together and holds it at the same time in a real physical world. The later poems seem to me not to be able to get hold of a symbol which will be a unifying thread. Here too in this poem a lot of what he says later on is said for the first time and said freshly. I often wonder whether in fact some of *To Circumjack Cencrastus* may not be passages rejected from the previous poem.

In a sense the dialectic seems to work for this poem partly because the symbolism helps it to. The basic groundwork of the poem which in effect is the struggle towards consciousness of a man and of a nation and of humanity is represented lucidly by the thistle and the moonlight. The thistle can be seen to stand for the man distorted by morality and the pressures of existence. The moonlight can be seen to stand for the Platonic idea, complete, unflawed and often deadly.

The fact too that the thistle is the Scottish symbol allows MacDiarmid to pass from the personal to the national very easily. It is clear also that to a certain extent he does allow the main character to be different from himself. The protagonist is not wholly himself though he does have a great deal of the knowledge of MacDiarmid. He seems to represent something essentially Scottish. He goes back to Tam o' Shanter, one supposes, and is a human being in whose twists and turns we are interested.

The change in mood and thought (which in others of the poems may seem arbitrary) does not seem so in this poem because the protagonist is after all a drunk man. It is a very gay poem, a very witty poem, the poem of a writer who has not allowed himself to be overwhelmed by the world. One senses in *Cencrastus* a kind of bitterness of which there is little sign in the *Drunk Man*. MacDiarmid in this poem is still able to objectify his insights without rancour. He can be playful in a very funny way, as for instance in the passage about the Chinese at the Burns supper.

The poem does not seem to me to reach any conclusion but it does not seem to matter very much for it is redeemed by so many other qualities, wit, humour, snatches of strange balladic verses, and in general a healthy tone.

Nevertheless in spite of all this and, in spite of the fact that in variety, interest in humanity, glitterings of wit, and sustained rhetoric this poem must undoubtedly be considered major and in spite of the brilliant use to which MacDiarmid puts his symbolism – externalising and internalising the thistle from one moment to another and doing the same with the moonlight (it is perhaps this he learnt from Rilke if he learnt anything) – in spite of the fact that there is a great richness in the poem, one still comes back to the earliest poems of all and one or two lyrics here and there among the later poems.

Essentially MacDiarmid is at his greatest in his lyric poems. Even the *Drunk Man* is itself a collection of lyrics to a great extent and this is proved by the manner in which MacDiarmid himself has presented the poem in his *Collected Poems*, by detached sections. In general he hasn't quite the architectural power necessary for the true long poem and it may be that this is no longer possible anyway.

It is a part of my argument therefore to say that in many of these long poems what he is in effect doing is setting up arguments and then knocking them down with others. Also they lack (these later ones) that which we look for in the greatest poetry, insights into human beings. I believe that it is in the early poems that MacDiarmid is concerned with people and their feelings and that later this disappears even when paradoxically he is claiming to be a Communist. But this is not the whole of my argument. I believe it goes deeper than this.

I believe that what happened to MacDiarmid is as follows. He began as a poet with both a masculine and feminine sensibility and eventually allowed the masculine elements in himself to dominate his work, therefore to a great extent becoming less human than he once was.

For what we find in the early MacDiarmid and miss later is a real tenderness, a real feminine love. It may be strange to say this about MacDiarmid whom one thinks of above all as masculine and a fighter. But I believe that he surrendered or lost a priceless thing when this disappeared from his poetry except now and again. It is for this tenderness and for a kind of hallucinatory quality which owes little to logic or reason that I above all value MacDiarmid.

I should like to say at this point before proceeding that this idea is not new, this idea of the poet being both masculine and feminine at his best. Coleridge remarked on it when writing about Shakespeare. In our own day Robert Graves talks about it. And I believe that it is this insight gained by using both sides of his nature that makes the greatest of all poets. I would maintain that on the basis of the lyrics alone MacDiarmid must be placed very high indeed and I think that in the last analysis when the judgment of literary history has been made that it will be on this side that the scales will come down.

It might also at this point be worth mentioning the distinction Coleridge makes between the Fancy and the Imagination, when one attempts an interpretation of MacDiarmid's lyrics. Some of MacDiarmid's lyrics are fanciful in the Coleridgean sense. Another way of explaining the distinction might be by an analysis of various types of jokes. Everyone knows the kind of joke which has been built up from a single point, very often foliated in order to disguise its point of origin. Most jokes are like this, inexorably labouring to a destination through the usual three stages. However, the jokes of the Goons for instance or the Marx Brothers reveal a new dimension to reality and in this sense are truly imaginative. They seem to take a leap into a new area beyond ordinary experience. The joke itself can be brief and unfoliated but nevertheless its implications with regard to reality are immense.

I would say that an example of the fanciful lyric is the one called 'The Diseased Salmon'.

> I'm gled it's no' my face,
> But a fozie saumon turnin'
> Deid-white i' the blae bracks o' the pool,
> Hoverin' a wee and syne tint again i' the churnin'.
>
> Mony's the face'll turn,
> Like the fozie saumon I see;
> But I hope that mine'll never be ane
> And I can think o' naebody else's I'd like to be.

Here as in the inferior joke the whole point depends on the resemblance between the colour of the salmon and the death colour of a man's face. The rest of the poem is merely a foliage around this. A poem which seems to me to be on the border between the fanciful and the imaginative is the one called 'Wild Roses'.

Wi' sae mony wild roses
Dancin' and daffin',
It looks as tho' a'
The countryside's laffin'.

But I maun ca' canny
Gin I'm no' to cumber
Sic a lichtsome warld
Wi' my hert's auld lumber.

Hoo I mind noo your face
When I spiered for a kiss
'Ud gae joukin' a' airts
And colourin' like this!

This poem is more complex than the previous one and the movement of the verse seems to suggest a greater complexity. But it is fanciful, in that the thought can be expressed in intellectual terms and the connections have a logic not far removed from that of the mind. But again this is not wholly true and this is why I said that it is on the border of the purely imaginative. When however we come to 'The Watergaw' we see that we are on a different level altogether.

Ae weet forenicht i' the yow-trummle
I saw yon antrin thing,
A watergaw wi' its chitterin' licht
Ayont the on-ding;
An' I thocht o' the last wild look ye gied
Afore ye deed!

There was nae reek i' the laverock's hoose
That nicht – an' nane i' mine;
But I hae thocht o' that foolish licht
Ever sin' syne;
An' I think that mebbe at last I ken
What your look meant then.

Here the whole poem is a continuous trembling analagous to the trembling on the verge of a revelation. All parts of the poem work to the one end. The poem vibrates like the rainbow. The phrase 'yow-trummle' anticipates without actually revealing the rest of the poem.

The second section of the first verse comes as an actual surprise so that one has to return to the beginning again. However no matter how often one goes over this poem one cannot understand by the reason alone how it was created or how the leap from the rainbow to the dying face was made. A kind of shock is achieved which goes beyond logic. MacDiarmid is pointing to something which he himself doesn't understand and we don't either, though at the same time we feel that the image is true and remarkable and is indicating something serious and important. It might be worth examining that single word 'wild' which MacDiarmid uses in the first verse. It seems that no other word would quite do and yet it is not intellectually clear why this should be so. One supposes it to mean 'distracted' in the sense that with the rain falling in front of it it is distracted from itself as someone's mind is often distracted by the downpours of life. But there is more to it than this. There is a kind of hint of the helplessness of the animal in that use of the word 'wild'. It is as if the being were a kind of animal dying and unable to communicate with the human being looking at it and the rain itself becomes the barrier to communication as if one were looking at the animal through a cage. And one might study the use of the word 'foolish'. Is MacDiarmid saying that there is no meaning to existence? Certainly it would be worth comparing with this poem other poems about the rainbow. One might for instance compare with it the closing lines of *The Quaker Graveyard in Nantucket* when one reads of God surviving the rainbow of his will. Again, the strictly fanciful poem by Thomas Campbell on the same subject, might show us by contrast the imaginative power of MacDiarmid's lyric.

The point is that the poem defeats the mind and yet the whole being is satisfied by it. There does seem to be a connection between the face dying and the rainbow beyond the rain. (Does the rain represent the tears of the person looking at the dying face?) The connection does not seem to be a religious one, though the rainbow of course has religious connotations. There was Noah's flood and the rainbow.

Whatever the imagination is, there is no doubt that it is what we require in poetry at the highest level. How it operates is incomprehensible. What it creates is, strictly speaking, incapable of being managed by the mind. This is true on a very slightly lesser level of 'The Bonnie Broukit Bairn'.

In this poem there are combined in a short space many of the elements which make MacDiarmid's poems distinctive – the concern with the universe and images of it, the intellectual wit, the class-distinction if one cares to call it that (the Cinderella theme in the poem). For the child is contrasted with the women in their beautiful dresses. (We might notice the hissing sound of the first two lines which might be there to reproduce the whispering and the gossip.) Then again he may be thinking that Earth is the only planet not called after a god. The daring ending is exactly right with the Scottish word 'clanjamfrie' which the women – Edinburgh women possibly? – might not know. Others of these lyrics which are roughly on this level are 'In the Hedge-Back', 'The Eemis Stane', 'O Wha's the Bride?' (from *A Drunk Man*) and above all 'Empty Vessel'. 'Trompe L'Oeil' is an example of the purely fanciful.

Along with 'The Watergaw' the 'Empty Vessel' seems to me to be on the highest level of the imagination. One points to the use of the word 'swing' – a word which one associates with children – but the mind is again defeated by this most moving poem. I have already said that in these poems there is a tenderness which the later MacDiarmid seems to have lost, surrendering himself instead to the masculine principle of reason. All these poems which I have mentioned illustrate this tenderness in some degree or another, this concern with humanity in an almost feminine way. In another of his poems MacDiarmid remarks how women will look after sick children when people like himself leave them because they are bored, and defeated by sickness. He talks of the patience of women in situations like this. There is a kind of patient looking behind these lyrics emerging later in a hallucinatory light and revealing what one can only call love. These lyrics are imaginatively in love with the universe. Whatever achievements MacDiarmid later made nothing comes near to the authority of these lyrics, an authority which rests only on themselves. They demand no proof and ask no questions or, if they do, they do not expect an answer. The poems themselves are answers on the imaginative level. The poems answer by music and language and the answer is love, the love which comes from tenderness and care. I know for instance of no poem like 'The Bonnie Broukit Bairn'. Here there is applied to the universe a parochial language, which seems to make it familiar and loved.

Poets of course will always undervalue poems like these because they are small but they are making a great mistake. The only authority poetry ultimately has is the imagination. If we cannot claim this power and see it now and again in action how can we defend ourselves against science? When the ideas in the poem are detachable they can be contradicted and often are. MacDiarmid can be contradicted when one discusses his *In Memoriam James Joyce*. He cannot be attacked at all on the level of these lyrics. They are the real proof of his genius. Their loss would be irreparable. The loss of much else of his work would not be.

The lyrics cannot be duplicated anywhere else in literature. In no other lyrics do I find their special combination of imaginative power, tenderness, wit, intelligence (but an intelligence which has not been divorced from the feelings). Clearly it would be difficult to sustain this achievement. However, though it is clear that it was necessary for MacDiarmid to move on, this does not prevent us saying that his lyrics are his greatest achievement. I can imagine most of his other work as being in a certain sense unnecessary, that is poetically unnecessary. The lyrics made themselves necessary. They appeared through him. The will cannot make poetry. Neither can intelligence. That is why poetry is so unfair. But then that is also why it is different from a craft.

MacDiarmid's Three Hymns to Lenin

SYDNEY GOODSIR SMITH

All Hugh MacDiarmid's three Hymns to Lenin belong to the 1930s, his most prolific poetical period. The 'First Hymn' was written for Lascelles Abercrombie's *New English Poems* (1930) and was subsequently published in *First Hymn to Lenin and Other Poems* in 1931. The 'Second Hymn' first appeared in T. S. Eliot's quarterly, *The Criterion*, in 1932, which says something for the editorial breadth of mind, and was published privately later in the same year by Valda Trevlyn from Sussex, and publicly in *Second Hymn to Lenin and Other Poems* by Stanley Nott in 1935. The 'Third Hymn', though composed during this period (*c.* 1935) in Shetland, did not see the light of day until 1955 in MacDiarmid's own quarterly, *The Voice of Scotland*, though he had quoted bits of it in his autobiography, *Lucky Poet* (Methuen, 1943). All three Hymns were eventually brought together in *Three Hymns to Lenin*, published by Castle Wynd Printers, Edinburgh, in 1957.

In almost all MacDiarmid's thought and work, two or three interrelated themes have been constant: Scottish Nationalism (which includes anti-Englishism), the literary revival of Scots and Gaelic (which was part of the general Renaissance programme) and Communism. The seeming contradiction between Communism and Nationalism is reconciled by MacDiarmid's belief that the U.S.S.R. encourages minority cultures and languages within the Soviet Union and grants autonomy with the right of secession to the smaller republics (see *Scots Independent*, August 1945). 'The Red Scotland line we advocate is in perfect keeping with the dicta of Marx, Engels, Lenin and Stalin, and with the practice of the Soviet Union in regard to minority elements. We too in Scotland must have an autonomous republic and equal freedom and facilitation for our Scots Gaelic and Scots Vernacular languages. Our minimal demand is to have Scotland on the same footing in all these respects as one of the autonomous republics of the U.S.S.R.' (*Lucky Poet*, p. 145).

Politically, this is the John Maclean line. John Maclean, first Soviet consul appointed by Lenin in Europe (his consulate was in a Glasgow tenement), stood out for a Scottish Workers' Republic and considered it would be a mistake for the Scottish Communists to join with their English brethren in forming the Communist Party of Great Britain. He believed the English movement would hold the Scots back if they combined; that Scotland would opt for Communism long before England would; that, in fact, England never would go Communist but that Scotland, by achieving this in separation, would pull her English comrades along behind her to the Promised Land.

In 1922 on Red Clydeside this was a perfectly tenable and even feasible theory, but Maclean, jailed for sedition four times, was frust-trated in his aims; his prophecy was realised only too accurately and he died in 1923 a disappointed man mourned by thousands of rebellious Glasgow workers. He became one of MacDiarmid's heroes and his policy is still rooted deeply at the heart of the poet's thought.

Scotland has had few men whose names
Matter – or should matter – to intelligent people,
But of these Maclean, next to Burns, was the greatest
And it should be of him, with every Scotsman and Scotswoman
To the end of time, as it was of Lenin in Russia
When you might talk to a woman who had been
A young girl in 1917 and find
That the name of Stalin lit no fires,
But when you asked her if she had seen Lenin
Her eyes lighted up and her reply
Was the Russian word which means
Both beautiful and red.
Lenin, she said, was 'krassivy, krassivy'.
John Maclean too was 'krassivy, krassivy',
A description no other Scot has ever deserved.

Communism as a force in British politics died the death in Hungary in 1956, but in the 1920s and 1930s it was very much alive, just as it was all over Europe during the German occupation; it was, as John Maclean and Hugh MacDiarmid thought of it, the hope of down-trodden humanity.

We are not here concerned with whether MacDiarmid was right or wrong in his beliefs any more than, at this date, we would be con-cerned with whether W. B. Yeats was in his opposite beliefs. The opinions and beliefs of a major poet (the case is often different with the minor ones) can be of interest, eventually, only in so far as they affect his poetry; we are not going to quarrel about them. You can still be a good Presbyterian and read and enjoy St. John of the Cross – at least, I should hope so. A Christian who cannot appreciate the pagan Parthenon or the glories of a Buddhist shrine is in sad case aesthetically, though his soul may rejoice in freedom from contamination.

Of course, this breadth of outlook, which we take for granted to some extent, is very much easier to indulge when contemplating works of the past in which, to our eyes, the issues that called them to birth have long been overlaid by those of the clamant but equally transitory present. It is sometimes not so easy to separate political from aesthetic views calmly when the subject is bang up in front of your face. We have all heard of the banning of Beethoven and Wagner from British concert halls in World War I and the sudden enormous popularity of Russian music and literature in World War II when Tolstoy's *War and Peace*, unlikely as it must seem today, sat almost permanently at the top of the Best Sellers List. When MacDiarmid and Roy Campbell conducted their public flyting they were not writing as artists altogether – if at all! That the closed mind can be a positive threat to a culture and to the production of works of the spirit (of art, in fact) is evidenced at home by the Reformation, the effects of which we have not yet thrown off after four hundred years, and abroad by the Socialist Realism creed in the U.S.S.R. The first years of the Revolution – the period that initially inspired such idealists as MacDiarmid – produced in Russia a great renaissance of poetry, music and film. Under Stalin and the imposition of political direction of the arts the inspiration dried up and even such world-famous masters as Prokofiev and Shostakovitch were on occasion banned and disciplined. Remember the history of *Lady Macbeth of Mtsensk*.

This is not to say that 'political' or didactic art must be inferior art: it can easily be shown that all ancient art is didactic. The bard educates the tribe by singing of its ancient glories in order to inspire emulation of its heroes in the present and future. Homer is didactic; Dante is didactic; Shakespeare's historical plays are didactic; Barbour and Henryson are didactic; Milton is didactic. All Christian art, indeed all religious art of any period or culture, is didactic. All royal portraiture from the Pharaohs to Queen Victoria, and even beyond, is designed to impress you with the power and glory of the ruler. This is not to say that Michelangelo's tombs of the Medici are bad art because they are directed art. In this century, much of Yeats's poetry is didactic, all Brecht's (call it *engagé* if you must), all Mayakovsky's, practically all of Attila Jozsef's; so is a great deal of Scottish poetry, Gaelic and Scots, ancient and modern. MacDiarmid's poetry is didactic, political, almost all the time, and the gospels he bears witness to are those seeming irreconcilables, Scottish Nationalism and Communism.

He has obviously been taxed with this evident inconsistency for he sometimes takes the trouble to answer such criticism. In August 1945 he wrote in the *Scots Independent*:

> I write as a Scottish Communist. These words mean exactly what they say. They do not mean Russian Communist. Russia stands at a very different stage of development from Scotland, and has a very different historical background. My Russian comrades can get on with their own affairs. I, on the other hand, am almost exclusively concerned with Scotland. The application of Communism in any country depends upon the accurate analysis of all the elements in its economic, political, cultural and social position and potentialities in the light of Dialectical Materialism. I accept that method of interpreting history, but I personally do not feel qualified to apply it myself to any country but Scotland, the only country of which I have the necessary first-hand knowledge and into whose problems and potentialities I have made the necessary intensive and comprehensive research.

A decade earlier, in 1936, in dealing with John Maclean's Scottish Republican line, he wrote (as quoted in *Lucky Poet*):

> Scottish separation is part of the process of England's Imperial disintegration and is a help towards the ultimate triumph of the workers of the world.... As against the all-too-simple cry that the interests of the workers in Scotland and England are identical, we have no hesitation in stressing that far more exact dialectical discrimination must be given to the alleged consequences of the identity of the interests of Scottish workers and English workers, since this in no wise conflicts with the question of Scottish independence nor necessarily involves any incorporating union of the two peoples, whose relationships signally illustrate the fact that, as Marx, and subsequently Lenin, insisted: 'No nation that enslaves another can itself be free.' The freeing of Scotland should be a foremost plank in the programme of the English workers themselves – in their own no less than in Scotland's interests.

With the bourgeoisification of the British 'masses' and the rise of

Russia's 'imperialistic' pretensions the Workers of the World bit may sound somewhat dated today, but that is the basis of MacDiarmid's political philosophy and certainly the Nationalist part of it needs little change to adapt it to the circumstances of 1962.

If the reader is unimpressed with the poet's reconciliation of these seeming inconsistencies I would suggest that, in any event, the inconsistencies of an artist are essential to his nature – as two such different types of poet, Keats and Whitman, understood very well. Inconsistency may be a characteristic of many artists but it is also a characteristic of all Scots – dare I add all Christians and all Communists? As MacDiarmid is an artist and a Scot, a Communist and – at any rate, by birth – a Christian, how could he possibly avoid inconsistencies? It is his reconciliation of these, his exemplification of the Caledonian Antisyzygy, in fact, that makes him MacDiarmid. In the Lenin poems Communism is naturally the dominant partner – as Scottish Nationalism is in *A Drunk Man* – but even in these, with their declared theme, the other half of the marriage is implicit – either by the use of the Scots language in the First and Second Hymns or in the subject-matter, Glasgow slums, in the Third.

Aesthetically, it can be argued that the adoption of English for the 'Third Hymn' is a mistake, formally speaking. But a poet of this stature does not make such a decision idly. Why then? All his life, and even today when most of his new work appearing is in English, he has advocated for Scottish poets the use of the two ancient languages, Gaelic and Scots. Why has the man who more than anyone else, indeed almost single-handed, promoted, stimulated and contributed to the revival or renaissance of the Scottish tradition ceased to practise what he preaches? Why in the 'Hymns to Lenin' did he use Scots for the 'First' and 'Second' and English for the 'Third'? Politically speaking, the use of the Scots language is part of his Nationalist programme, part of his original aim in the 1920s to revive the whole idea and soul of the nation, using a literary renaissance as the spearhead for an entire political and cultural rebirth. Almost all his early work was in Scots, once he had announced the programme in his monthly, *The Scottish Chapbook*, late in 1922. He continued to write a certain amount of poetry in English, but the proportion, as published, was not high until about 1934 in *Stony Limits*. *Scots Unbound* of 1932, for instance, contained only four short poems in English out of the thirty-odd pages of the longish philosophical and philological flights of 'Depth and the Chthonian Image', 'Tarras' ('This Bolshevik bog! Suits me doon to the grun'!'), the virtuoso piece 'Water Music' and the title poem, which are all in Scots and mostly in a very rich, even dictionary-dredging Scots. It should be noted, however, that the mostly English *Stony Limits*, which dredged the English geological dictionary, did originally contain an important long poem in colloquial Scots, 'Ode to All Rebels', which was rejected by the publishers – for other than linguistic reasons.[1] But the other important long poem in this book, 'Lament for the Great Music', was in English; it is one of his greatest works.

In his next book, *Second Hymn to Lenin and Other Poems* of 1935, the title poem, whose actual composition dates from a year or two before this, is the only one in Scots and it is in a much more dilute Scots than the 'First Hymn' of five years back. Perhaps it is significant that the collection includes, as separate poems, many extracts from the 'Ode to All Rebels', rejected from *Stony Limits*, which in their removal have suffered a sea change and now appear in English versions. One of these is a very short piece which, as printed in the 'Ode', runs:

Here at the heicht o' passion
   As lovers dae
I can only speak brokenly
   O' trifles tae.

Idiot incoherence
   I ken fu' weel
Is the only language
   That wi' God can deal.

As printed in the *Second Hymn to Lenin and Other Poems*, it reads:

Here at the height of passion
   As lovers do
I can only speak brokenly
   Of trifles too.

Idiot incoherence
   I know full well
Is the only language
   That with God can deal.

Some people would say there was not much difference here, just one word, 'ken' for 'know', and one bad rhyme, 'well' for 'weel'; the

[1] This poem was subsequently published in its original form in *The Voice of Scotland*, vol. 4, nos. 1 and 2, in 1947, and in book form in the Castle Wynd edition of *Stony Limits and Scots Unbound* in 1955.

rest is merely pronunciation. Maybe. Poetry is not quite so simple as that, but we have no space to delve. One question is, have these poems lost anything in their translation? I would say yes, but there is no doubt they are still effective and moving in their new guise, and the thought, profound or otherwise, is naturally unaffected. But they seem to have lost something of the full charge, their totality, and an immediacy, a vigour – their virr is what I mean – that they have in Scots. Others may not agree, but it seems to me as if a little of the heart has gone and a little of the head come in – as of course it must in the mere act of translating. I must admit I liked them well in English before I knew the Scots originals. This, however, opens up an irrelevant though exciting avenue that I will not explore here, not even turn a single stone upon it, for at the moment there is the other question, why MacDiarmid turned from Scots to English in the course of the 'Three Hymns', why likewise he translated those extracts from 'Ode to All Rebels' between 1934, say, and 1935.

The 'First Hymn' (1930) and, particularly, its accompanying poems are in a fairly rich Scots, the 'Second' (1932) thinner, more city vernacular than country, and in the 'Third' (1935) Scots is dropped altogether in favour of English. In the 'Ode to All Rebels' he is still using a rich but vernacular Scots, which seems to date it before the philological *Scots Unbound* of 1932. But the English translated extracts would seem to date from 1933 or 1934 because one of them, the famous 'O, she was fu' o' lovin' fuss', is printed in the original Scots version in Macmillan's *Selected Poems* of 1934 and in English in *Second Hymn etc.* of 1935.

It is only a guess on my part, but I think possibly his later turning to English was due to a desire to speak to a more international public than he thought he could reach in Scots, and this coincided with his increasing interest, at this time, in international or communist politics. In 1926, with *A Drunk Man*, he had conquered Scotland – the Young Chevalier at Holyroodhouse – but he sought a further throne and adopted the weapon of the enemy to secure it. Having achieved this – advancing beyond Derby – by getting his English poem, 'Cornish Heroic Song', published in *The Criterion*, the ark of the English covenant, which had already published the 'Second Hymn' in Scots, his eagle eye surveys the Atlantic and even the steppes of Muscovy and the plains of China and he becomes increasingly – and, for many, bafflingly – polyglot, at least in the use of quotation.

Whether, in fact, the use of English and other lingos is better than

Scots for this international purpose is not at all certain to my mind, though superficially it seems obvious enough. Yet Scots has always been acceptable in America, more so than in England, and, of course, Burns's Scots has not prevented him from travelling round the world. It is significant that the first *Collected Poems* of MacDiarmid should come out under an American imprint.

An interesting aspect of MacDiarmid's composition in the two languages is that when using Scots he inclines to a strict verse form and generally uses rhyme; when using English he inclines, not exclusively, to free, rhythmic, declamatory, rhetorical, sometimes positively prose-like verse. This seems to me to argue that the Scots language may release in him a vein of poetry as song – though much of it, as the 'First Hymn', for instance, is its very opposite, that of downright 'plain speaking' – whereas English prompts him to a magisterial, lecture-like delivery. Naturally, there are exceptions to this; I am thinking of the wonderful Shetland landscape, 'Island Funeral'. With English, also, he seems to require a much larger canvas and a longer line. Can it be that the Scots language, because richer in sound-words, is more apt for the succinct, telling, almost proverbial summing-up of an argument in a common, concrete, workaday phrase, whereas literary English, being bookish and removed from the common vernacular of the street, has become increasingly abstract and consequently feebler at the 'nutshell' phrase but more capable of enlarging on an abstract, rather vague intellectual idea?

Compare in the 'Three Hymns', for instance, the various means employed for the expression of comparable though not exactly similar thoughts about the minds of poet and man of action:

From the 'First Hymn to Lenin':

Descendant o' the unkent Bards wha made
Sangs peerless through a' post-anonymous days
I glimpse again in you that mightier poo'er
Than fashes wi' the laurels and the bays
But kens that it is shared by ilka man
  Since time began.

From the 'Second Hymn':

Your knowledge in your ain sphere
Was exact and complete
But your sphere's elementary and sune by
As a poet maun see't. . . .

Unremittin', relentless,
Organised to the last degree,
Ah, Lenin, politics is bairns' play
To what this maun be!

From the 'Third Hymn':

On days of revolutionary turning points you literally flourished,
Became clairvoyant, foresaw the movement of classes,
And the probable zig-zags of the revolution
As if on your own palm;
Not only an analytical mind but also
A great contructive, synthesizing mind
Able to build up in thought the new reality
As it must actually come
By force of definite laws eventually. . . .
Such clairvoyance is the result
Of a profound and all-sided knowledge of life
With all its richness of colour, connections and relations
Hence the logic of your speeches . . .
As some great seaman or some poet grasps
The practical meaning, ideal beauty, traditional fascination,
Intellectual importance and emotional chances combined
In any instant in his particular situation,
So here there is a like accumulation of effects
On countless plains of significance at once, . . .

As usual with almost all works of art, the historical context of these poems is important for a just appreciation. When the 'First Hymn' was written, romantic adulation of the Russian Revolution and a kind of parlour Communism was rapidly becoming the intellectual fashion in Left Wing circles; all Nationalism was equated with Nazism and Fascism. With the outbreak of the Spanish Civil War in 1936 and the forming of the International Brigade this had become an othodoxy with very few dissidents. It was dewy-eyed, but it was innocently sincere in the warm bosoms of the younger English liberal bourgeoisie. They were anti-Imperialist and anti-Fascist and when the Imperial British government at last agreed with them and declared war on their Fascist enemy they had theoretically nothing to grumble about, but it didn't seem quite right somehow, especially as their golden boy was sitting on the fence in the Kremlin and concluding a truce with the Fascist beasts. Many became pacifists to avoid the quandary; some went to America. Then Russia became involved, perforce, and everything was all right again. Throughout all this, and ever since, MacDiarmid never budged an inch from his original two-fisted position. If he now seems to be unique and stubborn in sticking to his principles of thirty years ago, when all the rest have changed sides with the tide, we must not on that account conclude that those principles were wrong at the time he wrote those poems.

To the leftish young, before 1939, Russia appeared the great white hope of freedom. One may consider that those hopes have been belied since, as all political ideals are belied in practice – but the poetry that those ideals inspired remains in the books. Wordsworth may have deplored the results of the French Revolution but 'Bliss was it in that dawn to be alive . . . to be young was very heaven' is still expressive of the aspiring dreams of youth and liberty. Art transcends the mutability of politics. Nobody today could applaud the violence of seventeenth-century life on the borders of Scotland and England – but who does not catch his breath at the balladry that society produced? The Greek pantheon was very different from the home life of our beloved Queen, but the horrors of a remorseless heathen deity visited upon Oedipus can still excite the pity of a non-believing welfare-state audience; great art even enables a monster like Macbeth to become positively sympathetic.

I do not suggest the 'Three Hymns to Lenin' are on this level, but the idealism of the first two and the humanitarian loathing of oppression and exploitation voiced in the third are still as viable now as when they were first written in the enthusiastic climate that surrounded Lenin's name in the 1930s – whatever future revelations may show of the true face of their hero. Would you dub Yeats and Pound black fascists and ban them from the libraries?

Lenin and Bolshevism as a theme in MacDiarmid's poetry is of course by no means confined to the 'Three Hymns'. It runs through all his work, especially his work of the 1930s, alongside and together with that of Scottish Nationalism, and it produced some of his very finest poems, as 'The Seamless Garment' from *The First Hymn, etc.*, and the well-known anthology piece, 'The Skeleton of the Future' from *Stony Limits*. During this period his monumental 'Lament for the Great Music', a celebration of the MacCrimmons and other great pipers, expressed his yearning, as a Borderer, for the resurgence and unity of all Scotland through an understanding and absorption of the

Gaelic ethos into the entire soul of the nation. This desire for greater understanding within Scotland then opens out wider to embrace the whole world through Communism and the defeat of the Bankers (Social Credit), and, at length, as at the beginning in certain poems in *Sangschaw*, would comprehend the universe and all within it. From this extraordinary vision, with its faint echoes of Whitman, evolved the huge fragments of the 1930s only now [1962] achieving publication – *In Memoriam James Joyce* (Maclellan, 1955), *The Kind of Poetry I Want* (Duval, 1961) – to which he gave the grand overall title of *Mature Art*, scheduled for publication by the Obelisk Press in Paris but cancelled on the outbreak of war.

This transcendental desire, beyond the ability of man to realise but within the secret potential of every artist's private dream, he has expressed often at great length. He has also expressed the same thing very simply and shortly – and beautifully – in one of the English poems in the *Second Hymn, etc.* which gains in impact, I think, over some of the grander expressions by its element of personality and the immediacy of the last two lines that draw all together with a wonderful compassion:

O ease my spirit increasingly of the load
Of my personal limitations and the riddling differences
Between man and man with a more constant insight
Into the fundamental similarity of all activites.

And quicken me to the gloriously and terribly illuminating
Integration of the physical and the spiritual till I feel how easily
I could put my hand gently on the whole round world
As on my sweetheart's head and draw it to me.

Does it matter whether a breathing of the human spirit such as that was written by an egotistical, pigheaded, atheistical Red or by a holy imperial teetotalistical Roller?

No; political theories and political empires can change the face of the world and affect the ways of life and thought of millions of mankind – but Sappho has outlived many tyrants and Virgil many empires. Who remembers Shelley's politics and who Ozymandias? MacDiarmid's politics are the chiefest inspiration of his poetry – you can like them or lump them, but you cannot have one without the other. If you are passionate in disagreement and unable to thole his opinions for the sake of his art you are unfortunate for you are cutting yourself off from one of the poetic pleasures of our time.

The 'First Hymn', as I have said, is downright plain speaking:

Christ said: 'Save ye become as bairns again.'
Bairnly eneuch the feck o' us ha' been!
Your work needs men; and its worst foes are juist
The traitors wha through a' history ha' gi'en
The dope that's gar'd the mass o' folk pay heed
And bide bairns indeed . . .

rising towards the end to a more exalted but still direct and simple utterance:

For now in the flower and iron of the truth
To you we turn; and turn in vain nae mair,
Ilka fool has folly eneuch for sadness
But at last we are wise and wi' laughter tear
The veil of being, and are face to face
Wi' the human race.

The 'Third Hymn' is a rhetorical outburst prompted by the poet's indignation at the living hell of Glasgow slums during the great depression of the 1930s:

Hard test, my master, for another reason.
The whole of Russia had no Hell like this.
There is no place in all the white man's world
So sunk in the unspeakable abyss.
Only a country whose chief glory is the Kirk,
A country with our fetish of efficiency and thrift,
With endless loving sentiment to mask the facts,
Has such an infernal masterpiece in its gift.

A horror that might sicken your stomach even,
The peak of the capitalist system and the trough of Hell,
Fit testimonial to our ultra-pious race,
A people greedy, lying and unconscionable
Beyond compare . . .

moving from this, through stages of satire and anger, to his final grand peroration:

We do not play or keep any mere game's conventions.
Our concern is human wholeness – the child-like spirit
Newborn every day – not, indeed, as careless of tradition
Nor of the lessons of the past: these it must needs inherit.

But as capable of such complete assimilation and surrender,
So all-inclusive, unfenced-off, uncategoried, sensitive and
    tender,
That growth is unconditioned and unwarped – Ah, Lenin,
Life and that more abundantly, thou Fire of Freedom,
Fire-like in your purity and heaven-seeking vehemence,
Yet the adjective must not suggest merely meteoric,
Spectacular – not the flying sparks but the intense
Glowing core of your character, your large and splendid
    stability
Made you the man you are – the live heart of all humanity!

Spirit of Lenin, light on this city now!

Light up this city now!

Admirable as this rhetoric is – and who dares nowadays to be so unashamedly equal to a grand occasion as MacDiarmid? – it is to the 'Second Hymn' that I keep returning. As a purely personal, indeed subjective, judgment I should say it is the most successful of the three, if for no other reason than for its memorable, even proverbial quality and for the homely and typically Caledonian ambivalence of the poet towards his master. MacDiarmid may or may not be a political philosopher, but he is a true poet who can remark to the great tyrant, with an odd mixture of arrogance and humility:

Sae here, twixt poetry and politics,
There's nae doot in the en'.
Poetry includes that and s'ud be
The greatest poo'er amang men.

It's the greatest, *in posse* at least,
That men ha'e discovered yet
Tho' nae doot they're unconscious still
O' ithers faur greater than it.

You confined yoursel' to your work
– A step at a time;
But, as the loon is in the man,
That'll be ta'en up i' the rhyme,

Ta'en up like a pool in the sands
Aince the tide rows in,
When life opens its hert and sings
Withoot scruple or sin.

Your knowledge in your ain sphere
Was exact and complete
But your sphere's elementary and sune by
As a poet maun see't . . .

. . . Freend, foe; past, present, future;
Success, failure; joy, fear;
Life, Death; and a'thing else,
For us are equal here . . .

Ah, Lenin, politics is bairns' play
To what this maun be!

MacDiarmid the Marxist Poet

DAVID CRAIG

When people speak of the 1930s as a time when poets were on the Left, they are thinking of W. H. Auden, Cecil Day Lewis, Stephen Spender, Louis MacNeice. Literary reputations are made (or suppressed) so exclusively in London that it is too often forgotten, or never realised, that while those others left barely one unquestionably outstanding piece of Marxist writing, there are among Hugh MacDiarmid's poems fully twenty pieces in which his Marxism or Communism found a style, an imagery and rhythm, that drew on the very fibre of that movement. While MacSpaunday was, or were, embedding the correctly ruthless and scientific imagery (pylons, aerodromes, rifles) in an incongruous basis of the old Romantic or the new clever-clever style, or forcing their verse to run with a jaunty popularness that remained painfully *voulu* because it had at its heart no fellow-feeling for the people, MacDiarmid rose to a truly Marxist intellectual content and a truly vernacular speech-idiom.

It is surely in his poetry, and nowhere else, that his Marxism lies. He has piled up a mass of other writing, the bulk of it polemical, but one looks in vain amongst it for coherent Communist thinking. His autobiography *Lucky Poet*, his biographical and literary essays, his many editorials and introductions cannot be said to amount to a body of thought that is capable of study. Rather it is a caddis-case of intellectual bits and pieces with a *personality* inside it, and it is the personality that dominates, not any firmly grasped material from wider life.

In the poetry, however, there is a great deal of clear, sound Marxism. In the fine 'The Seamless Garment' (from *First Hymn to Lenin*, 1931), he says:

> The mair we mak' natural as breathin', the mair
> Energy for ither things we'll can spare . . .

and in the 'Second Hymn to Lenin' (1932) he says, catching perfectly the thumping vehemence of the platform speaker:

> Oh, it's nonsense, nonsense, nonsense,
> Nonsense at this time o' day

That breid-and-butter problems
S'ud be in ony man's way. . . .

This faith that human experience and culture will expand immensely in an era of abundance and social ownership has been an essential of Communist thinking, from Marx's *Critique of the Gotha Programme* (1875) and Engel's *Socialism: Utopian and Scientific* (1880) to Lenin's *The State and Revolution* (1918), and it appears again, with confidence that it is on the verge of realisation, in the *Programme of the Communist Party of the Soviet Union* adopted by their 22nd Congress in October 1961.

Again, when MacDiarmid says in the 'First Hymn to Lenin' (1931),

Christ said: 'Save ye become as bairns again.'
Bairnly eneuch the feck o' us ha' been!
Your work needs men; and its worst foes are juist
The traitors wha through a' history ha' gi'en
The dope that's gar'd the mass o' folk pay heed
And bide bairns indeed.

he directly recalls Marx's description of religion as 'the *opium* of the people' and Lenin's fine expansion of this, both humanist and thoroughly militant: 'Religion is a sort of spiritual dope in which the slaves of capital drown the image of man, their demand for a life more or less worthy of human beings.'[1] And when MacDiarmid says in the second-last stanza of the 'Hymn',

. . . at last we are wise and wi' laughter tear
The veil of being, and are face to face
Wi' the human race,

he is surely putting into verse one of the deepest thoughts in Marx's *Capital*: 'The religious reflex of the real world can . . . only then finally vanish, when the practical relations of everyday life offer to man none but perfectly intelligible and reasonable relations with regard to his fellowmen and to nature. The life-process of society, which is based on the process of material production, does not strip off its mystical veil until it is treated as production by freely associated men, and is consciously regulated by them in accordance with a settled plan.'[2]

[1] Marx, Introduction to *Contribution to the Critique of Hegel's Philosophy of Right:* Marx and Engels, *On Religion*, Moscow 1957, p. 42; Lenin, 'Socialism and Religion', 1905: Moscow, 1954, p. 6.

[2] *Capital*, I, chap. 1, section 4, 'The Fetishism of Commodities'.

Those passages were written when MacDiarmid had just come to Communism, in the first onset of the Depression, when the lines of unemployed men stretched, I am told, from Motherwell to Wishaw. He had been a socialist of sorts for years. Before he was 20 he had served on a Fabian Research Committee on Land Problems and Rural Development, contributing 'valuable memoranda' to the report published in 1913. In the 1930s he was again doing practical work for the people, organising the cottars of Whalsay in the Shetlands to fight in the courts against the increased assessments of their houses.[1] W. R. Aitken's first check-list of MacDiarmid's works, in the section on books and periodicals announced but never published, consists mainly, for the years from 1935 to the war, of work specifically on socialism, and there is also mention in *Lucky Poet* (p. 204) of a promised biography of John Maclean, evidently in the mid-1930s. MacDiarmid's work in general, like Lewis Grassic Gibbon's, takes its place as a key part of the social movement that included the Clydeside Shop Stewards' Movement, outstanding political leaders such as Keir Hardie, Willie Gallacher and John Maclean, and the important contribution made by Red Clydeside to the founding of the Communist Party of Great Britain in 1920.

It would be misleading to draw a hard-and-fast line at the point where one supposes his pre-Marxist poetry ends and his Marxist begins. With one exception there is no expressed awareness of Communism in his poetry before the 'Hymns to Lenin'. But his very coming to Scots as the indispensable new medium for writers living and working in Scotland contained within itself the germ of a progressive trend. In writing his Scots lyrics in the mid-1920s, MacDiarmid was acting as a Nationalist, as he was when he helped to found the National Party of Scotland. In recent years, as the undeveloped countries – India, Ghana, Kenya, Algeria, Congo, Cuba and many more – have struggled for their independence from imperialism, we have become familiar with the truth that nationalism is often a first stage to socialism. Mao Tse-tung and Chiang Kai Shek could collaborate to defeat the Japanese, but the Communists had to fight and defeat the Kuomintang to establish socialism. Castro's rising in Cuba against native and American economic tyranny found itself, once it had to begin construction, turning into a Marxist-Leninist revolution. Such are the reasons why MacDiarmid's singling out of Scots, the language of a

[1] W. R. Aitken, 'C. M. Grieve/Hugh MacDiarmid': *The Bibliotheck*, vol, 1, no. 4, Autumn 1958, p. 3; MacDiarmid, *Lucky Poet* (1943), p. 87.

small, exploited, non-imperialist nation, as the vital medium for Scotland's poetry seems to me, in a potential way, progressive.

This trend in his thinking soon found, with the fertility of genius, its own style. There is a note in MacDiarmid's poetry of 1930–35 that can be heard nowhere else, and it is the very sound of his Marxism finding its voice. It occurs, for example, along with many other *timbres*, in 'Lo! A Child is Born' – a poem long ago picked out by John Speirs as outstanding.[1] It is an allegory in nineteen lines of the birth-pangs of history, and here is its superb close:

> . . . Then I thought of the whole world. Who cares for its travail
> And seeks to encompass it in like loving-kindness and peace?
> There is a monstrous din of the sterile who contribute nothing
> To the great end in view, and the future fumbles,
> A bad birth, not like the child in that gracious home
> Heard in the quietness turning in its mother's womb,
> A strategic mind already, seeking the best way
> To present himself to life, and at last, resolved,
> Springing into history quivering like a fish,
> Dropping into the world like a ripe fruit in due time. –
> But where is the Past to which Time, smiling through her tears
> At her new-born son, can turn crying: 'I love you'?

The peak of intensity is reached in the splendid double simile of fish and fruit. Here feelings are marvellously united: the measured, nearly Bibilical gravity of the repeated participles, 'Springing . . . Dropping', allied to the richness of the images, creates a feeling both springy and solid. The momentum at this point seems both to flow onwards and yet gather itself monumentally. With the unerring touch of genius the poet has evoked sheer vitality in nature and at the same time the experience of dwelling on it with steady intellectual intent.

The lines remind me strongly of Yeats's consummate passage from 'Sailing to Byzantium':

> . . . The young
> In one another's arms, birds in the trees
> – Those dying generations – at their song,
> The salmon-falls, the mackerel-crowded seas,
> Fish, flesh, or fowl, commend all summer long
> Whatever is begotten, born, and dies . . .

Both poets can make us feel how even as they experience nature in its

[1] Speirs, *The Scots Literary Tradition* (1940), p. 187.

full teeming power, their analytic intellects permeate their responses. But Yeats comes, deliberately, to the verge of an almost luxurious surrender to ripeness. MacDiarmid, characteristically, has less free flow of Romantic emotion; his impulses are subordinate to his long-range concerns.

'Lo! A Child' is less clearly socialist than other outstanding poems of that period; it could be just humanist. But the sense it gives of someone looking out over the whole of humanity's historic struggle to develop can be seen to draw directly from his Marxism. 'Strategic mind' is clue enough: Lenin's concern with strategy – the finding and co-operating with key trends of progress – has had a special fascination for MacDiarmid:

> Lenin was like that wi' the workin'-class life.
> At hame wi't a'.
> His fause movements coudna' been fewer,
> The best weaver earth ever saw.
> A' he'd to dae wi' moved intact,
> Clean, clear and exact.
>
> On days of revolutionary turning points you literally flourished,
> Became clairvoyant, foresaw the movement of classes,
> And the probable zig-zags of revolution
> As if on your palm. . . .

Lenin's mastery has evidently typified for MacDiarmid a kind of clarity he has desperately wanted since 1930.

At the very start of the 1930s he was writing his most concentrated, serious, and distinctive poetry, and in it that note I have mentioned can be heard time and time again. But I think it occurs first in *Penny Wheep* (1926), in a poem adapted from the German called 'The Dead Liebknecht'. MacDiarmid had nothing to do with revolutionary socialism in those days. Yet here he is coming onto his deepest vein in a poem on the German Communist leader who was murdered along with Rosa Luxemburg during the suppression of the short-lived revolution in Germany just after the Great War. The poem ends:

> The factory horns begin to blaw
> Thro' a' the city, blare on blare,
> The lowsin' time o' workers a',
> Like emmits skailin' everywhere.
> And wi' his white teeth shinin' yet
> The corpse lies smilin' underfit.

We bring up with a deep shock at the final image – saved from the merely creepy (the *Cabinet of Dr. Caligari* touch in German art of the 1920s) by its setting in a realistic contemporary environment. Closing on such an image makes us feel a potent force biding unshaken just under the surface of society; and this is the gist of the finest touch from 'John McLean (1879–1923)' (one of the revolutionary poems kept out of *Stony Limits* when Gollancz published it in 1934):

> . . . 'justice' may well do its filthy work
> Behind walls as filthy as these
> And congratulate itself blindly and never know
> The prisoner takes the light with him as he goes below.

This passage is fine also in the movement of the words in that last line – falling onto the page one by one as though forced out from the poet's depths, enacting the slow steps of the sentenced man. This is also the movement of 'Another Epitaph for an Army of Mercenaries' (from *Second Hymn to Lenin*, 1935), which is surely one of the finest pieces that speak out for socialism's traditional belief in peace:

> It is a God-damned lie to say that these
> Saved, or knew, anything worth any man's pride.
> They were professional murderers and they took
> Their blood money and impious risks and died.
> In spite of all their kind some elements of worth
> With difficulty persist here and there on earth.

Who else has written with quite that dogged toughness, every phrase doing its terse bit to establish an unanswerable logic, and without the least concession to the easy-flowing or the 'beautiful'? We can feel in this verse that grips so hard on experience and measures itself out so sparingly a rare mental stamina, the quality that could sustain, as Yeats did, a complex *argument* down many long lines – but with fewer flourishes than Yeats and greater earnestness:

> Christ's cited no' by chance or juist because
> You mark the greatest turnin'-point since him. . . .
> Certes nae ither, if no' you's dune this.
> It maitters little. What you've dune's the thing,
> No' hoo't compares, corrects, or complements
> The work o' Christ that's taen owre lang to bring
> Sic a successor to keep the reference back
> Natural to mak'.

This extraordinarily intent, intellectually concentrated vein is the perfect style for his key progressive ideas on culture:

> Gin I canna win through to the man in the street,
>   The wife by the hearth,
> A' the cleverness on earth'll no mak' up
>   For the damnable dearth.
>
> 'Haud on, haud on; what poet's dune that?
>   Is Shakespeare read,
> Or Dante or Milton or Goethe or Burns?'
>   – You heard what I said.[1]

It is also the right style for his core-idea of what he himself has had it in him to give to the progressive struggle:

> And as for me in my fricative work
>   I ken fu' weel
> Sic an integrity's what I maun hae,
> Indivisible, real,
> Woven owre close for the point o' a pin
>   Onywhere to win in.[2]

Again the words bind together with rare density, in a way that veritably enacts their content ('the seamless garment'). And finally there is the little poem called 'The Skeleton of the Future', subtitled 'At Lenin's Tomb':

> Red granite and black diorite, with the blue
> Of the labradorite crystals gleaming like precious stones
> In the light reflected from the snow; and behind them
> The eternal lightning of Lenin's bones.

Reading this, we realise that no other British poet has *cared* enough for politics to exalt a political leader as high as that – and not through empty rhetoric: 'eternal lightning' is an image full of meaning.

These examples have almost all been militant, revolutionary-socialist. But that is not why they have picked themselves. As poetry what they have in common is that utter intentness, the whole being focussed on its object, all self-regarding feelings burned away by the intensity of concern for a large objective purpose. The most comparable thing I know in British literature is the outstanding cluster of poems by Englishmen of the Civil War period in which we can feel the gallantry of the gentleman steadied and hardened into a new gravity by the dire epoch through which his class was passing – the

[1] "Second Hymn to Lenin" [Ed.]. [2] "The Seamless Garment" [Ed.].

poems I mean are Marvell's 'Horatian Ode Upon Cromwell's Return From Ireland', Shirley's 'The glories of our blood and state', and Lestrange's 'Loyalty Confin'd'. Like MacDiarmid's poems they typify what he himself calls, in the 'Second Hymn', 'Disinterestedness, Oor profoundest word yet'. It is by no means his only Marxist vein: for example, there is also a fleering radicalism, speaking out with a verve that recalls Burns flinging at genteel society, in the poem 'Tarras' (from *Scots Unbound*, 1932):

> This Bolshevik bog! Suits me doon to the grun'!
> For by fike and finnick the world's no' run.

But the intent and utterly serious vein does seem to be the core.

It still crops up occasionally in the 'Third Hymn to Lenin', for example the fine stanza that opens 'What seaman in the history of the world before'. This 'Hymn' seems to have been drafted in the middle or later 1930s. But apart from such fragments, the vein is finished. And nothing else takes its place. MacDiarmid's work runs out into a vast graveyard of ideas – the 'Cornish Heroic Song' (1939), *In Memoriam James Joyce* (1955), *The Kind of Poetry I Want* (1961) – terrible monuments to his final failure to fulfil a text from Lenin that he quotes twice in *Lucky Poet*: 'It would be a serious mistake to suppose that one can become a Communist without *making one's own* the treasures of human knowledge. . . . Communism becomes an empty phrase, a mere façade, and the Communist a mere bluffer, if he has not *worked over in his consciousness* the whole inheritance of human knowledge' (italics mine: Speech to the 1922 Comintern Congress).

The examples necessary to back this judgment are in the nature of the case so colossal that they would use up far more space than they deserve. Perhaps it will be enough, and fair to the poet, if I quote the end of 'On a Raised Beach' from *Stony Limits* – written at a time when creative rhythms were still moving in him (the preceding section, beginning '. . . if only one of these stones would move', is in fact very fine and characteristic):

> Diallage of the world's debate, end of the long auxesis,
> Although no ébrillade of Pegasus can here avail,
> I prefer your enchorial characters – the futhorc of the future –
> To the hieroglyphics of all the other forms of Nature.
> Song, your apprentice encrinite, seems to sweep
> The Heavens with a last entrochal movement. . . .

Is further quotation necessary? Do the forced, limping rhythms and musty poetic-diction encourage us even to look up in a dictionary 'auxesis', 'futhorc' and the rest? The Communist poet (he joined the Party the year that volume came out) is breaking down into the sort of chaos that was diagnosed by one of the profoundest English Marxist critics, Christopher Caudwell: 'Only when the bourgeois passes to the anarchistic stage where he negates all bourgeois society and deliberately chooses words with only personal associations, can rhythm vanish, for the poet now dreads even the social bond of having instincts common with other men, and therefore chooses just those words which will have a *cerebral* peculiarity. If he chooses words with too strong an emotional association, this, coupled with the hypnosis of a strong ryhthm, will sink him into the common lair of the human instincts.'[1] Just such a revulsion from instinctual experience – a desperation to get up into the free air of pure intellect – appears in 'Harry Semen' from *Stony Limits* ('A' the sperm that's gane for naething rises up to dam / In sick-white onanism the single seed / Frae which in sheer irrelevance I cam') and in many another poem of that time.

The reasons can hardly have been purely psychological. This most poignant occurrence, the running-out of a wonderful creative flow, must make us look back at the flow itself, and if we consider MacDiarmid as a Communist and a Communist poet, some very odd things come to light even in the 'Hymns to Lenin'. In the 'Second Hymn' MacDiarmid confides to Lenin that 'politics is bairns' play' to what poetry must be – a claim difficult to reconcile with responsible Communism. Babette Deutsch in *This Modern Poetry* interprets 'poetry' in the 'Hymn' to mean the whole distinctively human imaginative faculty. Of course, if you stretch terms far enough you can prove anything, and if 'politics' were so treated, it could easily be made to mean the whole human social organisation, in which case to exalt 'poetry' above it, or vice versa, could lead only to the inanest metaphysical speculations. Again, in the finely outspoken lyric from the second 'Hymn', 'Oh, it's nonsense, nonsense, nonsense,' the argument runs into this:

> Sport, love, and parentage,
> Trade, politics, and law
> S'ud be nae mair to us than braith
> We hardly ken we draw.

[1] Caudwell, *Illusion and Reality* (1946 ed.), p. 125.

This simple assertion deserves a simple reply: how *could* love and parentage, vital physical-emotional links between us as human beings, ever dwindle to mere reflexes, in any conceivable stage of mankind's development?

Surely the poet here is no Marxist, no historical materialist. He is using Marxism to license an almost maniacal wish to escape from the necessities of existence as we know it. In the 'Third Hymn', dating probably from a few years later, the self-styled materialist is writing:

> . . . only one or two in every million men today
> Know that thought is reality – and thought alone! . . .

But this is the most arrant idealism – treating the mental processes that depend on material existence as somehow higher than it, more 'real'. It is what the great thinkers in the Marxist-Leninist tradition have specifically fought against time and again.[1] They have fought it because they know that idealism cannot help being accompanied by reactionary tendencies when it comes to concrete social issues. And sure enough we find MacDiarmid writing in 'Reflections in a Scottish Slum', published in the anthology *Honour'd Shade* (1959) just three years after he rejoined the Communist Party:

> . . . It is good that the voice of the indigent,
> Too long stifled, should manage
> To make itself heard.
> But I cannot consent to listen
> To nothing but that voice.

Who asked him to listen to nothing else? The Aunt Sally he is knocking down is the merest figment from the bourgeois bogey-version of socialism ('levelling-down instead of levelling-up', etc, etc). Its occurrence suggests a quake in the foundations of his Communism. He is forgetting what every socialist should have forever in his mind, the words of Gene Debs, fearless pioneer of American trade-unionism: 'While there is a lower class I am of it, while there is a criminal class I am of it, while there is a soul in prison I am not free.'

If we consider MacDiarmid's Communism as a body of opinions, the inconsistencies typical of his thinking are as crippling there as anywhere. Politically he had started as a Fabian, turning Scottish Nationalist in the mid-1920s. Although fellow-feeling with the workers has certainly been strong in him, pure nationalism has been

[1] E.g. Engels, *Ludwig Feuerbach and the Outcome of Classical German Philosophy* (1888); Lenin, *Materialism and Empirio-Criticism* (1908).

even stronger. He is for workers' republics. But this turns out to mean a 'Celtic Union of Socialist Soviet Republics' embracing Scotland, Ireland, Wales and Cornwall![1] How could such a fantasy (usually unsupported by any evidence regarding the economic viability or convenience of such a union – or the desire of the peoples for it) ever have been put forward seriously?

The most objective reason for this must be that MacDiarmid was a victim of the confusions that have made unity of the Left so hard to achieve in Britain for generations now. Communists are banned in many cases from participation in labour institutions such as the Trade Union Congress, the Labour Party Conference and trades councils. Nationalism, even when it refuses to commit itself to any class and economic policy for the period after its precious Independence has been won, can still attract political support. Gallacher himself had a struggle before he understood why the Scottish Communists should go in with a British Party rather than remain in puny isolation.

Perhaps the most constructive way of making the point is to put MacDiarmid's work side by side with Bertolt Brecht's, as he too is a poet with that fine 'disinterestedness' permeating the very tones of his verse. He too was a Communist, and a man formed by the Great War and its aftermath. He too can base a spare stating (rather than evoking) poetry on a straight, terse vernacular: this stanza from 'A Worker Reads History' could almost have come from the 'Second Hymn to Lenin':

> Every page a victory,
> At whose expense the victory ball?
> Every ten years a great man,
> Who paid the piper?

Brecht too can make breathtaking transitions from 'low' language to a lofty style from classic literature – very disparate manners fused together by his sense of history and his position as an intellectual aligned with the workers. The passage from MacDiarmid's *A Drunk Man Looks at the Thistle* (1926) that begins in the old ballad way 'O wha's the bride that cairries the bunch / O' thistles blinterin' white' and works up through proverb-like couplets, coarse colloquial asides and gnomic folk-rhymes to the sardonically desperate 'song',

> O Scotland is
> THE barren fig –

[1] See for example *Lucky Poet*, p. 26; *Francis George Scott* (1955), p. 37 – here Ireland for some reason has been dropped.

this passage has many a counterpart in Brecht: the entire *Threepenny Opera*, for example, or (in a condensed way) the extraordinarily poignant 'Nanna's song' from *Round Heads and Pointed Heads* that gets its effect by modulating from jaunty folk-song to flat speech, mocking cliché and traditional refrain:

> And, though you may learn your trade well,
> Learn it at Lechery Fair,
> Bartering lust for small change
> Is a hard thing to do.
> Well, it comes to you.
> But you don't grow younger there.
> (After all you can't stay seventeen forever.)
> Thank God it's all over with quickly,
> All the love and the grief we must bear.
> Where are the tears of yester evening?
> Where are the snows of yester year?

But differences are equally marked. MacDiarmid wanted his poems to be 'spoken in the factories and fields'. Brecht's *were* sung in the Army, on United Front marches, in the workers' theatres. Brecht can bring poetry to the verge of prose – factual, barely rhythmical – but it never sounds like broken-down verse, it does not run out of control into delirious verbosity. 'The Rug-weavers of Kajan-Bulak Honour Lenin', for example,[1] could be 'prose'. But it is so controlled by its intentness on realisable social needs that it becomes a finished, lucid fifty lines such as we fail to find in any section whatsoever of MacDiarmid's *colossi*. Brecht could in fact dare to break up the poetic forms because he never lost his creative rhythm – the forms were not crumbling helplessly in his hands.

No doubt temperament plays its part in the difference, but full weight must be given also to the political situations of the two men. Brecht was forced to a deadly point of responsibility and a pitch of urgency by the most savage of all reactionary antagonists – German Fascism. The duties of a Communist poet could hardly have been clearer than in such a society. By contrast it is perhaps small wonder that MacDiarmid's gifts should have been allowed to splairge all over the place in the un-urgent, fumbling, amateurish *milieu* of Scottish Nationalism.

At the time when MacDiarmid's poetry was coming to grief, he

[1] All the Brecht examples come from his *Selected Poems*, trans. H. R. Hays (New York, 1959), pp. 109, 87, 135–7.

was obliged to leave the Communist Party because he had pursued narrow nationalist ends incompatible with the main purposes of the workers' movement. But there has also been continuity in his position. In the article he wrote for the *Daily Worker* of March 28, 1957, on 'Why I Rejoined', he used points that he had first made in the 'First Hymn to Lenin' of 1930: 'Even if the figures of the enemies of Communism were accurate, the killings, starvings, frame-ups, unjust judgments and all the rest of it are a mere bagatelle to the utterly mercenary and unjustifiable wars, the ruthless exploitation, the preventable deaths due to slums, and other damnable consequences of the profit motive, which must be laid to the account of the so-called "free nations of the West".'

So his convictions and the creative work that has depended so much on them have gone in and out, now clear, now muddied, often losing themselves, often failing to achieve wholeness. Setting that vein of rare intentness from the early 1930s in the perspective of his life's work, we can see that it was too much an evocation of only the *attitude* of seriousness and militancy. The subject-matter from social experience that should have been dealt with in the light of these attitudes never really appeared. The poems singled out in this essay are like a foretaste of what a masterly progressive poet might achieve – but the substantial doing of it never materialises. Yet even to have evoked the idea of such a poetry, to have brought it to the verge of realisation, is an achievement outstanding and unique (for obvious reasons) in the literature of the English-speaking world.

Hugh MacDiarmid and Gaelic Literature

DOUGLAS SEALY

> For what mess of pottage, what Southern filth,
> What lack of intricacy, fineness, impossible achievement,
> Have we bartered this birthright, for what hurdy-gurdy
> Exchanged this incomparable instrument?

An insistence on the study and restoration of Gaelic has always been one of the planks in MacDiarmid's platform. A knowledge of Gaelic was not only desirable but also necessary for the complete exploration of Scotland and for the understanding of its history. Scots, MacDiarmid has claimed, included English and even went beyond it; but Gaelic, so far from including English might almost be said to ignore it, and the elements of the Scottish psyche which are expressed in it are therefore the least likely to be contaminated by what MacDiarmid has called 'the wandering abscess of the English influence'.

Although Gaelic is not English, it might be wiser to regard it as contributory to the Scottish psyche rather than as the essence of it, for as T. F. O'Rahilly wrote in *Irish Dialects Past and Present* (1932), 'To the Gaelic-speaking Scotsman of the past Ireland was the mother-country, whose culture and whose traditions belonged no less to himself than to his kinsmen in Ireland'. Scottish Gaelic did not become independent till the middle of the eighteenth century and it was greatly influenced by the numerous Norse settlers, as can readily be seen in many place-names.

There were other reasons for MacDiarmid's interest in Gaelic. He was attracted by the recognised position of the poet in Gaelic society and by the fact that he had to undergo a stringent training in the details of his craft. A poet was a poet and a carpenter was a carpenter; there were no part-time poets, Sunday painters or do-it-yourself kits; there were only professionals. And MacDiarmid is fond of quoting from Henri Hubert's *Les Celtes*: 'Celtic literature was essentially a poetic literature. . . . We must not think of Celtic poetry as lyrical outpourings, but as elaborately ingenious exercises on the part of rather pedantic literary men. Yet Celtic literature was popular as no other was.' The first two statements are correct but the implications of 'popular as no other was' are completely misleading. To quote O'Rahilly again: 'Down to the seventeenth century our Irish writers, in so far as their writings have survived, belonged exclusively to the upper classes. . . . The poets of the schools rigidly retained to the last not only an archaic diction but also an old pronunciation. . . . In more than one Irish tale a king, before whom a poet has recited verses, is made to exclaim: "An excellent poem, only I do not understand a word of it." ' In a story about the seventh-century king Guaire we read of a poet reciting a poem in poetical jargon and then explaining it to the king before receiving his reward. And David Greene in *Seven Centuries of Irish Learning* (ed. Ó Cuív) writes on these poets or professional panegyrists: 'Their weakness was that they were, by the very nature of their calling, the paid propagandists of the existing order of things . . . When that order vanished, they vanished with it. They had no interest in the common people. . . . They made the Irish language a better literary medium than it had ever been before, while at the same time denying it all possibility of intellectual development.' There were occasional poems and poets of great talent, but the picture drawn by David Greene gives a correct overall impression. After the collapse of the Gaelic aristocracy the syllabic verse of the schools gave way to the accentual verse of the people, which had arisen from some of the older Irish metres under the influence of the French song metres of the Anglo-Norman settlers, and reached the peak of its technical development six senturies later with the poets of the Munster school, whose work has been ably championed and described by Daniel Corkery in *The Hidden Ireland.*

This book is another source book for MacDiarmid's ideas of Gaelic literature – 'he tells,' writes MacDiarmid, 'how men labouring in the fields all day entered again at night into full possession of the high Bardic tradition and rejoiced in complex literary allusiveness and intricate rules of versification.' In other words they were a literary élite and Corkery does not forget to tell us that there were other anonymous poets, living side by side with them, who wrote a very different kind of verse with simpler metres and a more frank and passionate message, and who neglected the tales of Troy or of Deirdre for themes of local relevance, where love and death and sorrow gained no added lustre from references to the past. It is this anonymous poetry that is one of the glories of our literature. So much of the more sophisticated poetry is spoilt by an excess of ornament, by long strings of alliterative adjectives, matter being so often subordinated to form, that while one can admire this poetry as a literary *tour de force* one must withhold the highest praise. This poetry loses everything when it is translated, not so the Amhráin na nDaoine or Songs of the People, as the anonymous songs are called.

> Do you remember going to Mass that day?
> A thin needle would not have gone between us.
> Now this year a man with a horse could go
> Or a ship in sail on a day of violence and storm.

The force of that is apparent even in prose translation.

It is by force and simplicity that many of the poems in Robert Conquest's collection of verse from the Soviet bloc, *Back to Life*, make their point. The Polish poet, Adam Wazyk, says of his own 'Poem for Adults'.

> This is a naked poem
> before it is clothed
> with vexations, colours and the smells of this earth.

The aim is to shed all irrelevance, all merely decorative detail. If there is ever to be again a popular poetry it will have to be like this, a 'naked' poetry. Irish songs are full of this nakedness, so are the Spanish Cantes Flamencos:

> The two of us in a little room
> If you were to give me poison
> I would take poison

and in Willard R. Trask's collection *The Unwritten Song: Poetry of the Primitive and Traditional Peoples of the World* one finds this nakedness continually, just as one finds it in the anonymous or obscurely authored Scottish Gaelic songs of the sixteenth, seventeenth and eighteenth centuries. Sorley MacLean in *Scottish Art and Letters, 3* (1947) compares them with the Border Ballads and says that 'in the Gaelic anonyms there is far more of the variety of life realised on a high level, and though there is often in them the same bare concentration, there is often a rich texture of imagery, and always the Gaelic music and finish which prevents them from being so unequal as the Ballads'. Although MacDiarmid would probably not care to write such poetry himself, as he has never retreated from the attitude expressed in 1926: 'The highest art at any time can only be appreciated by an infinitesimal minority of the people – if by any' (*Selected Essays*, p. 44), it seems to be something of this nature that he had in mind when he referred to 'a "bareness and coolness of expression" as in the Sagas, or the hardness of the ancient Gaelic classics – the literature of men conscious of their own reality as well as that of outer reality, because fully conscious of the society which makes them what they are' (*Islands of Scotland*, p. 27). It is certainly what Norman MacCaig means when he speaks of his own 'attempt to achieve the simple and direct, but highly charged statements which seem to me the greatest achievement of Gaelic, as of other poetry'. Could we take as a further example the words of Vergil?

> Venit summa dies et ineluctabile tempus
> Dardaniae. Fuimus Troes. Fuit Ilium et ingens
> Gloria Teucrorum.

Nevertheless, it is not so much these anonymous authors that MacDiarmid admires but the two great names of the eighteenth century, Alexander MacDonald and Duncan MacInyre, for he has translated, with the assistance of Sorley MacLean, the major poem of each and written a poem to each of these poets as well. His translation of MacDonald's 'Birlinn of Clanranald' is vigorous and probably gives as good an impression of the original as English could. The original describes, in Douglas Young's words, 'the voyage of a chief's galley across the Minch as if it were going from Heaven to Hell and back' and it does so with resource and energy, though to my mind eighteenth-century Scottish Gaelic poetry suffers from the same defects as eighteenth-century Irish poetry, though to a lesser extent; the Scottish Gaelic poems are much more alive and popular in the sense alluded to above. I suspect that what MacDiarmid admires is more the man than the poetry, for as he says in *In Memoriam James Joyce*:

> . . . the authors I love best are they
> Who have lived, knocked about in the world,
> Had a thousand adventures of every sort,
> And penetrated every kind of milieu,
> Feeling, watching, taking stock the whole time;
> Men for whom writing was first and above all
> A pleasure, men who, when they sat down to write,
> Had merely to let their pens run freely,
> So great was the pressure of memory
> And the weight of the thousand living images
> That dwelt with them.

MacDonald is said to have entered the pulpit of the Parish Church of Islandfinnan on a certain Sunday in 1745 to utter propaganda for the Jacobite cause, at one point removing his coat and displaying underneath it a tartan plaid, while he recited the couplet:

Sìos an clò dubh,
Suas am breacan!

He fought as a Captain in the Prince's Army and after the battle of Culloden took refuge with his wife in the wilds of Glencoe, where he remained till the passing of the Indemnity Act. MacDiarmid's exhilarating poem to MacDonald, 'To Alasdair Mac Mhaighstir Alasdair', ignores MacDonald's personal history and instead uses MacDonald and his poetry as a pretext for a description of all that a poet should be. MacDonald joins the other figures in the MacDiarmid pantheon, Lenin, Doughty, F. G. Scott, Korzybski, to name a few, and is seen as an apotheosis of MacDiarmid himself:

Jaupin the stars, or thrawin lang strings
  O' duileasg owre the sun
Till like a jeelyfish it swings
  In deeps rewon,
And in your brain as in God's ain
  A'thing's ane again.

The translation of MacIntyre's 'Praise of Ben Dorain' is less successful. MacDiarmid doesn't attempt to represent the original metric scheme and frequently uses far more words than necessary. It is interesting to compare MacDiarmid's version with some others.

I

I the band am admiring
  Defiling in order,
And with noise retiring
  Up the Strone's rocky border;
'Twixt Craobh-ainnis they tarry
And the mouth of Strong Corrie
A fed and horned quarry
  That buy not their portion . . .

(trans. George Calder, 1912)

2

Graceful to see to me was a group
Lined up in the order of march to troop
Down by the Sron rock south through the loop
'Twixt Craobh na h-ainnis moor and the scoop
Of Corrie-dhaingean; no goog* on that herd, * unfledged bird
And none with a staring hide covered,
That for bite and sup never begged or chaffered
Nor yet lacked though to that they'd not stoop.
That was the fine line to be watching oop
The seen parts of a path between noop and noop.

(trans. MacDiarmid, 1940)

3

That troupe was beloved
assembling in order –
ascending, bright hooved,
each cliff that's in nature.

Between the Poor Pastures
and the Corrie of Fastness –
not buying repast there
but eating it freely.

(trans. Iain Crichton Smith, *Akros*, 1969)

A prose rendering might run as follows: 'I thought the band was beautiful as it advanced in order, noisily ascending the rock of Srone; between the moorland of Craobh na h-ainnis and the mouth of Coire-daingean, it was a well-fed high-headed herd that doesn't buy its portion.' It is impossible to convey in English the music and elegance of the original, and MacDiarmid's translation is at its best when he forgets his original and writes:

Volatile, vigilant there
One with the horizon she goes
Where horizons horizons disclose,
Or lies like a star hidden away
By the broad light of day.
Earth has nothing to match her.

This is more reminiscent of the early MacDiarmid of 'A Herd of Does' than of MacIntyre. Although MacIntyre's poetry is perhaps finer than MacDonald's – Sorley MacLean says MacDonald 'realises dynamic nature with a vigour immediacy and exactness which would appear to me unrivalled if I could forget the delicacy which MacIntyre adds and which make the latter's poetry the very greatest of eighteenth-century Gaelic Nature poetry' – MacDiarmid is less in sympathy with the gentle simple deerstalker. 'How difficult to make out such a genius as yours,' he says in his poem to MacIntyre, which displays a learning that would have bewildered the unlettered Highlandman, but he does pay real tribute at the end of the poem in a moving passage describing deer browsing on twigs above the watchers:

> . . . only in *your* poetry can we feel we stand
> Some snowy November evening under the birch-trees
> By a tributary burn that flows
> Into the remote and lovely Dundonnell river
> And receive the most intimate, most initiating experience. . . .

MacDiarmid's translations from Gaelic are competent but not in the same class as his translations from twentieth-century continental poets. His method is to work over translations by other hands ('creative transcription' to use the words of K. S. Sorabji) and it is interesting to note in this context that a passage in the very fine translation from Rilke to be found in *To Circumjack Cencrastus* is given a lift by the use of the Gaelic word *caoin* (Anglicé 'keen').

> Surely the keening women should have keened
> In truth – women who weep for pay and whine
> The whole night through if they are paid enough,
> When there's no other sound.

> Ob man nicht dennoch hätte Klagefrauen
> auftreiben müssen? Weiber, welche weinen
> für Geld, und die man so bezahlen kann,
> dass sie die Nacht durch heulen, wenn es still wird.

No English word could have translated Klage as well as the Gaelic has done.

MacDiarmid, busy with poetry and politics, not to mention the task of survival, cannot have had much time to spare for the study of Gaelic and had to rely to a large extent on the writings of others in his efforts to keep the Gaelic tradition before Scotland's eye. For instance the requirements he postulates for Gaelic poetry:

> Cruadal (hardihood), gaisge (valour) and that sentiment
> For which English has no name, but which
> In Greek is αἰδώς and in Gaelic nàire . . .

are quoted verbatim from W. J. Watson's Bardachd Ghaidhlig and the passages dealing with Gaelic literature in *To Circumjack Cencrastus* are based on a reading of Aodh De Blácam's *Gaelic Literature Surveyed*. This is an excellent book but definitely propagandist, and it would not be wise to accept all its literary estimates, but this is what MacDiarmid has done and in an otherwise fine passage where the Gaelic poets are likened to peaks rising from the mist:

> The great poets of Gaelic Ireland
> Soared up frae the rags and tatters
> O' the muckle grey mist o' Englishry –

he then proceeds to list the poets – 'Raifteri, Ó Rathaille, Ó Súilleabháin, Feiriter, Haicéad and Céitinn.' Whatever about the others, Raifteri was no peak, at best he was a pleasant enough foothill. MacDiarmid was on safer ground when he merely borrowed or adapted quotations from the Irish poets, out of De Blácam's book, as in *To Circumjack Cencrastus*, and also in 'Lament for the Great Music' in *Stony Limits*, where there are at least a dozen citations from *Gaelic Literature Surveyed*. The Great Music is of course the classical music of the Great Highland Bagpipe, dating from around 1600, an extraordinary and unique survival of a sophisticated art from the mediaeval Gaelic world, with its own scale or scales, its own concept of melody as an intricate pattern of conventional motifs, its own rhythms and a mysterious appeal which no amount of theorizing or analysis has been able to explain away. The art of pìobaireachd lies on the very edge of improvisation and must still be handed down from piper to piper, for the written scores are unable to convey the subtleties of timing that make the pìobaireachd live. Its affinities would seem to be with the East rather than the West and there is a possibility that it may have taken over the classical music of the Gaelic harp. Here indeed was a link between Gaeldom and the modern world and MacDiarmid has made good use of it in the Lament.

In his efforts to discover the lost history underlying the present state of Scotland MacDiarmid has frequently mentioned Waddell's *Edda* and *The Chronicles of Eri* edited by L. Albert, with an essay establishing their historical veracity. Among the proofs of the authenticity of the

Chronicles offered us we are shown a portrait of the author, Roger O'Connor, a sturdy rubicund gentleman, and asked could the owner of such an honest face be guilty of fraud! MacDiarmid cannot have seen the original edition of the Chronicles, published in 1822 which contains a facsimile of a page from the 'original manuscript in the Phoenician dialect of the Scythian language'. This page shows some gibberish of a vaguely Irish character, written in Irish script, and could only have been concocted by O'Connor. Albert tells us that there are similarities between O'Connor's history and the old Irish manuscripts that describe the wanderings of the Gael before they reached Ireland, the 'faked and distorted versions of the Leinster or Tara records' as Albert calls them. But these old Irish manuscripts are as much a fabrication as the Chronicles, and are finally based on the Old Testament. (See R. A. S. MacAlister's *Lebor Gabála Érenn*, Vol. 1.) As M. A. O'Brien writes in *Early Irish Society*, ed. Myles Dillon, 1954; 'Some time after 431 Irish learned men became acquainted with world history from scriptural and classical sources. They must have been amazed at the silence of these works about their own country, and so, fired, no doubt, by an abundant patriotism they set about reconstructing the pre-Christian history of Ireland.' MacDiarmid was not the only one to be taken in by Roger O'Connor and L. Albert for in 1940, four years after Albert's edition, a book appeared about the Chronicles by R. Perry, a British Israelite, who found in the Chronicles support for the wildest of theories. Reviewing Perry's book in *Irish Historical Studies* MacAlister described the Chronicles, accurately, as 'actually an amalgam of bombastic paraphrases of Irish annalistic matter, irreverent parodies of Biblical excerpts, 'etymologies' (which have to be seen to be believed) and wildly irresponsible inventions resembling those in the closely analagous book of Mormon . . .' If the Chronicles had inspired MacDiarmid to write some poems all might have been well, but 'The Fingers of Baal Contract in the Communist Salute', to be found in the little pamphlet *Poems of the East West Synthesis* is among the contenders for the place of MacDiarmid's worst verse.

The British Edda, by L. A. Waddell, author of many books including *The Phoenician Origin of the Britons*, is a translation from the Icelandic of the Elder Edda which purports to show, by real or imagined resemblances between proper names, and by illustrations taken from ancient Sumerian seals, that the gods of Scandinavian mythology were originally human beings who lived in the Euphrates basin around 3380–3350 B.C. and that Adam, Thor, Dardanos first king of

Troy, Midas, St. George, the Indian god Indara, King Arthur and others were originally the same man. The whole concept seems on a par with proving by cryptograms that Queen Victoria wrote 'In Memoriam', and as for the Sumerian seals they could be used to illustrate many different kinds of books – here is the text accompanying the seal on page 82: 'We then find in the Edda that Eve as Freyia or "The Friend" is installed at home with Adam-Thor as Queen of the Goths, and holding receptions in a garden saloon [sic] in which we gain a glimpse of her happy, gracious, social life.' However *The British Edda* supplied MacDiarmid with one poem 'The Pot Hat or The Ballad of the Holy Grail', which is an adaptation of Scene XXIII: compare MacDiarmid's

> It sat at the feet of the witches
> Mair lurid than the nails on the toes
> O' yon nether maimers squat in their mess
> When he dirled it frae under their nose.

with Waddell's

> This titbit of Gull, Ullar (Cain) loos'd
> In the teeth of the three tied witches,
> Those nether maimers amid their mess,
> And he dirled out the beaker (afore) their nose.

It also supplied the title of the poem 'Larking Dallier' and a metaphor in 'Vestigia Nulla Retrorsum' – 'the sink of swords'.

These books have little to do with Gaelic Literature, but MacDiarmid is not a scholar, he is a poet; he intuits first and reasons afterwards. He imaginatively grasps the need for a renaissance of Gaelic and in order to present a case the world is then ransacked for supporting materials, not all chosen with equal care. It is important when one is reading MacDiarmid to separate what is of value from the merely silly, so let us return to the 'Lament for the Great Music', which MacDiarmid calls a key poem in his concern with Scottish Gaelic and his effort to bring out an underlying unity of the Scots and Gaelic elements of Scotland. He writes,

> . . . I know the root I am gripping in the darkness here
> Is the unstruck note that gives all the others scope,
> That deepest root from which even Freedom can unfold.

The important thing here is to notice that MacDiarmid is not seeking primarily or at all for a linguistic change. 'Freedom' means a Scotland

> 'where the supreme values
> Which the people recognise are states of mind,
> Their ruling passion the attainment of higher consciousness.

The Celts, as he tells us in 'Credo for a Celtic Poet' (*Agenda*, Winter 1967) 'never fell into that cardinal blunder of mistaking means for ends' and for MacDiarmid language itself, whether Gaelic, English, or Scots is only a means towards some end which he has adumbrated variously in political terms as Red Scotland and Pan Celticism, though these in turn are means towards 'higher consciousness'. MacDiarmid's earliest poems in *Northern Numbers* and *Annals of the Five Senses* showed nothing particularly Scottish, but since then his work has been so inextricably interwoven with the Scottish Scene that any dereliction of his country cannot but affect his verse. Ibsen felt bitter about Norway's betrayal of the Danes in 1864 and it is lines from Ibsen's *Brand*, written in 1865, that MacDiarmid goes on to quote in the 'Lament'.

> I too who have never become eingebürgert elsewhere
> Feel changed in Scotland, grown strange to myself,
> And waken to its realities as baffled Samson woke
> Shorn and tethered. 'My native land should be to me
> As a root to a tree. If a man's labour fills no want there
> His deeds are doomed and his music mute.'

This is not chauvinism. It is the faith of Joan of Arc, who would not look behind to see if anyone was following her. MacDiarmid is the piper who pipes himself and the troops 'through battle and into daith'; he is not the cook or the engineer or the ambulance driver. Despite the elegiac note of the 'Lament' his work does not look back, it looks forward, though in full consciousness of the past and all its traditions: he has brought science and technology into his poetry as an ingredient and not just as an exotic decoration. So his message for the Gaels is that they must bring their language up to date, they must catch up with 'machineries o' expression like the English, French or German'. It is a measure of the distance yet to go that when MacDiarmid wishes to make an important quotation he does not turn to Gaelic.

In Memoriam James Joyce, that cento of passages from other authors, contains less than a dozen references to Gaelic literature (mostly only a word or two, whereas there is a page on Racine, and there are five pages on Karl Kraus, borrowed from the *Times Literary Supplement*. It is plain that whatever sources MacDiarmid had at hand did not refer to Gaelic literature, and that his own background could not furnish the gap. In his poem 'A Golden Wine in the Gaidhealtacht' he admits, by implication, his ignorance of Gaelic:

> In Scotland, in the Gaidhealtacht there's a golden wine
> Still to be found in a few houses here and there
> Where the secret of its making has been kept for centuries
> – *Nor would it avail to steal the secret, since it cannot be*
> *made elsewhere.*

The long poem 'Island Funeral' does not refer to Gaelic language or literature at all. Ostensibly about the Hebrides, 'our Gaelic islands', it is an amalgam of a description of the Aran islands in Ireland (limestone rock, currachs, black shawls, crimson skirts, rawhide shoes), a description of certain isolated communities and their carpentry, and a critique of a cornet player in a jazzband. These disparate elements have been worked together to make a poem which is in effect an extension of the 'lament'. We are to understand that there has been at times in the past a 'Gaelic dynamic' which if it could be revived would lead to the MacDiarmid Utopia.

References to this 'Gaelic dynamic' run through MacDiarmid's work, but it is hard to build up a picture of exactly what he means. He quotes a review of Bringmann's *Geshichte Irlands* (1939): 'Gaeldom was moving towards – and but for the English would have realised – a real people's state', and also 'Irish must and will become once more the living language of Ireland'. It is likely that Bringmann had been influenced by a reading of the historians of the early 1900s. So was James Connolly, who believed that in Ancient Ireland there was communal ownership of land and equality and democracy, and that therefore the Gaelic Revival and Socialism should go hand in hand. These ideas are briefly touched upon in Connolly's *Labour in Irish History*, which he opens by praising Mrs. Stopford Green's *The Making of Ireland and its Undoing* (1908). Mrs. Green does say, on page 107: 'The propertied classes (i.e. the English) evidently feared the Irish land system as expressing what might be called the Socialism of the time. We may see their instinctive antipathy in the crude accounts they give of Irish customs. "They of the wild Irish as unreasonable beasts lived without any knowledge of God or good manners, in common of their goods, cattle, women, children, and every other thing. . . ."' This hardly proves that the ancient Irish were Socialists, but Connolly, and Bringmann, and MacDiarmid, were too ready to believe, on too little evidence, what they wanted to believe. It is also necessary to point out that the connotations of the German 'Volksstaat' and the English 'people's state' are not the same. In the second edition of Bringmann's history (1953) he has dropped the reference to Gaeldom moving towards a people's state. This curious book moves from 300 B.C. to A.D. 1921 in 37 pages and the remaining 98 pages are devoted to the period from 1921 to 1952, and the hero of the book is not the 'Volk' but De Valera, 'ihr Führer'.

MacDiarmid refers us to a book called *The Gaelic Commonwealth* by Father William Ferris (Dublin, 1923). Ferris regards the Catholic Church as the model for the Commonwealth. 'The statecraft of the Gaelic Commonwealth and of the Catholic Church, by their strong points of resemblance, mutually support each other in a most extraordinary manner. The sole difference between them is that in the Catholic Church all power comes from the Pope, as Vicar of Christ, whereas in the Gaelic State all power comes from the people. The religious power coming from above and the secular power coming from below dovetail into each other, as it were, and together produce the nearest approach to Utopia ever likely to be realised on this earth.' Ferris will have nothing to do with parliamentary rule, regards Socialism as 'this delirium and dotage of democracy', and wants a High King. Though Ferris wishes to abolish Rent, Wages, Usury and all forms of exploitation, his Commonwealth is hardly what MacDiarmid had in mind when he wrote, 'Only in Gaeldom can there be the necessary counter idea to the Russian idea. The dictatorship of the proletariat is confronted by the Gaelic Commonwealth with its aristocratic culture, the high place it gave to its scholars and poets', etc.

Recent historians have painted a less rosy and more plausible picture of Irish society in early times. Ancient Irish society was, according to D. A. Binchy (*Early Irish Society*, ed. Myles Dillon, 1954) 'tribal, rural, hierarchical . . . and the family, not the individual was the unit,' and in the grades of society 'the real distinction was between those of gentle birth, those whose family tree was preserved among the genealogies, and the commoner or churl'. The poets, men of art, men whose skill gave them a status beyond that due to their birth, belonged to a caste intercalated between the two grades, and 'in that aristocratic and rural society it was quite possible, owing to the system of patronage, to produce great literature and great art'. That society was 'a complete contrast to the unitary, urbanised, egalitarian and individualist society of our time', and 'the inequality of man . . . had been erected into a legal principle. . . . Most men were free – the number of slaves seems to have been comparatively small – but they were certainly not equal.'

MacDiarmid's acquaintance with Gaelic Literature and History is superficial, his readiness to believe in the bizarre surprising. Does this matter? He himself thinks not for he writes in his essay, 'The Caledonian Antisyzygy and the Gaelic Idea': 'It does not matter a rap whether the whole conception of this Gaelic Idea is as far-fetched as Dostoevsky's Russian Idea . . . The point is that Dostoevsky's was a great creative idea – a dynamic myth – and in no way devalued by the difference of the actual happenings in Russia from any Dostoevsky dreamed or desired. . . . It would not matter so far as positing it is concerned whether there had never been any Gaelic language or literature, not to mention clans and tartans, at all. It is an intellectual conception . . . It calls us to a redefinition and extension of our national principle of freedom on the plane of world affairs, and in an abandonment alike of our monstrous neglect and ignorance of Gaelic and of the barren conservatism and loss of the creative spirit on the part of those professedly Gaelic and concerned with its maintenance and development.'

The 'Gaelic Idea' is as much an aberration as Yeats' 'A Vision', or Graves' 'White Goddess', the defects of their ideas inextricably associated with their qualities as authors. The spirits gave Yeats metaphors for his poetry and perhaps the ancestors of the Clann Diarmaid have had an incalculable effect on Christopher Murray Grieve. MacDiarmid has shown the way, the onus is on the reader to read the classical Gaelic poets and for that the Gaelic language is a *sine qua non.* The old living patterns of the Gael are 'curjute and devauld' and disappeared with the social structures that gave birth to them. Only by retaining the Gaelic language – since every language of its own nature determines what can be said in it, can we be sure of cultivating the soil from which alone a Gaelic 'dynamic' or 'idea' could spring, without necessarily knowing or foreseeing what shape it might take. The men of the Irish Revival knew this and made their slogans 'Tír gan teanga, tír gan anam' (A country without its own language is a country without a soul) and 'Beatha teanga í a labhairt' (A language lives when it is spoken). Saunders Lewis in Wales has said that the Welsh tongue is more important than even the independence of his country. Only by speaking and reading Gaelic can we discover the truth of MacDiarmid's contentions.

> Today the spiritual values of Gaelic civilization have not dissolved.
> They have, however, shifted. They no longer form one
> With the flesh of human substance. We can still
> Attain to every one of the subtlest goods in Gaelic culture,
> But only mentally, analytically, or rationally. We must return
> To the ancient classical Gaelic poets. For in them
> The inestimable treasure is wholly in contact
> With the immense surface of the unconscious. That is how
> They can be of service to us now – that is how
> They were never more important than they are today . . .
>
> Le moment semble venu d'une résurrection de l'humain.

It is quite possible that the above impressive passage originally referred to something else and that MacDiarmid borrowed the passage and substituted the word Gaelic for whatever term was in the original, thus doing something 'similar to what is done when a green light on a railway replaces a red light, or vice versa, in a given lamp.' For as early as *Annals of the Fives Senses* (1923) he wrote that 'these perhaps strange fish of mine are discernible almost entirely through "a strong solution of books" – and not only of books but of magazines and newspaper articles and even of speeches', thus anticipating Thomas Mann who wrote in *The Genesis of a Novel* of 'my own growing inclination, which I discovered was not mine alone, to look upon all life as a cultural product taking the form of mythic cliché, and to prefer quotation to independent invention'. At different times in the past there have been men who possessed the qualities admired by MacDiarmid, and in the future such men would be found again, indeed if all went well, far more men of such a kind would exist. The men of genius we now have are the inheritors, the preservers and the carriers on of the proud tradition. The Gaelic world, and its pipe music in particular, were eminently suitable symbols for the process of the things of value in the past being transmitted to futurity. Both seemed to have had their day, yet the Great Music stubbornly remains, and Gaelic speaking Scotland has thrown up at least five poets of the highest excellence and greatest interest. Here indeed is an inestimable treasure, here is *The Kind of Poetry I Want*.

> A poetry – since I was born a Scottish Gael
> Of earth's subtlest speech . . .

Thirty years ago from Raasay and Kintyre and from the Desert War in Africa where they both fought came the voices of Sorley MacLean and George Campbell Hay, and their poetry was better than any English poetry written during the war. More recently, from Lewis, has come the poetry of Derick Thomson, Domhnall MacAulay and Iain Crichton Smith, the latter best known for his poems in English. Sorley MacLean and Crichton Smith have addressed poems to MacDiarmid, and MacDiarmid has undoubtedly been an inspiration to writers in Gaelic, as he has been to writers in Scots and writers in English. MacDiarmid's propaganda for the Gaelic dynamic has been justified in the work of these men, and the Gaelic Literature of the future will be in his debt.

Lament for the Great Music

TOM SCOTT

MacDiarmid published this poem of some 600 lines in *Stony Limits* (1934). It is in the lingua franca, not Scots, and together with the title poem of homage to that great epic poet C. M. Doughty, is his highest achievement in Sudron at least up to that time. His conception of the Scottish literary revival was then undergoing a sea-change from a purely national revival of Scots, in which he had already published three volumes which were the best work in Scots since the eighteenth century, to a pan-Celtic vision rooted in Gaelic. The problem of a Gaelic poet is different from that of a Scots poet: the Scots poet writes in both Scots and English and/or an amalgam of the two, whereas the Gaelic poet must choose between Gaelic and a translator's English or Scots. This shift to a pan-Celtic European vision influenced Grieve's return to a form of the Sudron tongue, which he has chiefly (but by no means entirely) used ever since with varying degrees of success and failure, but rarely with the tact and assured mastery of his poems in Scots. He has little native Gaelic to use.

The term 'Great Music' is a translation of the Gaelic *Ceol Mor* as applied to the pibroch music of the MacCrimmons, those traditional pipers to the clan MacLeod of Skye. They flourished in the late seventeenth and eighteenth century, creating in the pibroch one of the greatest achievements of all music, comparable to the preludes and fugues of Bach, and the most original contribution Scotland has made to European art of any sort. The mood of the poem is of heroic elegy, not only for the lost glory of the pibroch, but the high Celtic culture of which it was the culminating (apparently) expression – itself a mighty lament for a race oppressed and threatened with total extinction. The pibroch is of sonata or concerto length, of great classical dignity and simplicity of theme, yet moving through its succeeding variations to an almost incredible intricacy and complexity – and the mood of heroic elegy is its own most characteristic one. No other music known to me can match it for dignity and noble pathos, and it is astonishing that a Celto-Teutonic people (and all the British are more or less that, the Celtic strain dominant here, the Teutonic there) should be so unaware of the musical treasure created in these islands and held here by a few in trust for the human race.

MacDiarmid in his lament for a lament is here discovering the deepest historic roots of his own psyche, and is inspired by the majesty and pathos of the fate of aristocratic Gaeldom to a classical verse which has never been equalled, let alone surpassed, since Milton, in these islands. This is evident even in the quiet opening lines:

> Fold of value in the world west from Greece
> Over whom it has been our duty to keep guard
> Have we slept on our watch; have death and dishonour
> Reached you through our neglect and left you in lasting sleep?

Here already he has struck the theme he has been searching for in certain previous works, the theme which will allow him to explore the Celtic roots of Scotland. This theme became dominant in *To Circumjack Cencrastus* (1930), where he speaks of a European Fourfold Idea pillaring up European culture – the Teutonic Idea of the North, the Classical Idea of the Mediterranean South, the Russian Idea of the East, and the Celtic Idea of the West. In that poem he found no 'objective correlative' for his intuitive apprehension of the Celtic Idea, but here, in the *Ceol Mor*, he strikes it. It is significant, not only for Scotland but for Europe, that when he finds it, the mood is elegiac.

The *Ceol Mor* is at once reality and symbol, as the Thistle was to him. As I see it, the movement of European poetry leads up to the allegorical form dominant in the Middle Ages; and when that breaks up, takes the twin lines of realism and symbolism; and in the twentieth century (beginning earlier, probably with Goethe), the realist and symbolist lines re-integrate into a new polysemous art in which, instead of the abstract theology (or theory) of allegory proper, reality itself in the historical and scientific senses, becomes the adequate 'symbol' or allegorical term of a new vision. I call this new art, to which all modern art is moving. 'Polysemous Veritism', to distinguish it from Dante's 'Polysemous Allegory'. I have no scope here to develop this view, but MacDiarmid's work, like that of Pound, Joyce and many others, is a major contribution. Through the reality-symbol of the *Ceol Mor* he breaks through into the real Celtic world as Yeats never did. The ancient world comes alive to him, and this is at once manifested in the intensity of his rhythms – urgent, vibrant, strong, of classical nobility and dignity, like the Great Music itself. The heroic ghosts of the Celtic world rise to meet him, shadowy though they still are, and with them the Celtic Church, the Nynian-Columban root of Scottish Christianity, and the awareness of that extraordinary culture, compounded of heroism and an almost tender delicacy of feeling, which the Teutonic has never yet caught up with. Shakespeare comes near it, being himself the greatest product of the Celto-Teutonic blend (The Tempest is an almost purely Celtic poem, with Prospero an Arch-Druid) yet born.

As always when the Muse is ardently responsive, MacDiarmid plunges deep into thought, argument, discussion, proliferation of *aperçus* and concepts, rugging at problems others have scarcely thought of: he is on chatting terms with the perennial mysteries, the eternal questions. In fact, he is a natural theologian (i.e. a student of reality), and it is because of this that he has poured intense scorn on an orthodox religion that has lost all its inspiration (or murdered it) and is no longer anything but empty, alienated form, far-strayed from its own Christ.

But his chief concern, as always, is with Scotland, and it is to Scotland he returns again and again:

> These things will pass. 'The world will come to an end
> But love and music will last for ever.'
> Sumeria is buried in the desert sands,
> Atlantis in the ocean waves – happier these
> Than Scotland, for all is gone, no travesty
> Of their ancient glory lives
> On the lips of degenerate sons as here.
> This is what is hard to bear; the decivilised have every grace
> As the antecendents of their vulgarities . . .
>
> We who are strong think only in terms
> Of classes and masses, in terms of mankind.
> We have no use for the great music.
> All we need is a few good-going tunes.

The passion of utterance here is unmistakable, and is the one element missing, at this pitch of intensity, in most of the other poems in this volume (*Stony Limits*).

He can hear the great pibroch of the MacCrimmons in his ear as he writes, and the fire burns in him:

> The bagpipes commit to the winds of Heaven
> The deepest emotions of the Scotsman's heart
> In joy and sorrow, in war and peace.

He speaks of two of the greatest pibrochs, *The Lament for the Children* and *I gave a kiss to the King's hand*, marvelling at what he considers the triviality of the occasion that gave rise to the magnificence of the latter: and he tells a story of the quality of these pipers. The pipers of Lord Louis Gordon refused to play for him because, after the battle of Inverurie in 1745, Gordon held the great piper Duncan Ban MacCrimmon prisoner of war. What other army, then or since, has had such men? These 'barbarian' Gaels knew, as MacDiarmid puts it,

> That Kings and Generals are only shadows of time
> But time has no dominion over genius.

Their tribute of silence to a piper of genius is one of the most striking cultural gestures I have ever heard of. What indeed was the whole misconceived Rising of 1745, the right rebellion in the wrong cause of the obsolete Stewarts, what was war itself, compared to the genius of Duncan Ban? These men knew the meaning of reverence for art.

The poet goes on to muse on the impermanence of temporal things:

> Yet the waves will not wash the feet
> Of MacLeod's Maidens for ever, and all modern Science
> May vanish from human memory as the great days
> Of Assyria and Egypt and Rome . . .
>
> The State has its roots in time. It will culminate in time.
> Greater things than this will fall . . .

Even the great *a priori* principles may not be as eternal as they seem – who can guarantee that two and two may not make five in some other planet? They too may be wearable as the Skye rocks (MacLeod's Maidens) mentioned above. His musing leads on, as always, to language and he meditates on the 'language where language ends', saying it reminds him of a sunset he once saw in a highland place 'When the tide-forsaken river was a winding ribbon of ebony' and a great light suddenly lit up the foreground . . . and he had the sense of a man returning from foreign scenes to the place of his birth.

So his thought runs on, typically seeming to range away from the central theme, like a setter chasing up many cross-scents, yet still coming back always to the main one. For him this is not only the great music, the *Ceol Mor*, but the Celtic root it stems from: and he asks whether the apparent decay of Celtic civilisation is not just a shedding of dead leaves to prepare for a coming spring. To this root he grips in the darkness, and in a swift appraisal of his own situation as the one great Scottish poet in two centuries, he speaks of his bafflement at the lack of comprehension in his own countrymen, which estranges him from them and from himself:

> And waken to its (Scotland's) realities as baffled Samson woke
> Shorn and tethered. My native land should be to me
> As a root to a tree. If a man's labour fills no want there
> His deeds are doomed and his music mute.
> This Scotland is not Scotland . . .

There is the crux – the Scotland of to-day is no longer Scotland, but a philistine travesty of itself. It is Scotshire, a county in the north of England, an ex-country, an Esau land that has sold its birthright for a mess of English pottage. The Scotland of today would be a foreign land to the MacCrimmons. He, as poet, presents the Scottish people with their own image, the thing they have become, and he calls them back, like a true bard, to their own heritage. But so lost they are that they do not recognise it, or him. This is the measure of how deep the rot has gone since 1707.

At this point the note of elegy, the lament for the great music, modulates into an elegy for the whole of Scotland, the 'broken image of the lost kingdom' (it is Edwin Muir's phrase) that every Scot carries deep in his soul. But it is not only the lost kingdom that concerns MacDiarmid – he knows there is no way back to outmoded states – but with the lost freedom to create new forms of society and art. The great Scottish Idea, the one that Scotland gave to the world out of the agony of the Wars of Independence, is Freedom – the 'nobill thing' of Barbour's famous outburst in *The Brus*. This is the *sine qua non* of existence, whether of nations or persons, and the tragic irony of Scotland is that she, who gave birth to the idea of national independence and integrity out of the abstract ruling-class gangsterdom which was feudalism, owing allegiance to no country and no people but itself, should almost alone of European nations have betrayed and lost this freedom to live and change. Truly, such a Scotland is not Scotland: it is only a corpse breeding and spreading corruption.

He goes on to brood on what the MacCrimmons would think of our modern cities 'swollen huge with thoughts not thought, that should have been thought', and with songs unsung, with

> Tears unshed for ever and deeds undone beyond achievement now?
> These denationalised Scots have killed the soul
> Which is universally human; they are men without souls;
> All the more heavily the judgement falls upon them
> Since it is a universal law of life they have sinned against.

There, surely, is the answer to the particular kind of 'trahison des clercs' found in those Anglo-Scots intellectuals who bleat of false antithesis, 'internationalism, not nationalism' – as if it were possible to have the one without the other. They sin against the universal law of life which invests life in individuals, not conglomerations – yes, even in the ant-hill. In the place of living, separate identities having mostly their differences in common, these ghouls would reduce all to a horrible 'international', characterless, abstract fog, a devitalised non-entity. That phoney distortion of Marxism was given the lie long since and utterly by Tito. But their 'international' equals 'English', and behind the pseudo-internationalism of the Anglo-Scots lurks the face of the Auld Enemy – English imperialism.

His thought runs on round these 'eternal embers' of Scottish culture, and he says he feels he knows the pibroch music best when

> Away here I hold a glass of water between me and the sun
> And can only tell the one from the other by the lint-white quiver,
> The trembling life of the water . . .

That remarkable image of a real observation (compare Dunbar's description of the water in the fourth stanza of *The Goldyn Targe*) is typical 'polysemous veritism' – the image being the exact symbol, the real cohering with the apparent in vibrant meaning. This image of light is, at one level, the Great Music itself (and the greater music of reality beyond it); but radiating out from the actuality and reference, he sees the whole spirit of man as sunlike:

> Our spirit is of a being indestructible . . .
> It is like the sun which seems to set to our earthly eyes
> But in reality shines on unceasingly . . .

Thus – and it is typical of the man – in the very moment of deepest lamentation, instead of regret, he re-affirms the indestructibleness of the spirit, and the mood of elegy gives way to heroic affirmation.

In this mood he meditates on the source of this mighty spirit, and decides 'it is not lawful' to probe its sources (an unusual law-abidingness in him), as if it were a thing subject to space and time. We must wait and watch for it to reveal itself to us, as the eye

> Waits patiently for the rising sun. The mind creates only to destroy;
> Amid the desolation language rises, and towers
> Above the ruins . . .

And in the same way the music rises, its relations with itself rather than anything external. He reflects on the nature of pibroch and its relations to other musical forms; and the stupid neglect of pibroch leads back to himself:

> I am as lonely and unfrequented as your music is.
> I have had to get rid of my friends . . .
> If one's capital consists in a calling
> And a mission in life one cannot afford to keep friends.
> I could not stand undivided and true amongst them.

This is an extraordinary passage, and only those who know the weight of sheer negation the unusual individual has to try to bear up under, will understand it. 'Hell is other people' for the man of vision. Only those who conform are welcome in a group: the non-conformist, the man who bears the burden of the mystery, can only be smothered by its smug defensiveness. His solitude is a tragic and heroic fate which must be borne for the ultimate good of the race. Thus a Rilke is quite right in saying that a poet must love his loneliness and celebrate it with harmonious lamentations – and MacDiarmid was one of the earliest paraphrasers of Rilke.

The happiest of such solitaries are those who are 'companioned by a future', foreseeing the struggle of a nation into consciousness of its existence, and who sing out of that consciousness, animated and restrained by a mystical sense of the high destiny of a people. Such are not swallowed up by the petty cares of individual being. But is MacDiarmid one such? He thinks not:

> But I am companioned by an irrecoverable past,
> By a mystical sense of such a destiny foregone . . .
> Time out of mind . . . Oh, Alba, my son, my son!

The adaptation of David's incomparable cry over Absalom is startling and revealing. Alba, the ancient Scotland, is seen by this twentieth century poet as an Absalom son for whom he would gladly die. What kind of poet can utter such a cry? The answer is as direct as genius – a bard, a *fili*, a poet in the great Celtic tradition too long dormant and decayed, but at last showing signs of stirring among the scunnersome poeticules of our benighted age. Here MacDiarmid speaks with the eternal voice of the bard of his people, to whom all time is but a thought rooted in the mind of eternity. This is the voice of the keeper of the nation's conscience and traditions, the guardian of the welfare of the race. This is not the voice of C. M. Grieve speaking, but the timeless voice of Scottish poetry itself speaking immortally through him.

Yet even in this moment of realising his national identity, he looks beyond his own nation, out of his own nation, to the fraternal nations around him: for when one has found and is sure of one's own identity, both personal and national, the gaze no longer looks inward to the lost self but outward to the other selves. Thus in finding his national identity, the poet finds, as part of that identity, the between-nations, the socialist inter-national, and affirms both as aspects of each other. For through national sovereignty alone a people can come to full maturity and international responsibility. This is what our Anglo-Scots intellectuals, their bright heads darkened by their benighted souls, can never understand. Through self-realisation one comes to realise others:

> Not to one country or race, but to humanity,
> Not to this age but to all time,
> As your pibrochs that reached to Eternity . . .

The poem goes on for pages after that, but there, at its highest illumination, I must leave it. It is a great poem, one of his best, and the best heroic elegy written by a Scot in the lingua franca.

Poetry and Knowledge in MacDiarmid's Later Work

EDWIN MORGAN

In the Preface to the *Lyrical Ballads*, Wordsworth makes some striking comments on poetry and science which are quite often quoted but very seldom believed. After claiming that poetry is the 'impassioned expression which is in the countenance of all Science' (a phrase referred to approvingly by Hugh MacDiarmid), he goes on in no less confident vein:

> If the labours of Men of science should ever create any material revolution, direct or indirect, in our condition, and in the impressions which we habitually receive, the Poet will sleep then no more than at present; he will be ready to follow the steps of the Man of science, not only in those general indirect effects, but he will be at his side, carrying sensation into the midst of the objects of the science itself. The remotest discoveries of the Chemist, the Botanist, or Mineralogist, will be as proper objects of the Poet's art as any upon which it can be employed, if the time should ever come when these things shall be familiar to us, and the relations under which they are contemplated by the followers of these respective sciences shall be manifestly and palpably material to us as enjoying and suffering beings.

Wordsworth envisages not simply the acceptance by poetry of facts or things or attitudes which science may unavoidably set within man's future environment (once they have become an intimate part of that environment), but also a more positive co-operation by which poets will be 'carrying sensation into the midst of the objects of the science itself' – in other words, helping to further the process of assimilation instead of passively hoping that schools, television programmes, 'popular science', and the passage of time will float the new material some day into the trembling ambit of the sensitive but unknowledgeable muse.

A good deal of MacDiarmid's poetry, from the *Stony Limits* volume of 1934 onwards through *A Kist of Whistles* (1947), *in Memoriam James Joyce* (1955), and *The Kind of Poetry I Want* (1961), has been a practical exploration of both aspects of Wordsworth's ideal. His search, as he says in *In Memoriam James Joyce*, is for

> The point where science and art can meet,
> For there are two kinds of knowledge,
> Knowing about things and knowing things,
> Scientific data and aesthetic realisation,
> And I seek their perfect fusion in my work.

Some would deny that there is any such meeting-point, or argue that there may have been once but could not be today, or fall back on the belief that to press for such a fusion would be inevitably to dilute both science and art. One does not have to evoke the theory of 'two cultures' to feel that there is something unduly inhibiting about such views. A poetry of knowledge may be difficult to produce, but its challenge is present in our time, and its absence ought to tantalise and stimulate. It should not be necessary to apologise for such attempts as are being made within the arts to show man inhabiting a world of which science and technology are a formidable part. It should not be necessary but it seems to be; because we are apt to forget how unhelpfully and unhealthily antiscientific the dominant literary atmosphere has been. This is where the later work of Hugh MacDiarmid would have value even if only the value of a corrective to the onesidedness of (for example) Yeats and Lawrence. Such a corrective is surely to be welcomed, and studied carefully and without prejudice. Only those to whom 'a poem is a poem and I am not interested in anything else' can turn unconcerned from the spectacle of a man writing with the quixotic aim of seeing poetry, or one kind of poetry, accepted as

> A protest, invaluable to science itself,
> Against the exclusion of value
> From the essence of matter of fact.

MacDiarmid himself would readily admit that success in writing such poetry, and success in recommending it to others, can only be achieved gradually, and to some extent luckily. The 'lucky poet' is here the poet who chances his reputation by courting heavy odds. When a hard thing is beginning to be done, failures have to be accepted, but one moves ahead. The appeal to the future, either as a period when better poetry of the same kind will be written or as a period more likely to understand the value of the first stumbling efforts, is sometimes made in these poems of MacDiarmid's, and although it is not in itself the strongest of arguments it is an essential part of the evolutionary credo implicit in the poetry. *In Memoriam James Joyce*, as I have described elsewhere,[1] is concerned with the fragmentation of human cultures and the desirability of bringing together (as the 'imaginary museum' of modern photographic reproduction has done for painting and sculpture) the knowledge, achievement, and beauty left isolated and sterile in unfamiliar languages and literatures. The interests and faculties required to assimilate this material will grow, though slowly, until the ideal situation heaves in sight with

> Omnilateral aristology obligatory on everybody.

Appeal to the future, however, does not banish the haunting problem of communication, even for MacDiarmid, as is clear from a passage like the following, where he says he has

> spent many of my happiest busman's holidays
> In books like Leonard Bloomfield's *Language*,
> Happy as most men are with mountains and forests
> Among phonemes, tagmemes, taxemes,
> Relation-axis constructions,
> The phrasal sandhi-type and zero-anaphora.
> (What? Complaint that I should sing
> Of philological, literary and musical matters
>
> Rather than of daffodils and nightingales,
> Mountains, seas, stars and like properties . . .)

That comment shows him still on the defensive, which is hardly surprising when we consider the inaptness of the word 'sing' as applied to the preceding lines. This does not mean, however, that it is impossible to write poetry about phonemes and taxemes; only that in order to do so, one must replace a bare catalogue of terms by a more persuasive, sophisticated proof that these things can be related to us all as (in Wordsworth's phrase) 'enjoying and suffering beings'. In relying so much as he does on the catalogue, on mere mention of the thing itself, MacDiarmid is doing no more than initial spadework; he sacrifices 'poetry' for the sake of an advance in the art of poetry which

[1] 'Jujitsu for the Educated', *Twentieth Century*, September 1956.

he believes to be feasible, though others may carry it further than he can. The kind of poetry he wants is 'a learned poetry', and also 'a poetry which fully understands / That the era of technology is a necessary fact'. He is willing to accept the extremer implications of this, as in the short poem 'The Changeful World'.

> Earth has gone through many changes.
>   Why should it now cease changing?
> Would a world all machines be as strange as
>   That in which the saurians went ranging?

But this science-fiction mood is not so typical as his concentration on present knowledge (and theory) and his attempts to relate this to human experience and to his own aesthetics. In all his 'poems of knowledge', therefore, the method of analogy is widely used, sometimes with carefully worked out parallels, sometimes with an oblique hint thrown off to the agile reader. Although this method, which has become MacDiarmid's trademark, can quickly be ridiculed or parodied, it has at its best produced a very remarkable blending of fact and imagination. In *In Memoriam James Joyce* itself, there is the fine passage on the importance to the work of art of what is *not* present, led up to by the introduction of the haemolytic streptococcus which is 'in the sore throat preceding rheumatic fever' but at the height of the fever is gone, like the mysterious 'silence supervening at poetry's height' or an awesome pause in music. In many of the shorter poems there are striking illustrations of the same mastery of unexpected analogy: in *Stony Limits*, the elegy on Charles Doughty, where the growth of the poem that he wishes he could write to praise Doughty is described in terms of crystal growth in rocks and then, by a daring shift of perspective, in terms of the great rayed craters of the moon; in 'Dytiscus', with the mocking comparison between the water-beetle and man striving to breathe a 'diviner' air than that of his muddy environment; in 'Cornish Heroic Song for Valda Trevlyn', the buccal cavity of the white whale with its 'heavy oily blood-rich tongue which is the killer [whale]'s especial delight', and the analogy drawn between the Celtic genius and the 'hideous khaki Empire' of the English; the parturient, self-flyping guinea worm of 'To a Friend and Fellow-Poet' [Ruth Pitter], with its extraordinary description of a desperate yet delicate fecundity applied to the process of poetic creation; the extraction of mercury from cinnabar in 'Crystals Like

Blood', where iron piledrivers are crumbling the ore and a conveyor draws it up into a huge grey-white kiln –

> So I remember how mercury is got
> When I contrast my living memory of you
> And your dear body rotting here in the clay
> – And feel once again released in me
> The bright torrents of felicity, naturalness, and faith
> My treadmill memory draws from you yet.

Surely the main thing to be said about this poetry is not 'the details are not always accurate' or 'the process has not always been fully understood by the poet' or 'in any case these are only analogies or extended similes which are being used by the poet for normal aesthetic purposes'. To an expert in some particular discipline (e.g. linguistics in *In Memoriam James Joyce*,[1] geology in *Stony Limits*[2]) MacDiarmid is bound to reveal some inadequacies which betray the lack of an intimate familiarity with the subject. Such inadequacies seem, however, fewer or less damaging than one might suppose. Further investigation of the scientific background of these poems may qualify this statement, but it looks at present as if Wordsworth was right in assuming that the poet could still use his natural insight and mental tact in penetrating regions of knowledge as well as the more obvious regions of feeling. As for the objection that these analogies are no more than a refurbishing of heroic simile, it must be remembered that something more than illustration is at stake. The poem 'To a Friend and Fellow-Poet' is equally 'about' the guinea worm and the poetic process; if it shows the poetic process in a new light, it also throws poetic light on an extremely interesting bit of zoology.

The Kind of Poetry I Want affords the best vantage-point for considering the whole problem. A fair amount of technical material is

[1] The poem speaks about 'Vogule, / The smallest of the Baltic-Finnish language group, / Spoken by only 5000 people'; but there is no 'Baltic-Finnish language group', and even if there was, Vogul (which is wrongly spelt) could hardly belong to it, since it is spoken in Siberia, thousands of miles from the Baltic area; it is spoken by more than 5000 people, and even if it was spoken by only 5000 it would not be the smallest of the group MacDiarmid is referring to (under the wrong name). Vogul is a Ugrian (or Finno-Ugrian) tongue, belonging to the Uralian linguistic stock, and there are at least two smaller languages, Livonian and Vodian, in the group.

[2] To a geologist, 'crossing shear planes' are not 'extruded' as the poem says they are; and 'ultra-basic xenoliths that make men look like midges' (presuming that this refers to size rather than durability) would be exceedingly unlikely since most xenoliths are even smaller than man-size.

scattered throughout, but very often in reference to easily assimilable activities and pursuits – fishing, piping, dance, film, music – and the originality consists mainly in the precision with which things like 'a 3-inch anti-kink minnow, brown and gold' are mentioned. Most of these references are analogical: the activities described are models, in their richly ordered complexity and grace, for the sort of poetry MacDiarmid would like to see. At the same time – and this is what is distinctive – the analogies are intended to be themselves examples (not always successful, naturally) of such a poetry in its early stages of development. I say 'early stages of development' because it is more a 'poem of knowledge' than a 'poem of science': it opens out into various sciences, but is concerned to present the reader with thresholds and vistas rather than with entry and possession. It distinguishes its own aim, nevertheless, pointing clearly in a direction taken by few:

> The poetry of one who practises his art
> Not like a man who works that he may live
> But as one who is bent on doing nothing but work,
> Confident that he who lives does not work,
> That one must die to life in order to be
> Utterly a creator – refusing to sanction
> The irresponsible lyricism in which sense impressions
> Are employed to substitute ecstasy for information . . .

What in fact happens in *The Kind of Poetry I Want* – and it is a measure of the poem's great interest –is that a balance is struck between 'sense impressions' and 'information' which makes it possible for much of the information to be seen not in a textbook context but in a life context, and this, though not the poem's primary intention, helps the reader to edge his way in towards the more intellectual passion at the centre. The kind of poetry MacDiarmid wants to see is glimpsed through glasses of varying fineness and power. It is likened to the dancing of Fred Astaire (complex but apparently easy); to bagpipe music (involving skilled improvisation); to fishing (observation, choice, grace of action); to bending a piece of wire back and forward to breaking-point (an experiment with an aim – finding out how words, like atoms, behave); to the mixture of races in Spain and the mixture of cultures in India (a wide range and fusion of individual enriching factors); to the eleven-year cycle supposed by some to govern sunspots, Nile flood levels, wheat prices, tree-rings, measles epidemics, Bank of England discount rates, and many other phenomena (a Jamesian 'figure in the carpet', perhaps, though the analogy is not made syntactically clear); to living flesh suddenly touched in a mineral world (shock of the unexpected); to a busy, sparkling operating theatre 'in which the poet exists only as a nurse during an operation' (devotion of contributing to a larger, complex whole – no doubt the 'operation' of apathectomy on all mankind); to a documentary film about sheep-dogs in which physical setting and elementary natural movement are more important than the story being told (information better than ecstasy – though the information itself is a sort of ecstasy); to the ironic baa of a wild goat chased by man onto crags where he can't be followed (posing questions rather than giving easy answers); and to hedge-laying (craftsmanlike but abstruse).

From these analogies, two main and apparently contradictory models for poetry emerge. On the one hand MacDiarmid wants a poetry of great complexity, coupled with great order, 'organised to the last degree', a product of the 'crystallising will', subtle yet proportioned 'masterpieces of intricate lucidity' on the highest level, and on the lowest at least 'artful tessellations'. Where this conception is leading is seen in the admiring reference to Coleridge's 'coadunation' and 'multeity in unity', and in the autobiographical passage describing the changes in a man's life – and in all life – from less to more organic. Like the humble but exemplary lancelet which almost crossed the gulf from invertebrate to vertebrate and pointed the way as a prototype for others –

> If I have evolved myself out of something
> Like an amphioxus, it is clear
> I have become *better* by the change,
> I have risen in the organic scale,
> I have become more organic.

The poem as organism, as a complex structure ordered with such finesse that the code has swallowed the key, is of course a familiar model in recent aesthetic theory, but it would be surprising if MacDiarmid accepted it as it has usually been propounded, since he does not himself write, or apparently very much enjoy, poetry conceived on such principles. He does not, however, go the whole way with organism despite his praise of 'the more organic'. The important difference is that he demands lucidity (whereas in organismic theory ambiguity is welcome), and tries to ensure it by his insistence on reference to 'fact and science' rather than to (say) myth and mythmaking: that is, poetry should emulate the expository power of a T. H. Huxley or a J. P. Joule in making the abstruse stand out 'in cut-gem clearness'.

But as a far greater qualification of this model of poetry, other analogies lead MacDiarmid away from 'organising', though not necessarily from 'the organic'. We have his belief in poetry that is 'never afraid to leap', poetry improvising like expert pipe-music, poetry going up like fireworks, poetry with unforeseen Beethovenian modulations into remote keys, poetry that is 'wilder than a heifer / You have to milk into a gourd', the 'poetry of one like a wild goat on a rock'. We have the notable passage where he asks for a poetry

> With something about it that is plasmic,
> Resilient, and in a way alarming – to make cry
> 'I touched something – and it was *alive*.'
> There is no such shock in touching what
> Has never lived; the mineral world is vast.
> It is mighty, rigid, and brittle. But the hand
> That touches vital matter – though the man were blind –
> Infallibly recognises the feel of life, and recoils in excitement.

Yet this, and in the same sentence, is the poetry he describes as 'full of *cynghanedd*, and hair-trigger relationships'. Of a marriage between Wallace Stevens and Allen Ginsberg one might well say: No go. There is indeed a contradiction here, and it reflects a central contradiction in MacDiarmid's nature which shows elsewhere in the 'metaphysical materialism' of his philosophy. But although MacDiarmid makes it difficult for the reader to envisage in the abstract a poetry which is 'organised to the last degree' and yet 'the poetry of one like a wild goat on a rock', it is important to see that this is not a complete contradiction; nor is *The Kind of Poetry I Want* devoid of hints as to how we must bring the ideas together. Just as some extremely intricate Celtic interlace may gain, not lose, by being slightly asymmetrical; or as film-makers have found (or re-learned, after the great painters), how a carefully played scene will gain, not lose, power by having in the background something irrelevant which shows ordinary 'non-art' life going about its business: so, in poetry, Virgil writes a short line, Shakespeare sketches Parolles, Milton 'by occasion foretells the ruine of our corrupted Clergy'. And so too, although *The Kind of Poetry I Want* like most of MacDiarmid's long poems is loosely rather than closely organised, it shows in some passages how improvisation can still help to prove theme, and how 'irrelevance' can become relevant.

The wild goat, following its instincts in jumping from crag to crag, may be tracing patterns which science cannot yet describe. Is the passage on Mary Webb a 'digression'?

> A poetry abstruse as hedge-laying
> And full as the countryside in which
> I have watched the practice of that great old art,
> – Full of the stumbling boom of bees,
> Cuckoos contradicting nightingales all through a summer day,
> Twilight deepening with a savage orange light,
> Pheasants travelling on fast, dark wings,
> – Or like a village garden I know well
> Where the pear-trees bloom with a bravery of buds,
> The cydonia blossoms gloriously against its wall,
> And roses abound through April, May, and June,
> – And always with a surprising self-sufficiency
> Like that of almost any descriptive passage of Mary Webb's
> – The fact that she was not wholly herself in all she wrote
> Creating a sort of finality and completeness
> In each part of any given whole,
> The integrity of her experience revealing itself in many ways,
> In the fulfilment of rare powers of observation,
> In the kind of inward perception which recognised
> 'The story of any flower' is 'not one of stillness,
> But of faint gradations of movement that we cannot see',
> The outer magic and the inward mystery imaginatively reconciled,
> Her deep kinship, her intuitive sympathy with leaf and flower
> Extending without a break into the human kingdom,
> And flowering there in an exquisite appreciation
> Of the humours of single characters,
> And a rare power to make them live and speak
> In their own right and idiom.

Now Mary Webb's novels are not abstruse; but consider the modulations of the lead-in, if it is a lead-in. The abstruse art of hedge-laying quickly passes into the thick, complicated, rich-looking texture of the hedge itself, the rich living world and natural habitat of the hedgerow, the richness being a link between the 'abstruse' art and the 'full' countryside which is the next comparison; poetry should be full, as fouthy in its language as the English countryside is in sounds and colours or a village garden in flowers. Then comes the oblique move to 'a surprising self-sufficiency', a phrase which, added to the abstruseness and fullness, reminds us of the 'intricate lucidity' mentioned earlier in the poem but which hardly prepares us for the sudden illustration from 'almost any descriptive passage of Mary Webb's'. She has floated in, perhaps, on the wings of the pheasants, but very soon we become absorbed in what the poem says about her art, and probably we forget any analogy to poetry. If we stop at this point, we may ask ourselves whether the passage is not simply a pleasant interpolated tribute to someone who was a personal friend of the author's. When we read on, we see that it is, and it isn't. The quoted passage is followed by another thirty-odd lines which meditate generalisingly on the value of such a writer, who with her 'practical working knowledge' can 'capture the elusive spirit of a countryside':

> literary graces concealing
> No poverty of context, lack of virility, emptiness of thought,
> But, held in perfect control,
> Contributing the substance of poetry
> To subjects 'with quietness on them like a veil',
> A manifold of fast-vanishing speech,
> Customs and delights.

The only thing that links Mary Webb and MacDiarmid's aims for poetry is the idea of a rare, intimate knowledge being used for artistic purposes. Our first reaction when we see her name is that few writers could be more different, and we wonder how MacDiarmid could possibly enlist her among his Zouave acrobats and *cynghanedd*. She is brought upon the scene without premeditation, but having been brought, she justifies the suddenness, and we find ourselves looking at the main ideas of the poem from a new angle.

What MacDiarmid seems to be adumbrating in *The Kind of Poetry I Want* – it is nowhere made sharp and definite – is a poetry which is highly organised in parts, but not prescriptively with regard to the whole. It is not so much an organism as a colony, a living and in one sense formless association of organisms which share a common experience. Shape and architectonics are not so important as the quick movements of the thought – the feelers in the water, moved partly by the surrounding currents and partly by their own volition and partly in response to the movement of neighbour tentacles – while a succession of images, illustrations, and analogies is presented to it. As zoologists may argue whether a colony is an organism, critics may hesitate to say that the kind of *poetry* MacDiarmid wants is a kind of *poem.* A movement towards a more 'open' conception of the poem than has prevailed in the modern period is however gaining ground, and I see no reason why we should deny ourselves, for love of architectonics, the ingredient and emergent pleasures of a poetry in evolution.

> The ingredients resemble the things
> For which a woman with child longs.
> Like the juice of the oyster,
> The aroma of the wild strawberry,
> The most subtle and diversified elements
> Are here intermingled to form
> A higher organism.

The longings are perhaps not 'sensible', perhaps not 'compatible'; and yet they are a part of the great process of creation, they take their place in the effort to bring something new into the world. That is the value of Hugh MacDiarmid's later poetry.

Hugh MacDiarmid: Visionnaire du Langage

MICHEL HABART

Il y a trente ans que Hugh MacDiarmid, en publiant *Un homme ivre regarde le chardon*,[1] annonçait la renaissance littéraire écossaise en même temps qu'il lui donnait son plus beau poème. Le déclin pitoyable de la poésie écossaise – des grands jours de la poésie courtoise de Dunbar et Henryson aux exercices de style pour école du dimanche où elle avait fini par sombrer – faisait de ce réveil un événement surprenant.

Une première renaissance, illustrée au XVIIIe siècle par Allan Ramsay et Robert Burns, n'avait été qu'une brève illusion. En marge de l'évolution culturelle, vouée au 'pastoral', l'heritage qu'elle laissait était condamné à la stérilité. Et les écrivains écossais qui succédèrent, comme Walter Scott (en dépit de sa contribution aux *Border Ballads*), John Davidson, Robert Louis Stevenson, James Thomson (nom si injustement négligé), furent d'abord des poètes anglais.

C'est ainsi que *Sangschaw* et *Penny Wheep*, les premiers recueils de Hugh MacDiarmid écrits en *Lallans*, furent, pour la culture écossaise, un exemple salutaire et décisif. Une poésie véritablement moderne dans son langage et son inspiration pouvait-elle donc s'exprimer dans un dialecte traditionnel?

En réalité, c'était, pour la littérature écossaise, le problème capital du langage maternel en poésie qui de nouveau se posait. Puisque le *Lallans* était sans aucun doute mieux adapté aux exigences du tempérament écossais, étail-il sage et légitime d'y renoncer pour l'usage exclusif de l'anglais littéraire, dans le seul but de donner à l'œuvre une audience élargie? Il est certain que l'anglais littéraire ne répond pas entièrement à la gamme émotionnelle des peuples celtiques. Il suffit de voir avec quelle ferveur (mêlée de défi), l'Ecossais, une fois en pays anglais, cultive son accent d'origine, ce précieux vestige du dialecte natal, pour comprendre ce que celui-ci représente pour les complexes de l'exil. Plus qu'aucun autre, le poète souffre de ne pouvoir user du langage de son enfance, le seul qui lui donne accès aux zones subconscientes où

[1] *A Drunk Man looks at the Thistle.*

se forme le substrat affectif de sa personnalité, le seul qui puisse vraiment se porter garant de l'expression authentique de ses sentiments. C'est par les associations émotionnelles du langage maternel que le poète reste en communication avec les symbolismes collectif et infantile dont se nourrit son inspiration profonde. Pour Hugh MacDiarmid, l'abandon du Lallans se justifiait d'autant moins que ce dialecte est relativement accessible au lecteur anglais et que l'effort qu'il demande ne dépasse pas après tout celui qu'exige, dans sa propre langue, tout modernisme poétique.

Jusqu'à quel point d'ailleurs, l'usage des dialectes n'est-il pas en mesure d'enrichir, en la renouvelant, la langue littéraire commune d'une nation? Jusqu'à quel point ne l'aiderait-il pas à résister aux nivellements journalistique, universitaire ou administratif qui peu à peu dégradent un langage vivant en cette prose de mandarins qui est le mal chronique de la culture occidentale? 'Je pense', écrivait T. S. Eliot à Hugh MacDiarmid, 'que la poésie *Scots* est d'une influence fertilisante pour la poésie anglaise et qu'il est de l'intérêt de celle-ci que cette poésie fleurisse.'

Un usage mal compris du dialecte peut, il est vrai, encourager l'écrivain à limiter ses horizons et s'enliser dans le régionalisme. Hugh MacDiarmid a su en éviter l'écueil. Les thèmes qu'il traite sont d'une telle envergure que toute accusation de provincialisme semblerait absurde. Certains critiques se sont évidemment empressés de voir en lui le Burns du XXe siècle. La comparaison est injuste. L'amour de la femme, celui du whisky, une nationalisme obstiné, une coriace anglophobie, leur sont peut-être des traits communs. Ils ne touchent guère à l'essence de leur création. Le slogan de Hugh MacDiarmid: 'Non pas Burns, mais Dunbar', définissait son ambition. Son œuvre s'en est montrée digne. En dépit d'une certaine rhétorique 'coin de feu' qui, par instants, alourdit le poème, *Un homme ivre regarde le chardon* reste le chef-d'œuvre de la poésie écossaise moderne. En fait, Hugh MacDiarmid se compare plus justement à Rilke dont il fut le premier à traduire le *Requiem für eine Freundin*, et son poème *Vestigia Nulla Retrorsum* est un magnifique hommage au poète allemand.

* * *

Plus encore que les précédentes, la nouvelle œuvre de Hugh MacDiarmid – *In Memoriam James Joyce* – écrite peu de temps avant la guerre, apporte de nouveaux et importants éléments aux problèmes de la création poétique.

C'est une suite de méditations en prose scandée (en *chopped-up prose*, dira un critique mal disposé), coupée de passages lyriques d'une surprenante beauté, sur les rapports des premiers langages et de la pensée, sur l'universalité de l'œuvre d'art, et surtout sur les problèmes des relations linguistiques, qui, pour le poète, prennent une importance capitale dans un monde qui s'achemine rapidement vers l'unité. C'est en hommage aux fabuleuses explorations d'*Ulysse* et surtout de *Finnegans' Wake* dans les immenses et nouvelles possibilités offertes au langage que l'œuvre (dont le second titre est *A Vision of World Language*) est dédiée à la mémoire de Joyce.

Le poème apporte avec lui un formidable appareil de mots puisés à travers le monde, des Iles Shetland à la Chine, 'une sorte de jiu-jitsu pour l'homme cultivé', nous dit l'auteur.

S'il demande un effort de participation soutenu, cet effort trouve sa récompense. L'œuvre, en effet, réalise ce tour de force de donner au discours poétique une tension intellectuelle qui, l'animant du rythme intérieur de la pensée, soulève le lecteur au-dessus d'obstacles qui, sans cet élan, lui paraitraient infranchissables.

Ce style a la force nerveuse de celui d'Ezra Pound ou de Wyndham Lewis. Comment d'ailleurs ne pas penser aux *Cantos* et aussi à ce chef-d'œuvre ignoré, l'*Anathemata* de David Jones? On n'en reste pas moins surpris de voir que, dans son poème, l'auteur renonce à un dialecte auquel il doit tant pour l'anglais littéraire, si du moins je puis qualifier d'anglais littéraire un langage poétique qui apporte tant d'éléments nouveaux. Trahison? Désaveu? Aveu d'impuissance? Ou seulement la crainte d'imposer au lecteur anglais un fardeau supplémentaire? Dans sa préface, Hugh MacDiarmid, prévenant nos réserves, compare, non sans mélancolie, sa destinée poétique à celle de Hofmannstahl, qui, après la crise retracée dans la fameuse *Lettre de Lord Chandos*, devint, pour certains de ses amis, une sorte de renégat, pire, un faux Messie. C'est une crise de même nature, nous dit-il, qui a transformé sa méthode poétique. Non pas seulement une crise de style. Mais une crise affective, imaginative, d'une telle ampleur que pour lui les possibilités du langage et de la connaissance en furent bouleversées. Le problème particulier du dialecte, du même coup, passait au second plan.

Dans *In Memoriam*, le discours poétique – car il s'agit bien ici de discours – veut faire de chacune de ses phrases une phase déterminante de l'expérience humaine, cherchant à créer un champ d'idées multiples que seule l'épaisseur du langage poétique est capable d'engendrer.

Comment ne pas se référer là encore, aux *Cantos* d'Ezra Pound?

Pourtant la différence est capitale. Alors que l'esthétique des *Cantos* est essentiellement impressionniste, le discours d'*In Memoriam* est conduit de la façon la plus rigoureuse. Pour le poète, l'humanité est maintenant lancée dans une évolution intellectuelle destinée à faire de l'homme un être totalement différent, et aucune œuvre d'art – sauf peut-être celle de Joyce – n'a tenté de réaliser et d'exprimer cette transition dans les limites d'une seule vie. Nos langages et nos littératures ne sont pas à la mesure de cette mission. Il s'agit donc de leur donner une densité nouvelle, et ceci à l'échelle planétaire. Sans les efforts des quelques rares écrivains plus ou moins conscients de cette nécessité, comme Pound, Eliot ou Joyce, la littérature anglaise se serait irrémédiablement assoupie dans cette platitude, ce conformisme suburbain, qui est sa tentation majeure. C'est bien cet universalisme 'agissant' de la culture que Goethe annonçait lorsqu'il parlait de littérature universelle, et non une admiration platonique des quelques grands chefs-d'œuvre du passé. Une nouvelle tension est établie entre l'homme et l'univers. Elle peut, elle doit renouveler le langage du poète et ses rapports avec le monde. Cette conscience planétaire, dont on trouve déjà l'écho dans l'Iliade, la Divine Comédie, Don Quichotte, et surtout dans la littérature sanscrite, deviendra l'élément essentiel de l'expression littéraire, tout comme la nation était l'élément essentiel d'une littérature 'nationale'. Rendre présents à l'homme la multiplicité des âmes et l'abîme du temps, tel est ce que le poète appelle la 'nouvelle ambiance', ambiance dont *In Memoriam* est profondément imprégné

> Toutes les mélodies déjà entendues ou jamais proférées
> Résonnent ensemble de toutes leurs notes, pour nous soulever,
> Nous embrasser, nous emporter – mélodies d'amour et de passion,
> De printemps et d'hiver, de mélancolie et d'abandon.
> Esprits de millions d'êtres
> Sur des millions de siècles
> Vision de la Forme Universelle (Visva-Rupa-Darsanam)
> Devant laquelle Arjuna se prosternait, tout crispé de terreur.[1]

Les sciences linguistiques jouent dans cette tentative un rôle déterminant. Aussi bien n'est-ce pas de Glasgow que nous est venu, avec *The Principles of Semantics* de Stephen Ullman, l'ouvrage fondamental de la sémantique moderne? Le poème exalte les travaux

[1] *In Memoriam James Joyce*, p. 15.

de Rudolf Carnap, de Gardiner et Jespersen. Dans cette perspective totale, les différences formelles qui séparent la poésie de la prose, perdent leur sens. Hugh MacDiarmid fait sienne la thèse du grand poète juif Chaim Bialik sur 'la folie de différencier prose et poésie'. Il fait sienne aussi l'ambition de retrouver, en dehors de toute prosodie formelle, le rythme intérieur de la pensée, ce rythme qui court '*comme un fil rouge et brûlant*' tout au long du Deutéronome par exemple, réussissant à faire d'un simple report de chroniques et de lois un très grand livre poétique. C'est bien ce même fil rouge et brûlant que nous retrouvons à travers *In Memoriam.*

Voilà ce que signifie l'exploration des dictionnaires,
Tout les abîmes et les sommets de la pensée,
Tout les risques, toutes les épreuves de l'esprit,
Entre les débris des littératures passées
Et la matière première des littératures à venir.
Mais *tout* le langage? Un éblouissement de lampe-à-arc.
Plus d'illusions, ni de refuges pittoresques,
Ni d'ornières toutes prêtes où assoupir
Nos complaisances. Chaque instant est exigence
Reprise nouvelle de nos forces.
Plus de guenilles à partager
Avec ces aveugles aux cerveaux satisfaits
Qui cultivent, raillait Disraeli,
'Les âneries de leurs prédécesseurs',

* * *

Dont les âmes vivant dans une torpeur sacrée,
Prosternées devant des autels refroidis et des dieux trépassés

* * *

Tout le langage!
Et non pas distiller, à la Valéry, des mots comme 'pur'
Dans le goutte à goutte d'une minutie de chimiste,
Et non pas trouver l'essence du poème
Dans le maniement correct de l'e muet!
– Je pense ici à l'inconséquence de Chaucer
Avec sa prononciation de l'e final –
(Bien qu'il y ait *tout* la différence du monde
Entre whisky et whiskey, bien sûr!)[1]

[1] *Ibid.*, p. 90.

Il est aisé de reprocher aux complications de cette sorte de kaléidoscope culturel (qui prend par moments l'allure fâcheuse d'un répertoire), leur excès de didactisme, voire leur pédantisme. Pourtant une poésie résolument moderne – à moins de rester en marge et de se limiter, comme dirait William Empson, à 'quelque version de pastoral' – doit consentir à la complexité croissante des cultures et de la société, complexité favorisée par l'isolement du créateur dans un monde qui, cessant d'êtrel ocal, organique, hiérarchisé, ne peut plus lui fournir le cadre tout fait de traditions, de langage et de symbolique où venait s'ajuster sa sensibilité:

> Un langage qui serve nos ambitions,
> Merveilleuse lucidité, légère et ardente lumière,
>
> * * *
>
> Flexible comme une jeune baguette de coudrier,
> Sûre comme une aile de mouette,
> Claire comme une eau de montagne,
> Profonde comme des yeux de femme en présence de l'amour,
> Exprimant la complexe vision de toute chose en une,
> Laissant passer toutes impressions, toute expérience,
> toutes doctrines,
> Pour n'en retenir que le grain,
> En assumant l'innombrable promesse
> Qu'il porte en son germe.[1]

Si cette complexité poétique, qui en France date de Baudelaire, a pris un départ plus tardif en Angleterre (1910–20), le danger qu'elle représente pour l'unité de l'inspiration, n'en est apparu que plus soudain et plus urgent, en même temps que se découvrait le seul remède qui permit au poète de conjurer cette dispersion: une réconciliation de la culture et de la Société. C'est en effet dans un cadre culturel élargi que le poète anglais essaie d'échapper à cette dichotomie de l'art et de la vie, fatale à la civilisation comme à la poésie. Eliot, Pound, Empson, sont les meilleurs exemples de cette poésie érudite où l'obscurité (ou plutôt l'opacité) ne vient pas de l'usage d'un matériau subconscient, mais de l'extraordinaire diversité des allusions culturelles.

C'est dans ce développement qu'il faut situer, pour les comprendre des œuvres comme l'*In Memoriam* de Hugh MacDiarmid ou l'*Anathemata* de David Jones.

* * *

[1] *Ibid.* pp 88–9.

Embrasser, dans leurs diversités, l'ensemble des cultures pour les unir sur le plan cosmique, tel est bien le dessein d'*In Memoriam*. 'Mais cette unification, écrit le poète, ne peut s'achever que dans une société où la communauté d'action atteindra son expression maximum.' On s'en doute, cette société ne peut être que la société marxiste, puisque les contradictions de la société libérale sont décidément sans espoir. Que n'a-t-on dit du marxisme de Hugh MacDiarmid, dont l'œuvre apparaît à certains comme une provocation politique?

Ses 'Hymnes à Lénine' (dont le second fut publié par T. S. Eliot dans sa revue *Le Criterion*), ses poèmes activistes comme 'Fascistes, vous avez tué mes Camarades', ses appels révolutionnaires, forment une part importante de son œuvre poétique. C'est en cherchant à incarner ses idées politiques qu'il trouve, semble-t-il, ses accents les plus fermes et les plus émouvants, et il est singulièrement à l'aise dans ce mélange inattendu que constituent l'intensité intellectuelle d'un esprit moderne, et la féerie mystique de la ballade traditionnelle. On comprend que le poète se soit fait le traducteur enthousiaste d'Alexandre Blok.

Vu d'un peu plus près, ce marxisme, il faut bien le dire, n'a pas l'air très cohérent, et parait tenir beaucoup plus d'une sorte d'anarchisme philosophique, où surgissent des références aussi imprévues que Vladimir Soloviev, Keyserling, John Cowper Powys et même Gurdjieff, que d'un matérialisme dialectique orthodoxe. En tous cas, ce marxiste réalise cet étrange paradoxe d'être en même temps le seul grand poète mystique que l'Ecosse ait produit.

Tout aussi imprévue et paradoxale est la haine maniaque que le poète n'a cessé de nourrir contre l'Angleterre et qu'il déploie de nouveau dans *In Memoriam*, en dépit de son repentir vers la langue anglaise. Quel que soit le bien fondé des thèses nationalistes, il est difficile d'affirmer que la littérature écossaise représente une littérature autonome. En fait, elle dépend étroitement de l'histoire littéraire anglaise, dont elle reste un chapitre mineur. Même dans sa période la plus glorieuse, la poésie *Scots* tenait de très près à ses modèles anglais. Et à la question 'Qu'est-ce qu'un poème écossais?', les plus chauvins des Ecossais seraient bien embarrassés de donner une définition précise qui ne risquât d'en exclure leurs glories les plus sûres. Si le reniement total du dialecte natal est pour l'Ecossais une mutilation, l'anglophobie aveugle en est une autre.

Comment, d'ailleurs, Hugh MacDiarmid pourra-t-il bien empêcher qu'*In Memoriam James Joyce* ne devienne un grand poème . . . anglais?

Toute l'exécration qu'il voue à l'anglo-saxon ne peut rien contre cette ironie. Dylan Thomas évoque quelque part 'toutes les statues que l'Ecosse élèvera un jour à Hugh MacDiarmid', mais que celui-ci prenne garde plutôt que l'Angleterre, dans un accès d'humour, n'ait l'outrecuidance de lui élever à son tour un mémorial. Car devant quel méfait d'annexion reculerait cette 'race intensément vulgaire, et à l'esprit infantile'?

Hugh MacDiarmid: The Later Poetry

G. S. FRASER

I. THE NOTION OF THE DISCURSIVE POEM

This essay is a kind of appendage to Iain Crichton Smith's *The Golden Lyric* (Akros Publications, 1967), which was at once a wonderful appreciation of Hugh MacDiarmid's early poems, and a wonderful polemic against his later development. I am going to consider the longer, the later, what might be called the discursive poems. I want to consider first of all, in a way that I think MacDiarmid might approve of, the whole notion of a poem as *either* an imitation of a mode of discourse *or* a mode of discourse in itself.

Prose is written in sentences and paragraphs. Poetry is, by and large (there would be exceptions in some imagist and some surrealist poems), written in sentences and paragraphs, but it is also written in *lines*, which establish, even in free verse poems like Pound's *Cantos* or MacDiarmid's *In Memoriam James Joyce*, a greater expectation of regularity than prose tends to. Prose and verse both have inescapably rhythm; rhythm or prosody is a quality emerging from the fairly limited phonetics and vocabulary of all languages, from the necessity of our repeating either phrases or patterns of phrase. In verse, we draw attention to it; in prose, we try, usually, to distract attention from it towards a development and elaboration of something that we might call meaning, argument, or sense. In prose, we are trying to *say* something – in great philosophical prose, like Wittgenstein's, say, to *say* something at the very moment we are for the first time *thinking* it.

Poetry is not the most convenient or direct mode for either human saying or human thinking. The profoundest limiting remark about poetry as a mode that I ever heard was made by a post-office girl on a day-release course at Kingsway College, London. I had been reading some poems by Yeats and Eliot and others. 'Poetry,' this girl said, 'seems to be a very *round-about* way of saying things.' It is very difficult to say things; if we set before ourselves the barriers of rhyme and regular rhythm we make the saying more difficult. T. S. Eliot once remarked in a correspondence in *The Times Literary Supplement* on

Shakespeare's adaptations of North's Plutarch in *Coriolanus*, *Anthony and Cleopatra* and elsewhere, that we can find many examples of prose, with slight alterations, being turned into great verse (Yeats's verse setting of Pater's famous Mona Lisa passage at the beginning of *The Oxford Book of Modern Verse* might be another example); but that even very great verse, transcribed as prose, will not be even good prose. Milton's *Paradise Lost* is a very great poem; but a French translation into prose, however, in fact, scholarly and precise, would tend to be boring, since it would lose the special quality, the pacing and pausing of the verse paragraph, the modulation of feeling and tone, that makes the poem great.

The poem, as such, makes sense but its greatness is in how the limitation and narrowness of its rhythmical form, and yet the varieties of tone it achieves *within* that limitation and narrowness, controls our response of feeling more precisely than prose can ever control it. Poetry can perhaps never *convince* us of anything, other than its own internal coherence, and the validity of our final mood of response to it, if we have attended to it with enough patience and impersonal alertness. But MacDiarmid, in his later poetry, Crichton Smith insists, uses poetry as if it were prose (or even as if it were an inferior type of prose, polemical political rhetoric) primarily to *convince* us. To make us agree with him, about a variety of topics about which he holds strong and passionate, but also sometimes limited and cantankerous, views. MacDiarmid's later poetry, for Crichton Smith, is what Keats called 'poetry with a palpable design on us'. It tries to bully us, often, into taking up attitudes which it is not proper we should take up unless, in prose, or in unspoken thought, we had argued out the question for ourselves. It is demanding and peremptory, Crichton Smith thinks, in an essentially unpoetic way. *Style*, as in Dante or Milton, can properly be demanding and peremptory; *ideas* cannot. The poetry of the doggedly argumentative mood is a poetry demanding a doggedly argumentative answer, which the greatest poetry does not demand.

I agree with Crichton Smith that MacDiarmid's later poetry is extraordinarily uneven, and also that the unevenness comes partly from a demand for submission, for practical assent, upon the part of the reader, that is not a properly poetic demand. But I think one can make a much better case for much of MacDiarmid's later poetry, if one thinks of the argument in the poems as being directed not against a reader who is being bullied but against MacDiarmid himself. I shall try to illustrate this point by quotations and analyses. The element of greatness in MacDiarmid's later poetry lies in an inwardness, an unending inner struggle, in a strenuously lonely man, whose loneliness can, for the reader, be an emblem of his own. The true poet (and this applies to a poet as utterly in contrast with MacDiarmid as Yeats) is less an individual person, with a definite role in society, than an attempt at least at the universal role in a particular historical period. He is less like a man than like a country or even a great society; we witness within him the drama of a kind of civil war. The rhetoric of MacDiarmid's best poetry is not the argument with others but the argument with oneself.

The 'ideas', which to Crichton Smith seem so peremptory and cantankerous (so much the ideas of an aggressively self-educated man) are in the end elements in a total composition: like Yeats's 'images'. The pose of wanting to change the reader and the world radically and immediately is part of a properly poetic strategy; the building up of a *persona*, which is something like Hobbes's Leviathan, or the giant figures in Blake, a kind of composite emblematic Man. MacDiarmid is a poet of the 'egotistical Sublime': one who tries to include everything (including long passages lifted from other writers) in himself, rather than, like Yeats, to lose himself in everything. But I want, before labouring this point, to consider the nature of the discursive peom.

2. POETRY AS IMITATION OF DISCOURSE: POETRY AS DISCOURSE, NAKEDLY

'Poetry' – to repeat that phrase – 'is a round-about way of saying things.' And a widely acceptable definition of the discursive poem might be that it is an imitation of some human mode of discourse rather than, nakedly, discourse in itself. There are, of course, great English (I cannot, off hand, think of very many very great Scottish, but some of Burns's verse epistles are very good 'think-poems' as well as first-rate social-conversational pieces. He thinks in fits and starts.) discursive poems, very near the tone and mode of good plain prose. In one of these, *Religio Laici*, Dryden says:

> And this unpolished, rugged verse I chose,
> As fittest for discourse, and nearest prose.

But the real *thinking* has been done in prose, or silently, before the composition of the verse starts. As Pope says, in another great discursive poem:

True wit is nature to advantage dressed,
What oft was thought, but ne'er so well expressed.

The primary thinking that has gone into such traditional discursive poems as *Religio Laici* or *An Essay on Criticism* is not thinking about the subject matter (about that the author has made up his mind already) but the mode of poetical presentation. Dryden had a powerful mind and the arguments for and against a merely natural theology have rarely been more concisely and cogently expressed than in *Religio Laici*: but what the poem convinces us of is not of the necessity of joining the Church of England but of its plain eloquence. Pope had a much less powerful mind though a much more various and alert sensibility than Dryden. But, again, *An Essay on Criticism*, beautifully summarising and exemplifying what in prose were already becoming stale commonplaces of neo-classical criticism, would not alter a single one of our critical attitudes (as Dr. Johnson's critical prose might, perhaps). It convinces us, in its sparkle and variety and assuredness, of Pope's youthful genius.

After these, in a later period, the greatest discursive poem in the English language is, I suppose, Wordsworth's *Prelude*, and here the case is slightly different. This is genuinely inward, the exploration of the growth of a poet's mind; there is a sense, quite often, of fumbling and groping: the mind is a much more original and profound mind than Dryden's or Pope's, it is innovating a whole new period of subjective sensibility, of emphasis not on the poetic product but on the poetic process. Yet this Rousseauistic autobiography is, after all, written in the epic blank verse and often in the diction of Milton. The poet's mind has become a 'heroic' subject, in the traditional sense. I think that MacDiarmid's mind has become a heroic subject for him, in that sense; but also, of course, he is a polemical, a satirical, one might say an opinionated poet, as Pope and Dryden were, and as Wordsworth was not. And he differs from them all in not having a set mould, even the set mould of Wordsworth's loose and flexible autobiographical Miltonism, into which to feed an at least partly preformed discourse. He is attempting, one might say, not to write a poetic imitation of discourse, but to discourse *in poetry* freshly and nakedly. How far, and in what ways, does he succeed? Let us look at some examples.

3. SOME PASSAGES FROM 'ON A RAISED BEACH'

Duncan Glen, in his preface to a beautifully printed recent edition of 'On A Raised Beach' refers with regret to the fact that this poem, which was first published in *Stony Limits and other poems* in 1934, has received little critical attention (except from James Burns Singer, in a fine article in *Encounter*) and was cut to a few lines in MacDiarmid's *Collected Poems* of 1962. Burns Singer, with his own special tumbling-over eagerness of language, referred to *Stony Limits* as the first book which established 'those types of versification (that lack of versification) and the concatenation of antagonistic ideas which are (MacDiarmid's) most original and far-reaching contribution to English – as opposed to Scottish – poetry. Here', Singer went on, 'we find those lines larded with learned allusions, interpenetrated by a terrifying stoicism, rich with surface mines of the blackest hatred, categorical polysyllabic, aphoristic lines following one another in ungrammatical abundance. It is a very beautiful, noble, and well-balanced book.' Duncan Glen adds, in his own introduction, that it would be hard to find a better-balanced description of 'On A Raised Beach', taken in isolation.

The first few lines illustrate MacDiarmid's vocabulary at, for the ordinary reader, its most obstinately impenetrable. Fortunately, most of the words are in the two volumes of *The Shorter Oxford Dictionary*, which I happen to have handy (I wonder if he had?):

> All is lithogenesis – or lochia,
> Carpolite fruit of the forbidden tree,
> Stones blacker than any in the Caaba,
> Cream-coloured caen-stone, chatoyant pieces,
> Celadon and corbeau, bistre and beige,
> Glaucous, hoar, enfouldered, cyathiform,
> Making mere faculae of the sun and moon,
> I study your glout, and gloss, but have
> No cadrans to adjust you with, and turn again
> From optik to haptik and like a blind man run
> My fingers over you, arris by arris, burr by burr . . .

It took me about quarter of an hour with the *Petit Larousse* and the *Shorter Oxford English Dictionary* to gloss this, and even yet I am in doubt about *haptik*, which clearly by context refers to touch as opposed to sight but may or may not have something to do with the

Scots verb *hap* (preterite *hapt*), to wrap up someone warmly as in a quilt. A prose translation might be:

Everything is born from stones – or is a dead and messy after-birth. Fossil fruit of the forbidden, stones blacker than the sacred stone of Mecca, cream-coloured as the light yellow building stone of Normandy, glittering pieces, green like Chinese jade (or Chinese celadon porcelain) and crow-coloured, dark brown and bown, greeny-grey, frosty, cup-shaped, making mere bright spots the sun and the moon, I study your sulking, and making my commentary, but have no quadrant[1] (clock-face) to adjust you with, and turning from seeing to feeling, and like a blind man run my fingers over you, sharp cutting edge by cutting edge, hard boss in the freestone by hard boss. . . . The translation clearly lacks a certain quality, of sheer miscellaneous pebbly puzzlingness, that the original has. The words as much as the stones are for MacDiarmid poetic objects, and it is interesting also that in the first three lines there would be indirect reminiscences of the book of Genesis Eden, and Mecca, in the fourth line a reference to Normandy (medieval cathedrals?) in the fifth line French colour words and a word for Chinese porcelain, later on a word suggesting Latin poetry ('glaucous')[2] and two archiac words, one from Spenser, 'enfouldered' and 'glout', as well as the scientific word 'faculae'.

The stone beach, indifferent and hostile to man, yet suggests the whole range, or a wide part of it, of human religion, geography, culture. If the word 'hapt' is implied in 'haptik' there is a pathos in stroking tenderly with one's hands what can never respond. The stones, in this long poem, are rather like the notion of 'reality' in Wallace Stevens's poems – something which is a 'vacuum' and with which man was no *noeud vital*, but which the imagination must confront all the same, since it cannot live on the imaginary.

I think MacDiarmid is probably old enough to have read as a boy Hugh Miller's *Old Red Sandstone*, which combined the elements of popular geology with natural theology. At heart, MacDiarmid is still a kind of natural theologian. The broken stones are the most ancient and enduring part of the earth we can get at. They will outlast us. They are not to be glanced at and forgotten, but are endlessly 'open' to the curiosity of the scientist or the poet who can see them as things not

1 There is *cardoon*, French *chardon*, a kind of semi-artichoke, or edible thistle, irrelevant here. Also metathesis.

2 Glaucaus is also a technical term in botany, but I think the Latin poetic context is more to the point here.

of any obvious use to him, not in any sense flattering him, but as sacredly what they are. They can help the human soul by offering it an image of endurance:

> Deep conviction or preference can seldom
> Find direct terms in which to express itself.
> Today on this shingle shelf
> I understand this pensive reluctance so well,
> This not discommendable obstinacy,
> These contrivances of an inexpressive critical feeling,
> These stones with their resolve that Creation shall not be
> Injured by iconoclasts and quacks. Nothing has stirred
> Since I lay down this morning an eternity ago
> But one bird. The widest open door is the least liable to intrusion,
> Ubiquitous as the sunlight, unfrequented as the sun.
> The inward gates of a bird are always open.
> It does not know how to shut them.
> That is the secret of its song,
> But whether any man's are ajar is doubtful.
> I look at these stones and know little about them,
> But I know their gates are open too . . .

As compared with the first passage, what we notice here is deliberate plainness and ineloquence, an unornate reflective quality. It is not so plain as it seems; the word 'Creation', as often in MacDiarmid, suggests that a religious feeling outwardly denied is being sustained somewhere at the back of the mind. The 'openness' of the bird and the stones as compared to the 'shutness' of man – man at the most 'ajar'! – is not an easy concept, and indeed it takes the whole long poem properly to develop it. (Incidentally, Singer seems to me wrong about 'the lack of versification': look for four main sense stresses, as in *Piers Plowman*, forget about stress-syllable metre, and you will scan most of these lines easily enough. There is no doubt about how to read them aloud.)

There are touches in this poem that suggest to me certain elements in the English romantic tradition:

> These stones will reach us long before we reach them.
> Cold, undistracted, eternal and sublime.
> They will stem all the torrents of vicissitude forever
> With a more than Roman peace.
> Death is a physical horror to me no more.

Compare (and, as the examiners say, contrast) Wordsworth:

> No motion has she now, no force.
> She neither hears nor sees.
> Rolled round in earth's diurnal course
> With rocks and stones and trees.

My friend John Hayward once told me that in a reading life-time of, I suppose, between fifty and sixty years he had read all English poetry, I suppose he ment that bulk of the best of English poetry, twice over and hoped to read it three times over before he died. I shall never equal or begin to compare with his taste or scholarship, but one privilege of a teacher is to go over the few perfect and the many strong and moving poems in our language many times with students who are sometimes receptive. Both these passages are very strong; but the Wordsworth is perfect; the MacDiarmid is struggling and mannerist, with a touch not only of romantic feeling, but of the kind of abruptness and surprise one associates with Jacobean drama. One is showing no disrespect for the later MacDiarmid in saying that the poetry which, so to say, 'belongs to one's peace' is something other.

The old struggler compels admiration all the same:

> We must reconcile ourselves to the stones,
> Not the stones to us.
> Here a man must shed the encumbrances that muffle
> Contact with elemental things, the subtleties
> That seem inseparable from a humane life, and go apart
> Into a simple and sterner, more beautiful and more oppressive
> world,
> Austerely intoxicating; the first draught is overpowering;
> Few survive it. It fills me with a sense of perfect form,
> The end seen from the beginning, as in a song.

He goes on (and perhaps goes on too long, making explicit what he has already implied?):

> It is no song that conveys the feeling
> That there is no reason why it should ever stop,
> But the kindred form I am conscious of here
> Is the beginning and end of the world,
> The unsearchable masterpiece, the music of the spheres,
> Alpha and Omega, the Omnific Word.

He goes on to see in the crystalline world an example, though an almost impossible example, for mankind:

> These stones have the silence of supreme creative power,
> The direct and undisturbed way of working
> Which alone leads to greatness.
> What experience has any man crystallised,
> What weight of conviction accumulated,
> What depth of life suddenly seen entire
> In some nigh supernatural moment
> And made a symbol and lived up to
> With such resolution, such Spartan impassivity?

Well! (one half thinks of answering): the philosophy of Spinoza, the late sculptures of Michelangelo, Milton's *Samson Agonistes*, Mycenae. . . . Human culture, rich in many things, is not lacking in examples, if one's taste runs that way, of the austere sublime. But he goes on again and he reminds me again of the self-tormenting, rich, slightly forced self-communings (in the letters and in the *Reminiscences*, particularly) of Carlyle. Carlylean, a very late type of Scottish Calvinist, seeking a God as hard and testing and as cold as rock: anti-Goethean, ungenerous to the huge rich variety of what human life has been (and has achieved), MacDiarmid *is*: Hebraic, not Hellenic, a man seeking his peace among the mountains and the rocks.

He goes on:

> It is a frenzied and chaotic age . . .

(when was it not, and what else, if humankind retains any energy, would we ever expect it to be?) . . .

> It is a frenzied and chaotic age,
> Like a growth of weeds on the site of a demolished building.
> How shall we set ourselves against it,
> Imperturbable, inscrutable, in the world and yet not in it,
> Silent under the torments it inflicts upon us,
>   With a constant centre,
> With a single inspiration, foundations firm and invariable;
>   By what immense exercise of will,
> Inconceivable discipline, courage, and endurance,
>   Self-purification and anti-humanity,
>   Be ourselves without interruption,
>   Adamantine and inexorable?

This again is the voice of the prophet in the desert. If I were to allow myself to fall into the temptation of argument, I would say: many new buildings have been built in this century (mathematical logic, modular architecture, philosophy and science of language, art as analysis and reconstruction of forms): we need (and humanity would not have survived without) a multiplicity, not a singlness, of inspiration: courage and endurance (think of the wars, revolutions, and famines of this century and of all centuries!) are remarkably common: self-purification does not imply 'anti-humanity' but an insight into the human stuff we are all made of . . . and so on, the Erasmian view against the Lutheran or Calvinist view.

But how irrelevant these debating-society points are against the properly poetic eloquence: MacDiarmid as a brittle but determined version of Samson Agonistes: struggling not merely to submit to, but to *be*, some modern equivalent of the fierce Old Testament God of the *Book of Judges*. This is the poetry of the Elect:

Great work cannot be combined with surrender to the crowd.

It is a deeper struggle than that, that of the man who does not 'surrender to the crowd' but seeks to save its soul: of a man obsessed with the image of the stone rolling away from the tomb, and yet obsessed also with the idea that the meaning of life is acceptance of the fact of death. As E. M. Forster says in *Howords End*: 'Death destroys a man. The idea of death saves him.' Something like that is said towards the end of 'On A Raised Beach'.

> Detached intellectuals, not one stone will move,
> Not the least of them, not a fraction of an inch. It is not
> The reality of life that is hard to know.
> It is the nearest of all and easiest to grasp,
> But you must participate in it to proclaim it.
> – I lift a stone; it is the meaning of life I clasp
> Which is death, for that is the meaning of death;
> How else does any man yet participate
> In the life of a stone,
> How else can any man yet become
> Sufficiently at one with creation, sufficiently alone,
> Till as the stone that covers him he lies dumb
> And the stone at the mouth of his grave is not overthrown?

I would take this as one of the least successful passages. It is an orthodox Marxist sentiment that 'detached intellectuals' should not be detached, because in detachment they can see nothing truly, we must participate to understand. What I am questioning is not that (here) but the adequacy of the image. Why should anybody, even 'poetically', want to raise any of the stones on this raised beach? Nature has made them and Man often shows his best respect for nature by leaving her alone. The reproach seems inept. But then we see that lifting a stone is a symbolic Samsonic gesture; this dead weight we are straining to lift is the meaning of life, is – Heidegger rather than Marx! – death. (I think a good Marxian like a good Crocean idealist would not make too much fuss about death; I die, yes, but there will be other poets and critics; the kind of function I approve of goes on; or say the whole human race comes to an end some day: that is a long way off and meanwhile there are plenty of ways in which we can usefully occupy our time. These sentiments are flat, but they express also a common-sense view of things, which can conduce to useful and sane behaviour. More profoundly, is it not nobler to live eternally, as the artist and the thinker do, in time – for thought and art *are* timeless! – rather than to worry too much that one's own life in time must have an end?).

The point of that last passage is that MacDiarmid though a Marxist is not a humanist, indeed he could be described as an anti-humanist. He is preoccupied with death in what is essentially a religious way. It worries me a little, I must confess, that he uses the stones as symbols of death. Some of them of course are fossils. But many of them must be originally of crystalline formation, with their own principles of inner shaping, but not animate. It worries me also – and I mean from a poetic not an argumentative point of view – that MacDiarmid wants us to feel a self-reproach about the stones on the beach. We have done them no harm; could have done them no good. So the feeling seems artificial and strained.

One should note, however, that the central symbolism of this poem, at this point, is Christian, or anti-Christian: there will be no rolling away of the stone from the mouth of the tomb, no resurrection. But this becomes a lament:

> – Each of these stones on this raised beach,
> Every stone in the world,
> Covers infinite death, beyond the reach
> Of the dead it hides; and cannot be hurled
> Aside yet to let any of them come forth, as love
> Once made a stone move

(Though I do not depend on that
My case to prove).
So let us beware of death; the stones will have
Their revenge; we have lost all approach to them,
But soon we shall become as those we have betrayed,
And they will seal us as fast in our graves
As our indifference and ignorance seals them; . . .

Again, here, the feeling seems strained, for, to repeat, I cannot see what the stones want their revenge for, or what our ignorance and indifference is. Both geology and crystallography are in a thriving condition and, if one is looking for sculpture that respects the essential nature of stone, there is the work of Brancusi, say, and Barbara Hepworth and Henry Moore. To be very Scotch, what is MacDiarmid 'girning' about here? But it is true, I suppose, as the French poet Francis Ponge has said, that language, even poetic language, generalises and that no poet has ever described the unicity, the uniqueness, of some one particular pebble. This may be the sort of betrayal and ignorance that MacDiarmid has in mind, and it makes more poetic sense.

But let us not be afraid to die.
No heavier and colder and quieter then,
No more motionless, do stones lie
In death than in life to all men.
It is no more difficult in death than here
– Though slow as the stones the powers develop
To rise from the grave – to get a life worth having;
And in death – unlike life – we lose nothing that is truly ours.

I feel a fine eloquence here and there is no trouble about grammar – Jimmy Singer was as confidently wrong in saying that the grammar is bad as in saying that there is a 'lack of versification' – but I am puzzled because I can only make sense of this passage in relation to something like the Christian doctrine of the General Resurrection, and I suppose, at least, that as a Marxist MacDiarmid repudiates this doctrine, and from what I know of world religions it is silly to talk of 'something like' the Christian doctrine of the Resurrection. It is a unique doctrine, other world religions believe in a purely spiritual immortality or in absorption in a single cosmic spirit or in reincarnation, but none in the resurrection. Is MacDiarmid saying, like D. H. Lawrence in 'Bavarian Gentians', that out of Hades, the dead winter soil, new life, the life of the released Persephone, grows? I do not think so: there are only barren rocks in this poem, no humus, however thin. He means, I think, some personal doctrine of his own, whose feeling he conveys very powerfully, but whose intellectual nature baffles me. And this is one of the flaws in a powerful poem.

The very last short passage of the poem, like the very first, sends one hurrying to one's dictionaries. Perhaps, once I have deciphered it, it will throw some light on the whole structure?

> Diallage of the world's debate, end of the long auxesis,
> Although no ébrillade of Pegasus can here avail,
> I prefer your enchorial characters – the futhorc of the future –
> To the hieroglyphics of all the other forms of Nature.
> Song, your apprentice encrinite, seems to sweep
> The Heavens with a last entrochal movement;
> And, with the same word that began it, closes
> Earth's vast epanadiplosis.

Ébrillade must be a fairly rare French word, since my *Petit Larousse Illustré* does not have it; but let us guess that it is connected with *briller*, that the *e* is the Latin *ex* or *e*, and that it means something like 'a shining out from', perhaps because of the *ade* termination (like par*ade*, cavalc*ade*) a kind of processional movement or cavorting of Pegasus that makes him shine out from the sky. 'Enchorial' is used of the popular or demotic as distinct from the priestly or hieratic or hieroglyphic way of writing the ancient Egyptian pictogram-characters. 'Futhorc' – named from the first six letters, f, u, th, o or a, r, k, is the Runic alphabet, connected especially with ancient Scandinavia, but also the word Runic is applied to an interlacing type of ancient Celtic ornament. Runes were the kind of mysterious poems appropriately written in the Runic alphabet. The word *futhorc* can also be spelt *futhork* or *futhark*.

'Encrinite' is a fossil crinoid and a crinoid (the root meaning is 'lily-shaped') is an echinoderm, and an echinoderm is a sea-creature of the sea-urchin, sea-cucumber sort, its skin typically covered with spines; what is particular to the crinoid is that it has a calyx-like body, stalked and rooted. An entrochal movement is a wheel-like movement, but the adjective is particularly applied to the wheel-like plates of which certain crinoids are composed. 'Epanadiplosis' is not in either *The Shorter Oxford Dictionary* or, in its French equivalent, in *Le Petit Larousse*. I feel I may have come across it in books, like George Puttenham's, on Renaissance terms of rhetoric, and it could appropriately apply to a piece of writing, like *Finnegans Wake*, which begins in the middle of a sentence and ends at the beginning of the sentence so ideally you read circularly on for ever (you could go back now to the beginning of the 'Raised Beach'.) This guess that *epanadiplosis* is a rhetorical term of art is plausible because *auxesis* is one, also, meaning *amplificatio* or hyperbole.

With all these clues, could we attempt a prose translation of the final passage? I think that MacDiarmid is no longer addressing the reader but the stones (like Keats addressing the Urn): he is saying: 'Clock that measures the pettiness of the human struggle, conclusion of the long hyperbole of man's activity, though no brilliancy of poetic activity (no shaking of Pegasus's shining hooves in the sky) can avail me in this desolate rocky place, I prefer your demotic characters – the marks on the stones that will be the runes of the future – to the hieroglyphics of all other forms of Nature (including Man). Song, like the little fossil crinoid which has been your apprentice, seems to sweep the heavens with his plate-like wheels; and, with the same word that began it, Earth's circuitous rhetorical statement comes to an end.'

Perhaps here, as in Keats's 'To Autumn' the poetic attempt to escape from transience to the permanent ends in finding permanence in the very regularity of the transient, finds something like the music of the spheres. And a deeply troubled spirit finds escape from the 'fury and the mire of human veins' not like Yeats in monuments of man's intellect but in that aspect of the earth, the geological, which is at once the most obstinate, the most intractable, the slowest to change, and the furthest from ordinary human sympathies (poets identify themselves easily enough with birds, flowers, moving clouds, bright stars, the changing moon: MacDiarmid finds his final consolation in an image of rocky sullenness and stillness, which alone can quiet, for the time being, his rage at human folly and failure).

4. SOME GENERAL REMARKS ON THE CHARACTER OF MACDIARMID'S LATER POETRY

I have not expounded or in a detailed sense criticised this poem; I have done a little sight-reading and dictionary-construing: but the poem has raised certain general thoughts in my mind, which apply, I think, not only to this but to very much of MacDiarmid's later poetry, his poetry of self-communing, of naked discourse.

Wölflinn, in his great pioneer book, *The Renaissance and the*

Baroque, has much to say about the new characteristics of the Baroque as compared with the Renaissance: 'the massiveness, the enormous weight, the lack of formal discipline and thorough-going articulation, the increased animation, the restlessness, the violent agitation . . .' He speaks of Michelangelo's influence on the Baroque, and notes, for instance, that unlike a true Renaissance artist, it was not in Michelangelo's nature to express harmony or happiness: 'Michelangelo's men and women appear to be the unresisting victims of an inner compulsion, not harmoniously and uniformly, but fitfully, so that some are expressive to the utmost while others are almost totally lifeless and inert . . . Vitality is unevenly distributed . . . some parts are superhuman in their strength, others all weight.'

It seems to me that on looking over the passages I have quoted from 'On A Raised Beach' and still more on looking through one of the much longer later poems like *In Memoriam James Joyce*, one has an impression not dissimilar to that which Wölflinn describes: 'enormous weight and massiveness', a distinct lack of 'formal discipline and thorough-going articulation' – though they can be scanned, these long poems are not in any particular metre, and though they are argumentative, they have not, quite unlike *Religio Laici* or *An Essay on Criticism*, or even the *Prelude*, a ground-plan of structure, a reason in themselves why, and where, they should begin and end – and on the other hand there is, in the more striking passages, 'the animation, the restlessness, the violent agitation' of which Wölflinn speaks. In writing these long poems, MacDiarmid too appears to be the 'unresisting victim of an inner compulsion, so that some [passages] are expressive to the utmost while others are totally lifeless and inert . . . Vitality is unevenly distributed . . . some parts are superhuman in their strength, others are all weight.'

Even more relevantly, Wölflinn describes how in poetry too in the Baroque age 'the light and easy grace of the Renaissance gave way to seriousness, dignity, the gay playfulness to pompous rustling splendour.' He contrasts the lightness, quickness, and airiness of Ariosto's *Orlando Furioso* (1516) whose opening lines in Sir John Harington's translation are

Of dames, of knights, of armes, of loves delight,
Of courtesie, of high attempts I speake,
Then when the Moores transported all their might
On Affrick seas the Force of France to breake,

with the opening lines of Tasso's *Gerusalemme Liberata*, which, since the translation by Hoole is abominably flat and prosaic, I will endeavour to render myself:

> Those pious arms, and the Chief, I sing
> Who the great sepulchre of Christ set free;
> Much he with heart and much with hand did sway,
> And much he suffered in the glorious quest;
> And in vain Hell opposed him, and in vain
> Took arms the mingled Asian and Libyan throngs;
> Since Heaven was on his side . . .

Wölflinn notes 'the lofty adjectives, the resounding line endings, the measured repetitions ("much . . .", "much . . .", "in vain", "and in vain"): the weighty sentence construction, and the generally slower rhythm." But he notes also that the grandeur is not only in the expression; the verbal images become larger, and perhaps vaguer. Boiardo, in the early Renaissance, says: 'To Angelica shines the morning star, the lily in the garden, the rose.' This succession of quick distinct images does not suit Berni who is making a Baroque *rifacci-miento* of Boiardo: instead, we get: 'To Angelica shines the bright star in the east, yes, to be true, it is the sun.' The move from the Renaissance to the Baroque is a move from a love of details and particulars for their own sakes (such as we get, for instance, in MacDiarmid's *A Drunk Man Looks at the Thistle*) to something more monotonous but by intention at least grander:

'Now, however, we step further back and survey the general effect; we do not require grandeur in the individual part, but only a general impression; there is *less perception and more atmosphere* . . . The baroque has no sense of the significance of individual forms, only for the more muted effect of the whole. The individual, defined and plastic form has ceased to matter; compositions are in the mass effects of light and shade and the most indefinite of all elements have become the real means of expression.'

The expression 'The Scottish Renaissance' was not a mere slogan.

The best of MacDiarmid's early poems, whether lyrical, satirical, comical, or a mixture of all three things, have the qualities that Wölflinn assigns to Renaissance poetry (as, indeed, have the poems of the Scottish poets who can be considered as his predecessors, Dunbar, Robert Fergusson, Burns): a sense of the variety of things, a quickness and gaiety, an untroubled acceptance of life within its limitations, what we call humanism. MacDiarmid was the leader of the Scottish Renaissance. In his later work, he is anti-humanistic: he seeks transcendence, he tortures himself and strains: he can no longer represent, nor does he desire, the rhythms, the harmonies, the humours of ordinary human happiness. He has a sense of oppressive weight incumbent on him, he sometimes collapses under this inertly, he sometimes struggles against it with titanic energy. Like Michelangelo, he has a certain *terribilità*. There is much less perception, detailed perception, in his late poems, but a much more unified and grandiose atmosphere. He has moved from the humanistic to the religious; he takes on, deliberately, more burdens than he can well bear. He does nothing than can be done easily and gracefully. He is the lone representative of a Scottish (or, as Jimmy Singer suggested, of an English) new Baroque. The repetitions, the vagueness, the grandeurs, the movement and stress and the impatience with the limitations of the human condition itself are all there.

The late poems oppress us or impress us or bore us, sometimes, these abrupt alternations of the strenuous and the inert, but they do not offer us, anyway, any more than Michelangelo does, the ordinary kind of artistic pleasure. They are struggling beyond the limits of art. They are not what I turn to, when I am turning to poetry for pleasure. But let us admire the lonely effort that has gone into them, and let us admire the strong old man, stonily intransigent, implacable, struggling always for transcendence.

A Hugh MacDiarmid Bibliography

W. R. AITKEN

The bibliography of Hugh MacDiarmid is complicated enough, even if one limits the record to the books, pamphlets, and separate publications for which he has been responsible, leaving aside the complexities of his many contributions to books, periodicals, and the press. The poet himself is well aware of these complications; in a recent letter to the present writer he admits: 'I know I am a bibliographer's nightmare.'

The complications of MacDiarmid's bibliography have two main causes: firstly, his use of a number of pseudonyms, possibly not all yet revealed, and secondly, the activities of a number of his friends and admirers in sponsoring limited and other special editions, sometimes as broadsheets or pamphlets printing only one or two poems. These privately printed, limited editions of single poems, or of a few related poems, are mainly the work of K. D. Duval, publisher and joint-editor of the seventieth-birthday *Festschrift* (1962), or of Colin Hamilton, his partner, or of Duncan Glen, who has told the story of his concern with the printing of MacDiarmid's poetry in his essay, *A Small Press and Hugh MacDiarmid* (1970). They must not be dismissed as though they were irresponsibly conceived bibliographical curiosities, produced in deliberately limited editions more for the glory of the printer and publisher than for the poet. It is, for example, very doubtful if the poems contained in *A Lap of Honour* (1967), the first of the collections designed to supplement the *Collected Poems* of 1962, and perhaps the best-planned recent volume of his poetry, would be known but for Duncan Glen's succession of pamphlets, privately printed between 1964 and 1967. Hugh MacDiarmid acknowledges that 'Duncan Glen . . . has done a great deal . . . to recover many poems I'd lost sight of and forgotten I'd written'.

Some of C. M. Grieve's pseudonyms are revealed and discussed in a pamphlet Duncan Glen wrote and published in 1964, *The Literary Masks of Hugh MacDiarmid*. Hugh MacDiarmid made his first appearance in the first number of the literary review, *The Scottish Chapbook*, which Grieve founded in August 1922, and edited and

Reprinted from the *Border Standard*, 20th and 27th November and 4th December 1927. Among the other books by MacDiarmid listed in *Second Hymn to Lenin* (1935) this pamphlet is cited as *The Present Condition of Scottish Music*, but 'position' not 'condition' is the word in the title.

13 *The Present Condition of Scottish Arts and Affairs*. [Anon.]
Issued by the Committee of the Scottish Centre of the P.E.N. Club. Dalbeattie: *The Stewartry Observer*, [1928].

14 *The Scottish National Association of April Fools*, by Gillechriosd Mac A'Ghreidhir. Reprinted from the *Pictish Review*, 1 (6), April 1928. Aberdeen: The University Press, 1928.

15 *Scotland in* 1980, by C. M. Grieve. Montrose: C. M. Grieve, 1929.
Reprinted from the *Scots Independent*, 3 (8), June 1929.

16 *The Handmaid of the Lord*, by Ramon Maria de Tenreiro. London: Secker, 1930.
This anonymous translation is first listed among MacDiarmid's works in *Second Hymn to Lenin* (1935).

17 *To Circumjack Cencrastus, or The Curly Snake*, by Hugh M'Diarmid. Edinburgh and London: Blackwood, 1930.

18 *Living Scottish Poets*. Edited by C. M. Grieve. London: Benn, 1931. *The Augustan Books of Poetry*.

19 *O wha's been here afore me, lass*. With drawing by Frederick Carter. [London: E. Lahr, 1931.] *Blue Moon Poem for Christmas* 1931.
There was also a special edition of 100 numbered copies signed by the author.
This poem had appeared previously in *A Drunk Man Looks at the Thistle* (1926).

20 *First Hymn to Lenin and other poems*, by Hugh McDiarmid. London: Unicorn Press, 1931.
A limited edition of 450 numbered copies and a special large paper edition of 50 copies numbered and signed by the poet. There is an introductory essay by 'AE' (George William Russell) and a portrait frontispiece from a crayon drawing, also by 'AE'.
The 'First Hymn' originally appeared in *New English Poems*, edited by Lascelles Abercrombie (London: Gollancz 1931).
It was reprinted in *Three Hymns to Lenin* (1957).

21 *Warning Democracy*, by C. H. Douglas. London: C. M. Grieve, 1931.

22 *Tarras*. Edinburgh: *The Free Man*, 1932.
Limited edition of 20 copies with frontispiece 'Macdiarmid and the Horse Punchkin' from an oil-painting by William Johnstone.
'Tarras' originally appeared in the *Free Man*, 25th June 1932, and was reprinted in *Scots Unbound* (1932).

23 *Second Hymn to Lenin*. Thakeham: Valda Trevlyn, [1932].
Limited edition of 100 copies.

published from his home in Montrose. His first work was a semi-dramatic study, 'Nisbet, an interlude in post-war Glasgow'. The first poem of Hugh MacDiarmid's to be published in *The Scottish Chabpook*, 'The Watergaw', appeared in the third issue, for October 1922 (it had been printed previously in *The Dunfermline Press* for 30 September 1922), and in the same issue Grieve's editorial 'Causerie' drew attention to the new contributor:

> The work of Mr. Hugh M'Diarmid . . . is peculiarly interesting because he is, I think, the first Scottish writer who has addressed himself to the question of the extendability (without psychological violence) of the vernacular to embrace the whole range of modern culture – or, in other words, tried to make up the leeway of the language.

So, like 'Arthur Leslie' thirty years later, Grieve had to explain what MacDiarmid was trying to do.

The relationship between Grieve and MacDiarmid, as between James Leslie Mitchell and Lewis Grassic Gibbon, is difficult to define. Originally it seemed that Grieve wrote in prose while his 'distant cousin' MacDiarmid was the poet, but MacDiarmid later turned to prose and is now the acknowledged author of several volumes of essays and the like and Grieve is silent. Perhaps a clue is to be found in the inscription which that perceptive critic and early admirer, Denis Saurat, wrote in a copy of his *Histoire des Religions:*

To C. M. Grieve, who will criticize
and MacDiarmid, who will approve
Très amicalement,
D. Saurat.

It is also difficult to ascertain when and how it came to be known that C. M. Grieve and Hugh MacDiarmid were one and the same, but it is certainly true that in the late 1920s and even early 1930s their identity was still unknown to quite a number of people interested in Scottish literature. By 1934, however, when Eric Linklater portrayed Hugh MacDiarmid as Hugh Skene in *Magnus Merriman*, it was generally known that the two were one.

The bibliography which follows does not attempt to record the material about MacDiarmid and his work. One point can be made briefly here, however. Nine years ago there was still no book-length biographical or critical study dealing solely with MacDiarmid's life and work. The first to appear was the seventieth-birthday *Festschrift* edited by

K. D. Duval and Sydney Goodsir Smith (1962); it was followed by Kenneth Buthlay's study in the 'Writers and Critics' series (1964) and by Duncan Glen's historical and critical survey, *Hugh MacDiarmid (Christopher Murray Grieve) and the Scottish Renaissance*, published in the same year. MacDiarmid himself has written: 'It was in 1962, however, that the real break-through came.'

Periodical articles and reviews continue to appear, and there have been a number of essays, and studies, in books or pamphlets, and special MacDiarmid issues of such periodicals as *Agenda* (1967–68) and *Akros* (1970). The second part of the two-part MacDiarmid issue of *Akros* contained a notable contribution from J. K. Annand that puts the record straight regarding certain facts of the poet's early career.

This bibliography can be, of course, only an interim statement, the record of an already prolific writer who is still actively planning further publications with a greater expectation that they will in fact be published than at any time in his long literary career. Hugh MacDiarmid's importance is at last recognised.

A BOOKS

1 *Northern Numbers, being representative selections from certain living Scottish poets*. Edinburgh and London: T. N. Foulis, 1920.
The foreword is signed with the initials C. M. G.
Issued in two bindings, cloth and paper, and also bound with the second series in one volume.

2 *Northern Numbers, being representative selections from certain living Scottish poets*. Edited by C. M. Grieve. Second series. Edinburgh and London: T. N. Foulis, 1921.
Issued in two bindings, cloth and paper, and also bound together with the first series in one volume.

3 *Northern Numbers, being representative selections from certain living Scottish poets*. Edited by C. M. Grieve. Third series. Montrose: C.M. Grieve, 1922.

4 (a) *Annals of the Five Senses*, by C. M. Grieve. Montrose: C. M. Grieve, 1923.
(b) —— Edinburgh: Porpoise Press, 1930.
A reissue with a new imprint.

5 *Sangschaw*, by Hugh M'Diarmid. Edinburgh and London: Blackwood, 1925.

6 *Penny Wheep*, by Hugh M'Diarmid. Edinburgh and London: wood, 1926.

7 (a) *A Drunk Man Looks at the Thistle*, by Hugh M'Diarmid. burgh and London: Blackwood, 1926.
(b) —— With an introduction by David Daiches. New e Glasgow: Caledonian Press, 1953.
This edition omits the Author's Note of the original editio prints an 'Author's note to second edition' (p. vii–xi) as well Introduction by David Daiches (p. xiii–xx).
(c) —— Third edition. Edinburgh: Castle Wynd Printers, 1956 Issued in two bindings, cloth and paper.
This edition gives the Author's Note and the entire text as i first edition and prints as appendixes the Author's Note (Append p. 97–101) and the Introduction by Dr. David Daiches (Append p. 103–10) which prefaced the second edition, published in 195
(d) —— Fourth edition. Edinburgh: The 200 Burns Club, 1 Published on the occasion of the poet's seventieth birthday.
(e) —— Illustrated with eight woodcuts by Frans Masereel. Falkl Kulgin Duval & Colin H. Hamilton, 1969.
160 copies printed in Dante type by Giovanni Mardersteig on hand-press of the Officina Bodoni in Verona.
All copies numbered, ten not for sale with roman numerals, all signed by the author, the illustrator and the printer.
Although dated November 1969, the book was not published u summer 1970.
(f) —— Edited by John C. Weston. Amherst, Mass.: The Univers of Massachusetts Press, 1971.
In this edition the spelling of MacDiarmid's Scots is standardised the editor in accordance with the poet's statement in his letter pu lished in *The Scotsman* on 28th September 1968 and reprinted *Lines Review*, no. 27, November 1968, p. 33.

8 *Robert Burns*, 1759–1796. [Edited by] C. M. Grieve. London: Ben [1926]. *The Augustan Books of Poetry*.

9 *Contemporary Scottish Studies*, by C. M. Grieve. First series. London Leonard Parsons, 1926.
These critical studies originally appeared in the *Scottish Educationa Journal* (commencing in May 1925) and are reprinted 'practically in their original form'. A promised second series was never published.

10 *Albyn, or Scotland and the Future*, by C. M. Grieve. London: Kegan Paul, Trench, Trubner, 1927. *To-day and To-morrow Series*.

11 *The Lucky Bag*, by Hugh M'Diarmid. Edinburgh: Porpoise Press, 1927. *Porpoise Press Broadsheet*, 3rd series, no. 5.

12 *The Present Position of Scottish Music*, by C. M. Grieve. Montrose: C. M. Grieve, 1927.

published from his home in Montrose. His first work was a semi-dramatic study, 'Nisbet, an interlude in post-war Glasgow'. The first poem of Hugh MacDiarmid's to be published in *The Scottish Chabpook*, 'The Watergaw', appeared in the third issue, for October 1922 (it had been printed previously in *The Dunfermline Press* for 30 September 1922), and in the same issue Grieve's editorial 'Causerie' drew attention to the new contributor:

> The work of Mr. Hugh M'Diarmid . . . is peculiarly interesting because he is, I think, the first Scottish writer who has addressed himself to the question of the extendability (without psychological violence) of the vernacular to embrace the whole range of modern culture – or, in other words, tried to make up the leeway of the language.

So, like 'Arthur Leslie' thirty years later, Grieve had to explain what MacDiarmid was trying to do.

The relationship between Grieve and MacDiarmid, as between James Leslie Mitchell and Lewis Grassic Gibbon, is difficult to define. Originally it seemed that Grieve wrote in prose while his 'distant cousin' MacDiarmid was the poet, but MacDiarmid later turned to prose and is now the acknowledged author of several volumes of essays and the like and Grieve is silent. Perhaps a clue is to be found in the inscription which that perceptive critic and early admirer, Denis Saurat, wrote in a copy of his *Histoire des Religions*:

To C. M. Grieve, who will criticize
and MacDiarmid, who will approve
Très amicalement,
D. Saurat.

It is also difficult to ascertain when and how it came to be known that C. M. Grieve and Hugh MacDiarmid were one and the same, but it is certainly true that in the late 1920s and even early 1930s their identity was still unknown to quite a number of people interested in Scottish literature. By 1934, however, when Eric Linklater portrayed Hugh MacDiarmid as Hugh Skene in *Magnus Merriman*, it was generally known that the two were one.

The bibliography which follows does not attempt to record the material about MacDiarmid and his work. One point can be made briefly here, however. Nine years ago there was still no book-length biographical or critical study dealing solely with MacDiarmid's life and work. The first to appear was the seventieth-birthday *Festschrift* edited by

K. D. Duval and Sydney Goodsir Smith (1962); it was followed by Kenneth Buthlay's study in the 'Writers and Critics' series (1964) and by Duncan Glen's historical and critical survey, *Hugh MacDiarmid (Christopher Murray Grieve) and the Scottish Renaissance*, published in the same year. MacDiarmid himself has written: 'It was in 1962, however, that the real break-through came.'

Periodical articles and reviews continue to appear, and there have been a number of essays, and studies, in books or pamphlets, and special MacDiarmid issues of such periodicals as *Agenda* (1967–68) and *Akros* (1970). The second part of the two-part MacDiarmid issue of *Akros* contained a notable contribution from J. K. Annand that puts the record straight regarding certain facts of the poet's early career.

This bibliography can be, of course, only an interim statement, the record of an already prolific writer who is still actively planning further publications with a greater expectation that they will in fact be published than at any time in his long literary career. Hugh MacDiarmid's importance is at last recognised.

A BOOKS

1 *Northern Numbers, being representative selections from certain living Scottish poets*. Edinburgh and London: T. N. Foulis, 1920.
The foreword is signed with the initials C. M. G.
Issued in two bindings, cloth and paper, and also bound with the second series in one volume.

2 *Northern Numbers, being representative selections from certain living Scottish poets*. Edited by C. M. Grieve. Second series. Edinburgh and London: T. N. Foulis, 1921.
Issued in two bindings, cloth and paper, and also bound together with the first series in one volume.

3 *Northern Numbers, being representative selections from certain living Scottish poets*. Edited by C. M. Grieve. Third series. Montrose: C.M. Grieve, 1922.

4 (a) *Annals of the Five Senses*, by C. M. Grieve. Montrose: C. M. Grieve, 1923.
(b) —— Edinburgh: Porpoise Press, 1930.
A reissue with a new imprint.

5 *Sangschaw*, by Hugh M'Diarmid. Edinburgh and London: Blackwood, 1925.

6 *Penny Wheep*, by Hugh M'Diarmid. Edinburgh and London: Blackwood, 1926.

7 (a) *A Drunk Man Looks at the Thistle*, by Hugh M'Diarmid. Edinburgh and London: Blackwood, 1926.

(b) —— With an introduction by David Daiches. New edition. Glasgow: Caledonian Press, 1953.

This edition omits the Author's Note of the original edition but prints an 'Author's note to second edition' (p. vii–xi) as well as the Introduction by David Daiches (p. xiii–xx).

(c) —— Third edition. Edinburgh: Castle Wynd Printers, 1956.

Issued in two bindings, cloth and paper.

This edition gives the Author's Note and the entire text as in the first edition and prints as appendixes the Author's Note (Appendix A, p. 97–101) and the Introduction by Dr. David Daiches (Appendix B, p. 103–10) which prefaced the second edition, published in 1953.

(d) —— Fourth edition. Edinburgh: The 200 Burns Club, 1962.

Published on the occasion of the poet's seventieth birthday.

(e) —— Illustrated with eight woodcuts by Frans Masereel. Falkland: Kulgin Duval & Colin H. Hamilton, 1969.

160 copies printed in Dante type by Giovanni Mardersteig on the hand-press of the Officina Bodoni in Verona.

All copies numbered, ten not for sale with roman numerals, and all signed by the author, the illustrator and the printer.

Although dated November 1969, the book was not published until summer 1970.

(f) —— Edited by John C. Weston. Amherst, Mass.: The University of Massachusetts Press, 1971.

In this edition the spelling of MacDiarmid's Scots is standardised by the editor in accordance with the poet's statement in his letter published in *The Scotsman* on 28th September 1968 and reprinted in *Lines Review*, no. 27, November 1968, p. 33.

8 *Robert Burns*, 1759–1796. [Edited by] C. M. Grieve. London: Benn, [1926]. *The Augustan Books of Poetry.*

9 *Contemporary Scottish Studies*, by C. M. Grieve. First series. London: Leonard Parsons, 1926.

These critical studies originally appeared in the *Scottish Educational Journal* (commencing in May 1925) and are reprinted 'practically in their original form'. A promised second series was never published.

10 *Albyn, or Scotland and the Future*, by C. M. Grieve. London: Kegan Paul, Trench, Trubner, 1927. *To-day and To-morrow Series.*

11 *The Lucky Bag*, by Hugh M'Diarmid. Edinburgh: Porpoise Press, 1927. *Porpoise Press Broadsheet*, 3rd series, no. 5.

12 *The Present Position of Scottish Music*, by C. M. Grieve. Montrose: C. M. Grieve, 1927.

Reprinted from the *Border Standard*, 20th and 27th November and 4th December 1927. Among the other books by MacDiarmid listed in *Second Hymn to Lenin* (1935) this pamphlet is cited as *The Present Condition of Scottish Music*, but 'position' not 'condition' is the word in the title.

13 *The Present Condition of Scottish Arts and Affairs*. [Anon.]
Issued by the Committee of the Scottish Centre of the P.E.N. Club. Dalbeattie: *The Stewartry Observer*, [1928].

14 *The Scottish National Association of April Fools*, by Gillechriosd Mac A'Ghreidhir. Reprinted from the *Pictish Review*, 1 (6), April 1928. Aberdeen: The University Press, 1928.

15 *Scotland in* 1980, by C. M. Grieve. Montrose: C. M. Grieve, 1929.
Reprinted from the *Scots Independent*, 3 (8), June 1929.

16 *The Handmaid of the Lord*, by Ramon Maria de Tenreiro. London: Secker, 1930.
This anonymous translation is first listed among MacDiarmid's works in *Second Hymn to Lenin* (1935).

17 *To Circumjack Cencrastus, or The Curly Snake*, by Hugh M'Diarmid. Edinburgh and London: Blackwood, 1930.

18 *Living Scottish Poets*. Edited by C. M. Grieve. London: Benn, 1931. *The Augustan Books of Poetry*.

19 *O wha's been here afore me, lass*. With drawing by Frederick Carter. [London: E. Lahr, 1931.] *Blue Moon Poem for Christmas* 1931.
There was also a special edition of 100 numbered copies signed by the author.
This poem had appeared previously in *A Drunk Man Looks at the Thistle* (1926).

20 *First Hymn to Lenin and other poems*, by Hugh McDiarmid. London: Unicorn Press, 1931.
A limited edition of 450 numbered copies and a special large paper edition of 50 copies numbered and signed by the poet. There is an introductory essay by 'AE' (George William Russell) and a portrait frontispiece from a crayon drawing, also by 'AE'.
The 'First Hymn' originally appeared in *New English Poems*, edited by Lascelles Abercrombie (London: Gollancz 1931).
It was reprinted in *Three Hymns to Lenin* (1957).

21 *Warning Democracy*, by C. H. Douglas. London: C. M. Grieve, 1931.

22 *Tarras*. Edinburgh: *The Free Man*, 1932.
Limited edition of 20 copies with frontispiece 'Macdiarmid and the Horse Punchkin' from an oil-painting by William Johnstone.
'Tarras' originally appeared in the *Free Man*, 25th June 1932, and was reprinted in *Scots Unbound* (1932).

23 *Second Hymn to Lenin*. Thakeham: Valda Trevlyn, [1932].
Limited edition of 100 copies.

There is a cover drawing of the poet by Flora Macdonald and a portrait frontispiece by William Johnstone.

An Author's Note states: 'Like the contents of my volume, "First Hymn to Lenin and other Poems" (Unicorn Press, Ltd., 1931), this poem is a short separable item in my long poem "Clann Albainn" [*sic*] now in course of preparation.' In the event *Clann Albann* never appeared; but see notes on the 'complete scheme' in the *Modern Scot*, 2 (2), July 1931, p. 107, and 'Clann Albann: an explanation' in the *Scots Observer*, 12th August 1933.

The 'Second Hymn' originally appeared in *The Criterion* (vol. 11, no. 45, July 1932, p. 593–8). It was reprinted in *Second Hymn to Lenin and other poems* (1935) and *Three Hymns to Lenin* (1957).

24 *Scots Unbound and other poems*. Stirling: Eneas Mackay, 1932.

Edition limited to 350 signed copies.

There is a portrait frontispiece of the poet's head in bronze by William Lamb.

An Author's Note states: 'The poems in this volume, like those in my *First Hymn to Lenin and Other Poems* (Unicorn Press, 1931) and *Second Hymn to Lenin* (Valda Trevlyn, Thakeham, 1932), are separable items from the first volume of my long poem, "Clann Albann," now in preparation.'

The title poem, 'Scots Unbound', was reprinted in *Stony Limits and Scots Unbound* (1956).

25 *Five Bits of Miller*. Now for the first time set up and printed from the manuscript. London: The Author, 1934.

Edition limited to 40 numbered copies signed by the author.

Reprinted in *The Uncanny Scot* (1968).

26 (a) *Scottish Scene, or The Intelligent Man's Guide to Albyn*, [by] Lewis Grassic Gibbon and Hugh MacDiarmid. London: Jarrolds, 1934.

A cheap edition was issued by the same publisher in 1937.

(b) —— London and Melbourne: Hutchinson, for the National Book Association, n.d.

This reset edition was also issued by Readers Union, by arrangement with Hutchinson.

27 *Stony Limits and other poems*. London: Gollancz, 1934.

Reprinted, with the restoration of certain excluded poems and with the title poem of *Scots Unbound* (1932), as *Stony Limits and Scots Unbound and other poems* (1956).

28 *At the Sign of the Thistle: a collection o, essays*. London: Stanley Nott, [1934].

29 *Selected Poems*. London: Macmillan, 1934. *Macmillan's Contemporary Poets*.

A selection, by the poet himself, from *Sangschaw*, *Penny Wheep*, *A Drunk Man Looks at the Thistle*, *Scots Unbound* and *Stony Limits*.

30 *The Birlinn of Clanranald* [*Birlinn Chlann-Raghnaill*], by Alexander MacDonald: translated from the Scots Gaelic of Alasdair MacMhaighstir Alasdair. St Andrews: The Abbey Book Shop, 1935.

Limited to 100 numbered copies signed by the translator. Reprinted from the *Modern Scot*, 5 (4), January 1935, p. 230–47.

31 *Second Hymn to Lenin and other poems*. London: Stanley Nott, 1935.

The dust-wrapper carries a drawing of the poet by William Johnstone.

The 'Second Hymn' had been published previously in a limited edition in 1932. It was reprinted in *Three Hymns to Lenin* (1957).

32 *Charles Doughty and the Need for Heroic Poetry*. [St. Andrews: *The Modern Scot*, 1936.]

A reprint of an article published in the *Modern Scot*, 6 (4), January 1936, p. 308–18. It is reprinted in *Selected Essays* (1969).

33 *Scottish Eccentrics*. London: Routledge, 1936.

34 *Scotland, and the Question of a Popular Front against Fascism and War*. Whalsay: The Hugh MacDiarmid Book Club, [1938].

35 *Dìreadh*. [Dunfermline: *The Voice of Scotland*, 1938.]

Edition limited to 20 copies.

A reprint of a long poem published in *The Voice of Scotland*, 1 (3), December 1938, pp. 13–21. 'One of the shorter separable lyrics interspersed in an immensely-long as-yet-unpublished poem, *Cornish Heroic Song for Valda Trevlyn*.'

36 (a) *The Islands of Scotland: Hebrides, Orkneys, and Shetlands*. London: Batsford, 1939.

(b) —— New York: Scribners, 1939.

37 *Speaking for Scotland*. London: The Lumphen Press, 1939. *Broadsheet no. 3*, edited by Paul Potts.

38 (a) *The Golden Treasury of Scottish Poetry*. Selected and edited by Hugh MacDiarmid. London: Macmillan, 1940.

(b) —— London: Macmillan, 1946. *Golden Treasury Series*.

39 *Cornish Heroic Song for Valda Trevlyn*. Glasgow: Caledonian Press, [1943].

This 'opening section of an extremely long unpublished poem' was first published in the final issue of *The Criterion* (vol. 18, no. 71, January 1939, p. 195–203), where the poem is dated 1936. It was reprinted in *A Kist of Whistles* (1947).

40 *Lucky Poet: a self-study in literature and political ideas, being the autobiography of Hugh MacDiarmid* (*Christopher Murray Grieve*). London: Methuen, 1943.

There is a frontispiece portrait from a photograph by Helen B. Cruickshank.

41 *Selected Poems of Hugh MacDiarmid*. Edited by R. Crombie Saunders. Glasgow: Maclellan, 1944. *Poetry Scotland Series*, no. 6.

There is a portrait frontispiece from a photograph.

With the approval of the poet the editor of this selection made 'certain orthographical changes' in the 'texts of the poems in Scots'.

42 *Speaking for Scotland: selected poems of Hugh MacDiarmid.* Baltimore: Contemporary Poetry, 1946. *Distinguished Poets Series*, vol. 3.

This first American edition has an introduction by Compton Mackenzie and a portrait frontispiece from a portrait of the poet by Barker Fairley.

The selection, by the poet himself, is almost the same as the *Selected Poems* published by Macmillan in 1934, with the addition of three poems 'not previously published in book form'.

There is a glossary followed by notes on the pronunciation of Scottish words, a few general notes, and 'literal renderings into English' of five of the poems.

43 *Poems of the East-West Synthesis.* Glasgow: Caledonian Press, 1946.

Reprinted from *The Voice of Scotland*, 2 (3) March and 2 (4) June 1946.

44 *A Kist of Whistles: new poems.* Glasgow: Maclellan, [1947]. *Poetry Scotland Series*, no. 10.

The title is one that MacDiarmid first used in 1922 when a series of poems began to appear in the *Scottish Chapbook* under the heading 'From "A Kist of Whistles"'.

45 *William Soutar: Collected Poems.* Edited with an introductory essay by Hugh MacDiarmid. London: Andrew Dakers, 1948.

The introduction (pp. 9–21) is dated May 1944. It is reprinted in *Selected Essays* (1969).

46 *Robert Burns: Poems.* Selected and introduced by Hugh MacDiarmid. London: Grey Walls Press, 1949. *Crown Classics.*

47 *Cunninghame Graham: a centenary study.* With a foreword by R. E. Muirhead. Glasgow: Caledonian Press, [1952].

48 *The Politics and Poetry of Hugh MacDiarmid*, by Arthur Leslie. Reprinted from *The National Weekly.* Glasgow: Caledonian Press, [1952].

This pseudonymous essay is reprinted in *Selected Essays* (1969), where it is acknowledged to be 'MacDiarmid on MacDiarmid'.

49 *Selections from the Poems of William Dunbar.* Edited with introduction by Hugh MacDiarmid. Edinburgh: Oliver & Boyd, for the Saltire Society, 1952. *The Saltire Classics.*

50 (a) *Selected Poems of Hugh MacDiarmid.* Edited by Oliver Brown. Glasgow: Maclellan, for the Scottish Secretariat, 1954.

Issued in three bindings: paper, cloth and a de luxe edition.

(b) *Poems of Hugh MacDiarmid.* Selected by Oliver Brown. Glasgow: for the Scottish Secretariat, 1955.

Issued in three bindings: paper, cloth and a de luxe edition. A reissue of the above with a different title and imprint.

51 *Francis George Scott: an essay on the occasion of his seventy-fifth birthday, 25th January 1955.* Edinburgh: M. Macdonald, 1955.

52 *In Memorian James Joyce: from A Vision of World Language.* With decorations by John Duncan Fergusson. Glasgow: Maclellan, on behalf of the subscribers, 1955.

Issued in two bindings: a limited edition on special paper, signed by author and artist, and the ordinary cloth edition. A second impression (Glasgow: Maclellan, 1956) corrects a few misprints.

53 *Selected Poems of William Dunbar.* Edited and introduced by Hugh MacDiarmid. Glasgow: Maclellan, 1955.

A selection of Dunbar's poems by Hugh MacDiarmid was announced to appear in the Crown Classics series of the Grey Walls Press, but the firm went out of business before it was published. This, however, would appear to be the very book: it is printed by the firm who printed MacDiarmid's *Robert Burns* in the same series (see no. 46), and the title-page with Maclellan's imprint is an obvious cancel.

54 *Stony Limits and Scots Unbound and other poems.* Edinburgh: Castle Wynd Printers, 1956.

Issued in two bindings, cloth and paper.

Reprints, with the restoration of certain excluded poems, *Stony Limits and other poems* (1934) and the title poem, 'Scots Unbound', from *Scots Unbound and other poems* (1932).

55 *Three Hymns to Lenin.* Edinburgh: Castle Wynd Printers, 1957.

For the 'First Hymn to Lenin' see no. 20 above, and for the 'Second Hymn' see nos. 23 and 31. The 'Third Hymn' was first published in its entirety in *The Voice of Scotland*, 6 (1), April 1955, p. 12–20, although part had been printed in the poet's autobiography, *Lucky Poet* (1943).

56 *The Battle Continues.* Edinburgh: Castle Wynd Printers, 1957.

57 *Burns Today and Tomorrow.* Edinburgh: Castle Wynd Printers, 1959.

As well as the ordinary edition there was a special limited edition of 25 copies, signed by the author.

58 *The Kind of Poetry I Want.* Edinburgh: K. D. Duval, 1961.

Printed by Giovanni Mardersteig on the hand-press of the Officina Bodoni in Verona. Edition limited to 300 numbered copies, signed by the poet.

Parts of this poem first appeared in *Lucky Poet* (1943).

59 *David Hume, Scotland's Greatest Son: a transcript of the lecture given at Edinburgh University, April 1961.* Edinburgh: The Paperback, Booksellers, [1962].

There was also an edition on special paper and limited to 50 numbered copies, signed by the author.

60 *The Man of (almost) Independent Mind.* Edinburgh: Giles Gordon, 1962. Cover title: *Hugh Macdiarmid on Hume.*

61 *Bracken Hills in Autumn*. Edinburgh: Colin H. Hamilton, 1962.
25 numbered copies, signed by the author and the printer.
A long-lost poem, written in the early '30s. It is reprinted in the Penguin *Selected Poems* (1970).

62 (a) *Collected Poems of Hugh MacDiarmid*. New York: The Macmillan Company, 1962.
There is a portrait frontispiece from a photograph by Douglas MacAskill.
(b) *Collected Poems of Hugh MacDiarmid* (*C. M. Grieve*). Edinburgh and London: Oliver & Boyd, 1962.
A resisue of the American edition with a 'corrigenda' slip.
(c) *Collected Poems of Hugh MacDiarmid*. Revised edition with enlarged glossary prepared by John C. Weston. New York: The Macmillan Company (London: Collier-Macmillan), 1967.
A revision of the *Collected Poems* published in 1962. As Hugh MacDiarmid has himself said (in the Prefatory Note to *A Lap of Honour*, 1967), the title *Collected Poems* was a misnomer: 'The MS I sent to the publishers of that book was much too large for their purpose and only a portion of it was used.' Thus, although the Author's Note printed in all three editions of the *Collected Poems* states: 'This volume does not contain all the poems I have written, but all I think worth including in a definitive collection', MacDiarmid has had to point out repeatedly that that statement 'was written for the large collection, and unfortunately was not altered when only a part of that was published'. The *Collected Poems*, then, is 'only a big selection' of MacDiarmid's poetry, and it must be supplemented by the later collections, *A Lap of Honour* (1967), *A Clyack-Sheaf* (1969) and *More Collected Poems* (1970). (See MacDiarmid's letter in *The Times Literary Supplement*, 4th June 1970.)

63 *The Ugly Birds without Wings*. Edinburgh: Allan Donaldson, 1962.
There was also a large-paper edition limited to 30 copies signed by the author.

64 *Poetry like the Hawthorn. From* In Memoriam James Joyce. Hemel Hempstead: Duncan Glen, 1962.
150 numbered copies, the first 25 signed by the poet.
First printed, with the subtitle 'On the death of W. B. Yeats, 28th January, 1939', in *Wales*, no. 11, Winter 1939–40.

65 *The blaward and the skelly*. Privately printed [Hemel Hempstead, Duncan Glen], 1962.
10 copies only printed.
This poem originally appeared in the *Dunfermline Press*, 30th September 1922, along with 'The Watergaw'.

66 *When the Rat-Race is Over: an essay in honour of the fiftieth birthday of*

John Gawsworth [*T. I. Fytton Armstrong*]. London: Twyn Barlwm Press, 1962.

40 copies privately printed and signed by the author and John Gawsworth.

67 *Robert Burns: Love Songs*. Selected by Hugh MacDiarmid. London: Vista Books, 1962. *The Pocket Poets*.

68 *An Apprentice Angel*. London: New Poetry Press, 1963. *A New Poetry Broadsheet*.

This poem was printed in the *New English Weekly*, 1 (8), 9th June 1932, and reprinted in *Scots Unbound and other poems* (1932).

69 *Harry Martinson: Aniara, a review of man in time and space*. Adapted from the Swedish by Hugh MacDiarmid and Elspeth Harley Schubert. Introduction by Dr. Tord Hall. London: Hutchinson (New York: Knopf; Stockholm: Bonnier), 1963.

70 *Sydney Goodsir Smith*. Edinburgh: Colin H. Hamilton, 1963.

Edition limited to 135 copies; 35 copies signed by the author were issued in a special binding.

The text of an address at a meeting of the Edinburgh University Scottish Renaissance Society on 14th December 1962, when Sydney Goodsir Smith was presented with the Sir Thomas Urquhart Award for his services to Scots literature.

Reprinted in *The Uncanny Scot* (1968).

71 *Poems to Paintings by William Johnstone 1933*. Edinburgh: K.D. Duval, 1963.

There was also an edition of 100 copies signed by the poet. Parts of two of the poems were printed in *Lucky Poet* (1943).

72 (a) *Two poems. The terrible crystal: A vision of Scotland*. Skelmorlie: Duncan Glen, 1964.

55 numbered copies signed by the poet.

The two poems were originally printed in *Poetry Review* and both are reprinted in *A Lap of Honour* (1967).

(b) —— New Edition. Skelmorlie: Drumalban Press, 1964.

Approximately 50 copies.

73 *Six Vituperative Verses*. Privately printed [by Duncan Glen, The Satire Press], 1964.

25 copies printed 'without the permission of either Mr. MacDiarmid or Dr. C. M. Grieve'. One of the poems was later found to be not by Hugh MacDiarmid; others were absorbed into *Poet at Play* (1965).

74 *The Ministry of Water: two poems*. Glasgow: Duncan Glen, 1964.

125 numbered copies signed by the poet.

The poems, 'Prayer for a Second Flood' and 'Larking Dallier', had been printed previously in the *Modern Scot* and the *London Mercury* respectively, and both are reprinted in *A Lap of Honour* (1967).

75 *Poet at Play, and other poems, being a selection of mainly vituperative poems*. Privately printed [by Duncan Glen], 1965.

The printer's note records that 'these poems were rescued and fifty-five copies printed without the permission of either Dr. Grieve or Mr. Hugh MacDiarmid'.

76 *The Fire of the Spirit: two poems*. Glasgow: Duncan Glen, 1965.

Edition limited to 350 numbered copies, the first 50 signed by the poet.

The poems, 'By Wauchopeside' and 'Diamond body: in a cave of the sea', had been printed previously in the *Modern Scot* (1932) and the *Welsh Review* (1939) respectively, and both are reprinted in *A Lap of Honour* (1967).

77 *The Burning Passion*. Bishopbriggs, Glasgow: Akros Press, 1965.

35 numbered copies.

This poem, previously published in *First Hymn to Lenin and other poems* (1931), had been reprinted in the first issue of Duncan Glen's periodical *Akros* (1965). It is reprinted in *A Lap of Honour* (1967).

78 *Whuchulls: a poem*. Preston: Akros Publications, 1966.

100 numbered copies.

There are a portrait frontispiece of the poet and two illustrations by Duncan Glen.

First printed in the *Modern Scot*, 'Whuchulls' was reprinted in *Akros*, 1 (3), August 1966. It is reprinted in *A Lap of Honour* (1967).

79 (a) *The Company I've Kept*, [by] Hugh MacDiarmid (Christopher Murray Grieve). London: Hutchinson, 1966.

Autobiographical, with a portrait frontispiece from a photograph by Alan Daiches.

(b) —— Berkeley, Calif.: University of California Press, 1967.

80 *On a Raised Beach: a poem*. Preston: The Harris Press, 1967.

200 numbered copies, designed and printed by students of the School of Art, Harris College, Preston, with drawings by Alan D. Powell. There is an introductory note by Duncan Glen.

First published in *Stony Limits and other poems* (1934) and reprinted in *Longer Contemporary Poems*, ed. David Wright (Penguin Books, 1966) and in *A Lap of Honour* (1967).

81 *The Eemis Stane*. Northampton, Mass.: The Gehenna Press, 1967.

500 copies; printed on one sheet of paper, with the author's portrait by Takahara after Leonard Baskin.

Reprinted from *Sangschaw* (1925).

82 (a) *A Lap of Honour*. London: MacGibbon & Kee, 1967.

A collection of poems which do not appear in the *Collected Poems* (1962, 1967), mainly 'recovered' by Duncan Glen.

(b) —— Chicago: Swallow Press, 1969.

83 *Celtic Nationalism*, [by] Owen Dudley Edwards, Gwynfor Evans and Ioan Rhys, Hugh MacDiarmid. London: Routledge & Kegan Paul, 1968.
MacDiarmid deals with Scotland, p. 299–358.

84 (a) *Early Lyrics by Hugh MacDiarmid. Recently discovered among letters to his schoolmaster and friend George Ogilvie.* With an appreciation of Ogilvie by Hugh MacDiarmid. Edited with an introduction by J. K. Annand. Preston: Akros Publications, 1968.
Limited edition of 350 numbered copies, the first 50 signed by poet and editor. Wrappers with portrait of MacDiarmid.
(b) —— 2nd ed. Preston: Akros Publications, 1969.
The second edition has different-coloured wrappers and a different portrait of MacDiarmid.

85 *The Uncanny Scot: a selection of prose by Hugh MacDiarmid.* Edited with an introduction by Kenneth Buthlay. London: MacGibbon & Kee, 1968.
40 copies of the first edition were specially bound in buckram, each numbered and signed by the author.

86 *An Afternoon with Hugh MacDiarmid.* Interview at Brownsbank on 25th October 1968. Hugh MacDiarmid – Duncan Glen, with Valda Grieve and Arthur Thompson. Privately printed [by Duncan Glen and the photographers – James Bamber, Geoff Green and Arthur Thompson], 1969.
55 numbered copies signed by the poet, Duncan Glen and the photographers.

87 *A Clyack-Sheaf.* London: MacGibbon & Kee, 1969.
A further collection of poems not included in the *Collected Poems* (1962, 1967).

88 (a) *Selected Essays of Hugh MacDiarmid.* Edited with an introduction by Duncan Glen. London: Jonathan Cape, 1969.
There is a portrait frontispiece from a drawing by Rosalie M. J. Loveday.
(b) —— Berkeley, Calif.: University of California Press, 1970.

89 (a) *More Collected Poems.* London: MacGibbon & Kee, 1970.
'The poems in this volume were not included in *Collected Poems* and are collected here for the first time.'
(b) —— Chicago: Swallow Press, 1970.

90 *The MacDiarmids: a conversation* – Hugh MacDiarmid and Duncan Glen, with Valda Grieve and Arthur Thompson. Recorded at Brownsbank, Candymill, on 25th October 1968. Preston: Akros Publications, 1970.
There was also a limited edition of 50 signed and numbered copies.
Reprinted from *Akros*, 5 (13, 14), April 1970, which was a special Hugh MacDiarmid issue in two parts. Similar to no. 86 above.

91 *Selected Poems.* Selected and edited by David Craig and John Manson. Harmondsworth: Penguin Books, 1970. *The Penguin Poets.*

B PERIODICALS

1 *The Scottish Chapbook: a monthly magazine of Scottish arts and letters*. [Edited by C. M. Grieve.] Montrose. Vol. 1, no. 1, August 1922 – vol. 2, no. 3, November–December 1923.

2 *The Scottish Nation*. [Edited by C. M. Grieve.] Weekly. Montrose. Vol. 1, no. 1, 8th May 1923 – vol. 2, no. 8, 25th December 1923.

3 *The Northern Review*. [Edited by C. M. Grieve.] Monthly. Edinburgh. Vol. 1, no. 1, May 1924 – no. 4, September 1924.

4 *The Voice of Scotland: a quarterly magazine of Scottish arts and affairs*. Edited by Hugh MacDiarmid. Dunfermline: Vol. 1, no. 1, June–August 1938 – vol. 2, no. 1, June–August 1939. Glasgow: Vol. 2, no. 2, December 1945 – vol. 5, no. 3, June 1949. Edinburgh: Vol. 5, no. 4, January 1955 – vol. 9, no. 2, August 1958.

5 *Poetry Scotland*. No. 4. Editor, Maurice Lindsay. Guest editor, Hugh MacDiarmid. Edinburgh: Serif Books, 1949.

6 *Scottish Art and Letters*. Fifth Miscellany. P.E.N. Congress Number, Edinburgh Festival, 1950. Literary editor, Hugh MacDiarmid. Glasgow: Maclellan, 1950.